FLYING SHOES

FLYING SHOES

A NOVEL

Lisa Howorth

BLOOMSBURY

NEW YORK · LONDON · NEW DELHI · SYDNEY

Published by Bloomsbury USA, New York

Bloomsbury is a trademark of Bloomsbury Publishing Plc

All papers used by Bloomsbury USA are natural, recyclable
products made from wood grown in well-managed
forests. The manufacturing processes conform to the
environmental regulations of the country of origin.

LIBRARY OF CONGRESS CATALOGING-IN-PUBLICATION DATA

Howorth, Lisa.
Flying shoes : a novel / Lisa Howorth.—First U.S. Edition.
pages cm
ISBN: 978-1-62040-301-3 (hardback)
1. Women journalist—Fiction 2. Cold cases (Criminal
investigation)—Fiction 3. Sexually abused boys—
Fiction 4. Murder—Investigation—Fiction. I. Title.
PS3608.O95729F59 2014
813'.6—dc23
2013039124

First U.S. Edition 2014

1 3 5 7 9 10 8 6 4 2

Typeset by Hewer Text UK Ltd, Edinburgh
Designed by Simon Sullivan
Printed and bound in the U.S.A. by Thomson-
Shore Inc., Dexter, Michigan

Bloomsbury books may be purchased for business or
promotional use. For information on bulk purchases
please contact Macmillan Corporate and Premium Sales
Department at specialmarkets@macmillan.com.

for Richard

for Oxford

and for all the little ghosts

"It's a hard world for little things."

—Lillian Gish as Rachel Cooper
in *The Night of the Hunter*

One

MARY BYRD THORNTON knew that breaking things was not a good, adult response to getting sudden, scary news about a terrible thing in the past, a thing buried with the dead and kicked to the curb of consciousness; but that was what she'd done anyway.

She'd been unloading the dishwasher, killing time until school let out and half-listening to NPR. The IRA had broken a truce and bombed London, unwanted rape babies—"*enfants mauvais souvenir,*" NPR called them—from the massacres in Rwanda over the past two years were abandoned and dying, some scientist was predicting global chaos, calling it Y2K—planes would be falling from the sky and subway trains colliding in the year 2000. Basically it was the usual news; what she and her brothers called every new day's headlines: *More Dead Everywhere.* It always seemed like the world was a kitchen full of leaking gas just waiting for the careless match.

Even though it was February and the windows were closed against the cold, damp day, Mary Byrd could hear the knuckle-head frat boys over on the next street, hollering and floating around in their hot tub like beer-sodden dumplings in a testosterone stew.

The phone had gone off—more an electronic alarm than a ring that she'd never gotten used to. Answering with one hand and turning off the radio with the other, Mary Byrd received the startling but somehow, she realized, not unexpected news that the unsolved case of her nine-year-old stepbrother's murder, on Mother's Day, 1966, was being reopened.

The call was from a detective in Richmond—what was his odd name? The voice was calm and polite, but strict, like a school teacher dealing with a balky problem child. He suggested—strongly—that she not discuss the unwelcome news outside her family until he'd had a chance to meet with them all. And the sooner the better for that, he said.

"In fact, if you can get up here in the next couple days that would be great. What's happening is that we think we have some new information and we feel we can now go after, and try to convict, the suspect. If we . . ."

"Think?" Mary Byrd interrupted. "What do you mean? Like what new information?" She asked the question not feeling she wanted an answer.

"What I was going to say is that if we can get your family to look at some things, make an ID, we believe we've got this thing nailed."

Mary Byrd felt gooseflesh tightening on her arms. "What things?" Was he talking about her little green teen-aged diary, which had been confiscated and never returned? "Is it Ned Tuttle?" she asked. Tuttle, the creepy guy down the street who was the only suspect. She hated to say his name.

"I'm sorry, Mrs. Thornton," the detective said. "I don't think it's in anybody's best interest, or in the interest of working the case, for us to talk about details over the phone. But it is pretty . . . I'd say *critical,* actually, for you and your family to meet with me up here very soon if at all possible. There's a lot that needs to be discussed. I'm hoping that a meeting Monday morning will suit everybody. That gives you a little time, anyway."

Mary Byrd felt the belligerent asshole rising up in her. There was something else about the voice—slick? "What, it's been thirty years and now there's this big hurry?"

There was a reproving pause and the detective said, "Yes, exactly. I can apologize till the cows come home for this intrusion. I know this is difficult and unpleasant for all of you. But this is what I do here—try to solve cold cases. These . . . developments have just come up. I would think that you'd want to know, and to cooperate. Let's get this resolved once and for all, and put this guy away forever so no one else gets . . . hurt."

The guilt card. She wondered how many others had already been *hurt* over all these years. "Okay, I get it. Have you talked to my mother and brothers?"

"They're willing. Your mother was certain you'd want to be involved."

Why had her mother said that? She was overthinking; it was just her mom's normal bossiness and nothing else. But why hadn't she called to let her know? "Okay," Mary Byrd repeated. "I'll see what I can do."

"Thank you, Mrs. Thornton," the detective said. "I don't think you'll be sorry to be here. I hope that this will mean some closure for your family."

I *will* be sorry, she thought, and what the fuck is *closure*?

"And if I may ask once again," he said, "it's very important to the case that you not speak to anyone outside your family about all this. What we don't need is reporters and publicity mucking things up or scaring off people we need to be interviewing before we can get to them. There are a lot of complicated legal issues involved and we need to go strictly by the book on this one. Can I count on your cooperation with that?" She heard the snap of a lighter and breath being drawn. Maybe he was done with her.

"Yes," she lied, knowing she would discuss this grim turn of events with her friend Mann, or Lucy, if she could find her. And her husband Charles. But no problem about not talking to anyone else; it was all so unspeakable and always had been. But why did he care?

Cold and shaky, and guilty; a super-gravitational weight settled on her like a tractor tire and made her want to gimp up right there on the kitchen floor, fetally curled and impervious like one of her napping cats. That's when she went back to the dishes and picked up a piece of the crappy Corelle she used to feed her animals and children because of its alleged indestruct-ibility and threw it hard at the floor, where it shattered in an almost-satisfying way, just as she had always expected it would. Her heart flapped madly and she took some deep breaths to compose herself, trying to decide what to do next. Feeling an acrid thickness in her throat—bile?—she coughed a big, hair-ball cough of revulsion. As she filled a glass with water and considered adding some vodka, the phone sounded again. She looked suspiciously at the caller ID, which said RICHMOND VA. An unfamiliar number. Did she have to answer?

She did. "Hi! Is this Mrs. Thornton?" asked a too-cheerful, girly voice.

"This is she," Mary Byrd said.

"Oh, hi! My name is Linda Fyce. I'm a journalist and I'm calling from Richmond. Mrs. Thornton, are you aware that the murder case of your stepbrother, Steven Rhinehart, is being reopened up here?"

A *reporter*.

Mary Byrd went cold. After a moment, she lied, "No. Who is this?"

The woman, or girl, repeated her name and blundered ahead. "I'm working on a story about your stepbrother's case. I'm surprised, but actually not very, that the Richmond police haven't already contacted you. I was wondering if we could talk about it. I'm sure you'd like to see it finally resolved by *somebody*, which I hope to do. Is this a good time?"

"No," Mary Byrd said, not having any idea of what else to say. There was no good time. She sat down at the kitchen counter. "No, I'm really busy right now. And I don't think I have anything . . . useful to say about that."

"From what I know so far, wasn't there some . . . well, maybe *involvement*'s not the right word, but weren't there some questions about your boyfriend, and your relationship to the suspect?"

"I don't know what you're talking about," Mary Byrd said. "I'm sorry, I have to go now."

"Well, maybe I can call at a more convenient time? I'm sure this is important to you and your family."

Mary Byrd hung up. Anger welled up in her. There was something about the pushy snake-oiliness of the woman's voice that alarmed her. Was this reporter really going to write about the case, and put it all out there in public for her whole family to deal with? Again? She got it, now, about why the detective had asked her not to talk to anyone else. He didn't want the reporter scooping him, and making the police look like idiots. Which they had been. How could they possibly solve the case after so many years? And would she really have to go up to Richmond and look at . . . what? She was horrified at the thought.

Pale at no crime. The motto of her eighteenth-century crush, William Byrd, who believed that one must strive to right all wrongs but who was guilty of quite a few, came to her, and she gave herself a mental kick in the ass. *Take heart, thou indolent, indulgent wench. There is much ado.* In other words, don't be such a pussy.

Looking down at the "china" explosion on the floor, she knew she'd better get it up fast before Evagreen saw it. It was the kind of thing Evagreen expected from her and loved to see: further proof that Mary Byrd was a cradle fuckup. On her knees, collecting the shards—why had her creepy college anthropology professor called them "sherds," as if they'd been digging up turds—and wanting to lighten up, she said to herself, *Ladies and gentlemen, what a tragedy. Oh, the humanity!* This didn't much work, and out loud she said, "I knew this crap would break." Another myth bites the dust, like Teflon that got scratched and left gray, poisonous flecks in the eggs. Or stainless steel that stained, or insurance that didn't insure. American advertising bullshit.

Her first impulse had been to throw a piece of her Spode Queen's Bird, which might have felt better in the moment, but she had a maddening way of second-thinking her impulses, even split-second ones, making them non-impulses and therefore devoid of real satisfaction. Mary Byrd had a word for this self-thwart, another expression her brothers used to describe the last-minute bungling that made their teams, the Spiders and the Redskins, lose a game: *auto-cornhole.* But she was glad she hadn't thrown the Queen's Bird because she loved it; a wedding gift and charming play on her name from her dead mother-in-law, Liddie, whom she also loved. And then, if she had thrown the Spode, seeing the pale blue china, the almost-white color of the sky on a scorching Mississippi day, with the lovely little magenta and gold bird, smashed on the floor, that would only have made her feel worse. She'd already broken enough of the Spode over the many years of her marriage. Well, in an unusual fit of anger over something now forgotten, Charles, normally a model of comportment and restraint, had broken a plate once, and not on accident.

A skinny splinter of the bogus china had stuck in a cantaloupe on the floor next to the stove. The cantaloupe was there because one of the cats, Ignatius, was weirdly obsessed with them and rolled them off the counter and into corners where he could wedge them up and get at them more privately. She only bought the expensive, out-of-season fruit (which in February tasted more like pumpkin) for Iggy. The gnawed place with the shard oozed onto the heart pine.

Still on her hands and knees, considering crying a little bit, which she knew would help nothing, and then considering a Valium, which would, Mary Byrd had just finished picking up broken pieces and wiping up the juice puddle when she raised her head and saw that Evagreen, the Thorntons' late-middle-aged but ageless maid—housekeeper, cleaner, whatever you were supposed to call them now; all the labels for black help seemed either degrading, euphemistic, or just silly—stood in the kitchen doorway. One skinny arm was akimbo, fist on the hip of her shrimp-colored jogging suit, the other holding a stack of tightly and perfectly folded sheets and towels to her velour chest. There was no particular expression on Evagreen's face.

Sheepishly, kneeling before the woman, violated cantaloupe in one hand and paper towel wads and pieces of plate in the other, Mary Byrd said, "Evagreen, did you know that this Corelle stuff actually does break?"

"Don't break on *me*," said Evagreen, moving off. "Anything'll break, thow it down hard enough."

Evagreen never called her by name, never called her anything, and—Mary Byrd appreciated this—never called her "ma'am." She sighed. She was sure Evagreen hadn't seen her throw the plate, yet the older woman seemed to always have a sixth sense about things, especially if they involved Mary Byrd doing the wrong thing. *She* should work for the damn FBI, or somebody, solving cold cases, Mary Byrd thought. She tried to resist thinking, *What a bitch.*

She knew Evagreen disapproved of her and she sort of understood why. Whiteness was only a small part of it—that would be reason enough in Mississippi—but actually it had more to do with Mary Byrd not being white *enough,* or the right kind of white person. As far as she knew, Evagreen didn't do anybody else that way. Mary Byrd wasn't super-lazy; she'd worked most of her adult life. After Charles had gotten his gallery business going and they could afford for her not to work, she'd tried to be an efficient housewife, making beds, loading and unloading the dishwasher, getting up at the crack and making school lunches and breakfast (cold cereal and orange juice, but still), chauffeuring children, trying to keep up with things that needed keeping up with in their vast, overgrown yard, blah blah blah, holding down the fort when Charles was often out of town, and entertaining his photographers and clients when he wasn't. Before Evagreen came to work on Thursdays, Mary Byrd rushed around straightening, getting all the cat turds that hadn't been scarfed up by the dogs out of the litter box, emptying the trash of earwaxed Q-tips and Tampax applicators, getting the pubes off the commode rim, scraping dried toothpaste blobs out of the sink. One of not very many white Democrats in town, she didn't do ladies' lunches, didn't belong to the country club or play tennis or golf on its scrubby, eroded golf course, and her children went to the public schools. For Martin Luther King Day she and Charles went to the long, boisterous services at Second Baptist, where, as far as Mary Byrd could see, they all celebrated not how they were all the same, all in this crazy world together, but how insuperably *different* they all still were.

Still, Evagreen would cut her no slack. In fact, Mary Byrd felt that she might gain some ground with Evagreen by doing more of those white lady things; that their impasse had more to do with breeding and outsiderness, and with Mary Byrd's willingness to accept, if not embrace, guilt. Evagreen could sniff this coming off her and took advantage of it. To Mary Byrd, Evagreen was like one of the scary old bully nuns at St. Bernard's back in Richmond, except that there it had been okay to hate Sister Pascal because she was white, and because, by example, she had made it clear that hating was okay, like it was okay to scorn you if you had divorced parents. There'd been no pleasing her, and there was no pleasing Evagreen, except when you screwed up. Maybe it was nothing more than what used to be called, before psychobabble, and before everything had to be about race, simply a *personality conflict.*

Mary Byrd wondered if she needed to tell Evagreen now about this trip to Richmond she was apparently going to have to make and decided no, don't stir that pot yet; she could get back from Virginia before next Wednesday and could get the house in order before Evagreen came again. But Charles and the children, she'd need to tell them today. She should call her mother, too. But not now. She wasn't ready.

To escape her personal Quasimodo and to think, Mary Byrd wandered out of the house in a fog, onto the front porch where she knew a world of ugly winter yard detritus waited for her to deal with it. She should get busy doing something. Slimy yellow rags of elephant ear lay around the porch's edge, punctuated by shriveled caladiums. Pots of impatiens looked like the wet, wilted crap at the bottom of a salad bowl and the lady ferns, so emerald and luxuriant in July, had all frozen and were crispy and brown as toast. It all should have been cut back and raked out of the beds before Christmas, weeks and weeks earlier. The red honeysuckle, morning glories, and clematis vines she encouraged to grow up the white porch posts of the old house still clung there, bare and tangled—so gorgeously frothy and fragrant all summer and at the first frost good for nothing. Thank you, Jesus, for the Lady Banks rose and Jackson vine and Carolina jessamine which kept their verdant, skinny good looks all winter. Vines were her favorite plants; she gave them carte blanche in her yard. Even wisteria and Virginia creeper she egged on, although she knew they were hell on paint and woodwork and pissed Charles off. It was so, so worth it to have the wisteria's grape-scented purple haze in spring and the rusty red creeper that glowed like fire in the fall with the late afternoon sun. She liked to think that that's how her curly black hair looked, backlit, when she put some henna in it. Ha. More like a clown wig. The red honeysuckle would have to be moved, she noticed. It was competing with the clematis and she couldn't do without the sweet waft of that and its delicate white laciness in the worst part of summer. Clematis and crape myrtle and a few weedy things like false dragonhead were the only flowers with the balls to stand up to the relentless Mississippi late summers. If not for the small relief of those tough blooms she thought she might have blown her brains out one of those dusty Septembers. Not really, but the summers were so brutal, and the heat gave her bad headaches. It was no wonder all the horrible civil rights crimes had taken place in summer. It brought out the craziness, and the worst in people.

The frat boys were still thrashing in their tub, warming up for their Thursday-night throw-down. Thursday was the biggest party night of the week and when their weekend began. Classrooms were empty on Fridays; they all used to go home to Meridian or Jackson or wherever on weekends if there wasn't a game, but now there were so many bars and bands coming through town the students stayed around. It sounded like the boys were rapping along to a recent Snoop Doggy Dogg song. She didn't know the name of the song, only that Eliza, eleven going on sixteen, played it a lot, and it included the n-word loud and clear. She and Eliza had fought about it, but she had given up when Eliza had said, "But Mom, it's okay because he's a black guy. If *he* doesn't care, why do you?" And Snoop's mama and daddy, Eliza enjoyed telling her, were from Mississippi, too. What could you do? It had all gotten so confusing, southern white kids totally into rap and affectionately calling each other "niggaz," black kids doing the same, like it was now okay. But it was still not okay with Charles and Mary Byrd. Maybe they couldn't keep their children from hearing it, but they better not be singing or saying it; it marked you as white trash if nothing else.

By midnight, when the bars let out, the frat boys would be back in the tub again, the music with the n-word and worse broadcast across the neighborhood, punctuated by rebel yells— "WOOooo!"— the broke-dick war cry of the proudly defeated. Mary Byrd didn't really mind them—Charles and their friend Mann had been Greeks at Emory and Washington and Lee, after all. They added life to the neighborhood and their parents' dollars to the town. They were sweet and mannerly when you asked them to please get their beer cans picked up. They grew up to be all kinds of successful people —famous writers, doctors, and lawyers, a guy who invented a landmine detector, another founded that Netscape thing, a hotshot music producer, a guitarist in that new group Wilco—so somebody was learning something out there. If they just wouldn't drive around drunk, killing themselves. Their poor parents couldn't possibly have a clue about how close to the edge their kids were or they wouldn't be letting them come up here with practically new driver's licenses and giant cars that they didn't need in the small town. A skid away from death every weekend. Their precious boys.

Mary Byrd inhaled deeply to see if she could catch a scent in the chilly, wet air, and she could: the green vegetal smell of rotting stems and leaves. If this winter storm they were talking about was bad enough, she'd even lose the Jackson vine and Lady Banks, and the brittle azaleas. Maybe the ones that framed the house should be covered. She could scare up Teever, her yard man, and, she thought, friend, to help her, but he hadn't come around for a week or so; she hoped he wasn't in jail. Maybe she should go out to the trailers and see if she could find that nice Mexican guy, the one with the silver teeth, to help her. She liked that there were Hispanic guys around now; it made the town seem more in step with the rest of the country. They were work monsters, and giving them work made her feel like she was honoring her immigrant grandparents, or something like that. And maybe soon there'd be a decent taco place with those delicious Mexican Cokes. But it always miffed Teever when she had them do the jobs that he considered his.

Mary Byrd's mind went unwillingly back to the phone calls from the detective—what *was* his odd name?—and the reporter. She hated them both. Fyce—it sounded slightly familiar, but maybe only because it was such an *unfortunate* name, as her mother-in-law said about anything unappealing. Just because she couldn't find anything new to write about she starts dredging up people's private stories, things best forgotten or not spoken of, even if unsolved. It had been too long! It was too over! Wasn't there a statute of limitations or something? Mary Byrd could understand how the reporter couldn't resist the story. A suspect to whom nothing would stick. Neighborhood secrets. No one, particularly the Richmond police, had been able to figure it out. There hadn't been organized searches or milk cartons or Amber alerts or DNA in those days. It had been long before stories of missing and murdered children appeared practically every week in morning papers and on local TV news, and long before the whistle had finally been blown on predatory priests and the cardinals and popes who protected them.

Long before the ghoulish fascination with unsolved crime and mysteries and cold case files meant they were featured every night on TV shows. Then, it was unheard of—a front-page story in the Richmond *Times-Dispatch* with a banner above the regular headline: POLICE HUNT KNIFE SLAYER OF 9-YEAR-OLD BOY. Kids didn't disappear and weren't killed then. They weren't sex objects. They didn't get left to broil in parked cars and day care vans; there wasn't such a thing as *day care.* Newborns weren't found in Dumpsters. Dumpsters didn't even exist. Maybe then they were still bothering to put them in shallow graves like the Lindbergh baby. Or was it that the world just hadn't known before CNN or whatever that those things were going on? No, it was a simpler, better time, wasn't it? So even though the sixties had been a decade of death—the horror of assassinations, freedom riders buried in levees, the masses of men in Vietnam—when had the times turned on children? It had been a very big, very terrible thing that had befallen all of Richmond. And now Mary Byrd and her family would revisit it, especially if the reporter went with it, and who knew how long it would go on and what would come of it. As if even now, when she did have to think about it, was reminded of it, her part in it wasn't unlike the crick in her shoulder, that small but naggy pain in her left wing-bone—or whatever those bones were that would be where wings would be attached if she were an angel, which she surely wasn't—that little spot that always seemed to ache. A pinched nerve that stayed pinched.

And this total stranger would write a book or a TV script about it? Then she and her mother and brothers would be left to patch themselves up again and Fyce would walk off with a wad. She didn't want her mother or brothers or Eliza or William or even Charles to be touched by any of it. What if Tuttle wasn't in custody, and he saw Fyce's story, and came after her or her children, or her brothers? Was that just crazy, or possible? But she knew there wasn't going to be a choice. She'd go to Richmond and do what she had to do: look at whatever awful things they had to show, and hear whatever awful things they had to tell. But it was one thing to have to talk to police and another to talk to a reporter. She was not *required* to talk to Fyce. She thought about how good it would feel to punch her in the face, being sure not to tuck her thumb in her fist, the way Ernest had shown her. She was at least glad not to still be living in Virginia in the middle of things. Good *could* come of it, Mary Byrd's reasonable self knew, but *would* it? The case might finally be solved and who? Ned Tuttle? finally put away. She could stop being afraid of Tuttle still being out there somewhere. But she felt sure that like so many things in life, there had been too much time and too much bumbling for this meeting to come to anything.

Tuttle, the spooky kid down the street. A year older than Mary Byrd, but so gimpy that he mostly hung around the younger kids in the neighborhood. He had taken a lot of teasing at school, she remembered, and something nuts had happened to him—he'd gotten his dick caught in his zipper or something, in the boys' bathroom, and after that he had gone off to military school. He had a dead mother, and lived with his father and older brother. She'd felt sorry for Tuttle and had been nice to him. At least she *thought* she had been. They'd all played in the street on summer nights together when they were younger, but by the spring Stevie died, she'd started dating and running around and she couldn't remember seeing much of him. But the week after Stevie was killed, she'd gotten the weird little note from Tuttle, after he'd gone back to Charlotte Hall. So strange. Just hey, how are you, what's going on in the neighborhood— as if he'd known nothing about Stevie and hadn't been questioned by the police. The detectives had had a field day with the note, which Tuttle had backdated to make it seem like he hadn't been around the weekend of the murder. They'd had her write back; she couldn't remember a word of what they'd had her say. Then they'd taken her diary! Surely her mom and Pop, her stepfather, had known this but they'd never said a word about it. They had waited every day for Tuttle to be arrested. And then, nothing. Until now.

Oh, god. Mary Byrd could not think about it. Her chest hurt when she tried to draw a deep breath and she hoped she wouldn't have a heart attack or something. Should she run take an aspirin? No, she'd keep on thinking about her yard. It steadied her. A few small round morning glory pods still were on the vine and she reached and pinched them, letting the tiny black pyramidal seeds fall into her open hand. They needed scattering in sunnier spots and maybe they'd take, and the little magenta trumpets would volunteer around the yard. An incorrigible seed poacher, she'd stolen the seeds a few years earlier from a friend's Manhattan fence. Why hadn't the Heavenly Blues, so startlingly and luminously azure, done well this year? Squirrels had probably gotten onto their hallucinogenic properties and were hoarding seeds and tripping on them. She'd certainly seen them doing some insane things—swinging like monkeys and stunt-fucking on bouncing limbs in the big water oaks that stood solidly at each corner of the rambling Victorian house. Sometimes they would drop like stones onto the tin roof, scaring the hell out of you if you were watching TV or quietly drinking or reading in the living room. At least they didn't peep in the upstairs windows at night, like the raccoons and possums, terrorizing William and Eliza. Mary Byrd herself had tried a few Heavenly Blue seeds, crunching them up in her teeth. They'd made her feel like barfing, but nothing else.

A blue jay who'd been picking at the last few red berries that clung to the old dogwood cawed—or whatever they said—at her. Why did everybody hate them? They were badass—she loved their tiny bandit masks—and bossy to other birds, maybe, but so beautiful and military with their regimental striped tails, white collars, and heroic crests. And they didn't wuss out and go south in winter; they stayed around and were welcome spots of color in the drab yard. They took no crap off Iggy and Irene, either; she'd never seen any telltale blue feathers strewn tragically around. Well, maybe once or twice. Mary Byrd threw the handful of morning glory seeds at the jay, saying, "Go with the flow, man." She wished she had some Valium; it wouldn't make her as dopey as a Xanax but would take the edge off the nasty afternoon. Hoping, she fished with one finger in the coin pocket of her Levi's, only coming up with a few four o'clock seeds she'd filched somewhere, and she tossed those to the jay, too.

She wondered when Jack Ernest would come up to town again. She could call him; he'd have something maybe even better than what she had. But she did not need to be thinking about Ernest, the Big Bad Wolf to her Little Red Riding Hood. She was drawn to his manic dementedness and balls-out, absurd—or absurd*ist*—(he knew the difference) bravado. In a way, talking to him might be easier—he was so on another planet. He had nothing to do with anything real in her life. If she was weak enough to call Ernest and tell him what was going on she knew he'd probably offer to go up to Richmond and whack the killer and then the reporter but first fuck Fyce in some humiliating way. Or at the very least he'd say something like, "Baby doll, that truly sucks, what you need is to come over here and let Jack Ernest give you some of his medicines and special TLC." Either offer would be so ridiculously disingenuous that it would cheer her up. Not that she would follow through on the latter offer. She might be crazy, but she wasn't *that* crazy. Yet. Was she? But she really did want to get a few nerve pills to get through this mess in Richmond. She had one or two of something and some crumbs, and she was going to need handfuls. But then she'd be obligated to him, and nobody wanted to be obligated to Ernest. So, no, she couldn't, wouldn't, call Ernest. Bad idea. That had to be over. Or actually, that absolutely could not begin.

On the sidewalk just below the yard she spotted some chalk graffiti. Uh oh. No doubt the work of William and his posse, Other William and Justin. LAUREN HAS BOZOMS. SCHOOL BITS. A crude, rear-view perspective of a dog with a bull's-eye butt hole bore the curious caption: THIS DOG WILL BITE AND DODO ON YOU. WWJD? Damn it. Neighbors and passersby had had since yesterday afternoon to consider the question, and Evagreen would have seen it when she got out of her old maroon Cadillac. She was surprised Charles hadn't noticed it picking up the morning paper and raised some hell. Those crazy little dudes. Last week they had gotten themselves into trouble when they discovered a horde of *Playboy, Penthouse,* and *Hustler* that had been thrown in the Dumpster by a student vacating the ramshackle hippie hotel across the street. It had been a windy day and the boys, in a frenzy, had climbed into the Dumpster to get at the treasure. In seconds boobs and beavers were everywhere, slick pages and centerfolds gusting up around the boys' heads and down the street, beaching up in the hedge around Walnut Hill—or Nut Hill as the kids called it—the geezer apartment complex. They got mildly punished, but you could tell they thought it had all been well worth it. It wasn't so bad that they had seen, at eight years old, ladies' private parts, it was just a little disturbing that their first glimpse of them was gigantic silicone breasts and shaved landing strips. Oh, boys. Boys, boys, boys. It wouldn't be long before these little guys were in a hot-tub scrum too. If nothing happened to them before then.

Mary Byrd let herself think of Stevie, something she tried never to do, although she kept his tiny School Days photo on her dresser mirror where she saw it every day: his blond, crew-cut head and thin, goofy smile, his brown and orange striped T-shirt against a cheerful sky-blue background. The photo was like a scar on her face: not pleasant, she saw it in the mirror every day, but it did her no good to notice it. But still she kept it.

A sweet, transparent little guy, practically a baby when her mother married his recently widowed father. He'd been her real-life baby doll and he'd adored her, following her around, trying to hang out in her room, letting her dress him up in ridiculous costumes, listening to her records. He was crazy for her Beach Boys and Coasters 45s—"Surfin' U.S.A." (Pop called it "Sufferin' U.S.A." and always made her turn it down), "Charlie Brown," and "Poison Ivy." She'd tried to teach him to Twist and Swim, but all he really wanted to do was the Monkey and the Monster Mash but he couldn't get the foot-work on the Monster Mash. His dancing was so hilarious. Sometimes she'd get on her knees and slow-dance with him, swaying back and forth to "In My Room," the big make-out song, pretending she was dancing with Richard or John or Joe, whoever it was that week. He was a big suck-up and loved to hug her legs and be adored in return. When he began to annoy her, she'd scooch him out, and he'd sit outside her door, sing-ing or talking to himself, the pitifulness of which annoyed her even more, and she might let him back in. As he got older, naturally his allegiance switched to her brother Nick, who had all the cool boy stuff—plastic guns and models and sports equipment. She and Nick would mess with him some, but he could give as good as he got. Mary Byrd became a teenager, and Stevie became a boy. She supposed he never even remem-bered a time when he wasn't in his new family, he'd been so little when he and Pop moved in.

Mary Byrd decided she could wait on cutting back the vines

and ferns—save it for Teever or the Mexican guy—but she looked forward, sort of, to yard work, its practicality, its be-here-nowness and the pleasure of actually getting something done with visible results. Too little that she did all day lasted: the food she shopped for and cooked got eaten immediately, laundry and floors got dirty again overnight. And there was the simple physical satisfaction of lopping things off with big, sharp shears. Even the wing-bone ache that would be aggravated by the wide scissoring of the shears would be satisfying. Actually, *extra satisfying* because then she'd *have* to take a pain pill and the world would be a better place and any unpleasantness would seem far away. And points for yard work might be scored with Charles and Evagreen. But one of the things Mary Byrd did best was putting *off*. Off-putting too, but she was the Great Procrastinatrix. At any rate the most obvious thing to do right now was hose the walk off before someone complained.

Her life was a matter of domestic triage. First things first. Or trying to figure out exactly what the first things even were. She began to scuff around on the sidewalk, scumbling the chalk and water to obliterate the goofy messages. She jerked at the hose to get it to the side of the house where the dogs stayed. Why were hoses such dumb colors having nothing to do with nature? Kelly green just showed up a neglected lawn. Why weren't there brown ones to match crappy winter yards? Or if they were going to be some unreal colors, why not something fun like pink or clear with glitter? Or python print? How fun would *that* be to see lying around in the grass.

Mary Byrd turned the hose on the dogs' water dish, which they never drank from, clearing it of oak leaves and refilling it. Green slime filmed the inside of the bowl; she needed to clean it and maybe the dogs would prefer it to the toilet, which they rushed to the second they came in the house.

Puppy Sal and the Quarter Pounder dozed in the holes they'd

dug, and hearing the splashing in their bowl but not the desired clatter of kibble, they lifted their heads in mild interest. They were the best of dogs, she thought with a surge of affection. Nondescript mutts, not too smart, not too dumb, but with all sorts of endearing quirks. They could both lie down and die when you cocked your fingers at them and shouted, "BANG." They could shake. Puppy Sal had a nervous tic—some kind of neuro-damage from contracting distemper before they had found her—making her jaws snap constantly, like a heartbeat, even in her sleep. She was a reddish golden-brown color, so they told people her breed was Golden Snapper. Puppy Sal had been famous in town, before the leash law came down, for bolting to the Holiday Inn, where she would scrounge in the restaurant garbage area and, after she was completely slicked up with bacon grease and funk, take a little swim in the hotel pool. Then the ladylike manager, Mr. Selff, would call and practically have a nervous breakdown. He claimed she left a *dithguthting earl thlick* on the pool. Of course she did. The Quarter Pounder, Sal's son by an awful science experiment of a Corgi-Bassett mix, could also sing. Mary Byrd would croon in a falsetto, "*It's over, it's over, it's o-o-o-ver,*" stretching out the end on a high note, and the Quarter Pounder would throw back his head and howl.

"Good dogs," Mary Byrd said to them. The dogs rose expectantly, plumy tails slightly wagging. "Good puppies." She wanted to pat them but didn't want her hand to smell doggy. She loved these guys without really being a dog person. The children and Charles would allow the dogs all over them, even letting them lick their faces, but Mary Byrd could never get past all the butt-sniffing, shit-eating, and carcass-rolling that dogs did. She constantly caught them guiltily slinking around with kitty litter sprinkles on their noses after snacking. And when Eliza and William were little and threw up or when the cats horked up hairballs, one of the dogs would be on it like a hornet. Rancid deer legs and dead armadillos, which Mary Byrd had heard could have leprosy, had been hauled up into the yard by Puppy Sal and her accomplice son. Dog germs were a huge reality—one of the major cootie groups—right up there, in her estimation, with those in salad bars, airplanes, New York subways, and on William's hands. For some reason it didn't bother her at all that cats licked themselves all over. She'd bury her face in a cat's fur any time. You'd never, *ever* see a cat chew dirty socks or underwear crotches or bloody bandages or roll happily in roadkill.

She would have to make sure that Charles and the children could see about the animals and themselves while she was in Richmond. All the drills: food, school, walking the dogs on time, dealing with any piles or puddles, dealing with homework. Odd that her mother hadn't called.

The impulse to whine to someone came over her, but at the same time the last thing she wanted was to talk about it. Her family had been sucked up into a tornado of grief and fear and the unknowable, and when the storm subsided, their bodies fell scattered about their house and they were zombies; the walking dead. The awful thing had never been discussed with her mother or with her brothers, and certainly not with her stepfather, who died not long after. They'd all chosen not to know; newspapers went straight to the trash, news channels were quickly changed. That day, those days, were rarely spoken of again. The implications and the volatility of the matter within the often touchy, so-called blended family—it had just been too big a risk for any of them to take. The price in terms of their necessary relationships with one another was too high. But was it *still*? Over the years, each of them had hunkered down into their personal pods of regret and sadness. And ignorance, and, she supposed, blame. Although life had changed forever and Stevie's loss, the terrible way they'd lost him, gripped them all, they tried to put it aside. It was easiest. That much they all seemed to understand.

No one had ever brought up the question of her part—her *alleged* part—in it. How much her mother and stepfather had known about what the police knew, or guessed, Mary Byrd had never known. She suspected that each of them had different pieces of information, or misinformation, about the murder, as if they all had the same disease but different symptoms, or were in different stages of it, and there was no cure.

Mary Byrd began to feel an old creepiness, a poisonous smog of bad feeling, leaving her in a black, blank space that would easily fill up with all kinds of ugliness. She *should* talk to someone about the day's news, to make it seem real, and navigable. Well, it wouldn't be her mom, or Charles, who did not invite conversations about feelings.

She was afraid of bringing on the old bad dreams again. They didn't come to her often anymore, but when they did, they were paralyzing and heart-squeezing and sleep-sucking and day-ruining. She'd never said a word about them. Back then, after Stevie died, she'd slept in the basement of the new house they'd moved into to start fresh, to get away from the fearful neighborhood, their haunted house on Cherry Glen Lane with Stevie's empty room, and the horrified neighbors who avoided them because they had no idea how to act or what to say. Who would? Her basement space in the new house with its own bathroom, which her mother said would give Mary Byrd more privacy from her brothers, only isolated and spooked her. Her mother had really been thinking, surely, of keeping her out of the way of her despondent stepfather, his crazy binge drinking, his rage and resentment. So for a long time Mary Byrd, the big sister, slept with her light on, a nine iron by her bed and a knitting needle and a barbecue skewer easily reachable, sticking slightly out between the box springs and mattress. She had been afraid of everything. Tuttle. Creepy detectives. Her stepfather and her mother. Herself. Her memories were like her nightmares, but she'd always been able to slam the door on them. Now that door swung wide, wide, wide as hell open.

RAIN HAD BEEN falling down that evening, seemingly at the same rate and density as the cherry blossoms. The spent petals— it was early May—had fluttered down with the sparkly drops and been illuminated by the streetlight so that Mary Byrd, not wearing her glasses, had imagined that the dark woods across the street were a deep blue, almost black prom gown studded with luminescent pale pink pearls and rhinestones. From time to time her boyfriend's head had obscured the view. They were making out, necking, it used to be called, struggling with heavy petting, reclined in the backseat of his little blue Chevy convertible, steaming up the back windows. They'd had to put up the top quickly because of the rain, which had surprised them; it had been such a gloriously bright Sunday, and they'd taken a drive once the Rhinehearts' afternoon dinner was over. It was Mother's Day, but she'd been allowed to go riding with the boyfriend because he no longer had a mother, and maybe Mother's Day was not such a good day for him. Eliot Nelson. What had ever happened to him? He'd been a senior, and she'd never seen him again after that spring. Quiet and handsome-ish, and not as interested in her as she was in him. She'd pretty much initiated the make-out session; he'd seemed aloof . . . Maybe because she was too young for him?

She'd been late; she should have been home, but it had been hard for her to quit, and the night had been so balmy and beautiful, even, or especially, with the rain. They'd each had a couple warm beers. She was fifteen and only a few weeks earlier on her birthday she had finally been allowed to "go in cars with boys," and it was the most exciting, fun thing in the world.

What she hadn't known, there in the backseat with her boyfriend, was that her family had been out looking for Stevie for hours. And what none of them knew, and wouldn't for another day, was that in the dark velvety woods, not a hundred yards away from Eliot's convertible, Stevie lay dead.

Two

MARY BYRD SHUDDERED and drifted deeper into the yard, glad to kick clods of clay that Teever had left around after transplanting some red Midnight Flare azaleas that clashed with the Coral Bells. She picked up fallen sticks and it felt good to snap them into kindling size, and to viciously stomp some pooched-up mole tunnels. Any animal with fur, generally, she liked except for voles, or moles, or whatever they were, the ones with those creepy hands. They must have been eating her Naked Lady bulbs, because she'd noticed them dwindling; the previous July there hadn't been the usual cheerful pink crowd.

She thought about the only two people, really, she could or would call. Actually only one—Lucy was touring with her band somewhere. Austin? Chicago? It would be hard to reach her even if she knew; they were on totally different schedules. It was too bad she'd never made any close friendships with other housewifey women. Most women scared her. Their neat, wholesome lives. Their judgment. She didn't really trust herself, so why would she trust other women?

But there was Mann, as always. Mary Byrd supposed that what Mann got out of their friendship was mostly entertainment. There was enough dysfunction and drama and artiness in the Thornton orbit to keep him endlessly amused. And he cared about Charles and Eliza and William and the animals as well: his old prep-school friend, the children he'd never have, and the pets he could enjoy but never have to fool with. Mann was practically family, devoted to them all. But he was just a tiny bit more devoted to Mary Byrd, she thought, no doubt because she needed him more. Lucy was a better ear for complaints about Charles because she wasn't close to him. Not that there was ever much to complain about. So as usual, she'd call Mann. Almost always upbeat, with a lot of free time, he tolerated her whining or rants, he sometimes had useful things to say, and when he felt she'd indulged herself enough and she was boring him, he'd stop her. Mann was the perfect surrogate husband when you left out sex and reproduction. He was also so precious and tiny—collectible—with his beautiful coppery hair, violet eyes, and perfect little clothes that he often let her wear. What would she do without him?

Hubard Mann Valentine Jr. was from Dundee, a decrepit, crumbly river port town—"Home of the World's Largest Bream"—where his Virginia forbears, like so many Mississippians, had migrated after losing the considerable fortune they had made importing liquor and wine into Richmond before the war. It wasn't that after the war there was no longer a need for booze; in fact, there was an insatiable need—the desperate need of big-time losers. But the Valentine home had been burned with much of Richmond by General Goddamn Weitzel, and so had their James River dock and boats, and the Richmond and Danville railroad had been torn up, and the Yankees had taken their horses, wagons, and mules, and the slaves had bolted, and anyway nobody had had any money anymore to buy good liquor. Bootleggers, who never went to war, took over with their jinky distilling contraptions made of cottonseed oil drums and hog intestines (the ones that weren't eaten), producing unguinous, toxic swills that they sold in used bottles that they painted so that customers couldn't see the sick color or the varmint hairs and bug pieces that might float within. Deciding on a fresh start, the Valentines descended to Mississippi and bought into the newly rebuilt Mobile and Ohio Railroad as minor shareholders. The family scraped along in considerably reduced circumstances for a couple generations until Mann's daddy met his mother, Carusa, a hard McComb girl with ambition. She took the genteelly impoverished and feckless Mr. H. M. Valentine Sr., who had been *reading for the law* at the university for thirteen years and making and drinking his own small-batch shine, and steered him away from alcohol and law. Thanks to Carusa Valentine, the reconstruction of southern railroads, the advent of trucks, and the South's addiction to fried chicken, the family built another fortune.

Mann had grown up in the chicken plant, cleaning up, hosing down, packing, wearing waders and slogging through offal, feathers, cigarette butts, tobacco cuds, and blood. Carusa insisted that he learn the business from the bottom up, and she meant this very literally. Every time in his adult life that something unhappy occurred, Mann rated it against the summers he had had to work the conveyor belt, seizing slippery, naked dead birds by their drumsticks, spreading them, and sniffing their private cavities for freshness. He had kept a bucket by his feet for when he puked on the bad ones, and was happy when he was promoted to the chick pens, where he became the only non-Vietnamese at the plant who could sex a three-day-old chick.

After prep school at Woodberry Forest, where he and Charles were roommates, Mann was sent off to business school at Emory, where he very belatedly realized his sexual preference amongst the gaggles of fluffy blond Hitler-youth, Jesus-adoring boys. Some *were* and some *weren't*. If he could only sex them or sniff them out, like his chickens. He learned soon enough. But, confused about the nature versus nurture controversy surrounding homosexuality, and worried about all the hormone-dosed poultry he'd come in contact with, Mann had wondered if his chicken experiences had marked him. To Mary Byrd he described his early hetero encounters in terms of chicken; a date situation he'd gotten into once had been "exactly like putting my hand in a bucket of hot, throbbing, just-harvested chicken livers." Although Mary Byrd assured him that it wasn't a choice—"You just hatched out of your own queer little egg just the way you are"—Mann never felt completely convinced that the chicken work hadn't turned him gay.

After college, he was invited back to Dundee and into the office where he spent long, nutty days on the phone dispatching trucks and fussing with buyers in Russia or Mexico or dealing with shitweasels like Elvers Hartay. A nasty bantam of a man who called himself a preacher, Hartay also ran a dirty little farm where he raised roosters that he somehow, Mann was convinced, stole from the vast chick pens at Valentine Chickens. Mann also suspected Hartay of doping rooster chicks with huge amounts of steroids, and then, when they grew scarily gigantic, selling the roosters, big and mean as turkey vultures, back to Mann as "good breeding stock." What Hartay's Cocks LLC was *really* doing was providing most of the champion fighting birds at work in the Deep South. Even at the end of the twentieth century, a chicken thief was still a chicken thief and one of the lowliest of assholes. Mann was determined to bust Hartay someday, somehow, preferably in his own church pulpit, where

Hartay railed every Sunday morning and Wednesday night against cold beer and in less public places about *lower-echelon nigras and hummasekshuls.*

At any rate, now Valentine Chickens was enormous, operating internationally, and Mann was one of the most successful chicken brokers in the country. A *revendeur de poulet,* as he snarkily referred to himself. He actually even loved some aspects of the job. He employed his highly evolved decorating skills to create gorgeous, eye-catching graphics for his trucks, packaging, and advertising. He chose two colors: an old red and a beautiful meadowy green—more Martha Stewart than John Deere—stolen from the shutters of the Soniat House, his favorite place to stay in New Orleans. The Valentine logo he designed himself, inspired by an old paper valentine from the 1940s and a cake shop in New York: a cozy-looking farmhouse and pasture done in the green, framed by clover and hearts and a kitcheny checked border in the soft red. Across the top of the logo, in Hollywood newsreel lettering, was VALENTINE CHICKENS and beneath that the slogan FROM US TO YOU WITH LOVE. Used on the chicken packages, the green of the logo brought out the fresh pinkness of chicken meat, and made the chicken of rival companies seem to be a sickly yellow. But the trucks were Mann's magnum opus. The billboard-size flanks of the trucks were done entirely in the lovely green, and the logo appeared in cream and the pinky red that looked vintage even when freshly painted, the whole thing evoking wholesomeness, World War Two, Valentine's Day, and Christmas as the semis rocketed down the highways with their raw, frozen loads of legs, wings, tenders, breasts, necks, livers, hearts, gizzards, and random pieces-parts for America's tables and dog bowls.

In spite of all his money, Mann wasn't pretentious, or snobby. How *could* you be uppity about being a chicken man? He didn't give a rat's ass, actually; chicken money spent just as well as any other kind. Chickens afforded him a tiny jewel of an apartment, his pleasure dome in the Marais and a charmed life with the occasional lover, clothes from Barneys and Bergdorf's, good restaurants, and travel. With the exception of a few jerks like Elvers Hartay, Mann was pretty much accepted, in fact, well respected in their town, where he'd chosen to live because he loved college sports, and in Dundee, where he commuted to his office when he had to.

In spite of the rest of the world's perception, small southern towns knew how to tolerate difference. There was always an old queer or lesbian couple, or a Boo Radley in town. You just had to not be *from away*, and stay within the unspoken boundaries, and you would have grown up knowing what those were. There was a place—a role—for everyone, and there actually had to be a few marginal types to provide the entertainment that kept everyone going and feeling that they were what *normal* was. Your chance of social success was greater if you were somebody's smelly, addled uncle or transvestite cousin than if you were a stranger from California or Chicago trying to accrete in.

Mary Byrd loved Mann and she knew that's who she'd call. Back in the house, she listened for Evagreen, who she thought was upstairs. She was so stealthy, you never knew. Picking up the phone in the study, she yanked it and its cord into the small booze closet and closed the door. She didn't need J. Edgar Evagreen listening in. She dialed Mann's number, which always gave her a soupçon of happiness: 328-2449, or as Mann enjoyed telling select people, EAT-CHIX. His head was charmingly miswired, and he got things backward or confused: "chopsticks" might come out "foresticks," the Longshot Bar might be "The Shothole," or he might describe a color as being "egg-robin blue"—but he was very smart in ways that Charles and Mary Byrd appreciated.

Mann answered the phone and Mary Byrd said what she always said when things, for one reason or another, weren't going well: "Come get me."

"What now?" he asked.

"God," she sighed. "The worst. Well, of course not the worst, but not good."

"Tell me," he encouraged.

"You know that stuff that happened with my stepbrother? When he died?"

"Of course."

"And you know they never got the guy who did it? A guy right down the street, but they could never prove it, and oh, god, I don't know, it just never got solved. We . . . we didn't keep up with it. We just wanted it to go away." Mary Byrd could hear Mann fiddle with his stereo, turning down his music. Sade. It bugged her when he did certain trademark gay things—profiling himself. "But now some reporter in Richmond has apparently been going back through files, cold cases, and digging around for stuff to write about. She's going to do an article or book or something."

Mann exhaled loudly. "How do you know all this?" he asked.

"Because she—the reporter—called me. I guess she turned something up, and the police don't want to look stupid, or have her fucking up the case. A detective called me, too, and now they want to talk to my whole family. On *Monday*." Her voice broke a little on *family*.

"Aren't you glad that they might finally solve things? And it will all be over?"

"No!" she said, and quickly added, "I mean of course I am. I, we, *are* sort of over it, as much as we can be, you know? I mean, it was thirty years ago. I don't want to have to do all that again."

Mann asked, "So maybe they've got new evidence. DNA. Or a new suspect."

"I don't know. The detective wouldn't say, and I don't know what the reporter knows. I wouldn't talk to her."

"Just think: whoever it was could still be walking around committing more . . . crimes, and messing up more lives. It's got to be a *good* thing that they're bringing the case back up."

She sniffed hard to steady her voice. "Of course I get that. I just can't tell you how much it will suck to go there again. And if it's true—did I ever tell you this?—one of the *theories*," she said the word with sarcasm, "one of the stupid ideas the police had was that this guy who they thought killed Stevie did it because of some twisted fixation he had on *me*. That I led him on. What if that's true?"

Mann said firmly, "Look, I don't think that can be what happened. We talked about this before. Child molesters who go after boys are *not* interested in teenage girls. They don't make substitutions. That is a fact. They want what they want, like animals. Or like everybody else! You know that, M' Byrd. I can't believe a detective or whatever would tell a teenage girl something like that."

"A lot of things were going on with me and my family, and what fifteen-year-old wouldn't believe a cop?" Her exhaled breath whistled in the receiver.

"What was the name of the guy—the guy down the street?"

"Ned Tuttle."

"Look, this is *not* about you! Maybe it's true that Ned Tuttle had a crush on you, but that doesn't mean he killed your stepbrother, right? And maybe he *did* kill your stepbrother, but that doesn't mean it had anything to do with you. Did you not ever watch *Car 54* or *Andy Griffith*? Those cops in Virginia were probably just hicks. Do you think they knew anything about criminal psychology? They're just guys who can make mistakes.

Probably they'd never even had a crime in Richmond like that. Not back then."

"They took my diary," Mary Byrd said. It was hard to keep the tremble out of her voice. Why did people mostly only cry if they had an audience. "I don't know *what's* in that thing. I didn't even remember then. They still have it. Mann, I'm scared of Ned Tuttle."

There was silence on the line. Then Mann said softly, "Jeez, M'Byrd. I don't know what to tell you, except that I can't believe anybody would pay much attention to anything in a teenager's diary, and I don't think it makes sense for you to be scared of the guy. You just feel upset and paranoid. I'm really sorry. Please don't blubber."

"I'm not," she said, snorting back hard to abort her sniveling. "You know I don't cry. But—maybe I did say or do something to . . . piss Tuttle off or something. Anyway, it doesn't matter if it was true or not, or made any sense, I just know my stepfather probably believed it. He was always giving me crap about being boy-crazy, guys sniffing around. It didn't take much for him to blame my sluttiness for—whatever. We really didn't get along anyway and we pretty much stopped talking after Stevie died."

"Man," said Mann. "I hate it for you. I'll go up there with you if you want," he lied.

"Yeah, right." Mary Byrd paused. "Thank god my stepfather is dead. Okay. I've gotta get my ass in gear and get the kids and tell Charles what's going on. I'll call you later. Thanks, Mann."

"You okay?"

"Course. Always am."

"Tough girl," he said.

"Ha."

"You know what that guy—what's his name? Don Walsh?— says on every *America's Most Wanted* show? 'And remember: YOU can make a difference.' Just do it."

"*John* is that guy's name," she said. "I don't know if you watch too much TV, or not enough."

They hung up. Mary Byrd didn't feel any better. It wasn't about feeling better, there wasn't any feeling better about Stevie. It was a matter of feeling *less* as time went on, but not *better*. She guessed it felt safer for somebody to know what a little hell she was in. She couldn't even stand to mention the note that Ned Tuttle had written her, which seemed to definitely point to her . . . *involvement*. How was it that the reporter seemed to know something about all that?

Mary Byrd stepped out of the booze closet and wandered back into the study, heading for a box of old family photos. She dug through the piles for a small manila envelope that held the few family snapshots with Stevie. She hadn't looked at them in forever. All but one was black and white and she supposed had been taken with her old Brownie. Here was the only shot of the whole family together at the bay, standing in the sand in front of the family cottage. Pop, smoking a cigar, handsome and fat, her teeny mom with cool shades and a Jackie Kennedy scarf over her hair, holding Baby Pete. Nick stood sideways, flexing his biceps, practically black with a tan, holding a dead crab; that was his MO, picking up dead crap on the beach and pretending he'd caught it. James and Stevie knelt in the sand, James imitating Stevie who was imitating Nick, all flexing their pathetic muscles, squinting into the sun like they were badasses. Everyone was in a bathing suit but Mary Byrd, who wore a sweatshirt and cutoffs; she'd rather have died than be in her two-piece in a family photo. She stood off to the side, looking enormous—as big as Pop! It must have been the summer before Stevie died. Who'd taken that picture?

Here was another shot of her, Nick, Stevie, and James stacked up in order on the sliding board in the backyard. She wore a madras kerchief and one of her mom's old bathing suits, a black tank she could barely squeeze into. She'd loved it because it had great falsies. The big boys were shirtless in shorts, and James wore only a droopy, probably damp, cloth diaper. Boys never wore clothes or shoes in summer back then. William and his friends never went shirtless or barefoot, or even wanted to. Funny.

The other two pictures were just of Stevie. In one, the color photo, he sat at the kitchen table, leaning on his crossed arms, smiling a tight-lipped, satisfied smile. Lined up before him was a row of his little metal trucks. He was obsessed with them, especially his yellow and green dump truck, whose doors opened and the dumper thing actually dumped. He had a thing he'd say to himself over and over, down on the floor or in the yard, playing intently, "Pickin' up dirt, brrrrooom, *dump truck*," as he made the dumper dump. It looked like he'd loaded it with—what? Peanuts? Or maybe pumpkin seeds; her mother toasted the seeds in salt and butter at Halloween. Stevie loved them. Mary Byrd noticed that the truck was worn nearly silver with use. The last shot was Stevie in a gigantic cartoonish bonnet she'd made for Baby Pete. He was making a goofy monster face and raising his fist at the camera. His big, blocky head looked ridiculous on top of his scrawny little neck and shoulders. Oh god, she thought, his pitiful, pitiful little birdy shoulders, where his killer had cut the letter N. Mary Byrd put the photos back in the envelope, wondering how long it would be before she'd look at them again.

She startled, hearing the school buses grinding their gears on the steep hill at the intersection of their street and Jefferson. She'd be late to get William and Eliza. What else was new. She could think this trip crap through later.

Where *was* Evagreen, she wondered. She didn't hear the vacuum, so she was probably still upstairs doing the bathrooms. Feeling too sapped to climb the stairs, and not wanting to catch

Evagreen possibly smoking out the window, Mary Byrd cupped her hands around her mouth and yelled up at the air vent, "Evagreen! Going to get the children!" Pausing a second for a response that she knew wouldn't come, she put on her coat and pulled on her gloves and left the house by the back door. Some slugs had left a big map of shiny rainbow mucus on the steps, she noticed. What were slugs doing around in the winter? Why did slugs even exist at all? So gross, she said to herself. Were slugs just escargot without shells? And why did so many disgusting things feature rainbows? Slug tracks, spoiled ham, fly wings, greasy starlings, oil on a fish pond? Aloud, she said, "Assholes," knowing how the slugs spent luxurious nights devouring her hostas. William would be happy to salt them, or make them a little beer hot tub. Poor slugs, just trying to get by like everybody else, and, like everybody else, they couldn't help it if they did some asshole things.

FROM THE WINDOW on the landing upstairs, Evagreen watched the driveway until she saw the Ford Explorer backing out through the bare crape myrtle trunks. Pushing the window up, she muttered, "Hmph. Never gone put this screen back in. Wonder so many bugs always be around in here, matter *how* I clean." From the pack of Salems in the pocket of her warm-up jacket she took a cigarette and lit up, exhaling the first delicious, minty draw into the cold air. She sat down on the windowsill with her feet on the roof.

"Hollerin' up through the vents!" She was indignant. "Like trash." From blocks away, she could hear the squeals and shouts of children being let out at the elementary school. Three squirrels ran up and down, chasing each other high up in a leafless chinaberry tree she could barely see off in the woods. Look like they on wheels, or a rollercoaster, they move so smooth and quick, up and down. Chinaberries in winter, with their round gold seed pods, always reminded her of a crayon drawing one of her twins had made for her a long time ago, with clusters of polka-dot fruit grouped in the branches. She still had that drawing, probably Tommy Smith's; John Carlos never too big on coloring, even though the boys identical. She had *all* the twins' and Ken's and Angie's old school things in the deep bottom drawer of her bedroom chest. Beyond the woods the school bus engines rumbled and groaned as they climbed the hill, and somewhere in the neighborhood college boys were carrying on. "Not studyin', that for sure," she tsked. She wished her own boys had stayed close, gone to Delta State, even Valley, instead of going to college in Atlanta. Had to go where the most money was, though, and at least they got to go together; keep each other out of trouble and focused on playing ball. They'd been a little wild, not solid like Angie or Ken, but they seemed to be straightened out now, and she thanked the Lord for that. Evagreen suddenly felt as chilly and gray as the day outside, and shivered, but instead of closing the window, she pinched out the cigarette butt between two leathery fingers and lit another. The butts would be stashed in the pocket of her warm-up pants, and later when she cleaned one of the bathrooms she'd flush them. Air things out, then close the window.

In the master bedroom—Mary Byrd just referred to it as "her" room, or "our" room, but Evagreen insisted on calling it the "master" bedroom to Mary Byrd's aggravation—she picked up a bottle of lavender body oil and some Q-tips from the dresser top and headed to Eliza's room.

The room, a messy pink lair, gave off the bright message that a girl child who considered herself to have outgrown the room's furnishings and décor lived here. Somewhere between a dorm and a nursery, faded pink eyelet curtains hung at the windows and a gauzy mosquito net floated above a bed piled with gaily printed Home Barn pillows. Three big bulletin boards covered the walls, and each was thickly shingled with snapshots. Every photo was the same as the others: tight gaggles of pubescent girls grinning ferociously with glittery, braced teeth, arms around each other, mostly blonde heads pressed tightly together, the girls on the ends with one leg, toe pointed, raised coyly behind. Mardi Gras beads, beer huggies with fishing jokes, invitations, ticket stubs, and words and phrases clipped from magazines festooned it all—masterpieces of new-hormone collage. Alicia Silverstone vamped from a *Clueless* poster on the closet door. In a corner, a number of dingy, matted stuffed animals were mounded carelessly next to a battered dollhouse that vaguely resembled the Thorntons' Victorian home.

"Breaking a perfectly good plate," Evagreen muttered, stiffly lowering herself to her knees in front of the dollhouse. "Not even on accident." From beneath the diminutive claw-footed bathtub she pulled a paintbrush and began gently dusting the dollhouse surfaces. When this was complete to her satisfaction, she took a Q-tip, dipped it in the lavender oil, and carefully swabbed the tiny rosewood and cherry furniture and the walnut wainscoting and chair rails, turning the Q-tip to the dry end to buff it all down to a rich, miniature luster. Sometimes Evagreen would arrange the rubbery play people and beds, tables, and chairs, narrating to herself: "They's a new baby. Everyone got to move around." Or, "They mama died. Good riddance. They grandmama got to move in an' take over." She longed to redecorate the old dollhouse, to cheer the place up and paint over the faded old miniscule forget-me-not wallpaper in a warm, bright color, peach or aqua or sunflower; crochet some cozy acrylic granny squares for rugs—you could *wash* those—and throw away the stiff, stained little "Aubussons" with their ugly moth holes.

The dollhouse furniture was quality, Evagreen knew that, and although she herself preferred furniture styles that were more substantial and more comfortable, she appreciated the beautiful woods and craftsmanship of the pieces. All the little drawers worked, tiny gateleg tables opened, the cast-iron oven door folded down; it was something for things so small to work so well. "Hmph. Not like around here in *this* house. They's some nice furniture, family things, but knobs gone, veneer peeling, drawers warp and don't close, even if I do run over 'em with bar soap. Don't nobody care. *Umn.*" Although Evagreen was happy to fail to notice cobwebs and dust bunnies and fingerprints around the real house, and tarnish could darken the Thorntons' silver and brass, for Evagreen, the dollhouse and its family was a model of good housekeeping and family behavior, and she planned to keep it that way.

Eliza took little notice of Evagreen's efforts except to remark to her mother, "Mom, my dollhouse smells like you when you get out of the shower."

"Does it?" Mary Byrd had answered. She'd vaguely noticed the scent in her daughter's room, too. "I thought you were just poaching my lavender."

"Right, Mom. Like I would *really want* to smell like you."

"What was I thinking?" her mother had lightly replied. It never paid to take a daughter's insults seriously.

Evagreen finished straightening in Eliza's and William's rooms and very casually cleaned their bathroom. The children's environment was a mixture of filth and persnickety hygiene. Socks could be worn for days, hair and toothpaste slobber could coat the tub and sink, boogers could be wiped on the corner of the bed sheets, William even had what he thought was a secret booger crop on his wall, but yet each child *had* to have a clean towel every day, and in Eliza's case two: one just for a hair turban. Despite what she perceived to be a spoiled upbringing, Evagreen felt a strong, if not deep, affection for the two Thornton children and blamed their shortcomings and flaws on

Mary Byrd. "Don't go to church, that's why. Animals live in the house, eat and sleep on the table, the chair, everwhere. Things be pile up all over." There was a long, long litany of cause-and-effect about the Thorntons—at least this generation—that Evagreen recited to herself every Thursday. Basically it came down to how far white people had fallen, and how foolishly they brought so many of their problems all on themselves.

With her own family, her own four children, Evagreen had been strict to the point of military: church, school, after-school jobs, college. She and L. Q. were there for them in the mornings, after school, and at night, even though it meant L. Q. had to take the graveyard shift at Chambers Stove. Maybe "The Dream" hadn't quite been theirs, but it sure was going to be those kids'. No doubt.

Evagreen had been cleaning house for Mary Byrd and Charles since they married, and she was something of a legacy. Her Auntee Rosie had taken care of Charles's old great-aunt Rosalie for most of Rosalie's spinsterhood, the two becoming like an old married couple as their years together totted up. Totally in tune with one another's personalities and foibles and tricks, and united against outside interference, they became a formidable two-headed beast, not to be taken lightly or for granted. The two roses: a thorny totem of the Old South. Occasionally there would be a falling-out. When Rosalie's health began to flag, they almost broke up over Rosie's desperate attempt to trick Rosalie into eating. After exhausting every nourishing excitement she could think up or cook, Rosie had offered Rosalie ants on a log—celery sticks slathered with peanut butter and studded with raisins, the heinous "salad" of elementary school lunches—and this had been such a grievous affront to Rosalie's sophisticated palate that she had rallied and regained strength out of sheer indignation, a response that Rosie had probably anticipated. The two didn't speak for weeks. When Rosie's family asked why she tolerated Miss Rosalie's uncalled-for wrath, Rosie only replied with a wink, "That all right. Ever mornin' I spits in her coffee." They were much more like Gertrude and Alice than Morgan Freeman and Jessica Tandy. In fact, they were both more like Alice B. Toklas: small, sinewy, dark, and prickly as mock orange.

Evagreen had a lot of her Auntee Rosie in her. Mary Byrd, someone from away who had just married in, with no breeding, no idea of how things worked in an old family in a small Mississippi town, did not know her place, was never going to measure up to the examples set by the women in the Thornton family, most notably Charles's sainted mother, Lydia—everyone called her Liddie—and her sister, Evelyn. Evagreen knew that Mary Byrd knew the truth of the matter, too. Didn't count that she was from Virginia; as far as Evagreen was concerned, anything north of Louisiana, Mississippi, or Alabama was *north*. Even Georgia. "Atlanta full of gangster trash, pervert baby-killers. Might as well be Chicago," she'd say. And even Alabama didn't hardly count: "Not enough black folks to make it a decent place to live. Just rednecks and cracker trash, mud and clay," was her feeling about it.

Evagreen gathered up a bag of bathroom and bedroom garbage—empty Gatorade and shampoo bottles, Mountain Dew and Coke cans, a few empty bubble packs and Styrofoam chunks that some of the children's mysterious electronic gadgetry had come in. She stomped on the garbage bag to mash the cans and plastic down so that Mary Byrd wouldn't notice that things weren't being recycled. "Recycle—more crazy white people's notions. What the matter with the dump and burning, way it always been done?" She gave a last satisfied look at the dollhouse.

Downstairs Evagreen surveyed the kitchen, taking a moment to stick one pointed fingernail into her small, perfect helmet of a hairdo for a thoughtful scratch. She began to rinse and wash the coffee machine, taking the cleaned drip basket and placing it far back in a little-used cupboard. It *could* be seen but would have to be looked for. She considered that this might be pushing it a little, since just the previous week she had hidden one of Mary Byrd's favorite earrings in the same way, and not long before that she had allowed—had *encouraged*—one of the dogs to chew up a high heel, a prized Jimmy Choo, by rubbing the tiniest dab of bacon fat around the inside. "Only a ho gone wear a shoe like that, anyway. Four hundred dollar shoe. *Umn,*" Evagreen rationalized. "It be Jimmy *Chooed* now, all right," she'd laughed. Even though Mary Byrd had the sense to put two and two together about these mutinies she was still not in a position to do without her, Evagreen knew. Charles wouldn't have it. She began loading the dishwasher, noticing with grudging approval that this morning anyway the family had apparently had bacon and eggs for breakfast instead of sugary cereal for the children or that birdseed mess Charles and Mary Byrd ate. No meat, nothing hot, that part of the problem, she thought. Don't have strength to get through the day. And bring in pizza, Taco Bell, that nasty fish for supper—terrible square little bites—not even cooked. *Japanese—umn.* The world done had enough *Japanese.* Pitiful, just pitiful. Evagreen moved on to the drier and began removing warm, fragrant bed sheets. She said out loud, "And don't know how to fold a bottom sheet, hang a towel. Nasty things round the house and on the walls. *Art,* she say. *Umn.* I say *pestilence.* Just pestilence."

In the master bedroom, the phone rang.

Three

JACK ERNEST CAME to with the sickening but sexy sensation of something foul and warm and wet on his face. His aunt's shameful little Yorkie was standing on his chest, feet four-square, lapping at Ernest's mouth. With one hand he chucked the dog across the room where it landed with a wheezing squeak like a child's rubber squeeze toy. He reached for a Marlboro; after a smoke he'd consider full consciousness. Since his return from Bosnia he'd switched to filtered, not entirely unconcerned about his health. Eventually he would rise, shower, and descend to the kitchen where he would have breakfast with his aunt and grandmother. Then he would go back into his room and write about the war. He did this eighteen days out of the month and had accumulated most of his novel, to be titled "It Tolls for Me." Every other weekend or so he went up to town, where the university was, to party. That was what he planned to do Saturday.

In a not-so-far-back part of his mind he hoped to cause his path to cross that of Mary Byrd Thornton, whom he enjoyed imagining he loved because he should not. If not Mrs. T, there might be a splendid array of substitutes. But it took something away for Ernest if it came without enough resistance. It was as much about the hunt as anything else. Like a Pink Palace steak never could taste as good as something he'd stalked in the woods for hours, brought down himself, dragged out, field dressed, and grilled under the stars. He relished things that tried to get away. That's why they called it game, right? Trophy meal, trophy fuck. Elusion and trouble were his condiments of choice. He cared about Byrd in his own way. He *liked* her. She was smart enough and fun and cynical; she shared his view that many things in life were bullshit. She looked good enough—she was pretty in a schoolmarmish way—but there was a sort of animal, wildlife thing about her that Ernest found enticing. He supposed he was just pussy-struck, as usual, but he could detect something dark about her that needed encouraging; something wounded and self-destructive that would be so sweet to take advantage of and would make her his perfect partner in sexual crime. She'd asked him to back off, and he could, but it was more interesting not to. She didn't mean it anyway.

From downstairs, women's kitchen chatter wafted up with the warm aromas of bacon and coffee. Best smell in the world, he thought, then re-thought: well, maybe second best.

Ernest sat down at the table with the women. Sisters, but they could not have been more different. Aunt Anna, Ernest's grandmother, whom he called "Antenna" because as a kid that's what he thought his older cousins were calling her, was conservative and provincial in all her notions but first with the latest fads at the mall, wore a wind suit—a plastic abomination of turquoise and fuchsia geometric designs. Ernest thought that after jogging suits, which people now actually wore out in public as if they were real clothes, wind suits were one of the most hideous affronts to the human body since leisure suits. He had not forgotten the jarring sight of those, like garbage men outfits, worn with white shoes and white belts by his grandfather and uncles, or the cheesy feel of their polyester Sansabelt slacks. Even at six or seven, running around shirtless and shoeless, he wanted to look like a frat guy: khakied, tweedy, clubtied; the perfect rebelsexual. Or like his mother's brother, Uncle Pothus, who never wore anything that he hadn't bought at the Brooks Brothers or Rosenstein's in New Orleans.

Antenna had had only one husband, Toy, who had simply sat down under a pine on the fifth hole of the Hatchatalla Country Club golf course one day and never got up again. She was as sad and prim and prissy as her sister Ella King was loose and generous of disposition.

Ella King on the other hand looked like Aunt Bee—henbreasted, tiny of foot and voice—but she held advanced ideas and had a sharp sense of humor. She had had two husbands and four children and was never without an escort for a movie or church event. She enjoyed David Letterman and smoked Parliaments. The recessed filter kept you from getting lip cancer.

"You know, Jacky, if you're going to party this weekend, there's a big winter storm coming—it's all across the TV," said Antenna.

"It's true—Dolores called and she watches that new weather channel day and night," said Ella King.

"You might could use those tire chains," Antenna said. "The ones we had for that last ice storm in nineteen seventy-three." She rocked the skillet back and forth to distribute the grease.

"I've got plans for those chains, my good grandmother," Ernest said. "And they don't include putting them on the car." He winked salaciously at Ella King, who laughed.

"Honestly, Jack. What a white-trash thing to say," said Antenna. She sniffed to signify indignation.

Ernest ignored her, slurping his coffee and wondering how he could find Teever to drive him around up there. He hoped he wasn't in jail again. His mouth full of a third egg-and-bacon biscuit, he asked, "Whersh Pothush?"

"Well, he had a . . . restless night," said Ella King, smirking.

Ernest said, pushing back his plate, "Yeah, I'll bet he did." Pothus had pounded most of a bottle of Maker's watching old movies.

The insectoid dog crept nervously into the room.

"And why is this dog acting like he's been beaten?" asked Antenna. The wind suit gave off a lot of irritating noise as she moved toward the coffee pot. "Come here, Ashley," she said, making little air smooches. "*Mwa.*"

"That dog is a loser," said Ernest.

"Ashley, oh Ashley," she said. She scooped up the little dog. "Don't listen to him. You're such a gentleman. And so handsome."

"He might look handsome at the end of a fishing line, or on the lazy Susan at the Ruby Chinese," Ernest rose from the table. "But there is no other way he would."

Upstairs, Ernest took a pair of Duck Heads from a clean, ironed stack of a dozen, and a crisp white shirt from a sizable row in his closet. He added a blazer and shades and the look was complete—the relentless and correct uniform of the Mississippi boulevardier and how he dressed every day. To get the creativity and testosterone percolating for a day of writing, he decided to take his gun out and shoot some stuff. From under his bed he pulled an AK-47.

It was an older gun; the folding butt stock had been painted red at one time, for identification, he supposed. The gun had been handled so much that the paint had worn away, leaving the wood with a rich cherry patina. It was lovely to look at and even better to feel. Ernest petted it, tracing a whorl in the grain with his finger. He had bought the gun for almost nothing—fifteen American dollars and a couple packs of Marlboros—from a wounded teenager returning from some Bosnian skirmish.

The kid, broken in every way, had had no wish for anything other than slivovice and cigarettes. He had laughed weakly, and had spoken in a gargly voice in spite of the neck wound that leaked Marlboro smoke. Ernest had said that he himself was headed out to write about the war. A Red Cross medic, a Texas girl of Ernest's acquaintance, had translated the soldier's exhausted remarks. "He's more or less telling you to *go on, get on up in it*," she said. "*Get you some*." He had smuggled in the AK by sending it home FedEx—you could send anything FedEx, bless them. The Mercury of the twentieth century. In Bosnia, Ernest had known guys who had sent amazing things stateside. He met a GI whose great-great-great grandfather was the Cherokee chief, the Ridge. The soldier had scalped a Serbian prisoner's unit, taking away pud, pelt, and balls, and sent it FedEx to his girlfriend. Another GI had sent exotic mushrooms and rare plants to his boyfriend in Mobile.

The AK under his arm, Ernest stomped downstairs again. He casually aimed the gun at Ashley and said, "Boom!"

"This dog is worth hundreds of dollars at stud," Antenna said. "So please point that thing somewhere else."

Ernest said, "You're crazy, Antenna. You know that dog has failed at love." He didn't get it about a dog that couldn't hunt, fight, or scare people, especially a dog that couldn't even mate with a real dog who could do those things.

"I know no such thing," Antenna called. "A random Rottweiler twice his size is no test of his abilities."

To Ernest, if you couldn't get it up for exotic, strange pussy, even if it was large, what was the point? Instead of saying this he said, "Well, I wish he'd quit testing his abilities on my hunting boots." He filled his coffee cup with some Tanqueray from the flask in his blazer and went out back.

AT MOLLY BARR Elementary, Mary Byrd got her Explorer in the long line of cars that wound up the school driveway to its entrance. Because she was a little late—most of the mothers came early to park in the line and check out the day's slick batch of catalogs—she was at the bottom of the long, stupid line. As usual. Through the oak and cedars she could identify every single car: the Chadwicks' Range Rover, like a playhouse on wheels, the Blounts' Toyota, the Morrisons' and the Lewises' Volvos, the smattering of BMWs and Mercedeses that belonged to new people—those who had recently moved in from Memphis or Jackson or the Delta, in search of the town's crime-free, arty, sports-possessed, boozy, barbecued college-town life, where white people were enlightened but still in charge. It refreshed Mary Byrd a little to see the other smattering of cars in the line: a few banged-up or rusty hoopties and the earth-toned, carpeted vans from the 1970s with little ladders to the roof. What were those ladders for anyway? Stargazing? Rock concerts? NASCAR infields? The hoopties and vans had trickled down to the poor white and black families, and now were starting to be acquired by the Mexican workers who had come to construct the crappy condos that were cropping up all over town like poison ivy blisters on a careless ankle to accommodate the students, weekend football people, and retirees who didn't want to pay taxes for things that didn't benefit them directly, like schools. Now that tornado season was just around the corner, the regular townspeople wondered if the clusters of cheap condos would hold up with the first big rains and winds of spring. Mary Byrd hoped they wouldn't. Let 'em wash away down the ditches they were built in or blow all over the county. Maybe condo developments would be the new mobile home parks—tornado magnets—and if they did remain standing they would be tomorrow's tenements when the real estate thing busted, which, Mann said, was definitely going to happen.

On the other side of the school building, Mary Byrd could see the orange train of buses all lined up. If she were queen of the world, school buses would still have the usual orange fronts and backs, but their sides would be painted in beautiful and cool ways, like psychedelic hippie buses or those crazy things in Ceylon. Or was it Sri Lanka now? Maybe kids would be happier about going to school if they could climb into a submarine, or a rocket, or a pioneer wagon, or onto a magic carpet. She could hear William saying, "Bye Mom! Got to get in the space shuttle *Endeavour* now and blast off for school!" No—not a space shuttle—bad idea. She thought of the *Challenger* and was glad William hadn't been one of the millions of children who'd watched that awful launch. God. Maybe kids could paint the buses themselves. Why not? As they were, except for their colors, school buses were identical to the prison buses at Parchman. Maybe that's why buses were so institutional and boring: to keep convicts or children from feeling too good about things.

Charles and Mary Byrd saw the bus as the great equalizer. Kids whose parents worked, whether at the hospital or the university or Chambers Stove, were relegated to the school buses, which had always been a sort of rolling microcosm of the real world and a rehearsal for life's realities. Every day zillions of American children were encapsulated in smelly, seat-belt-less tin cans piloted by drivers who could easily be stoned, hopped up, deranged, or worse—twenty-one or sixty-four. Every day they could have fun and socialize and make joyful noise and see and hear things they'd remember nostalgically their whole lives, or they could be robbed, tortured, or humiliated, or all of the above, for twenty minutes twice a day, every day. Maybe it made them tougher or maybe it broke them. Who knew. Mary Byrd hoped that by comparison, maybe riding the bus might at least make kids, even the ones with sketchy families, glad to get home and deal with whatever they needed to deal with when they got there. Well, all of them should ride the bus to school. Or walk. Too many of them were fatties already.

Charles and Mary Byrd were willing to sacrifice Eliza and William so that they could have this democratic experience, but out of some instinct for self-preservation, or just being spoiled, the Thornton children refused to ride the bus. They were okay with walking; but she admitted to herself, the idea of them walking alone, even just a few blocks, made her worry, and so, hypocrite wuss that she was, she caved and slavishly drove them. At least this line of cars seemed emblematic of what a decent mixed bag the town was. Charles always said, "A town is only as good as its public schools," even though he'd been sent off to Woodberry Forest because he'd been something of a problem. In the days of integration, most white townspeople had taken their medicine, opened the schools, and dug in to make the system work for everybody. Not like over in the Delta, for instance, where white people had abandoned the public schools and still perpetuated an un-Christian cycle of failure that would mean, everyone knew, that children would keep leaving and one day there would be nothing left in the Delta but vast corporate farms, computerized machinery, and destitute people, black and white.

It was true that a white academy had opened in their town, too, back in the sixties, subsidized by a wealthy backwoods family that had sold their land in the remote north corner of the state to Weyerhauser. Wanting to "protect their heritage," the family had usurped the university's name to add dignity and the suggestion of scholarship. University College Academy—*double* dignified—had opened in an old country store with seven students, learning their reading, writing, 'rithmatic, and racism. Now UCA was still up and running and operated out of a big new steel building that housed both the library and the gymnasium, and three new Jim Walter homes smushed together for classrooms. But at least UCA absorbed the kind of people who would otherwise be banning books and evolution, creating cotillions and sororities, complaining that black kids got all the playing time on the field or the court, and raising hell about prayers.

But the Delta, Mary Byrd thought sadly. You could go over there, to Shaw or Jonestown, and just looking around was enough to make you cry. The most beautiful, haunted landscape she knew, where every built thing in the tiny cotton-crossroad towns seemed from another time, or another country. She understood its hard past, but for her generation to have turned their backs on it—it sucked. They had had a chance to change history. It was as if crop-dusting poison had eaten their hearts and brains and they were all moving or dying out with all the birds and frogs and bears. Nothing alive but beans, cotton, and farmed catfish. A mosquito empire. Everybody loved the blues, loved to go to the festivals, but go to school with them? Ha. Well, easy for her to say; the university had made their hill town an oasis.

For a second Mary Byrd let her thoughts turn small, to the day's unhappiness. She suddenly couldn't wait to see her children. She had her catalogs, and the previous day's mail had brought her favorite: *Home Trends: Practical Products for Practical People*. The catalog was so lovable and entertaining because it was exactly the opposite of what it advertised. It should have been called *Home Crapola: Unnecessary Make-Work Gadgetry for the Sunset Years*. Mary Byrd was always

enthralled; the main concerns of the catalog seemed to be dealing with bugs, unruly baseball caps, sleep problems, soap scum,
and the protection of wall-to-wall carpeting. Random, name-
less cooties were definitely the enemy for these customers. Who
were they? The terminally lazy, germ freaks, people with that
obsessive-compulsive thing, the really, really bored or the really,
really old, or hopeful people with stock in plastics? Teddy bear
cleaners. A thing that enabled you to wash baseball caps so
that, the description said, they came out of the washer
"unscathed." Sock clips to "end one of the world's greatest
mysteries—missing socks." Mary Byrd knew this wouldn't do
her any good—socks in her house were hopelessly estranged
before they even got to the washer. A shower cap–like thing
with a gel pack—you could put it in the freezer then snap it
onto an electric fan and *voilà*— personal air-conditioning. A
long catch-and-release Bug Buster Wand. The Blanket Support
was a jinky under-the-covers rig that kept the feet of restless
sleepers from touching the bedding. Even weirder was the
personal between-the-sheets Bedfan that for only $79.95
"creates a cool personal microclimate between your bed's
sheets." What was that really about—bed farts? Some products
bordered on snake oil, like the Episal Overnight Drawing Salve
which purported to "draw out foreign substances from beneath
the skin" while you slept, so that in the morning acne and
ingrown hairs would be gone.

As if American products weren't overpackaged anyway, there
were plastic containers for plastic containers. A pancake
dispenser for "accurate" pancakes. A brush with more than a
thousand bristles for removing corn silks. Forks with serrations
on the inside edges of the tines to "stop slippery noodles from
falling onto the table or your lap." Maybe this stuff was for the
handicapped and she should feel bad for ridiculing it. Maybe
one day she would actually *need* the Acid Reflux Pillow (on sale

for only $59.99). Possibly the purpose of the catalog was to give meaning and purpose to life in geezerland. She imagined the process: waiting for the catalog, perusing new products, deciding that there were pressing needs and good bargains, ordering over the phone, taking time to ask a lot of questions and meticulously describing problems. Waiting for the order and the excitement over its arrival, trying to open boxes with arthritic hands (where *is* that special Big Grip Box Cutter ordered last month?), phoning friends to describe a product's success or failure, maybe going to the P.O. to return an item with a long, dissatisfied note. Days could be filled. Why didn't they think of the things *she* needed: an engraving tool for putting ineradicable IDs on eyeglasses or bicycles, or contact paper art, maps, or TV screens for the ceilings of gynecologists' offices, or lady-size Bobcats for big garden jobs. Ha. For burying nosy reporters.

She appreciated the fact that *Home Trends* didn't carry things like that horrible torture tape for mice, whose tiny feet stuck to it making them struggle to death for days. She wouldn't even wish that on moles. Or voles. She thought about her mother's zealous hatred of squirrels. Her mom bragged about trapping them in her Havahart trap and then popping them with her BB gun as they quivered there. Mary Byrd had asked her to please not do it around William and Eliza, who loved Beatrix Potter when they were little—and besides, she had said to her mother, did she want them to think Nana was crazy? Her mom did scare her sometimes. What was the difference between chipmunks and mice, squirrels and rabbits, deer and horses? What was a squirrel but a bunny in Spandex, with short ears? They were all just trying to make it, right?

The car behind her honked, jolting Mary Byrd out of her *Home Trends* musings, and she rolled the car forward to first in line. The school doors disgorged William, entangled with his guys, and then the girls. Mary Byrd focused on William—eight years old, she thought, nine next October. Stevie had been only nine, and was still only nine. Precious in a 1950s way, Stevie, so pink and golden, easily sunburned, had looked nothing like William, whose eyes and hair were deep brown and whose skinny body turned so dark in the summer that they called him the Brown Skeleton. Her heart gave a big chug, and she couldn't be sure if it was guilt, anxiety, or love, or for which boy she felt it. Both.

The boys body-slammed the car, pretending she'd hit them, and William clambered in. The usual carpool boys, Other William and Justin, peeled off to catch a ride to their Boy Scout meeting. She'd had misgivings about Boy Scouts, and William hadn't seemed to care about joining. Eliza and Meggie, Other William's sister, flung themselves into the car, backpacks and girl junk flapping and banging. They were always snappish and kinetic after school, like dogs left on leads too long. Lately, William and Eliza had ratcheted up their surliness; not just after school, but it had become standard, round-the-clock behavior. Even at their ages—Eliza was only a sixth grader—they both seemed to have tapped into teenage viciousness already. Eliza, finding Mary Byrd up late one night upchucking violently in the bathroom after a night of too many cigarettes and Beefeater martinis, olives taking the place of dinner, had regarded her mother coldly and in a manner curiously like Evagreen's, saying "Oh. My. God. Is that *vomit*?" As if Mary Byrd might have been on her knees in front of the toilet doing anything else. "Go back to bed," she had told Eliza. "I've got a stomach virus." The next day Mary Byrd had overheard Eliza telling a friend on the phone, "Mom blew chunks last night. So gross. She *said* she had a stomach virus."

In her own day children respected, or were afraid of, their parents. Why *would* they be afraid now, when they had learned from the Berenstain Bears that dads were bumbling fuckups, and from *Roseanne* that mothers were for fighting with. Charles, formal and aloof, might have commanded more respect had he been around more, but Eliza and William knew better than to mess with him much. She regretted that the Eddie Haskell model of teen rudeness that she and Nick had grown up with was gone—an art kids had developed of behaving offensively without seeming callous or mean, exactly. Just smarmy and punk, like Eddie.

Mary Byrd turned the Explorer slowly up Jefferson, watching for stray kids that might, frantic to get away from school, run into the road.

"Mom, Taylor got the Jansport backpack that I wanted to get, so now I can't, and I know you won't go to the Athlete's Foot to let me pick out another one, and this one *sucks*," Eliza said. "Even Meggie has one."

"Meggie sucks," said William.

"Everyone named William sucks," said Meggie.

Looking into the rearview mirror, Mary Byrd could see her daughter's lovely face, framed by stringy blonde hair and still padded lightly with fat that had not quite settled on her bone structure, pulled into a puffy pout accented by her new red-and-blue rebel braces. "*And* mine still smells like deer pee." Some boys who liked Eliza had put some crap—deer musk or some kind of hunting jizz—on her backpack, and despite a number of washings in everything from tomato juice to, yes, Dog Gone Pee Remover from *Home Trends*, the faintest whiff was still discernible. The children themselves smelled meaty and stale.

"*My* backpack sucks *more*, and if she gets a new one, I do, too! I'm tired of Ninja Turtles." William, who preferred to be squeezed in back between the girls rather than in the front seat where he couldn't annoy them effectively, sprawled out, deliberately putting a leg on Eliza's side. "She always gets everything all the time."

"Always everything all the time!" Mary Byrd said. "How about, 'Hi Mom.' Or, 'How was your day, Mom?' And please don't say *sucks*—I don't know how many times I've asked you this—outside the privacy of our own house. Or how about the privacy of your own *head*? Just think it, don't say it. You know what that expression really means, right?"

"Yes, Mom, we *know* it's about wieners. Big deal," said William, sighing with exaggerated boredom. Meggie giggled, and Eliza looked at them both with disgust.

"And isn't this the privacy of our own *car*?" Eliza said, and then, with almost no sarcasm in her voice, added, "So, Mom, how was your day? I hope it didn't absolutely *blow*."

Mary Byrd thought about reaching behind her over the seat and just smacking randomly at whatever she could hit, like her own mother used to do. Another day, she would have. Today, she thought to herself that whatever assholes they were, these children were hers, so far alive and well and as far as she knew unmolested and maybe pretty happy, probably more out of luck or fate than any good care or protection she and Charles had given them.

"Oh. My day? I guess I'd have to say it sucked," she conceded. "It sucked big-time."

The children looked at each other wide-eyed and laughed. "What's for dinner?" William asked.

Dinner. Good question. The bad day had knocked the sense out of her and she hadn't planned a meal. She'd drop Meggie off and make a quick stop at the Jones Food Center. She wanted to scare up Teever, anyway, if only to see if he could work in the yard while she was gone, but also to ask if he'd drive her to the airport so Charles wouldn't have to. She cringed at the thought of a plane trip. An idea occurred to her: was it total insanity to get Teever to drive with her to Virginia?

She only had a few things to get and hoped Eliza and William would stay in the car, but that wasn't happening. William jumped out and ran ahead, while Eliza walked slowly enough to distance herself from William but quickly enough to appear not to be with her mother. Having a locally owned downtown grocery store was such a luxury, but Mary Byrd also thought that its handiness encouraged her poor planning. Because it was only three blocks away at the end of her street, she found herself running there constantly, sometimes two or three times a day, for whatever. A big Kroger had opened recently out by the highway—the condo people were all over that—and she did shop there for certain things like seafood or panty hose, and Kroger's prices were sometimes lower and they had seafood and better produce, but she was devoted to the Jones Food Center and valued all that it meant, as much as any ancient Athenian had valued his agora. The corner candy store for the children; the place where she could cash a counter check at midnight to pay the babysitter, buy a bale of hay or a sack of manure or a *Mad m*agazine or Baby Tylenol or Tampax, or tiny new potatoes from Mr. Hollowell's farm. If the JFC didn't have it, you probably didn't need it all that much. From the checkers and sackers, some of whom were challenged in various ways, you could get a five-day weather forecast, gardening or cooking tips, or a rundown on who was in the hospital (published every day in the *Mercury*) and why. If you needed your garden turned, Mr. Johnny could conjure up a guy with two mules who would come and do it. There was also a bulletin board where just about anything was posted: cars, services, hunting dogs, house parties, church events, messages, and bad checks. On the way out she was going to leave a message for Teever.

William and Eliza had probably gone off to the cooler in the back for chocolate Yoo-hoos and Jungle Juice. Mary Byrd headed toward the meat counter for pork chops, passing disorderly shelves with products bearing vintage labels that could pass for stuff that had been sitting there for decades: School

Days English Peas, Red Bird imitation Vienna sausages, Possum brand sardines (when she'd first come to town they'd still carried canned Negro Head Oysters), Picayune and Home Run cigarettes, Tulip brand snuff, King Leo stick candy, and Rock'n Roll Stage Plank cookies with Pepto-pink icing showing through the wax wrappers. Grabbing a jar of pasta sauce, she approached the meat, breathing shallowly. The meat bins stank weirdly of the paradoxical aromas of Clorox and spoilage. In them were stacked fatback, souse, Day-Glo–red hot dogs, and nearly every part of a cow or a hog: feet, stomachs, ears, jowls, neck bones, tails, and giant testicles labeled BULL FRIES or PORK FRIES, which were inexplicably packaged three to a pack. There were other things just labeled MEAT. Mary Byrd looked through the chops for a set that wasn't too gray or rainbowy and then headed to Produce.

In deep summer or early fall the produce department was a wonderland overflowing with the bounty of local farmers. In the dead of winter, other than greens, there wasn't much: dinged-up apples, expensive avocados in a basket with a sign saying ADOVACODS, slightly wrinkled, flaccid peppers; the usual stuff trucked in from wherever they grew and trucked that stuff in from. Mary Byrd lusted for the summer's beautiful chartreuse cranberry beans streaked with magenta, or the fat, mottled Georgia rattlesnake beans; crisp, tart, lopsided York apples; Nancy Hall sweet potatoes from the town of Vardaman, the Sweet Potato Capital of the World; vaguely sexual yellow squash with fused necks and the not-so-vaguely-sexual Big Boy tomatoes with mutant, Nixon-faced protuberances. She'd give a lot, in February, to see the JFC's grungy bushel baskets piled with the sweetest Pontotoc peaches, tomatoes labeled SLICERS, rusty carts full of bowling ball–size LOPES, and YELLOW MEAT MELONS lined up on the dirty floor. And pint baskets of figs and blackberries, and sometimes muscadines and scuppernongs packaged in cellophane meat trays. All of it piled high, over-flowing, a carnival of fresh, brightly colored, delicious fruits and vegetables brought into town every day, summer after summer, from the same Mississippi hill country farms.

Mary Byrd frowned, picked out a less-wrinkled pepper and a muddy onion, paid for her stuff and the two Jungle Juices that the children had already absconded with, and stopped at the bulletin board. She tore a big piece off her grocery sack and wrote:

and stuck it up with a pin, hoping Teever would notice but not too many other people would. She hurried to the car outside, where in just the few minutes they had been in the store it had gotten nearly dark, and much colder. As they pulled away toward home, the light inside the Jones Food Center glowed greenly on the empty, wettish sidewalk outside. There were no trays of flowers, fern baskets, tomato plants, or herbs in pots, no bales of hay or pine straw, no pumpkins and gourds and cornstalks and homecoming mums, no fragrant Christmas trees, no stacked firewood, even. This really is *the dead of winter*, Mary Byrd thought. *The dead, the dead, the dead.* She sighed. She hoped Teever would see his message tonight, or at least in the morning. *If* he was even around.

TEEVER BARR WATCHED from the County Co-op as Mary Byrd parallel-parked her car and entered the JFC across the street. It would be an hour or so before it was dark enough to sneak back to his hooch in the cemetery, and he couldn't stay there in front of the Co-op because Mr. Jimmy, the Co-op boss, would run him off. He had about one swig of Amos's shine left but he would save that for later. Mudbird might have some smokes; she always shared and bought him beers at the bar, but she wasn't regular with her smoking. He did have a couple half-smoked ones down in his sock. Best thing about Mr. Jimmy was he could only have a few drags before he started coughing. His cough was way worser than Teever's—man, did he look pretty ill—and he would stop and throw his practically unsmoked butt in the coffee can where lots of folks would get 'em—Dees, Pokey, some of the water-heads from the halfway house, if they came around.

Teever thought he'd stand there a little longer near the space heater 'til they put the chicks and ducks and seed sacks and tools up for the night. He liked to watch the little birds under the heat lamps. Too bad one of the halfway-house dudes did, too; one of them who thought he was a rock star—liked to dress up like a hair band—had bit a head off a chick one time. Teever had heard from Joey at the sally port that that dude had been sent back to Starkville to the *big* rutabaga ranch where they couldn't go around normal folks. Or chickens. Teever did want to speak to Mudbird, just to check on her, see how she doing, what's going on, she need some things done in the yard. Maybe she had a pill. He wondered if Jack Ernest was coming to town soon. He would have pills, booze, probably would need a driver. Mudbird would know when he coming back, though she and Ernest never hung out around people too much; some drinks maybe at the Bear, maybe a late-night. He knew Ernest chased Mudbird around some, but Ernest chase *all* the mossyjaw. He thought, personally, that Mudbird could do better. Wasn't nothing wrong with Charles, neither; not as far as he could see, anyway, but who knew what in a woman's mind. Some people probably thinking she crazy. She was nice. She was funny. Little old maybe, but not bad looking. Too bad she wearing those glasses—make her look like what's-her-name, Murder She Wrote, or somebody. No tits or ass, but Teever enjoyed hitting on her, playing, get her all bothered and who knows, maybe one day. Everybody like secrets. Well. He wasn't sure Ernest was doing her anyway. Maybe so, maybe not. So hard to tell sometimes *what* white people up to.

Teever, né Tolliver, was just about the last black Barr left in town. His people said they were descended from a slave of Pinckney Taliaferro of Goose Creek, South Carolina, who had come west to Mississippi when Taliaferro was accused of salting a competitor's rice crop. The Barrs said they had some Native American in them, too. "Yeah, I got Indian," was Teever's response when asked about it, letting loose his extremely loud, throaty laugh. "*Blackfoot* maybe."

He was also a Vietnam vet. Although no one could be sure that he could read or write, he was plenty smart. His company was made up almost completely of destitute Delta kids, mostly sons of sharecroppers from those sad old towns like Panther Burn or Marks, where the slogan chiseled into the courthouse lintel was OBEDIENCE TO THE LAW IS LIBERTY. Those guys had little to lose. At Hamburger Hill something bad had happened with a second lieutenant, it was rumored, a white West Point boy from North Carolina. No one really knew what had occurred, but some of the black guys, Teever included, had gone to Parchman. Whenever anyone had the balls to ask Teever about it, he'd simply laugh and say, "Ain't no shame in my game." You did not want to press Teever too hard on things.

Now Teever was mostly a driver and yard guy. People around town—often some of the writers who drank a lot—paid him to drive for them. Took people to Memphis to the airport, drove kids to summer camp, picked up college kids at the bar or a party if they were too drunk, took old ladies to church and bridge, picked up "special deliveries." He didn't have a driver's license. Why would he? He didn't have a car. Nobody really knew where he lived, but if anyone needed him they could put the word out, stick a note on the wall at the JFC, and he would turn up. In a really cold winter he might do something blatant in public—openly sell some crack on the square, steal a King Cobra from the B Quick—and end up in the cozy Lafayette County jail where his old bud Papadop would cook him Philly cheese steaks every day and give him Cost Cutter smokes. He'd just repeat his mantra, "Ain't no shame in my game," and wait until spring, when the judge, who Teever knew to have a gay black lover in Memphis, would let him back on the street. Teever traded on the secrets he knew; it was the only currency he had. Why not? Everybody was trading on something. "Everybody got something somebody else want; pussy, drugs, famous, secrets, whatever. We all buying and selling. Every *day*. Every single goddamn day," was the way he felt about it.

Teever took one of the butts from his sock, trying to hold it to the orange and blue flame in the Co-op space heater to get it lit without burning himself. Before he could, Mary Byrd hurried out of the JFC with a sack and jumped in her car. Teever hollered "Mudbird!" but she didn't hear him and drove on off. Oh well. Catch her later. Maybe she had stuck a note.

He crossed the street and entered the Jones Food Center. Mr. Johnny in there, just standing, watching his new electric doors. He was really proud about his doors.

He said, "Teever. Teever, you want to help me and Big Dan bust up some ground tomorrow if we don't get that freezing rain?"

"Might. You gone use them nasty mules or the tiller?" The mules were about a hundred years old and one of them, Lars, kicked and bit if you weren't careful. They'd originally belonged to two old Norwegian twins who were just as ornery. Mr.

Johnny had bought them at the Sale Barn and named them for the men, even though, or maybe because, they were alleged communists.

"Mrs. Shaw has Yim and Lars out at her place doing some clearing," said Mr. Johnny. *Yim* was Jim, the good mule, but they all pronounced it like the Norwegians had. "So— the tiller. You want to work, be here six o'clock."

"Patty fix me some breakfast?" Teever asked.

"Sure. On the go. Lunch too."

"Okay, then. I'm here."

That's good, Teever thought. Hang out tonight 'til Dead Jerry's close, maybe a late-night, back to the graveyard, sleep a few, get warm and get some coffee and a hot Hen's Nest and a honeybun, make a little cash. Okay then. Thinking about a Hen's Nest made his mouth water. It was a JFC specialty and he wished he had the cash for one right now. Take some three-day-old chicken salad with an ice cream scoop, mash it down some, break an egg on it, fry it a little, *umm*. Too bad. He'd have to settle for his bread and peanut butter stashed at the graveyard shed. But he wasn't complaining. He was just glad he had the hooch and almost everything he needed there.

Above the pay phone, which was hung at midget height for kids and old folks in their chairs, was the bulletin board. All kinds of things were posted there for all the world to see. Teever looked them over. He *could* read, but he found it more convenient for people to believe he couldn't. Bad check for this one, that one, some students from other towns, oh man, one for Booger Britches, the worst landlord and biggest asshole around. Lots of folks love to see that. He was not very surprised to see the little note from Mudbird posted too. He thought she was on to him about the reading thing, but when she wanted to get in touch she'd still just post a note with TEEVER and a little drawing of a bird and some other scribblings if she had a big message, like in Egypt. Wonder what she want. Maybe Charles need some help, need a ride to the airport. He'd check on her later. Maybe tomorrow, next day. He liked her little drawings. This one said:

which he knew meant "Meet me at the Black Bear Bar (the only bar in town with stairs) at five and I'll buy you a beer. Mary Byrd." Okay then, I can do that. He looked over at the pile of the day's *Mercury* to check the date. Today the ninth, so she mean tomorrow.

Putting the message in his jacket pocket, he left the Food Center and crossed the back parking lot just as an old Valentine Farms pickup pulled in behind the apocalyptic JFC Dumpster. It was always overflowing and unbelievably foul, and at night it came alive with critters: possum, coons, dogs, cats—an animal juke joint. Out of the truck came a Vietnamese guy that people called Cong, even though he was a refugee. He carried two clear sacks full of yellow crap that Teever knew was chicken feet or beaks, or both. Chinese students ate them, which disgusted a lot of people, but in Nam, Teever had seen it *all* with food. Anyway, it wasn't any nastier than chitlins or crawdads. What folks ate and what folks fucked their own business. As Cong turned the corner of the building, Teever saw the heads of some live chicks sticking out of his jacket pocket. What up with *that*, he wondered.

Four

WITH THE SACK of groceries in one arm, Mary Byrd groped for the kitchen light. She set the groceries down and noticed that the crappy little kitchen TV was off. Huh, she thought. Usually at this time of day Evagreen would still be here, watching Oprah or her stories as she ironed Charles's shirts. William and Eliza dumped their backpacks that sucked on the floor and ran off to the bathrooms. No one ever went to the bathrooms at school if they could help it. The bathrooms weren't as bad as the buses, but they were often sketchy and disgusting; another no-fly zone in the education experience. Mary Byrd grabbed two leashes and went back outside to walk Puppy Sal and the Quarter Pounder so they could come in and spend the evening relaxing with the family.

When she returned, the children were at their places at the counter, intently watching *Forrest Gump* as if they hadn't seen it ten times and shoveling in big spoonfuls of Frosted Mini-Wheats.

She said, "Okay, thirty minutes and *one* bowl, that's it." They didn't reply. William, the Cereal Killer, consumed two or three boxes of Frosted Mini-Wheats and Honey Nut Cheerios per week and would be perfectly happy to exist on nothing else. Maybe the occasional potato chip and Miracle Whip sandwich on white bread. The brown and white diet. Mary Byrd unclipped the dogs, who rushed over to sniff Eliza's backpack. Picking up both packs and setting them on a stool so the dogs wouldn't hose down the reeky deer-piss one, Mary Byrd noticed a note on the counter, weighted down with an empty can of Magic Sizing. In that curious handwriting that a lot of black people had—a mixture of upper- and lower-case letters—Evagreen had written: "Get more. I'm gone. Call you husband." She wondered a little; Evagreen rarely left early and she almost never left notes. Just leaving the empty starch or Zud can or Pine-Sol bottle on the counter would let Mary Byrd know she needed to buy more. And since Evagreen had left without her day's pay, Mary Byrd supposed she'd need to run it by her house. Well, she heaved a sigh, it'd have to be later. Right now she needed a drink while she started dinner.

Where was the damn phone? Portable phones were not necessarily a technological advance in her book; you could never find them, and usually they ended up in Eliza's room. Looking around, she spotted it under a pile of neatly folded dish towels. She checked caller ID, quickly deleting one she ruefully recognized as Ernest's and beeping through a few more. One was a Virginia number she didn't know; had to be the reporter calling again. She clicked back to confirm it. She had a bad feeling about that woman. Why was Ernest calling when she'd told him not to? Looking in the freezer, she wondered what to make, a decision she ought to have made at the JFC. She had the pork chops, easy enough, but what to go with them? Eliza hadn't really liked "piglet meat" ever since, when she was a little girl, she had fallen in love with Wilbur in *Charlotte's Web* and with Pooh's friend Piglet. Pigs *were* adorable; Mary Byrd also wished they didn't eat them. Maybe dice the meat and do stir-fry? As long as meat was served to her in a form that was not a body part, Eliza would eat it. Mary Byrd was suddenly weary. Fuck it; she'd just do the chops the way Nonna did—seared, quickly simmered with a sliced bell pepper in the sauce she'd bought, all of it dumped over pasta. Eliza could just have the pasta and Mary Byrd could add the anchovies to her and Charles's pasta after. William would have to pick the pepper pieces out of his. Nonna would spin—sauce out of a jar. But sauce had come a long way since Chef Boyardee, even it if wasn't from scratch. She did wish they wouldn't put sugar in it.

"What about pasta tonight?" she asked.

Eliza said, "Again?"

William said, "Wow! Look at the TV! A giant snowstorm!"

"Actually, the other night we had spaghetti and meatballs," Mary Byrd said. "Or was it alfredo? It would be rigatoni tonight."

Eliza said, "Those are the tubes with the lines, right? We used to have all the time?"

"We stopped having them because *someone* insisted on putting them on all of his fingers. We might be over that now," she said. How they could make it without pasta, the staff of their family's life, their culinary lingua franca, the noodly duct tape that held their lives together, she could not imagine. It often seemed to be the only thing the four of them had in common and upon which they all could agree. That, and watching old *Little Rascals* tapes. And Mary Byrd, like her grandmother, almost always had meatballs in the freezer, like silver dollars socked away for an emergency. She'd have to replenish her stash soon. Meat *cakes*; her grandmother could never bring herself to say the word *balls*. Thinking about telling this to the children, she finally poured herself a glass of Chianti. Nope. They'd think it was funny if anybody but their mother told the story. Well, William would laugh.

William hopped off his stool to get his face three inches from the TV screen. "Some people already got frozen to death. I hope it's coming here."

"Get your dumb lice-infested head out of the way so I can see," Eliza barked.

"His problem is taken care of, Eliza," said Mary Byrd. "Stop being so rude. William?"

Eliza sneered, simultaneously sucking in a piece of cereal from her upper lip.

"No mushrooms, no whitish sauce, and no green things in it, 'specially English peas. And no throw-uppy cheese on mine," he paused. "*Please*. I wish we could get some killer snow. But no. *We* get black streets and hot rain."

Mary Byrd had to smile. "It's Parmesan, William. Or Romano. It's just a very ripe kind of cheese. It's aged. Same kind we get on pizza," she lied.

"That's what I mean. I don't like stuff that's *very ripe* or *old*. *Barf* is very ripe. And on pizza you can peel the whole flap of cheese off, like skin."

"Maybe I could just melt down some Cheese Cousin and pour it over your pasta," Mary Byrd said. Cheese Cousin was what they called Velveeta.

"Please!" complained Eliza. "Some people are trying to eat here."

"Some people are dorks and are getting big, Frosted Mini-Wheat butts," William said.

"Mom! Do something about him!"

"That's enough. Knock it off," Mary Byrd ordered. "Enough cereal *and* fighting. Go do your homework." William began backing out of the kitchen in his moonwalk approximation, singing "Woolly Bully," a performance calculated to detonate his sister, who had lots of gold, fuzzy body hair and had just begun shaving her legs. Eliza jumped up to chase him, yelling, "Yeah, you better *run, For-ray-est, run*, you little retard!" After hearing one door slam, shouts, and another slam, Mary Byrd picked up the phone and dialed her husband's office. "Don't say retard," she said to herself while she waited for Charles to pick up.

"Hey. Evagreen left a note that you called."

Charles's voice was pleasant and businesslike. "Yeah, I wanted to be sure you remembered that Wiggsby is coming by tonight with those prints."

Mary Byrd sighed, "Oh, *god*. I completely forgot."

"And I'll be late. I'm still in Memphis with Carl, from the Callahan. He's got to go back to D.C. in the morning and he wants to take back some of June Law's and Minnie's new stuff for a show he's putting together on women photographers in the Delta. But don't tell Wiggs that. We're just finishing up."

"Chaz, do we *have* to?" Mary Byrd complained. "He's so exhausting. It's a school night."

"You'll be fine. The children will be fine. Get Mann over for drinks to help you, and I'll be home in an hour and a half and we'll go out to the Pink Palace," Charles said. "That way, we can just dump him back at the hotel after."

"He's always rude to Mann. And he creeps the children out." Once he had reached over Eliza's shoulder as she ate spaghetti, forked a wad, and, raising his arm high, somehow neatly dropped it into his open mouth. The children were used to their parents' friends' eccentricities and didn't mind them much as long as they stayed out of their personal spaces.

"It'll be okay. I've got to get those prints of the casino photographs from him, and we've got to get him to agree to a late spring or summer show. It'll be fine. Get out the cream cheese and pepper jelly," he said, trying to lighten up.

"Ha ha. So he can eat it off his big German knife again?" They both laughed, but just a little.

"And what's with Evagreen?" Charles asked. "She seemed . . . *weird*, when I called."

"I don't know. She left early."

"Well, I'll see y'all later."

"At some point I've got to tell you about the call I got today from a detective in Richmond."

"Jesus. Will that never be over?"

"I *know*," Mary Byrd moaned. "Now some woman is writing an article, or something, I don't know, and so now the police have got to reopen the case, and I've got to—"

"Try not to worry about it. We can talk later. If I don't go now I'll never get home. Just tell Wiggs I got tied up with our accountant. See y'all in a little while."

So much for getting his attention. Actually, she was relieved not to have to go into it again. It could keep. They'd be too busy to talk about it tonight, and maybe same thing tomorrow, and she'd be putting the whole unhappy conversation off, and Charles would have forgotten it, and all of a sudden she'd be leaving to go up there and Charles would be furious, claiming, "Nobody ever tells me anything around here." She knew the drill. Her avoidances and his busy priorities kept their communication level very low, sometimes a good thing, sometimes not. It worked for Mary Byrd to have Charles be too busy to discuss lots of things; they could be easily put off or "forgotten" altogether. In this way it was actually the negative spaces—the inaction and noncommunication—that helped keep their marriage together. In spite of the fact that she and Charles had failed to become much of a comfort to one another, their union was long and without major trauma, both of them understanding that a marriage was what two people make it, like a business. You had to make it your own and try not to let it be prescribed. Pretty much their unspoken thing was, *whatever worked.* By both accounts they would say that they had a happy marriage. If there was even such a thing as *happiness* at all, Mary Byrd often wondered. *Contentedness* seemed like maybe the best a couple could do. At any rate, Charles and Mary Byrd both abhorred the small-town inevitability of private life stupidly made public, and so they carefully avoided the trashy and tragic messes that others stumbled—leapt—into, not seeming to mind that their foibles showed for all to see like dingy, holey under-wear on a clothesline.

There were always temptations, and failures. Women loved Charles's sexy preppiness and reserve. He had very thick brown hair that his mother, Liddie, referred to as "hair-colored" hair shot with silver and hinting of no ethnicity, neither the swarthy nor the fair, not curly and not straight, with a perfectly situated cowlick at his hairline that came from generations of good WASP breeding and created an alluring, natural wave that matched his eye-colored eyes. He was tall and slender, but not so tall and slender that people described him as skinny, and he looked mannish rather than manly; he had a youthfulness that Mary Byrd, as she counted her liver spots and crow's feet, found annoying. Charles didn't encourage women particularly but they were often attracted to his chilly aloofness, which seemed to challenge certain women or pique their interest by raising questions rather than answering any. She didn't think much about him and other women, maybe because she didn't, or couldn't, care enough. Or she was too busy. She'd heard other women with children or jobs or both talk about not having *quality time* with their husbands, but it wasn't that—she had plenty of quality in her life with Charles, she thought. He approached everything in their marriage with the surgical precision he'd inherited from his dad, Big William. He made things work: sex, money, arguments; it was all sort of like lighting the grill, making coffee, or cutting a mat for a photograph. And he didn't hold grudges, and god knows she'd given him plenty to grudge.

Mary Byrd did love Charles. What was not to love? Handsome, intelligent, cultured in a charming Old South way, a good father, and a pretty straight shooter, as far as she knew, and she thought after all the years she really did know him. He was an incorrigible do-gooder, a Dudley Do-Right with an edge. No hobbledehoy, he liked his minor vices and carousing as much as Mary Byrd liked hers, but somehow he never got confused about issues of *honor* or *morality*, like she did. For Charles, things were black and white, while Mary Byrd floundered constantly in a confused gray fog. They both saw life as being too short, but Charles thought the challenge was to leave a strong, clear footprint; Mary Byrd was drawn to kicking up dirt, but wanted to get it all smoothed over and cleaned up again. And not get any on her, as they said. But she had never even thought about being married to anybody but Charles, that was for sure. Well, maybe Jack Hanna, or the dad on *The Waltons*. Or Christopher Walken, but that might be too scary. And why discard a perfectly good husband just because he wasn't paying attention?

She was glad Charles had been married before to a beautiful, rich Delta girl whose daddy had the biggest John Deere dealership in the state, and one of the first catfish farms. Way younger, way prettier, and way dumber than Mary Byrd, she'd feigned pregnancy to get Charles to marry her, and then left him almost immediately to "have a career" with Wachovia in Charlotte, to Charles's great relief. Charles's sense of duty would never have allowed him to dump her. Of course, "having a career" meant that she quickly married a Wachovia CEO and probably was still up there, growing a fat ass and being a lacrosse mom and gloating over having transcended her humble Delta roots. At any rate, that first marriage had made Charles a better candidate for the second, of course. He'd quit thinking with his dick, if a man ever actually could quit doing that, and gotten a taste of how much marriage could suck, and was primed for a mate like Mary Byrd: attractive enough, nice enough, understood that there was a dark side to everyone, and had no ambition really, other than getting by and only occasionally pushing the fool button or the envelope to keep from dying of boredom.

But too much contentment made Mary Byrd discontent; too much comfort made her uncomfortable. She wasn't much used to happiness and security. Before her children, there'd been a medical student she liked because he did little but study, fish, and shoot ducks. His profile was low, he knew few people in town. Tall and skinny, serious-looking and unlike most of the silly, fat-assed boys out on the campus, he was a farm boy who had grown up working his father's fields in an air-conditioned combine, high up above the lush soybeans and cotton, beating off to Warrant's "Cherry Pie" when he grew bored. He was safe. He was clean, he understood disease; and their worlds did not intersect. At his little rental house as often as not she'd simply sleep a deep sleep while he studied. Sometimes he would read to her from one of his medical books—his only books. Once it was about the chemical analysis of sexual passion. "Chemistry, that's all it is," he said. "Dopamine, norepinephrine, and phenylethylamine—natural amphetamines. Then the endorphins, morphine-like substances, kick in and people settle down for the long haul. Think about that, M'Byrd. Love is nothing more than a dope trip." Mary Byrd found the idea of it all being science oddly affirming. It was like taking acid back in the day: part of the thrill of it had been knowing that you would eventually come down—you couldn't sustain that intensity forever—and get back to normal. She'd cut the boy loose when he'd started to badger her for butt sex. It was natural, she supposed—maybe a med student *needed* to explore all the options, or orifices. Lucy, who was single and still on the market, said that ass was the new pussy, due to too much easily available porn. Mary Byrd was also generally against hanging with younger guys: *memento mori* fucking. Who wanted to see her loosening, dry skin pressed against the taut, peachy flesh of a twenty-five-year-old? And really, she decided, it took *adults* to commit adultery, and he wasn't quite one.

There was the professor with a pygmy-haint wife. Whenever he saw Mary Byrd he would stare hungrily at her bony parts— her clavicles and wrists and knees, her sternum exposed by an unbuttoned shirt. After a drunken party, they had stepped behind a pool house and he had cupped her elbows, lightly brushing his palms across them, around and around. Then he'd gripped her hipbones, and kissed her. Did that even count as adultery: a mercy hump against a shed? After that they'd avoided each other for months. And anyway she knew that an affair with a married guy would suck; it would be like stealing a great piece of jewelry that would excite you and make you happy until you realized that you weren't going to be able to wear it anywhere in public.

Then there had been the semi-famous filmmaker who had passed through town scouting locations for a Civil War movie. She didn't know why she'd bothered—boring. The whole time the Chubby Checker "Limbo" song had played in her head, all Zildjians and tom-toms and Chubby's hoarse, high encouragement: "*How looow can you go?*" She hadn't really minded the indifference, it was just *difference* she had seemed to want, and maybe, she recognized, the guilt. Later, he had sent her a picture he had taken of her that he wanted to publish in a photo-essay for *Harper's*. He'd gotten her about half-right. In the shot she was framed by the sharply limned leaves and deep shade of a magnolia tree. She herself was in full sunlight, her eyes averted and her face unfocused; it might have been any thirtysomething woman with a guilty, tentative look. She looked more intelligent and interesting than she was. A critic described the photograph as "sparkling" and "brilliant." Maybe the tree had been that, but she, anyway, looked neither.

After her children, she hadn't felt the old joneses and self-destructive compulsions. At least not as much. And of course with babies around there wasn't a lot of time for clowning around. It wasn't that she was such a devoted mother, into reading ridiculous "parenting" books and "making memories" and her own baby food and crap; in fact she was a little afraid of her children, she loved them so much and their very existence had so much power over her. She mooned over them and worried about them, but fought it, following Liddie's advice: "Treat children like house plants. A little neglect is good for them." Which was in direct opposition to her own poor mother's MO, to overprotect, at least after Stevie died. When Eliza and William were born it became crystal clear to her what love was. What you felt for your children was the purest, most intense, most primal and true feeling a person could have. Everything that you felt for any other human being was about something else: lust, convenience, vanity, power, neediness, companionship, pity. What you begat was as good as it got. That was just about the only thing in this world of which Mary Byrd was one hundred percent confident and convinced. But there still were the challenges—disturbing jack-in-the-boxes like Ernest, an oddball who sniffed out the weakness of character in her and preyed upon it. At least she didn't, as she heard that a couple of ladies in town did, go down to Sneed's Hardware and troll for some of the hot workmen who came in and out all morning, or go up to Home Barn in Memphis, the new place for guys to hook up with bored housewives hobby-shopping for lamps and pillows. Anyway, it wasn't her business.

They'd grown up so differently, Charles Byrd Thornton and Mary Byrd D'Abruzzi. She wasn't sure if those differences had eased or afflicted their union, but it kept things interesting. On his mother's side, Charles's family, the Byrds, went right back to the seventeenth century when they'd arrived in Virginia from London to what would become Richmond with little but some family expertise in goldsmithing, and no gold—and with the intention of establishing themselves as aristocrats. Who would have been around to challenge the notion? The Indians with whom they traded furs? Of course, that pretense was abandoned by the Revolution. Charles's great-great-great grandmother was a daughter of William Byrd II, who'd founded Richmond and built himself a beautiful house with the James River lapping at its front door. A fortune was made in tobacco farming and shipping, and in establishing Richmond as a port and commercial center.

Not a lot was known, or talked about, anyway, of the less illustrious Thorntons, Charles's father's people, but like all white Southerners, they knew, or made up, something. A Thornton had come over to escape some *unpleasantness* in Warwickshire, England, and had built a log cabin and settled a tiny place called Coldfield in the mountains in the northwestern part of Virginia. His progeny became talented gunsmiths working in the Harpers Ferry Arsenal, where one of them supposedly designed the Harpers Ferry Rifle, a sort of magic wand to disappear Indians, Tories, and other frontier resistance, although the arsenal superintendent there, an associate of George Washington, took all the credit for the invention. Subsequent Thorntons worked there, too, and after John Brown's bloody foray and then when the Confederate army claimed Harpers Ferry, they were only too happy to remove themselves and the arsenal's machinery to Richmond, where they developed the Richmond Rifle, a copy of Harpers Ferry Model 1855, which proved somewhat less successful at beating back and disappearing Union troops. After the devastation of Richmond, and there not being enough money or business to go around, some of each family—Byrds and Thorntons—had gone west to Mississippi to start over, trading in their farms and ships and guns for law and medical degrees and academic appointments.

Charles, like Mann, had been sent back to Virginia for prep school—Woodberry Forest was a good choice for smart, bad boys from Mississippi—and college at Washington and Lee.

By Byrd and Thornton standards, Mary Byrd D'Abruzzi—she'd never taken her stepfather's name, Rhinehart—was a latecomer to Virginia. All four of her grandparents were right off the boat from Italy at the turn of the century, settling first in Norfolk, where her D'Abruzzi grandfather had worked selling fish, then pots and pans, before moving on to Richmond. There, he'd gone to work for the Velatis, an old Italian family that had been making caramel candy since before the Civil War. He'd done well enough with that that he started a little business repairing, then making, shoes. His pièce de résistance was the D'Abruzzi Boot, a heavy-duty but light leather brogan that was cured and softened with olive oil, making it very comfortable to wear, and the rich, rustic color of walnut pesto. The grids of fine steel cleats on the soles made them tough and durable, and in the 1960s and '70s, "Bruzzi Boots" became popular not only with workmen but with trust-fund hippie kids who wanted to create the illusion of work with their carefully negligent, proletariat wardrobes. Mary Byrd's dad joined him in the business. There wasn't exactly a fortune, but the D'Abruzzis became firmly and proudly middle-class, moving from Oregon Hill to the West End, acquiring a summer cottage on the Chesapeake, and sending Mary Byrd, the first grandchild, to William and

Mary and her brothers, Nick and James, to the University of Richmond. Her D'Abruzzi grandparents had died—her grandfather of something in his brain, maybe the French disease, or maybe tanning chemicals; Mary Byrd hardly remembered them—and her parents had had their marriage annulled and both had remarried when she was just a kid. She rarely saw or heard from her father; not, she chose to think, because he didn't care, but because he was so busy with his new family and new life in New Jersey, where he'd relocated the business. It was just coincidence that she and Charles shared the name Byrd. Or almost. Mary Byrd's mother thought that the association with a First Families of Virginia name, and a double name at that, sounded uptown, and heritage-y, and perhaps would give her daughter an advantage in life. Perhaps.

Mary Byrd had met Charles and Mann at a fund-raiser for the Valentine Museum in Richmond, where she had a part-time curatorship. Charles was learning about photography and the gallery business, coming out of his bad, short first marriage, and Mann was trying to come out of his closet. She was charmed by them both. She and Charles married two years later and they all settled back in Mississippi, Mary Byrd and Mann connected by their outsiderness and secretive natures, Charles and Mann connected by their prep school boyhood, and who knew what else, and all of them connected to the Virginia Tidewater.

Welcomed graciously into the Thornton clan, Mary Byrd tried to adjust quickly, striving to become more WASP than wop. More stoic, more civil, more reserved, less self-focused. More Melanie than Scarlett. Raised to disdain temperamental outbursts, Charles could ignore yelling, door-slamming, and, years ago now, tears. In fact, on the occasions that Mary Byrd had employed crying to get Charles's attention, it had backfired, and Charles had clammed up and withdrawn. Emotions, particularly the unhappy ones, in his view were somewhat tacky.

Charles had grown up with his family's disbelief in headaches, naps, or psychiatric help; god forbid one would talk to—pay money to talk to!—strangers about private matters. Self-indulgence, drinking excepted, was not good, either. And so, from the Thorntons Mary Byrd had learned to live more serenely, not think so much about herself, and to drink seriously. She believed it was a more civilized day-to-day existence. Gin and tonic in the insane hell of a Mississippi summer, bourbon or martinis in the damp, bone-chilling winters. Wine was nice but just more of a pleasant accompaniment to a meal, and plain old beer was more suitable to most Southern cooking. In Charles's family neither wine nor beer constituted drinking anyway, and were actually more of a pain in the ass to procure: the peculiar liquor laws in the town permitted buying and consuming gallons of hard liquor but not even one single can of cold beer. Go figure.

So Mary Byrd had settled in to the sort of nineteenth-century, Deep South way of her husband's people. And she had to admit that a little of her Italianness had rubbed off on Charles. It didn't happen often, but when he found himself with her family, he learned not to be alarmed at the aggressiveness and hyperbole that was part of their DNA: they weren't *really* angry all the time and didn't *really* want to kill each other, and food was to them what booze was to the Thorntons: civilization. Charles loved the succulent peasant dishes that Mary Byrd cooked; perhaps his biggest concession to her messy, Mediterranean soap-opera upbringing.

MARY BYRD DIALED Mann again. It rang a long time; she wouldn't blame him if he was screening her calls. Even Mann had his limits, and if he had any idea of why she was calling, he should not pick up the phone. But he did, asking a cautious, "What?"

"I forgot that Wiggsby is supposed to come by, and we've got to take him to dinner."

"*We*, white man?"

"Mann, you have to! Charles won't even be here for drinks; he's doing some stuff with a gallery guy from D.C. He said he'll meet us at the Pink Palace. Please! You *have* to come over. He's got some new prints we can look at—those ones he's been taking at the casinos."

"I just rented a movie. And he's such a Nazi."

"*Please.* I'll be your best friend."

"You already are my best friend. Lot of good it does me."

"Please, Mann. I won't let him be mean to you."

"*Ugh.* You *so* owe me." He hung up.

Mary Byrd put half the spaghetti back in the box and the chops in the freezer. No time for that; she'd have to downgrade again. Reaching for two plates for the children—the shamed Corelle—she noticed that one of her favorite knickknacks was a little bit broken. Just a little bit—the tip off an ear of one of a pair of dancing kitties. Probably one of Evagreen's "accidents," the hallmark of which was an object just a teensy bit lost or broken, or scratched, or dinged in some barely perceptible way. Nothing, of course, was ever said. For Mary Byrd it was a small price to pay for Evagreen's efficient, military presence and, she would have to admit, the consistency she provided in their chaotic lives.

She looked in the fridge to see what she could scare up for hors d'oeuvres. Not that Wiggs ever ate anything, the fistful of spaghetti excepted. And she did have plenty of liquor. She wished she could call Mann back and ask him to pick up some of his favorite yummy triple-cream cheese that he had caused to be present in the funky cheese shelves at the JFC, but he was already too pissed at her to be either hit up for another favor or appeased. Just as well; the children couldn't stand the oozy sight or smell of it. They called most adult cheeses "fromunda—you know, from unda your butt. She found some little green tomato pickles she'd put up last summer, some huge capers, a little soppressata, and a nub of rat cheese and arranged them on a plate. She heard the front door open and Mann walked slowly down the hall to the kitchen, dragging his feet dramatically as if he were headed to the dentist, or the electric chair at Parchman. His petite self did look precious wearing a very tailored jacket, jeans, and a yellow and pink bow tie.

"I really hate you," he said wearily.

"I know you do. But I *love* you and I will make it up to you."

"You can't possibly."

"Yes, I can. What about my precious little lawn dog?" she said. "Little Jimmy T?"

"Shut up," Mann said.

She was busily fooling with the boiling pasta, tearing salad greens, and buttering bread.

"Well, if you were only interested in *me* giving you a payback blow job."

"You know what? If you'd just wear that dykey Armani jacket and put a bag over your head I might go for it."

From a distance, or not even from a distance, Mary Byrd could look scarily like a myopic fifteen-year-old boy. Once, when she was helping out in Eliza's first-grade classroom and her moppy curls were cut too short, a kid had made Eliza cry by announcing loudly, "Yo mama look like a *man*."

From then on, for school functions, Mary Byrd tried always to wear a mom costume: a dress, or at least slacks and a froufrou sweater, dangly earrings, plenty of eye makeup and lipstick.

Mary Byrd drained the pasta, spooned sauce over it, and added a Wishbone-dressed salad, which she knew would be ignored, and a slice of leathery JFC French bread to each of the plates.

"I'm going to let the children eat upstairs to minimize the chance of horror," she said to Mann. "Get whatever you want to drink."

"What do you want? 'Tini? I'll make it."

Leaving the kitchen with a big tray, she said over her shoulder, "Oh, hydrocodone on the rocks for me, please."

Mann poured himself a glass of the already-opened mediocre Chianti on the counter, almost wishing he had brought one of the delicious bottles he had sent from Mr. Brown, his wine guy in New Orleans. But then he wouldn't have wanted to waste any of it on Wiggs. Or on Mary Byrd, for that matter, who'd guzzle anything.

Maybe, for helping to entertain Wiggs, Charles would give Mann one of Wiggs's beautiful photographs. It was annoying but a fact of life that some of these brilliant artists could be such a pain in the ass. Plenty of the writers and artists who came around town were just *boring*, apart from their work, Mann thought.

Mann mixed the martinis, adding an extra olive to Mary Byrd's. She was anemic; she always needed more protein. Weren't olives protein? He looked around the nutty kitchen. Like the rest of the place, it was full of stuff. Interesting and in some cases valuable stuff, but still—*stuff*. Mann did not see how Mary Byrd functioned in this kitchen, or in this house, for that matter. The kitchen was more of a crazy little museum than a work area. The windowsills were lined with miniature animals, cars, guns, and candlesticks; there were souvenir spoons, plant cuttings, feathers, wishbones, small novelty fireworks, old pill bottles and tins. A Museum of Tiny Crap. She was a magpie. The walls were hung with vintage political posters, old pie plates, madeleine molds, masks, maps, and a huge wooden cutout of a smiling green devil giving a thumbs-up and saying, BLAME ME. There were always flowers or at least greenery on the counter, not always in their prime. The refrigerator door was a chaotic assemblage of dozens of photos and magnets and bumper stickers and clippings and invitations and kids' art. Mann loved stuff, too, but wherever Mann lived, there were lots of cupboards and closets and drawers where things could be hidden or stashed quickly so that his places always looked right out of *Architectural Digest*.

Mann suspected Charles hated the clutter, too, but for some reason Mary Byrd had to be surrounded by it. It owned her. She just loved *things*. Her house—her kitchen especially—was just a metaphor for her life: messy, a little out-of-control, a little arty, full of *objets* and sometimes people she didn't need but continued to accumulate. He and Charles had decided she had Compulsive Curiosity Syndrome; she couldn't get out of gas stations or shops without more fart machines or novelty lighters, and in an antique store she *had* to inspect every single item, every little drawer and display case. Charles, Mann knew, had once taken Eliza and William on a Tour of Piles around the house: the Ungiven Pile, consisting of wedding and baby presents that had yet to be wrapped and sent; the Unpaid Pile, the Unfolded Clean Laundry Pile, the Future Yard Sale Pile, etc. A little mean, but funny, and he sort of didn't blame Charles. He also knew that part of his own appeal for Mary Byrd was his tininess. She'd collected him, too, but he enjoyed it. Usually.

Mary Byrd reappeared wearing her signature red pleated skirt, little black roach-killer boots with almost-high heels, and the shreddy Levi's jacket that she was probably too old for but looked cute in. They sat on stools at the counter to knock off a round of drinks before Wiggs arrived.

"The children have science fair proposals due tomorrow," she sighed. "I should stay here and sit on them."

"Those children will be fine. Eliza's old enough to be in charge," Mann said, picking up a caper by its stem and sucking it delicately before putting it in his rosebud mouth. "Anyway, you *hate* the science fair."

"I know—but they still have to do it." In the Thorntons' house it was known as the science *un*fair, because everyone knew that the kids who either had access to their parents' labs at the university, or had computers and fancy programs that generated cool graphics, or had plenty of money to spend on decorating their prefab display boards with grosgrain ribbon and glitter were the ones who won. The kids whose parents didn't have extra cash or extra time got their dicks left in the dirt, science fair–wise. For a project in the category of Behavioral Science, Eliza had once carefully documented the process of teaching their old orange cat, Big Boy, to play a toy piano. It was a brilliant project for a second-grader, but it got disqualified for involving a live subject. What the hell *was* the Behavioral Science category, then?

"And you're right. *I* certainly babysat all my brothers at her age. But we'll be miles out of town, you know?" Mary Byrd knew the children were fine without a sitter—at eight and almost twelve, a sitter now just offended them—and when alone together, possibly because they were a little spooked and uneasy and glad for each other's company, they got along fine. It was very hard, often, for Mary Byrd to permit them these little freedoms, to resist the urge to overprotect, because she certainly knew all too well that sometimes any amount of protection or vigilance couldn't keep bad things from happening. Bad things were like dog shit: it could be anywhere and you had to look out for it all the time. So Mann wouldn't hear, Mary Byrd went into the dining room booze closet to call Ashleigh from down the street to babysit.

Mary Byrd and Mann sipped their drinks and looked over the daily police and fire reports in the *Mercury*. The crime report was all the usual: MIPs, DUIs, public drunkenness, smoky kitchen, possession of paraphernalia, suspicious activity, driving without a license, animal rescue, animal complaint, cemetery desecration, malicious mischief, domestic disturbance, welfare check fraud, speeding, no vehicle tag, possession of controlled substance, and any combination of college and small-town crap that was testimony to the easy, relatively untroubled life of the town, although Mary Byrd knew that some of these innocent little items probably represented trauma, shock, and heartbreak for some family. It was mean to enjoy it, but they liked to discover the occasional bizarre entry, such as this latest: *uttering.*

Mann said, "What on earth is *uttering?*"

"I don't know," Mary Byrd said. "If I weren't so bummed out I'd go look it up. Maybe it has something to do with lying? Or cussing?"

"Then we'd all be in jail. Maybe something kinky—like with cows?" He was actually semiseriously asking.

"No, dopey. That would be *uddering*, with two ds, not ts." She laughed at him.

"I knew that," Mann said.

"Sure you did," Mary Byrd said. She bit a cracker and sipped her drink, scanning the paper. "This is the way things used to be in Richmond. Like you said: like Mayberry. There wasn't real crime too much, right?" She had a sudden sinking spell, thinking of the trip ahead of her.

"Everywhere was like that," he said. "It was Planet Donna Reed."

There was some noise at the front door: not really knocking, but a barging-in sound, and then, a few heavy steps, then nothing.

"He's here," Mary Byrd said, resignedly. "Bottoms up."

Mann put a hand over his eyes. "Please don't say anything like *that* around him and get him started on me." He threw back the last of his martini.

Edward Wiggsby had arrived, and apparently had paused in the hallway to take things in, maybe taking a photo or two. It would be something that nobody else would ever have noticed: a ding in the woodwork showing a century's layers of old paint, or one scuffed but richly hazel Bruzzi Boot at the bottom of the stairs, or the plastic sheen on Mary Byrd's purple "lizard" raincoat hanging on the hall tree. It might also be a pale apricot coughed-up hairball on the worn Serapi rug, or a big dead cockroach, Mary Byrd knew, and she thought about rising to intercept him but didn't. Who cared. Whatever he shot would be a beautiful, intriguing photograph worth tons of money, and the prestige of having him photograph *your* hairball in *your* home would be priceless. Wiggs's photographs were celebrated for their sublime subtleties of color and subject, and for his uncanny ability to notice things, or conditions of light, in a way that normal people didn't, as if he had the sight and perceptions of another species. But all his exquisite sensitivities went into his art, and people permitted him his social breaches because of their worshipful dumbstruckness. Charles and Mary Byrd were friends with him because it was good business, but also because his insane, unpredictable life was so fascinating and out of another century, when artists had been celebrities and treated like royalty. He was an *artiste roué* alky like Toulouse-Lautrec who exalted the ordinary and insisted on pushing everything and everybody in his life to the limits. Whatever limits were.

Mary Byrd and Mann sat silently, looking at each other, eyebrows raised, waiting for the next sound. It was the echoey wooden thud of the piano cover being raised and then the rapid play of scales, then arpeggios. The cover thudded again, and in a second, there he was, Edward Wiggs, in all his splendor. Striking a theatrical but easy contrapposto in the kitchen doorway, he announced, "I'm here now. Let the fun begin. Your piano is abysmal."

"Hey, Ed," Mary Byrd said, getting up and crossing the kitchen to give him a loose, bent, no-pelvic-contact hug. In return she got an air kiss on each side of her head. With one hand he scrambled her curly hair affectionately. "Darlin'?" he said, and then, "Mann," almost turning to acknowledge him.

"Hey, Ed," said Mann. "How are you?"

"I'm wonderful. Couldn't be better." Wiggs's speech was slow and halting; haughty, drunk, or both. There were so many Mississippi accents and his was the melodic, archaic drawl of white Delta planters of a couple generations earlier. "I'm just back from Japan. It was *fabulous*."

"What would you like to drink?" asked Mann, ever the surrogate husband and host.

"Well, I have been indulging in a little Laphroaig. But a martini might be wonderful. Fresh horses. Or changing horses in midstream. Something like that."

"Vodka or gin?" Mann asked and flinched like a kid realizing a dumb mistake at a spelling bee.

"Must you ask?" Wiggs sniffed. "There are *only* gin martinis."

"Right," Mann said flatly. "What was I thinking?" He reached for Rosalie's old beat-up, silver cocktail shaker.

"And I'm so delighted to see Beefeater. Why are people drinking that abominable blue swill these days." He paused. "Just on the rocks, please. And where is Charles?"

"He got caught in a powwow with our accountant," Mary Byrd answered, keeping her face turned away to ease the lie. "Some problem came up that had to be fixed right away. He's going to meet us."

Wiggs's old camera hung around his neck like a big chunk of *moderne* jewelry. While Mary Byrd put out more crackers and Mann mixed another round of drinks, he drifted around the kitchen, taking everything in. At the stove, the old Chambers handed down from Liddie, he turned on the gas and bent to light a Nat Sherman from a pack that magically appeared in his hand. For a second he watched the blue flame, and moving slightly to the side, he raised the camera with his right hand: *Click. Click. Click.*

"I love this stove. It is so gloriously Lucille Ball," he said.

"Yep, that would be me," Mary Byrd said. "Many a tuna casserole has issued from its bowels." She examined Wiggs. He wore a very luxe-looking black cashmere crewneck over a crisp white shirt, lean khakis tucked neatly into the cognac-colored German engineer boots he always wore. The high boots made his long, thin legs seem even longer. Storkish, really. She—everyone—was always awed by Wiggs's appearance. He was gorgeous—murderously gorgeous—probably the most beautiful man Mary Byrd had ever seen. Or woman, for that matter. He had this amazing skin, pale and translucent; the kind of pallor that always made her think: *blue blood*. Even Mann and Charles didn't have it, although they were both WASPily handsome.

Wiggs's silver hair was collar-length but combed back and high, with a wisp that fell over his forehead, so slight as to suggest nonchalance and roguery, or to mock the notion of roguery. A baronial coif. His hands were long and delicate and blue and seemed to exist solely to be set impatiently on his hips, to raise his camera to his eye, or to gracefully bring booze and Nat Shermans incessantly to his thin, often curled lips. The very picture of icy gentility, dissipation, and arrogance, he was a cross between a preppy fop and some Weimar libertine out of 1930 Berlin. Sexy, too, Mary Byrd thought, in an aging, Jeremy Irons sort of way. That such a creature had ever surfaced from Freeman Bayou, like the first feathered reptile slouching out of the primordial ooze and taking flight, was astonishing to Mary Byrd, but as Charles had once said about Wiggs, the Mississippi

Delta was the only place on earth where such an exotic rara avis of a man could have been hatched.

Wiggs would descend on them from Clarksdale every month or two, bringing his camera, esoteric audio equipment, and guns. Settling into the same nonsmoking room at the Holiday Inn every time, he would smoke, disassemble the stereo and the guns for a few days, put everything back together, and leave.

Mary Byrd glanced at Mann, who was making Wiggs's martini with an expression of faint terror, probably wishing he could pee in it. She would have to do her best to protect him. You don't grow up gay and not have a thick hide, though. Mary Byrd knew Mann could take care of himself. She just didn't want him to get pissed and leave.

Wiggs walked to the windowsill, where Mary Byrd had her tiny-crap display.

"M'Byrd. *Wonderful* tchotchkes. Where do you *find* these bits?" He picked up a thumbnail-size pot of lip gloss in the shape of a toilet.

"Oh, you know, here and there. Gewgaws-R-Us. June Law gave me that one. Tell us about your trip," she said, glancing at Mann.

Like a dog pissing in all the corners, he snapped a few more shots and said, "They *love* me over there. I can't say why. I hardly remember a thing."

Mary Byrd and Mann exchanged looks. Through the fecund grapevine they had already heard about Wiggs's trip. It was true: the Japanese did love him. And to repay their love, Wiggs had stood on stage, addressing an audience of hundreds of the most sophisticated photography enthusiasts in the world, and crooned "Love Me Tender." Incredibly, he had received a standing ovation.

"Inscrutable, the Japanese, don't you know," Wiggs said, smiling devilishly and tilting his elegant head slightly as if he were actually pondering this conundrum.

"And Mops?" Mary Byrd asked. "Did she go with you? How is she?" Mops was his glamorous, longtime Austrian lady friend, also a famed photographer, who as an intrepid ingénue had run with Castro and Hemingway back in the day. Charles and Mary Byrd—everybody—loved her. Wiggs did not deserve her.

"She did not," Wiggs said. "She had a show of her own in London. She is fabulous, as always."

Mary Byrd was just passing the little Queen's Bird plate with the crackers, cheese, and giant caper things when the phone sounded.

"Here, take this," she said to Mann, handing him the plate, but the phone didn't ring again. The non-ring seemed to her to echo more loudly than the actual sound.

"Huh," she said. "Weird." She handed Mann a stack of cocktail napkins.

She was reminded that she needed to call her mother, and Evagreen, but instead she said, "Y'all. We need to get going if we're going to eat. Let me call the sitter to come on. She's just down the street. I'll be right back. No fighting, no biting."

Mann had risen to transfer the martinis to go-cups and gave Mary Byrd his slittiest, hairiest evil eyeball. "Hurry up," he mouthed.

Wiggs watched Mary Byrd cross the room and said, "M'Byrd, are you wearing underwear? I haven't seen a north-south configuration in *weeks*." He raised his eyebrows, although his eyes were practically closed.

Mary Byrd turned and gave him the finger and a sarcastic smile and said, "You're a bad man, Wiggs. I'm telling your *good friend*, my dear husband Charles, that you are—*besmirching* my honor." Why did he always have to provoke everybody? It was like his hobby. It was pretty funny, but she was too tired to appreciate it.

"Darlin'," he said. "You don't think for a minute that Charles will think your . . . *honor* is worth more than those prints he wants, do you?" He grinned evilly.

"Wiggs," said Mary Byrd wearily. "Don't make me come over there and beat your ass." She'd knew she should be brownnosing him but she just didn't want to.

Wiggs's steely, alien-blue eyes opened wide. "Oh, that would be *too* lovely," he said. She and Mann rolled eyes at each other. Wiggs took a long draw on his cigarette and exhaled in Mann's direction. "I love these people," he said.

Five

Upstairs, Mary Byrd didn't call Ashleigh, who she knew was on her way; instead, she called Evagreen, wanting to be sure she was at home. Jeez—still busy. The children were watching TV in what had been their little playroom. Hearing her approach, the Quarter Pounder, who knew he was in violation of the house rule about dogs on furniture, tried to skitter back downstairs, passing her on the steps with guilt in his eyes. Puppy Sal was afraid to go upstairs at all in winter because the cats lurked there in the warmer air.

Eliza and William were stretched out and propped up on over-size pillows, side by side on an old comforter. Notebooks and textbooks were arranged around them to simulate working on science fair proposals, but neither one budged to assume a study-ing pose. Two spotless dinner plates and forks were pushed back into the corner, she knew, by the Pounder, who'd licked them clean. William, a mouth-breather, stared gape-jawed at the tube, absently stroking Irene, who was curled in a ball next to him.

"*William*," Mary Byrd said, and he immediately snapped his mouth closed. Poor fella. "What are y'all watching?"

"Nothing," they both said, which meant they were watching *Real World*, or *E.R.* reruns, neither of which they were supposed to watch.

"What's wrong with the History Channel?" she asked them.

Eliza looked at her scornfully. "You mean the tank and aircraft channel?"

William looked up at her and said, with irritation, "That's what I wanted to watch but Eliza wouldn't let me." Eliza cranked her forearm against his chest, rising to change the channel to Nick at Nite.

"Ow!" he yelled, making Irene startle and run off. "Look what you did to Irene!"

"Okay, quit," said Mary Byrd. She wanted nothing more than to lie down and watch *Real World* with them even though she hated it and would die if her kids turned out like those people. She just wanted to crawl up with her babies in their little nest and breathe their not-very-fresh smells. Of course, she knew if she attempted to do so they would both be gone in seconds.

"Ashleigh will be over in a minute so get your showers and get ready for bed," she said. "Soon." She added, "And I will look at your science fair things when I get home, so leave them out, okay?"

No one responded and Mary Byrd said pointedly, "*Okay, Mom.*" She made the overhead light strobe to get their attention.

"Not *Ash-hole* again," said William.

"*William.* I hope you don't call her that."

"He did once," said Eliza. "She thought it was funny."

"We're going out to the Palace for dinner."

"Where's Daddy?" asked Eliza.

"He's in Memphis with a gallery guy. He's supposed to meet us."

Eliza refocused on the TV. "Okay," she said, "luvyabye."

On her hands and knees, Mary Byrd kissed one, then the other. She picked up the plates, forks, and ubiquitous large bowl from which William topped off his pasta with his nightly fodder of Honey Nut Cheerios. You have to choose your battles, she thought. Today was not a day for carping at children, your dear, darling, alive children, about dogs on furniture and TV and homework. "I'll check on you when we get home. Love you both."

"Okay," said William, transfixed by the tube.

"Luvyabye," Eliza said again, dismissively.

She wondered about Evagreen. She could just leave her money in the mailbox, she supposed, if she wasn't at home.

At the bottom of the stairs stood Mann, a bottle of wine tucked under his arm.

"Mann, what are you doing? Get back in there and keep an eye on him!"

"I'm starving. I want to eat and go home. This is promising to be a very long night." Mann was so small, with the metabolism of a hummingbird, and he could get very surly if he did not eat every two hours. "Can you please get your act in gear and let's go?"

From the kitchen, a girl's voice called out, "Hey-ay!"

"Here's Ashleigh," Mary Byrd said, coming quickly down the steps.

The teenager came through the hall and started up the stairs. In an accusatory voice she said, "Who's that guy in the kitchen? He's like, *way* hammered." She didn't stop for an answer.

Wiggs was indeed hammered. He sat on a kitchen stool and was leaning back against the wall with his eyes closed and his arms folded over his chest.

Mary Byrd put a hand on his arm, saying, "Wiggs, let's go! We're starving. And Charles might already be waiting at the Palace by now."

"Yes, darlin'," Wiggs said, barely opening his eyes. "And we can all go back to my room later and see the casino prints. I have scotch and Stoli." Wiggs, usually snobby about booze, preferred the medium-priced Stoli because, he said, it was "distilled with the passion of the Russian soul."

"Great," she said, hoping that would not happen. "We're dying to see them. Charles is really excited. And he wants to talk to you about a new show." Mary Byrd knew she wouldn't be going anywhere later but the blanket show. Charles could go back to Wiggs's room, or they could do their business in the morning. Some time had to be taken to think about going to Virginia, to make some arrangements, but she couldn't do it now. I'll think about that tomorrow, she loved to tell herself. She was amazed that her mother hadn't called. Maybe she didn't want to think about it any more than Mary Byrd did.

Finally in the car, headed down the old Fudgetown Road, they all felt a little better, out of the house and refreshed by the night air. The night was cold but clear. It was hard to believe that a winter storm was coming. An orange moon was rising but still hung up in the trees, not giving off much light. Mary Byrd had the urge to fuck with Wiggs and punched off the headlights. Even with the moon they could see the Milky Way, which was a luminous cloud in the deep country darkness. To her surprise, it was Mann who shouted, "M'Byrd! Stop! You're scaring me!" He laughed, though. "Fool!"

From the backseat the reclining Wiggs, who actually seemed to have sobered up a bit, snorted, "My, but we're easily frightened, aren't we, petite monsieur Valentine?"

Mann ignored him. "Turn those lights on, you dumbass. We'll get stopped or end up in the ditch." She switched the headlights back on at the thought of being stopped and subjected to the most dreaded weapon in the county, the Breathalyzer. It wouldn't matter that she wasn't drunk, but if she registered at all she'd be dead meat. Charles would kill her.

"I'm sorry, y'all, but I've got to go by Evagreen's and give her her money. It's on the way and will just take a second."

"Fine, but I hope we're not eating at that charred-mystery-meat emporium in the odious shack that everyone thinks is so wonderful," Wiggs said loudly. As if he were going to eat anything.

"Yep," said Mary Byrd. "That's exactly where we're going. You'll enjoy it, Ed. The steaks *are* really good."

"*Mis*-steak, you must mean," he said. "As long as we can bring the bottle."

The Pink Palace was eight miles away and a place people liked to go for a change of pace. Or just a meat fix. The Palace was just a board-and-batten shack from the outside, but inside it was all painted raw-flesh pink, and the low ceiling was covered in white glitter. Dozens of bass trophies lined one wall. The place was known for its perfectly grilled steaks, the most popular cut being a twenty-ounce T-bone that was about the size of a flattened baby. The Pink Palace motto, beloved by frat boys who regularly stole the sign and put it in front of the Tri Delta sorority house, was THE PINK CENTER YOU CRAVE. The Tri Delts, pretty, cheerful girls (they answered their house phone with, "Delta, Delta, Delta, can I help ya, help ya, help ya?") who were known for liking to do it ("If you've tried everything else, Tri Delta"), had had a surveillance camera installed, but all that ever came of it was footage of guys in various costumes—gorilla heads and E.T. and Darth Vader masks—planting the sign again and again. Occasionally the sign went to the Bowheads' house, the Delta Gammas, who were prissy and wore giant ribbons stuck in their hair, but they were no fun and would call 9-1-1.

Mary Byrd went on. "It's sparkly and colorful. You might want to shoot something. Or somebody."

Wiggs sighed. "Maybe. If I were Diane Arbus or Shelby Adams."

Mann said, "Well, I, for one, can use some red meat. I've been feeling puny. And I am sick unto death of chicken."

"I imagine so. Bok bok bagok, here chickee, chickee," said Wiggs. "I . . . had a fahmm . . . in Affreekahh . . ."

"Do you have to be such an asshole?" said Mann.

"Horrors. An attack. Let me get my cuirass on," Wiggs said. "Oh, no, I'm sorry, that's what *you* wear."

"Oh, fuck yourself, Ed," said Mann, almost amiably. To Mary Byrd, he said, "What's a cuirass?"

"I have no idea."

"If you and your little friends could buy them at Barneys, they'd be all the rage in New York," Wiggs said.

"You sure seem to know a lot about me and my little friends, Ed."

"One must know the enemy, don't you know."

"Oh, I know all right," said Mann. "*Don't* I know."

Mary Byrd turned off onto the King Road, headed to the old Beat Five community called McCrady Hill. Many of the oldest black families had been living there since slaves were freed. There were Pegueses, Dixons, Carotherses, Isoms, and Barrs out there—black representatives (and in some cases, descendants) of all the first white settlers in the county.

McCrady Hill was a neat, close-knit neighborhood with its own church and playground. They had even had their road

paved at their own expense because the ignorant county super-
visors, all white, had found dozens of excuses not to do it.
McCrady Hill children were bused into the city schools to
comply with all the convoluted integration laws even though
the county schools were much closer. The small, modest homes
were mostly the same, although some urban renewal federal
architect had attempted to make them distinctive by using
different, and maybe less expensive, brick than those in white
neighborhoods: some houses were yellow brick, some black
and yellow, some red and black. Here and there some of the
original shotgun houses remained, although they were altered
and added onto and patched with siding or shingles or tar
paper, and had newish tin roofs. All the houses had iron grill-
work storm doors. West St. Peter Methodist Baptist church
stood at the end of the dead-end road, a plain, white-frame
building with a small steeple and a new brick fellowship hall
tacked to one side.

To Mary Byrd, the few times she'd been to the church for
funerals or weddings in Evagreen's family, it had always seemed
as close to the medieval idea of the cathedral as the center of life
as any church could get. For so long, churches had been the
only places black folks were allowed to gather, and even so,
how many black churches had been bombed or burned? It
always made her sad, going to West St. Peter M.B. and thinking
of those four little girls in Birmingham.

She did love to come out here and enjoy the difference between
the houses and yards in McCrady Hill and the houses closer in
town. Wishing wells, windmills, an old black kettle or a tire
planter, fancy brickwork around a flower bed; even the plants
in the neighborhood were different. Showier, pass-along stuff:
clumps of red president cannas up against porches, wine-colored
barberry sculpted into tuffets, exploding fountains of pink
pampas grass, elephant's ear, tall stands of variegated cane.

Scabiosa and dinner-plate hibiscus and creepy-looking but rich, velvety coxcomb. Abelias pruned into globes. Diamond-shaped beds of Day-Glo lime and cherry gladiolus. There weren't any fences, and it wasn't so different from the yards of white folks out in the county, but it was a refreshing change from the faddish wreaths, pineapple banners, and organized *landscaping concepts* in town.

Tonight every house on McCrady Hill seemed to have yellow porch bug lights on. Several houses still had strings of colored Christmas lights or the webbed, faux-icicle kind strung around, and two or three had translucent red Valentine hearts plastered randomly on the picture windows. The street had a warm, hearthlike glow.

Wiggs sat forward in the backseat, thrusting his head right up between Mary Byrd's and Mann's, scoping out the neighborhood. "This is too wonderful," he said.

Mary Byrd pulled up to Evagreen's neat little brick ranch house where several cars were already parked. The front door was open, and through the glass-and-grill storm door she could see people sitting around. She turned to Mann and said, "I'll be right back." To Wiggs, who was already climbing out of the car and fooling with his camera, she added, "Wiggs, please don't wander off. This will just take a second."

Mann, hungry and pissed, lowered his window and said to him, "Look, don't embarrass us, Ed. We have to live here."

"What are you two? The PC police? Nigras love to have pictures taken. But I am not the least bit interested in these *people*. Look at this *light!*" He snapped a few pictures of the Bons' house and moved off down the street in a purposeful slink, suddenly sober and as intent as a sniper on a mission.

Mary Byrd tapped softly on the glass door with a corner of the envelope that held Evagreen's pay. A short, round black man ejected himself from a recliner to open the storm door, which made a loud sucking sound. The man looked at Mary Byrd, almost, but not quite, in the eyes.

"Hey, L. Q.," she said. "How are you?"

"All right, then," he said, stepping back and holding the door open with one arm. "Come in, Miss M'Byrd." This seemed a little odd. She'd never actually been in Evagreen's house and normally she would have just handed over the envelope at the door. It was so strange that black people often saw white people as they really are, in their homes, sometimes in their most intimate state, but whites had so few clues about the private lives of black folks—their home life and families.

"Everything all right out here?" she asked, stepping into the hot, bright living room, immediately realizing it was not.

Evagreen sat on the sofa with two women Mary Byrd didn't recognize. In the kitchen she could see a man talking on the phone. The furniture in the room looked clean and new and comfortable, every wall and horizontal surface displaying china knickknacks and framed photographs, things Mary Byrd knew Evagreen had received every birthday and Christmas or acquired by attending every yard sale in town every Saturday at dawn. Not unlike her own kitchen windowsill stuff. She thought she detected the very faintest note of lavender in the stifling room. There was silence. Mary Byrd could sense that no already-spoken words even hung in the air.

"Evagreen, is—are you all right? Is something wrong?" She studied Evagreen's impassive face, from which she knew she'd learn little.

From a room in the hall emerged Evagreen's son, Ken, a tall, handsome guy with a shaved head, half-dressed, or half-undressed, in wrinkled military clothes, a standard-issue pale green dress shirt and dark green pants. He looked tired. Joe Tex was faintly singing "Skinny Legs and All" somewhere down the hall.

"Hey, Ken," said Mary Byrd. "I didn't know you were home."

"Hey, Miss M'Byrd," the man said. "We've had some bad news. Mama?"

Evagreen's hands lay in her lap, pale palms upturned. "Angie done kill Roderick," she said flatly, as if she were saying, "Angie just ran out to the JFC."

"Oh, my god, Evagreen, no!" Mary Byrd cried. "Evagreen! How could that have happened?"

She flushed and instantly felt beads of sweat on her scalp and face. How many fucked up things could happen in one day?

"She say he wouldn't stay out the street. She was afraid he'd make her and the baby sick." Evagreen opened her mouth to say more but nothing came out. Then, "He wouldn't quit runnin' in the street. Wouldn't quit, wouldn't quit, wouldn't quit." She looked directly at Mary Byrd and added, lower, "He beat her, too."

L. Q. looked at the floor and shook his head. "There was a girl," he said quietly, "an' other things."

"Oh, Evagreen, L. Q., I'm so sorry. What about Desia? Where is she?"

"She with Angie's friend. Cookie gone up to Memphis to carry her back, but Rod's people up there, too," said L. Q. "Don't know what's gone happen."

"There's going to be a hell of a custody fight, among other things, that's what's going to happen," Ken said quietly.

"Oh, god. Evagreen, Charles knows lots of people in Memphis. We'll find Angie a really good lawyer. With a good lawyer maybe she won't—Angie won't—"

"Get the 'lectric chair?" Evagreen looked at her with something almost like amusement in her eyes. "Go to jail? She already there. Maybe she *need* to go."

"*Mama*," Ken said firmly.

One of the other ladies put her hand on Evagreen's leg and patted.

"Lawyer ain't gone bring Rod back to his mama," L. Q. said.

The two families were neighbors and friends. Rod's people, the Kimbros, lived close by the Bons on the King Road. She remembered Rod when he and Angie had dated in high school. He was a nice kid—a bastketball player? Maybe a little wild. What kid wasn't. For a second she measured her own family's tragedy against Evagreen's. There was no doing it. Who could ever know or weigh another's suffering? Her heart ached for the Bons and for the Kimbros; they all would now have this terrible gravity affixing them to this moment, this day, this turn of events, and to each other, forever.

"Evagreen, I wish you'd called me! Please let us help. Let us help you find a lawyer, okay?" Mary Byrd pleaded, instantly thinking of how proud Evagreen was, wishing she hadn't said it. Oh, was it *ever* going to be okay between blacks and whites? Probably not; not any more than it would ever really be okay with Muslims and Jews, or Tutsis and Hutus.

Evagreen bent slightly toward the coffee table and picked up a big framed photograph of Angie on her high school graduation day and placed it in her lap. "Don't need no help. Ken can take care a us." She rubbed two fingers softly across Angie's cheeks. One of the ladies rose and stepped out the front door.

Mary Byrd's face burned with regret and the heat of the room. "I . . . I know that. Of course he can. I know he's a great lawyer, but it might, you might—" Her voice trailed off. She could not say, You might need a white lawyer.

Ken stepped forward and took Mary Byrd's hand in both his own. "Miss M'Byrd, we will figure this out and we won't hesitate to call y'all if there's anything you can do." Mary Byrd remembered Ken when he was a kid, too—a serious but sweet boy with a quick smile full of teeth, and later, braces.

Amazing how good-looking and poised he'd become. She remembered that Ken's full name was Hamer Martin Kennedy Bon, named for Evagreen's heroes: Fannie Lou Hamer, the mother, sharecropper, and civil rights leader from Sunflower County who famously said, "I'm sick and tired of being sick and tired"; and, of course, for MLK, and for JFK, who'd been assassinated the year Ken was born. Evagreen named all her babies for heroes. Why not. If she could have gotten away with it, Mary Byrd might have named hers Mick Jagger and Aretha Franklin. From Liddie she knew that while Ken was a newborn in the hospital, one of the nurses, seeing only "HMK Bon" on his birth papers, had labeled his little plastic nursery tub HIS MAJESTY THE KING BON. And that's what he was to Evagreen and L. Q. Evagreen had wanted his calling name to be Kennedy, but L. Q., who normally knew better than to cross Evagreen, had said, "You crazy? Might as well call the boy *Khrushchev*. Uh-uh. No way, Evvie." So he was just Ken. Always a smart kid, he won the high school Latin prize, played second base, went to the university on a full ride and then joined the Air Force. The Air Force paid his way to Tulane for his law degree, and now he was a captain in the JAG Corps. Ken and his German wife, Irmgard, lived in Wiesbaden and he was often in Somalia or the Middle East, helping soldiers sort out their legal problems and make their wills before they were sent off to be killed or handicapped in some stupid war that no mother would ever have started. Charles had always thought that Ken was CIA, which made sense, he traveled constantly. There were two children Liddie had seen occasionally. They didn't seem to visit often.

Mary Byrd felt her eyes welling up. "Okay, Ken," she said. "But please keep us posted. We'll be worrying like crazy."

"I will. I'll call you when I've gone up to Memphis and we know more."

"And if you—if you need—" She held up Evagreen's envelope. "Charles will insist."

"Thanks, but don't worry," Ken said. "We're okay for now."

Mary Byrd hesitated for a second and then went over to Evagreen and hugged her. Evagreen didn't resist, but she didn't hug back either. Her lips moved a little, but she said nothing.

Mary Byrd retreated, laying the envelope on a small stand near the door. "Okay. We'll be thinking of y'all. Night." She gave Ken a rueful, tight-lipped smile, and left.

The lady outside was smoking and she exhaled a white cloud into the purple dark. "Shouldn't be such a beautiful night, should it?"

"No, it really shouldn't," Mary Byrd said, and then, "Good night," thinking, Bad night. Bad day. *Horrible* day.

Mary Byrd plopped herself into the driver's seat as Mann said, "God, this pleasant evening is getting longer by the minute."

She put her head down on the steering wheel and told Mann what had happened.

"Oh my god! That's so awful," he said. "*Angie?* How did she do it? Jeez. Where is that asshole?" He looked down the street where Wiggs had disappeared. "Here. Switch places. Let me drive."

They swapped seats and Mann turned the car around. He pulled on the headlights, illuminating Wiggs coming up the street, walking stiffly.

"What's he doing, a goose step?" asked Mann. "Fucking maniac."

They heard a huge, angry voice shout, "Come 'round my family again, I'll shove that camera right up your skinny white ass! You'll be looking at a snapshot of the dark side of your tonsils, cracker!"

"Oh no," said Mary Byrd. "That's Roderick's house. Shit."

Wiggs threw himself into the car. "You wouldn't have believed it. There's a house down there—the one that's all lit up like a juke joint, where all the cars are. There's something awful going on—I don't know what—a wake or some wretched thing. You can hear the wailing from the street. I went into the yard to get some shots and all of a sudden, this—this fucking *animal* was on me! He nearly killed me! He nearly broke my back! He thought I was a fucking *newspaper reporter*! He grabbed my Leica—I'm sure this lens is ruined."

Wiggs blew his nose into a handkerchief and looked at it. "I wanted a picture of the window. Not those *creatures*. Wonderful. Now my nose is fucking bleeding."

"Well," Mann said, lighting a cigarette from the dashboard lighter, "There *is* a god. So much for your new coffee table book, '*Nighttime in the Quarters*.'"

Startled by this salvo, Mary Byrd said, "Mann! Don't."

"You'd feel a little differently if that baboon had given *your* candy ass a turkey stride," Wiggs said through his hankie. "Give me a smoke."

"I need one, too," said Mary Byrd. "And another drink. Or three or four."

Wiggs wanted to go straight back to the Holiday Inn to nurse his patrician nose and medicate himself with vodka. He wouldn't eat anyway, but they stopped and got him a chicken-on-a-stick and tater logs at the Chevron. Mann cautiously negotiated the downtown traffic; students were beginning to come out and were careening around in their big, fat death chariots on their way to the first parties of the night.

When Mann and Mary Byrd returned to the house, the sitter had *Emergency 911* on and didn't want to stop watching long enough to be walked home. "Some guys were scuba diving and a pipe fell on one guy's air hose. His girlfriend saved him. He has a cool Rolex," she said.

"That's why she wanted to save him," said Mann. "Gold diggers, all of you." The sitter eyed him suspiciously for a second and turned back to the TV.

"Let me cook something quick, M'Byrd. I'm vanquished," Mann said.

Mary Byrd looked around the counter for the science unfair proposals that of course weren't there. She called the Pink Palace looking for Charles but he hadn't come in yet. She asked the Palace to give him the message that they couldn't make it and were home, then she went upstairs to check on the children. Charles wasn't going to be happy with her.

William was asleep in his bed, hair still damp from his shower. She sniffed it and didn't smell shampoo, so he'd just faked a hair-washing. He'd better not get the damn cooties again.

Mouth slightly open, he lay on his back with a few of his favorite gadgets and models arranged by his head: pocket knife, binoculars, and a small model war plane still in his hand. Beside him, open, was *Jane's Guide to Fighting Aircraft*. Mary Byrd knew he had conked out—no one conked out like little boys—midflight, on some dangerous, epic bombing mission to Nagasaki or Dresden or Pearl Harbor. He didn't favor Japs or Germans, of course, but he loved their planes and tanks. His favorite, the one in his hand, was a little Russian Seagull, a plane so primitive that at Stalingrad it had flown so low and slow that Messerschmitts couldn't hit them. Peeking from under his pillow were his tanks: a German Mark VI Tiger, and a Shturmovik that William could tell you had destroyed the Third, Ninth, and Seventeenth Panzer divisions at the Battle of Kursk. Where the hell was Kursk? William could go straight to the huge world map on his wall and show you.

For a minute Mary Byrd imagined William dead, and shuddered. She kissed him, and, knowing he would knock his stuff to the floor in the night, she moved it all to the bedside table, picking up some empty Skittles boxes and throwing them in his Ninja Turtles trash can.

Eliza was still awake reading a trashy teenage novel that no doubt involved dope in lockers, heinous, clueless parents, and lots of near-sex. Mary Byrd lay down beside her. Her bed was so comfortable and poofy. There were about six inches of down underneath the sheets and comforter, and two feet of down on top, and several big, squishy pillows piled at the head.

"*Mom.*" Eliza protested. "Why are you home?"

"Don't read that junk, please," said Mary Byrd. "Read something classic or uplifting." She wound a piece of Eliza's damp blonde hair around her finger.

Eliza jerked her head away. "Like what? The *Weekly World News* that you always look at at the JFC?"

"I have to keep up with what's going on in the world, don't I?"

"Yeah," said Eliza, "Like what Bat Boy and Misbehavin and that guy Nostrildamus are up to?"

"Exactly. Let's see your hands." Mary Byrd put her daughter's hand against her own, remembering Eliza as a new baby and her hands that had looked like tiny stars when she was full and happy, and when she was hungry—practically always— had been knotty little fists pressed up against her cheeks, those huge chipmunk pouches and that precious potato head, like Charles's. She was surprised that Eliza had prettied up so much.

"My nails are *clean*," Eliza protested.

Mary Byrd ignored her. "Wow. Your fingers are as long as mine already. That means you're creative. You'll be a pianist or a painter, I'll bet."

"A surgeon. Like Big William. Who cares about creative?" she sniffed. "Mom, *get up.*"

"I care. Dad cares," said Mary Byrd. From downstairs came the smell of hot olive oil and garlic. "You go to sleep."

"Why are you home? Where's Dad?" Eliza asked.

"Ed had to take some pictures, and we decided not to eat out, so I guess Dad is on his way home."

"Why do you and Daddy hang around with him anyway? He's always drunk and creepy and says mean things to Mann."

"Drunk and creepy? Ed? You can't mean that." They both laughed.

"No, for real," said Eliza.

"You know why. He's a really great photographer, one of the most famous in the world, and Dad sells a lot of his work."

"Yeah, but what good is being famous if you don't know how to act?" asked Eliza.

"That's a good question. But when Ed's not drunk and acting up, he is really, really smart and interesting and, I swear, charming."

"*Huh.*"

"Maybe brilliant people *should* get cut a little slack, do you think?"

"Nope. Liddie wouldn't have liked him."

"Probably not. But Liddie would have tolerated him and been polite to him anyway, right?"

"Maybe. But she wouldn't *hang around* with him. And she would have said something like, 'He is such a *bore*. Have you *evah?*'" Eliza was great at imitating her grandmother. They laughed again.

"But I bet he would straighten up around someone like Liddie and be the perfect gentleman. She had that effect on people."

"Why don't *you* have that effect on people, Mom?"

"Not cut from the same cloth, I guess. Liddie's silk, and I'm . . ."

"Polyester," said Eliza.

"Thanks, pal. I was going to say denim, at least."

"Whatever."

Mary Byrd wondered if she should tell Eliza about Evagreen—she might hear about it at school in the morning—but decided against it. She reluctantly got off the bed and bent and kissed Eliza's face seven times, all over. Eliza narrowed her eyes and scrutinized her mother.

"Madison said her mom saw you kissing someone."

Mary Byrd stiffened a little. "Oh yeah? Who was that?"

"Some old man. One of those guys of Dad's."

"Pfft. I kiss those guys all the time. Is there a law against *kissing*? Is that the eleventh commandment or something? *Thou shalt not kiss?*"

"A *gross* kiss."

"If it was one of Dad's guys, I was probably giving him CPR. And besides, the Durthes are Church of God or Church of Christ or one of those religions that believe that *dancing* is a sin, for god's sake."

Eliza was silent.

Mary Byrd said, "Look, sometimes you just *have* to kiss people. Some people are needy."

"On the lips?"

"Oh, jeez, Eliza. Yes, on the lips. Lots of people kiss on the lips. Liddie and Evelyn and Big William kissed on the lips. Europeans kiss on the lips. Big deal. *Dad* kisses people all the time."

Eliza said, "Yeah, Dad kisses *Mann.*"

This gave Mary Byrd pause and she tried to read her daughter's face. Kidding? Charles and Mann often joked that they were a couple, and that it took both of them to be a husband to Mary Byrd. Then she said lightly, "Exactly. Ha ha. Be sure to tell Madison *that.* Stop making things up to worry about."

"Well, stop doing embarrassing things!" Eliza practically shouted. "Stop wearing that stupid FUPA skirt!'"

"God, you're insane!" She couldn't help but laugh. "What's wrong with this skirt? What's FUPA mean?"

"That's for me to know and you to find out," Eliza said. "Why don't you ask one of your *supposedly cool* friends?"

"Okay, I will. Now go to sleep before I call Whitfield to come get you."

"Hmph. They need to come get *you*."

"Fine. At least then I might find some people down there who'll be nice to me for a change."

"Yeah," said Eliza viciously. "You might find some slobbery retards and head-banger psychos you can kiss all the time, too."

"O-kay!" Mary Byrd turned to go, saying cheerfully, "Don't say 'retards.' Night-night, Miss Mean. Seepy-seep!" She turned off the light and closed the door. "Love you!" she called.

Eliza yelled back, "Yeah, *right*!"

Mary Byrd understood that possibly her most important function as a mother was to be a punching bag. Fine. Who else would Eliza take her hormone-driven insecurities and rage out on? Well, William, of course. Poor little guy.

When Mary Byrd got to the stairs, Eliza jerked open her door and said, "I already know about Evagreen. Roderick's sister works in Mr. Barksdale's office and the twins told me." Her lovely face looked vulnerable now.

"Okay," Mary Byrd said tiredly, and sadly. "We'll talk about it in the morning."

Mary Byrd thought she knew about children, about taking care of them, anyway—the nuts and bolts. She'd taken care of her brothers since she was Eliza's age. She'd certainly *thought* a lot about children all her life: about being one, about being a stepchild or a half-sibling, about having a child, and about losing it. But she did not know how to show her children how to be happy, or to give them happiness, which seemed to be the most important thing of all—certainly more important than piano lessons or Sunday School or SAT scores. Did any parents know? As Liddie used to say, "You're only as happy as your unhappiest child." Eliza and William were good kids—intelligent, warm-hearted, stable. Except for Eliza's preteen surliness, she thought they were fine. Mary Byrd hoped deeply that they'd stay that way, and she believed that with a little luck, because luck seemed to have everything to do with it, they would.

She and Mann sat in her kitchen and ate the fried egg and sautéed pepper sandwiches on stale French bread that Mann had constructed, and drank red wine. Mary Byrd wasn't very hungry. She lit a Camel Light.

"Pretty good, if I do say so myself," said Mann. "But I was kind of craving the pink center. And I think Wiggs was craving *yours.*"

"Shut up. He is not the least bit interested in me." She sipped some wine. "And things are too screwed up for one of those conversations," she said. "Anyway, he doesn't even seem sexual, somehow. Like a lot of people who are, you know, interested mostly in themselves and what they do." She didn't really want the smoke and stubbed it out.

"Yeah, I guess," said Mann, sopping olive oil with a hunk of bread. "This Chianti isn't bad," he said. "Even if it doesn't have the black cock on the label." He examined the bottle. "Hey, did you notice he was wearing the bulge exaggerator again? Dressed on the left this time, which I think is a signal."

"I thought you didn't like him, butt head." She ate a few bites of fried egg. They were delicious. What would the world do without eggs?

"Of course I don't." He started singing sillily, "What's *like* got to do, got to do with it?" Then, "He's just so incredibly good-looking, all I'm saying. And you know what we say out at the coops: cock's cock, even on livestock." He picked up a box of matches. "I'm like these. A strike-anywhere kind of guy."

She couldn't help but give a little laugh. "You are *so not* that. You are more afraid of cooties than I am," she said. "Now I *am* wondering where Charles is. If one more fucked-up thing happens today, I'll kill myself."

"You didn't even get those prints or anything, did you," said Mann, stating a fact.

"No," sighed Mary Byrd. "Charles will be pissed. But I have the excuse about the Bons. Maybe Charles can get with Wiggs in the morning." She bit off more sandwich. "Is it my idea that almost everything revolves around or happens because of sex? Either too much of it or too little of it or the wrong kind of it? Or did I read that somewhere?" she said. "I mean, Angie killed Rod because he had a girlfriend. My stepbrother got—"

Mann cut her off, waving his little hands. "We are not going there now. You might have bad dreams."

"I've been feeling all day like I'm *in* a bad dream!" Mary Byrd sighed loudly. "This stupid trip, and now what are we going to do about Angie?"

"What *can* you do?" Mann said. "You don't even know what's really happened."

"I bet Teever will know something, if I can scare him up." She wondered if he'd seen his message at the JFC yet.

"Yeah, but will it be true?"

"I don't know—his information is surprisingly reliable."

"Okay, so you know the details, then what?" Mann shrugged his shoulders.

"God. What a mess." Mary Byrd said, absently scraggling up her hair with both hands. "And what good is it going to do for *me* to hear new crap about my stepbrother?" she asked.

"Because *duh*—didn't we already do this? There will be one less bad guy in the world," Mann said.

"How am I going to get up there? I can't be ready to go 'til Saturday, and the airport might close."

"Hmm," said Mann. "We've got a truck going up north on Saturday. Maybe that could work?" He laughed. "I'd love to see it!"

"Very funny."

He cocked his head and said seriously, "Actually, why not? Foote Slay—you know him—we took some papers to his house that time. He's our best driver."

"Uh-huh. And what do you think Charles will say?"

"I'll take care of Charles. Let me look into it."

"You're nuts. I can't think any more about it right now." She was so tired. "I'm sorry to drag you into all this, Mann. Thanks for coming over. I don't know why you hang around with me—I'm depressed and depressing."

"I know," he said. "I guess I just always want to see what's going to happen next."

Mann left, walking the sitter out with him. Mary Byrd picked up the Spode plates, oily from the drippy peppers, and ate the rest of her egg with her fingers before putting the dish in the dishwasher. In went the silverware; she shouldn't have used the sterling because the eggs and the stainless stuff would tarnish it, but she liked to use her nice things for Mann.

Charles should be home any minute, she thought. Where *was* he? Maybe he *was* up to no good, but she let the thought go. She was too exhausted and distracted. Besides, Charles was almost exclusively up to *good*. She just wanted him to get home and help her deal with Evagreen's mess, and talk about going to Richmond, and she wanted to admit to her failure to secure what was needed from Wiggs and take her licks for that.

She wondered what Ernest had called for. Drunk again, she supposed. There was nothing to say. Still, it would be nice to hear him say nothing right now. Crazy thing.

Mary Byrd didn't bother with the greasy pan and began making her nightly rounds turning off lights, locking up, making sure Mann had turned the stove off, situating Puppy Sal and the Pounder and making sure Iggy and Irene were inside for the night. She left the driveway floodlight on for Charles even though he deserved to come home to the reprimand of a dark house and fumble his way around the bikes and dog bowls and possible eviscerated voles and garden tools on the porch.

Passing though the hall on her way upstairs again, she paused, as she often did, at the engraved portrait of Charles's ancestor and her crush, William Byrd, and the framed manuscript page from his amazing diary. Of all the lovely, heirloomy things Charles had, this was far and away her favorite. Using a seventeenth-century shorthand textbook called *La Plume Volante*, Byrd had written his entries in a cryptic scrawl that hadn't been transcribed and published until 1941. But long before that, some manuscript pages with horny entries had gone missing from the original text in the Virginia Historical Society. How Charles's family had come by the manuscript page was sketchy. Charles suspected either his very prudish Victorian great aunt or her infamously lecherous husband—an uncle only by marriage—of having pilfered the pages, or at least this particular page. They really ought to give the page back to the VHS. But then, why? It belonged to the family, didn't it? She would hate to give it up. The translation of the entry was penciled on the back—the children hadn't discovered this, or didn't give a rat's ass. Mary Byrd knew it by heart, anyway.

[September 26, 1711] I rose about 6 o'clock and read a chapter in Hebrew and some Greek in Lucian. I said my prayers and ate milk and rhubarb for breakfast. I danced my dance. I settled several accounts and wrote some of my journal. It was fine warm weather but there was great want of rain for the grass. I ate roast pork for dinner. In the afternoon I rogered my wife on the billiard table.

Captain H-n-t came and told me he had but 70 hogshead
on board and the reason was because people gave notes
for tobacco which was not ready. About 4 o'clock I took
a walk with him to Mrs. Harrison's to inquire when she
would send her tobacco. She gave us apples and wine and
told me that Colonel Harrison was very much indisposed
and drooped without being sick and believed that he
should never see Williamsburg again. In the evening we
returned home where my family and people were well,
thank God. At night I had several people whipped for
being lazy in the morning. I said my prayers and had
good health, good thoughts, and good humor, thank God
Almighty.

In spite of his colonial cruelties, somehow Mary Byrd had
long adored William Byrd—had known him longer than she'd
known Charles, since her William and Mary days. In fact, she
knew that some part of her initial attraction to Charles had to
do with his being descended from Byrd, and that he and his
ancestor, who had been born more than three hundred years
earlier, seemed so much alike. Not the cruelty, but his stoic
swashbucklingness, or something.

She knew Byrd intimately. At William and Mary she'd pored
over Byrd's insanely extensive and anal-retentive diaries—
volumes and volumes he'd written detailing life on his James
River plantation, participation in the House of Burgesses, laying
out the cities of Richmond and Petersburg, acting as colonial
agent and diplomat in London, commanding the militia for two
counties, and surveying the boundary between Virginia and
North Carolina. He wrote in it *every fucking day* about *every
fucking thing* that was going on, from his bowels and his wife's
periods to the state of his tobacco crops. It was irresistible to
Mary Byrd that she could get such an intimate glimpse into

early eighteenth-century life; the diaries were practically a time machine and fed the voyeur in her. She'd read other early American diarists in American lit class, but the bloodless, spiritual ruminations of the chilly Yankee, Cotton Mather, couldn't touch the earthy, sticky, and stinking humanity of Byrd's diary.

In the day, they'd called him the Black Swan because of his dark and dashing good looks—his portrait, an etching after a Kneller painting, was framed side-by-side with the yellowed hieroglyphic page—and Byrd looked charmingly swarthy; a little like Stanley Tucci in a wig. Byrd himself had used the pen name Steddy in his prime. His family crest was crowned by a swallow, a bird that she discovered symbolized perpetual movement and safe return: he'd crossed the Atlantic a few times. *Ten* times! A trip that sometimes took more than two months! Mary Byrd loved him so much—she could remember when she was a little girl feeling the same way about Fess Parker as Davy Crockett, King of the Wild Frontier—that she'd chosen to write about Byrd for her senior thesis: "Ague, Flux, Blue Wing, and Sallet: Healing and Foodways on an Early Eighteenth Century Virginia Plantation." If he wasn't walking about Westover checking on his mill or his orchards or unloading hogsheads full of tobacco or bossing his people around, Byrd was worrying about bad New England rum, sloops and tides, making business deals, arguing politics, writing letters back to England, raising the militia for a smack-down on the Tuscaroras, or complaining about his wife, who was a poor household manager or just lazy, and was frequently *"out of order."* Ha! They argued a lot: once, because he wouldn't let her pluck her eyebrows. This didn't stop him from *rogering her vigorously* or *giving her a flourish*, sometimes on the library sofa or wherever. Other times he *committed uncleanness*, or kissed or felt up someone else's wife or a maid, and when he went up to sessions of the House of Burgesses in Williamsburg, he and the other burgesses were *merry* on *canary, syllabub, mead, sack,* or *persico* and *played the fool* or *made good sport* with girls, or just *spoke lewdly.* Talked trash! He was a control freak and super-industrious, like someone else she knew, and read the classics in five or six languages every day, but also found time for gambling at *piquet, hazard, basset, cudgels, whisk,* and horse races, seeming often to lose some shillings, but never more than fifty, which was his limit. He dealt with characters who had crazily Dickensian names, like Billy Brayne, his dumb nephew; his friend Dick Cocke; and a French pirate named Crapeau! Believing that one should only dine on one dish at a meal, he was always having milk (he said he *ate* it), *caudle, sallet, chine, sheldrake, neat's tongue, pease porridge, water gruel,* and calf's head. Everyone, black or white, rich or poor, was always indisposed with *quartan fever, distemper, bloody fluxes, gripes, gout, dropsy,* and *impostumes, vapors,* and worms, and they came to Byrd for purges of *scurvy grass* or *laxative salts, tincture of snake root, jesuit's bark, beaver mineral, spirits of juniper, red lead plasters, burnt hartshorn, Venice treacle, stupe,* or laudanum. Often, he'd *salivate* them for rheumatism, or *let blood*—whole pints of it—for whatever, or have them take a *physic* or a *glyster.* He gave his slaves and servants no choice—Mengele had nothing on him—but his wife often sensibly resisted his quacky, experimental cures. For his own terrible piles, he had his wife *anoint his fundament* with tobacco or linseed oil and balsam or saltpeter. What a guy. No wonder he had 'rhoids: he was always doing stuff like slogging across the Great Dismal Swamp because he wanted to buy it and drain it and grow hemp!

Byrd was crazy busy managing his practically medieval, gigantic estate; he owned something like two hundred thousand acres. If he'd been born twenty-five or one hundred and twenty-five years later he would have been a revolutionary or a confederate. He didn't like being fucked with and even in 1709 he was already pissed off at the governor and the king for all the cash they were squeezing out of Virginia. *Nulla pallescere culpa*, he had adopted as his motto. "Pale at no crime." It was a good thing Byrd hadn't been around to see his beloved Westover first ravaged by Benedict Arnold and Cornwallis, and then used as headquarters for Union troops in the War of Northern Aggression, as he surely would have called it.

Imagining herself as Lucy Parke, Byrd's put-upon wife, she saw herself in her *undress*, meaning a sort of housedress; she'd rather have been in the fancy *mantua* that Byrd had brought to her from England, thickly embroidered and beautifully *scroddled* in swallows and flowers, with its lovely *scroop*, the train tucked up in back, but he wouldn't have stood for all that froufrou on a workday. She did have on a lovely new lace cap.

"Could you please get off your ass and do something around here?" he'd say.

"And what is it that my lord and master would have me do?" Mary Byrd would reply, lounging on some fabulous piece of furniture, picking sadly at a sweetmeat.

"I'll have you unloading some hogsheads, if you can't find anything else to do. God in heaven, woman," he'd say.

"I'm indisposed at the moment," she'd say. "I'm overwhelmed and despondent, having just lost my only son."

"*Work* is the best cure for that," he'd say. They'd fight a little more. Then, he'd say, "I know what you need, my good wife," and he'd yank her up, toss up her skirts, and bend her over the billiards table.

In William Byrd's mind, she'd enjoy it, and he'd believe that they were reconciled, but Lucy Parke probably faked it. Mary Byrd would've straightened her cap and gown, smiled weakly, and gone upstairs to lament her lost baby, do up some laudanum, and nap.

"Fuck this guy," she'd think, hoping he wouldn't follow her and have her anoint his fundament.

Byrd was a hard-ass. He had to be! When their baby son had died he barely mentioned it in the diaries, which had led some famous, dumb-ass feminist historian to offer this as further proof of his misogyny, or some silly crap. Mary Byrd knew Byrd better than that: it didn't mean that his heart wasn't broken. A teeny coffin was made from one of his walnut trees, and his baby boy was buried in a hard summer rain. William Byrd couldn't afford the twentieth century luxury of grieving. Hundreds of people depended on him. He just sucked up his gripey, colicky, hemorrhoidy guts, swallowed his tears, and attended to what needed attending to. Got back to work.

Mary Byrd's very favorite thing about him was the daily notation: *I danced my dance.* He mentioned it nearly every single day. No matter what wildness was going on around him—Indian uprisings, incompetent overseers and public officials, unpaid bills, shipwrecks, crop-ruining or sloop-stalling weather, people sick and dying—he got up at the crack, read his books, ate some milk, and danced his dance. Of all the Merchant Ivory vignettes of Byrd she carried in her mind, it was this one that fascinated her most. She pictured him shedding a Chinese silk wrapper, and then his billowing white shift—rough flax to mortify himself—and in front of a blazing fire, he'd do a sort of combination minuet, tai chi, and yoga, his longish colonial balls and mauve, sheathed cock bobbling and slapping against his strong, capable, and no doubt hairy thighs. Maybe there was a merkin, too. She couldn't remember if he ever mentioned lice. How did they stick merkins on, anyway? Call it exercise or exorcism, his dance got him prepared for, or through, his days and years. It seemed to give him what he needed to *go on.*

The truly bad things about him, though, Mary Byrd hated knowing. He not only had slaves but was part owner of a slave

ship. He bought political favors. He lost his temper and sometimes resorted to yelling like a maniac or cruelly punishing
people; Evagreen would not have fared well in Byrd's household. He suffered remorse and guilt, though, about these things,
and at the end of each day's entry, he'd usually write, "*I recom-
mended myself to God.*" But just as often, no doubt completely
exhausted by his responsibilities and busting his ass all day,
he'd regret that he'd "*neglected to say his prayers.*" Then, he'd
always close with that same upbeat entreaty, "*I had good
health, good thoughts, and good humor, Thank God Almighty.*"
She loved Byrd anyway because he wasn't exemplary but struggled to be, even knowing that perfection was never going to
happen. Was he so much worse than Thomas Jefferson?
Historians—about whom Mary Byrd often wondered, because,
despite seeming to have boring little faculty lives, they made
careers out of examining the lives of guys like Byrd who lived
large—had kicked around the question of what would inspire a
man to keep such an obsessive, personal diary every day of his
life, but she totally got it. *Duh.* It was a way, like praying or
keeping an expense account, to try to impose some order on a
scary, random, calamitous universe where the overseer was a
vengeful, Old Testament God. By keeping his diaries Byrd had
used every way he could think of to make sense of things.
Diaries were great until other people read them. She was certain
that Byrd had never intended for other people to read his. Why
else would he have written them in a secret language? Too bad
she hadn't done that back in 1966.

   Giving the portrait the lightest kiss, just touching the glass
with the tip of her tongue, Mary Byrd went upstairs to bed,
hoping that wherever he was, the Black Swan wouldn't hold it
against her for peeping.

Six

As the cold night wore on, things grew quieter on McCrady Hill Road. Cars that had parked at both houses, first the Kimbros', then the Bons', on opposite ends of the street, gradually went off into the night, one by one. The two little brick houses, almost identical, remained brightly lit, glowing yellow like lanterns, a blue flame inside: TV screens in the front rooms. There were so few streetlights in this part of town, and all the other houses had gone dark hours earlier, so that from a distance, the two homes might have looked afire in the blackness.

Inside Evagreen and L. Q.'s house it was hot and still. The phone had stopped ringing, and the ladies had put up all the food that needed putting up, and covered and arranged the breads and cakes and pies for whoever gathered the next day. People were shocked and confused as to what to do. It was Roderick Kimbro who was dead, not Angela Bon, but having a child who was a *murderer* and in jail in Memphis might be worse for a parent to bear than death. They all knew one another and both families attended West St. Peter M.B. Church. Everybody was making *two* pans of macaroni and cheese and praying two sets of prayers.

Evagreen and L. Q. had gone to bed after Evagreen finally consented to eat something: a skinny slice of Haseltine pound cake and a glass of buttermilk, into which Ken had mixed a teaspoon of Benadryl. Normally, Evagreen's sharp tongue enabled her to deconstruct any recipe after sampling just one bite and to name off every single ingredient in it, but she drank her buttermilk in two swallows without seeming to taste it. Ken gently wiped her lips, and L. Q. firmly led her to bed. Ken stayed up, sitting in the La-Z-Boy and writing on a yellow legal pad. Early in the morning—although it was nearly morning already— he'd go to Memphis and see Angie and get her a good lawyer and begin sorting this thing out. He had some ideas. He had some hope.

His baby sister. After all the tragic, senseless things he'd seen in New Orleans, and then in the Air Force, he still couldn't believe this. Angie had been the cutest, fattest baby and the prettiest, skinniest little girl. Ken had been gone, pretty much, by the time she was a teenager, but he'd remembered how proud he'd been of her. Cheerleader, homecoming court, working weekends at the bakery, principal's list. Sassy, too, but in a sweet way. Same thing with Rod: smart, great basketball player, good to his folks, nice guy. Didn't seem like a player. Everyone but Ken had been so glad when they'd married after graduation and headed to college. Not too far away, both going to Memphis State; Rod playing ball on his scholarship and Angie going for Communications. They had seemed so happy, but Ken had hoped she'd go off somewhere to school, see more of the world, get to know herself. He didn't care for Memphis much. What happened to people there? There was nothing up there but crossfire, crack, and barbecue, as far as he could see.

New Orleans had plenty of crime when he was at Tulane law school, but that's not all it had. A beautiful, funky, historic city—it was *worth* its problems: too many poor folks and the kind of trouble they had. He'd worked with many of them as part of his legal training. He and Irmgard and their kids weren't even noticed down there when they went back on vacations. Ken wished Angie had gone to Loyola, a good school that wanted her, but no, she had to follow Rod and Rod had to follow the money. It was hard to imagine that drugs had been a part of his—or their—problem. Hell, now he was going to be fooling with their mess, the same kind of messes he'd had to deal with in New Orleans: Ninth Ward crack hos and crack-head trash, and now with pot and pills and meth heads in the military. How had this happened in his own family?

Ken could only imagine what his poor mother was going through. And his dad, although his dad's expectations for Angie had been, if not lower, at least not verbalized so relentlessly as Evagreen's. Having seen some of the things he'd seen, many of which were unknown to Evagreen and the others in the family, he *thought* he'd learned not to let anything take him completely by surprise. Evil was a way stronger force than good in this world. Ken knew it. Give the devil a wink or a smile, next thing you know you'd be dancing cheek to cheek.

Whatever Angie'd done, he was going to work for the best possible outcome. He hoped not to have to ask Charles Thornton for help. His Auntee Rosie and his mother had worked for the Thorntons forever, and they'd helped the Bons many times. In his legal work, he had no problem getting help from white people, but here it all felt a little too down-on-the-plantation. Ken knew his mother had "issues" with Miss Mary Byrd, maybe unjustified, but issues all the same, and she might resent the

Thorntons' involvement. But if he had to ask them for help, he would. Whatever it took. He'd ask whoever he needed to to help Angie. And he had an idea about who that whoever might be.

In their small, neat box of a bedroom, Evagreen and L. Q. lay side by side in the dark. L. Q. held Evagreen's hand between them on the thick, velvet-like duvet cover that Evagreen had just bought the week before. She'd been sprucing things up—"freshening," as *Veranda* called it—and she'd redone the room in rich burgundy, hunter green, and gold. The window treatment matched the wine duvet cover and the cushion, shot through with gold threads, on the white wicker chair in the corner. L. Q. squeezed her limp hand every so often, and finally said, "We don't know why these things happen, Evvie, but they can happen to anyone, even nice folks. Part of God's plan, we have to believe."

"You think that, you a jackass," Evagreen said very quietly.

"Evvie, Evvie," L. Q. said. "We can't know what the Lord has in mind. You know that. We got to keep our faith."

"Why."

L. Q. rose up on one elbow and stroked Evagreen's cheek with his hand. He tried to turn her face to look into her eyes, but she stiffened her neck and refused to turn to him.

"Because that all we got, girl. *That is all we got.* You turn loose your faith, you be adrift on a ocean without a paddle, any kind of flotation devices, and sharks *will* be circlin'. Sure as I know my name."

"Don't talk at me with that mess *no more*," Evagreen said flatly. "You can shut up with it right now." She closed her eyes. From the front room they heard faint TV noise and the sound of Ken in the kitchen. "And don't y'all be slippin' nothin' in my food again."

L. Q. sighed. "We'll see Angie tomorrow. Hope we'll be able to talk to her." He took a deep breath. "I hope. But for sure

Ken will see her, Evvie. You know how smart Ken is and you know he gone do everything he possibly can do. That's another thing you can have faith in."

"I don't know can I see her." Evagreen pressed her eyes and her lips tightly together.

"Course you can. She *need* you. You still her mama, no matter what she done. *Course* you can see her," L. Q. said sternly.

Evagreen's chest swelled and she opened her mouth wide to expel a long, lowing sound out of the back of her throat. L. Q. scooped under her shoulders with one hand and with the other gathered his crushed, empty wife into his arms. She continued crying, her skinny frame heaving violently against him, with almost soundless sobs now, in spite of how tightly L. Q. held her.

"My poor girl," he said. "My poor, poor girls."

CHARLES HAD COME in sometime during the night and did not wake Mary Byrd up. Or so he thought. She was actually always semi-awake. Who could sleep with children and animals in the house? He was still asleep when she got up to set all the day's work into motion, banging on the ceiling with the broom to wake William and Eliza, then going upstairs and thwacking them with William's Styrofoam boffers to get them to dress, eat something, remember their lunches, and pile into the car for the ride to school. Alarms didn't work with them because of the OFF button.

In the car William asked, "Why are we taking the Vulva?" He was too sleepy to snicker. Eliza disgustedly squinched away from him as far as she could get. She was now grossed out by their family nickname for the car, although she had been the one to name it when she was little and she first heard the word from her grandfather. Always in every way correct, especially anatomically, Dr. Big William corrected her when she had fallen on a toy and had come crying to him. "The *vagina* is the internal part; what you hurt is actually your *vulva*," he'd said. "The outside part." "Okay," she had whimpered, "I broke my vulva, then."

"We're taking it because my car is almost out of gas," Mary Byrd said. "And the backseat's full of junk for the animal shelter and the Salvation Army."

"Just like it always is," said Eliza.

William said, "That's not a real army."

"*Duh*, William." Eliza gave him a disgusted look. "*Gah*."

He thrust a palm in her face, saying, "Talk to the hand!" Eliza swatted it away.

"Stop it!" Mary Byrd said. "You guys know about Evagreen's family, right? About Angie?"

"Yeah," said William. "What kind of gun did she have?"

"William! We don't know exactly what's happening but we need to help her if we can," said Mary Byrd. "That includes keeping your rooms under control and stuff like that. Evagreen might not come for a while."

"Mom, that helps *you*," Eliza pointed out.

"You know what I mean. And there's something else we have to talk about. I've got to go up to Richmond to talk to some people about Stevie. You know, my stepbrother who died."

"Why?" they asked together.

"I'm not sure. They've reopened the case and they want to talk to me, Nick, James, and Nana again. I don't really know what's going on yet."

Eliza huffed. "Too bad they didn't catch the guy when it happened."

"Exactly. But they didn't, and it's possible he could still be out there hurting people."

"I wish I had a flame thrower," said William.

That's my boy, Mary Byrd thought.

"Do they all of a sudden have a suspect?" Eliza asked.

"They say they do. Apparently some reporter has been poking around, trying to write about the case—you know how that cold-case stuff is getting to be the big thing now on TV. She can make money publishing a magazine article or a book, or selling the story to a TV show."

"Do we get any?" William asked.

"Course not, dumb-head," said Eliza.

"Anyway, it's just something I've got to take care of. It's the right thing to do. I'll probably go tomorrow and I'll be back right after." She slowed to the curb. "Okay, beat it. Just beat it. Love you both. Have a smart day." She watched them hustle into school as the way-too-loud bell from hell rang. William turned around for a last wave and a quick moonwalk.

But Mary Byrd wondered if that would happen—going tomorrow. She turned the radio up to hear the weather report. Freezing rain, possible snow, a winter storm moving through late tomorrow night or the day after, parts of Texas and Missouri were already in a mess, roads and airports closed, cars stranded, six killed already. Jesus.

What she really wished was that Liddie were still around. Mary Byrd did not get the clichéd jokes about mothers–in–law being bitches and haints. Ernie K-Doe had it wrong: Liddie was the *best* person she knew, mother-in-law or not. Mary Byrd loved her own shrimpy mother, Havnohart squirrel executions aside, but so much baggage came with the mother-daughter relationship, especially if mother and daughter were only eighteen years apart. And, of course, a mother *had* to love you no matter what, and a mother-in-law didn't. Mary Byrd had certainly given Liddie plenty of reasons and opportunities to *not* like or accept her, a footloose hippie chick in black tights

when Charles had first brought her around—not even a city
girl, but suburban, who took forever to catch on to the gentle,
byzantine manners of which Liddie and her regal, spinster sister,
Evelyn, had been masters. Or mistresses. One did not express
opinions, especially negative ones, directly, for instance.
"Daddy" or "Grandmama" or "Uncle Semmes used to say."
Not that *Liddie* thought this thing or that thing was tacky, or
just not done, but that's what *they* had thought, and perhaps
their point of view was worth considering. All unpleasantness
was to be skirted carefully. Behavior or people that were disapproved of were "unattractive" or "unfortunate," or were
dismissed with a pause, a meaningful stare, and a firm "Have
you *ever?*" She had an artist's sensibility and painted her house
a color she called "edible pink," a dusty, pale hue that matched
the old cedars on their place. Only partially reconstructed, she
would tell her grandchildren, with gleeful restraint, how *her*
grandmother had found a picture of Lincoln in her school book
and ripped the page right out. Every July Fourth Liddie would
subtly remind them that until 1945 and the end of World War
Two, Mississippians did not celebrate the Fourth of July
because, after all, Lee had retreated on July 4, 1863, from
Gettysburg, where the University Greys had suffered one
hundred percent casualties, and Vicksburg had fallen on the
very same day.

But the injustice and violence of the civil rights era had
wounded her and Big William's humane sensibilities. Liddie
had died the most rabid yellow-dog Democrat in the old meaning of the expression; not a Dixiecrat, but a populist, a believer
in taking care of all the people, not just the ones who were rich
and white. She had taken a beating at the bridge table for voting
for McGovern in 1972. A huge Watergate wallower, she had
insisted that not one, but *several* photos of Nixon resigning on
TV be added to the family album. And she had firmly believed

that "America the Beautiful" should be our national anthem, not a jingoistic battle hymn.

Mary Byrd had loved her sense of humor. Liddie had disapproved of the Midwest and the West, referring to *The Joy of Cooking* as "the Miz Rombauer," in which the recipes had too much sugar and not enough salt or Tabasco, and to the Rocky Mountains as "tacky." Her classic London Fog raincoat was her "lesbian coat," and the droopy skin under her neck that she deeply regretted was her "goozle." Kind to most, Bilbo and Nixon and his *apeheads* excepted, she had taken zinnias or fresh bread and pimiento cheese to the ill, the bereaved, or the just plain terminally pitiful.

Liddie had never interfered, and Mary Byrd knew that she did not want to hear about your problems, or even that you had any; but she would let you know that in general, she got it. No one knew better than she did how difficult Charles, for instance, could be to live with. Even when he was a baby they'd called him Ti-Mule, Creole for *petite mule.* Liddie had been Mary Byrd's model in the world; she thought of her as a kind of southern Lady Marjorie from *Upstairs, Downstairs,* and she was sorry that she wasn't more like her. She felt like the show's crazy-ass Sarah, the Cockney parlor maid. Mary Byrd wished she could be near Liddie now. They'd talk *around* what was going on in Virginia, but Liddie would give her strength and comfort. "Buck up!" she'd say, and Mary Byrd would.

TI-MULE WAS UP when Mary Byrd returned from the school and was sitting at the kitchen counter drinking coffee; stiff, chicory-laced, Community brand, black as tar—definitely not Midwestern coffee.

"Hey," he said, glancing up briefly from the *Commercial Appeal* sports page. "How is everything? How was last night?"

"Horrible. Did you hear about Evagreen?"

"No," Charles said, reluctantly lowering the paper to look at her. "What?"

Mary Byrd gave him what she knew about Angie's trouble and the Wiggs debacle with Rod's family.

"Oh my god. Poor Evagreen and L. Q." He folded the paper and put it down, conceding to the necessity of conversation. "What can we do? They'll need money. And a good lawyer."

"No. Of course I tried to offer. Ken's here, thank god. He said he'd call us. I don't know how he got here so fast."

"He's an Air Force officer. And whatever else. But that's so terrible." He thought for a moment. "What about Ed? Could you make any of that happen?"

"No," she said. "I hardly got to talk to him at all before the shit hit the fan on the way to the Palace. I'm sorry. He's probably still at the motel, this early. Maybe you can catch him?"

"Yeah," said Charles. "Damn. I'll jump in the shower. Sorry I missed y'all; I just couldn't get away from Callahan to get back here in time. If I'd been there Ed wouldn't have pulled that crap. "

"Oh, it would have been just as screwed up if you'd been here. He was just going to do his thing while I tried to talk to the Bons."

Charles stretched and started away, shaking his head.

"Chaz, wait. We've got to talk about this stuff in Richmond."

Falling back on his stool, he said, "What's the deal?" He arranged his features to read patience.

"I really do have to go up there as soon as possible, like tomorrow. This guy—the detective I talked to—said that time was really important. We need to meet with him Monday, he said." She grasped for more reasons, but why did she have to? "And Will and Eliza have science unfair stuff and games and drama club at the end of next week, and I want to get it over with."

"Okay. So *go*. Flying?"

"Not if I can help it." Flying scared the crap out of Mary Byrd, so much she had to take a pill to do it, which would give her a hangover. She knew that it was ignorant and lame to be afraid of flying, almost as stupid as worrying about something like cats sucking the breath out of babies, and of all the things in the world to worry about happening to you, a plane crash statistically wasn't high on the list. Probably lightning striking, or being eaten by a lion was more likely. Surely riding with Teever had to be way up there on the potential catastrophe scale. And all those hijackings in the seventies weren't happening anymore. There was the train; she loved trains and had taken the Southern Crescent to Virginia, and she and Charles and the children sometimes took the City of New Orleans. But the Crescent took too long, and someone would have to drive her the three hours to Birmingham just to get on it.

But she was pathologically afraid of planes. Bad things were less likely to occur if you could keep your feet flat on the ground, or at least on the floor boards of a vehicle that was in contact with the ground. When she was absolutely forced to fly, she would implement a complicated protocol that involved all kinds of checks and cross-checks.

First, she developed a fervent love for the airlines and its employees. She needed them all to be her best friends and like her very much so that they would be looking out for her and keep her well-being in mind before all others. There was humor and chitchat with reservation agents so they would give her a good seat. She liked a window seat. Not so she could see out, but so she could yank down the shade and pretend the sky was not out there. An aisle was okay, too, for faster escape and better bathroom access. No middle seats. Never sit way in the back:

tails could snap off, and it made you airsick. Don't sit over the wings because they wiggle flimsily, and you didn't want to be reminded of the *Twilight Zone* episode where William Shatner sees the abominable snowman thing hanging around out there. Sit near, but never *in*, the emergency exit aisle in case the door suddenly pops open and you are sucked out. This had happened! Someone had written a great poem about it.

No flammable or synthetic materials were to be worn because they would melt onto your skin if—*when*—the plane became a flaming cartwheel. Shoes must be sturdy with traction for running away from the wreckage—should you happen to survive initial impact. Her special necklace must be worn: a simple chain with mojos given to her by her mother (a little suitcase from the Hôtel de Crillon) and father (a gold heart locket, engraved with "To Mary Byrd from Daddy 1973," that held William and Eliza's photos) and a small crucifix from an old friend. A devout nothingist, she was hypocrite enough to keep it on the chain. She looked for coughers—spewers of germs that might bring her down with pneumonia, or worse. Famous passengers were a good sign. What plane would dare crash with Shelby Foote or Isaac Hayes or Eudora Welty on board?

The mechanical crew readying the parked plane also had to be scrutinized: were there slackers on the tarmac stoned out of their minds, playing chicken with their golf cart things, making monster faces at each other with their flashlights and forgetting to make sure no screws had metal fatigue, or that there was plenty of hydraulic fluid? Boarding the plane she examined the door hinges and exterior: were there a lot of dings? Was there rust? She'd crane her neck to get a look inside the cockpit: both pilots needed to be neither too old nor too young, nor too fat, and they should be wearing wedding rings; surely one with a family would work harder to keep the plane aloft. They should not be laughing or fucking around, but running down their own pre-flight lists and protocols. Mary Byrd didn't know whether it was better or not that flight attendants could now be middle-aged, oversized, and unattractive, but then she decided it was good: they were more businesslike now and there was probably less chance that they'd be horsing around or giving pilots midflight blow jobs. On the plane, you warmly greeted the crew and they became your family. Or maybe it was more like a hospital: pilots were the doctors into whose hands you entrusted your life, and the attendants were the nurses who cared for you; they would be the ones from whom you could glean clues about how the flight was *really* going. Before takeoff, you waved from the window at the stoner mechanics, who you hoped would think, "That's a nice lady! I better check those bolts one more time."

It was good to have a seat next to, or near, any deadheading pilots because you could watch them for signs that something might be wrong. Count the rows to the emergency exit in case there might be smoke and always have a little flashlight. Listen for noises that didn't seem normal, but try not to ask your seatmate if the noises seemed normal to them. Don't spaz out and grab their knees if there was a bump. Always wear a gauzy scarf to wrap around your face to thwart airborne macro-organisms zipping around the cabin trying to be breathed in.

Mary Byrd had never actually deplaned because of her fear, but she almost had. Back at William and Mary, on a trip to the Soviet Union to see the wooden cathedrals in Kizhi Pogost, she'd been on a domestic Aeroflot flight where a dog was seated in first class. Then in steerage, her seatmate's armrest had fallen off. If she hadn't been more terrified of being left behind in the insane disorder of a provincial Soviet airport, she would have bailed.

She was slightly less afraid of flying by herself or with the children; they would be fine with one parent if something happened to her, and it wouldn't be too bad if they all went down together. Flying alone with Charles when the children were little had made her the most anxious—the idea of William and Eliza as orphans. There was lots of stuff that Mary Byrd feared, most of it things that might happen to the children, or that might damage or warp them. Things that could just happen out of the blue.

She wouldn't bring up her pointless craziness with Charles. "It would cost a million dollars to fly with no notice, anyway," she said. "I could drive, I guess, but I can't make it in one day by myself, especially if the weather's bad." She paused. "What if I got Teever to drive up with me?"

Charles looked at her with a look that was his special face of incredulity and disdain. "Are you completely nuts?"

She laughed, slightly embarrassed. "Why not? We could drive straight through." Of course it was nuts.

"Have you been paying any attention to the news?" he asked angrily. "The weather predictions, for *one* thing. Jesus, M'Byrd. *Teever?*"

"Yeah, I *know.* But if I fly, the airport will probably close anyway, and I'll get stranded or something and freak out."

"Do whatever you need to do," he said, without meaning it. "Teever is just a really, really bad idea, seems to me. Or it would seem to any sane person."

"I'm going to turn around and come right back. Do you think it's really so crazy?"

"Yes, I think it's really crazy! What would you do with Teever when you got up there?"

"Let him stay at Mama's. It'd just be a couple nights. I *hope.*"

"I'd like to hear what your mother would say about that. Figure it out and do what you have to. The children and I will be fine." He turned and tried to get away.

"Chaz! I'm *scared*. I don't want to go." She hated to resort to melodrama and actually begging to get Charles's attention. Well, she didn't hate it; she did it all the time. It wasn't that he didn't care about her or sympathize with her fear and sadness, he just wasn't programmed for discussion; it wasn't in his genes. Global impoverishment, genocide, social injustice, famine and disaster and sad movies made his heart bleed, and he would write letters and send money, but break it down to one-on-one and you wouldn't get a whole lot. Mary Byrd had the advantages and resources to figure things out. It wasn't really his fault. It wasn't even a fault, it just *was*. The same would have happened if you'd gone to Big William with a minor but disturbing medical problem. He'd smile and say, "I guess we'll have to amputate below the ears," and that'd be the end of it. If you were a person of intelligence and privilege, you had no problems that couldn't be cured by outright surgery, and most things could be taken care of with a cocktail or fresh air, soap and water, and dignity.

Charles went to Mary Byrd and put his arms around her. His sweater, a handsome old green one, one of several knitted by Liddie while she was glued to the tube that Watergate summer, smelled faintly of mothballs, the indoor fragrance of the South.

"I'm sorry, M'Byrd," he said giving her a hug. "I know you hate it. But you're tough."

"I just feel so bad, and scared."

"I know this stuff is hard for you and your mom and everybody, but think about it—it was a long time ago, and people get through."

"I *know* that," she said, a little pissed now.

"Well, it's your duty to follow through on it. You should try not to brood so much, M'Byrd."

She understood he was trying to comfort her in his way, and she did appreciate it. Charles benevolently allowed the hug to continue, and she clung.

"You'll be all right," he said, lightly kissing the top of her head. He released her, pushing only just a little bit. "I've got to get going to catch Wiggs, okay?"

"Okay," said Mary Byrd, knowing that she'd squeezed the last drop of blood out of that turnip. And he was right that she needed to stop feeling sorry for herself. Like Mann said, it wasn't about her.

If she was going to make the trip she needed to be getting her shit together *now*. Make some calls: the carpool, get some groceries in for Charles and the kids. Bring in a little firewood, get water and batteries and put the emergency radio and candles out where they could find them if the storm knocked the electricity out. Go to Dog and Lena's and get wine, vermouth, gin, bourbon, and cognac. She and Charles loved cognac in their morning coffee when it snowed. Cover the tender plants in the yard in case they really did get a hard freeze, put down the sisal runner in the hall so slush and mud wouldn't get tracked in, put kitty litter on the steps and walks, blah blah. Remember to leave notes around reminding everyone to put the trash out on Sunday night, walk the puppies no matter what the weather was like, keep the front room closed off so the heat bill wouldn't be ridiculous and the puppies wouldn't pee or make a pile in there, remember to feed Mr. Yeti, their feral but devoted cat, and tell them to trap him in the big Havahart and bring him inside if it got really cold. Change the litter box for the spoiled homeboy kitties who wouldn't go outside if it was cold. They could do most of these things themselves but if she got it all done, and spelled out, she could leave without too much guilt and worrying.

FOUR THIRTY. ELIZA had drama and William had soccer practice, so she didn't need to pick them up until five thirty, giving her a few minutes to herself before she ran by the Bear to talk

to Teever at five. Charles would be home around six, and she'd
made a Dutch oven full of chili for him and the children to have
while she was gone. A little cast iron was good for them. Iggy
was bunting against her legs seductively. She wanted to pretend
that he was trying to comfort her, but she knew he was just
hoping for a treat. Her hands shook as she picked him up and
hoisted his fat, tailless body over her shoulder and began petting
his sleek black and white fur, which calmed her, and he purred
loudly, pulling out all the stops. "You're just a selfish slut like
everybody else, Iggy," she said. "You just want what you want,
and don't really care about anybody else." She kissed him deep
in the fur and fat around his neck, and with a finger tinkled the
little cowbell she'd put on him because he looked just like a
miniature Holstein. "Yep, you're just a slutty old heifer,
Ignatius," she said, dumping him to the floor. "It's not dinner-
time yet."

She was afraid Teever hadn't gotten her message and wouldn't
show. Maybe she should call Ernest and see if he knew where
Teever was. She had to find Teever, and she would like to have
some nerve pills for the trip. That couldn't hurt, could it? It
wasn't like she *had* to have them, but it was nice to know they
were there. She swigged a little Chianti out of an unfinished
bottle from the previous night and, seeing only an inch left,
glugged it down for courage. Ernest's number was written on a
ten-dollar bill, still rolled in a tube, at the bottom of her purse.
Mary Byrd didn't fully understand why she was attracted to
him, or vice versa. His inappropriateness was a big factor. She
knew that he knew that she knew the allure of sex that was
wrong. He had the preppy pretensions some Mississippi country
boys affected, mostly in dress. He always had a gun, but not the
kind that a farmer or hunter would have—he had some scary
military stuff and pistol things like gangsters would carry. Ernest
was kind of good-looking but in a hillbilly-come-to-town way.

Not inbred, exactly, but without even a drop of any kind of non-WASP blood to fortify his watery gene pool (not too different from Charles's, really, but without any money), too many generations of hookworms, poor diets, hard drinking, and smoking had given him a slightly sickly look. His blond hair was slicked back like it was still the eighties, although at least it wasn't a frat-boy Tuscaloosa Swoop. A soft, dissipated bod. Not her physical type at all. She liked long and lean and medium-well. Fair-skinned blonds with alcoholic bloat were kind of a turnoff. Sexy shadows under his eyes, though, and great wrists, and she loved men's wrists. His looked strong with pale, thickish hair curled around his Rolex. Wrists that seemed like they had character and competence. She knew it was just a mirage. Her friend Lucy had heard that he had what she described as "a smushed Coke-can pecker." Not good. She just had a thing for misfits and fringe people to whom conventional rules and situations did not apply. Flattered by the attention, she knew that Ernest wasn't someone you would leave home for, or fall in love with— Mary Byrd got that. He was a poor risk for a *thing*, perfectly likely to challenge Charles to a duel or a showdown. Discretion was not the better part of his valor.

Nobody much liked Ernest. She'd heard him described as "an asshole's asshole." But he cultivated his assholeness as a way of distinguishing himself from his slacker barfly friends who were amateur assholes. He loved to fight over bar tabs, girls, the state flag, literary heroes, whatever. Don't ever tell him *Chinatown* was not the best movie ever made, or that Gun Club's *Fire of Love* wasn't the best record. But in his too deeply set pale blue eyes, Mary Byrd thought there was often a demented twinkle signaling his amusement and the knowledge of how cartoonish he was, but the entertainment value made it worth it. If he took a notion, at the Bear he'd scoop a woman up like a fireman and carry her down the stairs, managing to slip a hand under her skirt before she knew what was happening—a redneck satyr in a blazer. Or he could pick up and go to the Bosnian front in his khakis and tweeds without a word to anyone. He was funny, which counted for more with her than anything else. He was smart in an idiot savant way; he'd read some books, and he and his pals had started a literary rag and had big plans for it. Unplugging the stupid current that buzzed between them, Mary Byrd had asked him to back off, but when she was blue or bored the flesh was weak. She hesitated, and dialed the number on the bill.

The ring was hollow and rattly. Wallett was way out in the country. "Hello!" said a loud, happy voice.

"Hello," said Mary Byrd. "This is a friend of Jack's. Is he around?"

"Why, I believe he is," the man said in mock surprise. "Just a minute, please, ma'am. Jacky!"

"*What* Pothus?" Mary Byrd could hear Ernest respond in an annoyed voice she'd never heard. He was hard to annoy.

"Tel-lee-phone," came the now-amused singsong.

"Hello?" said Ernest, businesslike.

"Hey, Ernest," Mary Byrd said. "What's up? Just checkin' in on you. And I wanted to run something by you."

"Well, hey, darlin'! How are you? I was just thinking about you."

"I'm sure." She already regretted the call. "Who's that who answered the phone?"

"Pothus, my uncle, my dead aunt Aleda's husband. Quite a character. He puts on a blazer just to answer the phone. Not even four o'clock and that knucklehead's already three sheets."

"And you're not? By the way, it's nearly five."

"I, as you know, have been working on my novel all day. I lose track of time."

"And you haven't had a drink?"

"Maybe just a drop," said Ernest. "To grease the wheels." They laughed a little. "So, what-all have you been up to?"

They chatted casually, staying in shallow water, giving each other a little more shit. She told Ernest that she was about to go to Virginia, hoping to get in front of the weather. Realizing it would not be smart to give Ernest any extra personal info that he could parlay into an advantage, she said she needed to "see about her mother," who "wasn't doing well."

"I'm sorry to hear that," Ernest lied back, as if he cared about her mother, and as if he hadn't already heard from a girl who worked in Charles's gallery what was really up. Did she think there were any secrets in town? "How're you getting there? I know you hate to fly," he said.

"Well, I was thinking about asking Teever to drive me," she said. She waited for the silence.

"Girl, that is *suicide*. I ain't lettin' you do that. Are you on crack?"

"You've got nothing to say about it, do you?" she taunted.

"I can make sure Teever's in no condition to walk to the square, let alone drive to Virginia," he said.

"He's *never* in condition."

"What if *I* take you? If you're going to take chances, why not me? I'm going to be in town anyway tomorrow for that Lords of Chevron party. I was hoping you might be around."

Mary Byrd laughed. "What, drive to Virginia in an MG? If it's icy? It's supposed to precipitate big-time."

"We'll take your car. I'll be a perfect gentleman, I promise."

"My husband will be happy to hear that plan. Who's on crack now?"

"That storm *is* supposed to be a motherfucker, though. My grandmother won't shut up about it."

"I might just try to drive myself. I've done that drive a million times."

"If you wait 'til Sunday, I'll take you," he said.

"I just can't quite conjure up that image: you and me in your clown car, going to Virginia."

"But yet you *can* picture yourself driving with Teever," Ernest said.

"Teever is at least . . . you know perfectly well what I mean."

"I haven't seen that old boy in a while now," he said. "But you should seriously consider going on Sunday instead and showing up at this party."

"Okay, I will," she said. "But I've gotta run. I'll talk to you later."

"No you won't."

"Did you call me here last night?"

"I don't remember."

"Ernest, I asked you to *please* not do that. Please."

"Why not? We're just *friends*, right? Aren't you allowed to have friends?"

"Can we please not drag this old dead horse across the road again?"

"Hey, *you* called *me*, darlin'."

"I know," said Mary Byrd. "But it's an *informational* call." She shouldn't have called him. Stupid.

"Well, here's some information, M' Byrd: I love you. I miss you. I miss you *hard*."

"There's nothing to miss, is there?"

"I liked it when I thought I was going to have something to miss," he said. "When I sell my novel, I'll give you twenty-nine thousand dollars to run off with me. No—make it thirty-five thousand. Don't go to Virginia tomorrow. Meet me at this party. You can go the next day. *If* you can tear yourself away from me."

She laughed. "You are nothing but trouble, and I don't need any more of that right now."

"I'm a wonderful guy upon whom you can pin all your hopes and dreams, girl."

"What you are is a grenade with the pin half pulled."

"C'mon now, M'Byrd. You're too hard on me."

"I'm sorry," she said. "*Not.* But I do hate to miss that party; the Lords of Chevron are always so fun." What she really hated to miss was some medicine.

"So I'll be lookin' for you, then?"

"Look, I've got to go, okay? Bye." You could lie and hang up on Ernest; it had no effect. Five minutes after five. She grabbed her purse and keys and ran out of the house, almost tripping over Irene, who rushed up behind her to take advantage of the open door.

LATE AS ALWAYS, Mary Byrd took the stairs in twos up to the Bear. It was deserted; at this hour the students were taking naps, resting up for the night. It was just a couple lawyers having a few after work and Teever and Chip, the adorable bartender who was Mary Byrd's favorite of the many adorable bartenders in town. They were silently watching some game on ESPN.

"Ayyy, Mudbird!" Teever said in his loud, gravelly voice. She gave him a hug. He always looked pretty dapper somehow, and today he had on a slightly too large tweed sport coat, expensive-looking weave, over a Greek black T-shirt.

Chip was drinking coffee and leaned over the bar to give her a kiss on the cheek. The Bear guys were well trained to make the of-a-certain-age ladies feel loved and wanted and in the mood to give tips.

"Teever's already running you a tab," Chip said with a grin. "Beefeater 'tini straight up?" He reached for the shaker. He was sort of unbelievably precious, Mary Byrd thought.

"You know what? I hate to be a pussy, but I think I'll just have whatever red's open," Mary Byrd said. "I'm only here for a minute." Turning to Teever, she asked, "So, how are you?" She lightly punched his arm.

"I'm cool, baby," said Teever. "Wassup? You seen Ernest?"

"Nope, but I talked to him. He says he's coming up here for that birthday party tomorrow." She made sure to add, "I haven't seen Ernest in weeks, though, maybe even a month. Guess he lowered his profile."

"Yeah, I might go to that party," Teever said, thinking that if Ernest was going to be there, he'd be holding all kinda shit, no doubt.

"I need to ask you something. Would you be interested in driving me to Virginia? Pay will be good."

"*Virginia?* Virginia? No way. No way. That is *too* far away," Teever said, lifting his beer and shaking his head. "Why you got to go there in such a big hurry?"

"Some family business came up all of a sudden that I have to take care of," she said. "You sure?"

"Yeah, I'm sure," said Teever, thinking of Ernest's certain stash in his near future. "'Sides, already told Mr. Johnny I'd bust up some ground for him. He won't call on me no more if I don't show up, hire some Mexicans instead. Sorry, Mudbird. That is *too* far off."

"That's okay," she said, not too disappointed. "I'll figure out something. I might just drive myself." With Teever out, it was down to driving solo.

"Charles won't go? Can't fly?"

"Nah. He's so busy. And he needs to be here to see about the kids and stuff. And I'm not crazy about flying." She lit a Camel Light and offered one to Teever. "But here's the other thing. What about Angie Bon? Do you know what happened? With Rod?"

"Sure do," he said, shaking his head again. "Sure do. That *somethin'*." He made a face at the smokes. "Why can't you smoke real cigarettes? Lights cut with arsenic, what I heard."

He expected her to beg a little. "Well, come on, Teever, tell me, please? I went to see Evagreen and L. Q. but it had just happened, and it was too awful and crazy over there. Ken said he'd call me but he hasn't."

"Well, the usual. The usual. Rod running 'round, getting up with the wrong people, usin', sellin', steppin' out." He signaled Chip, who was setting up for the evening. Chip brought another Bud. "Might a beat on her a little, what I heard. You know—ramshacklin' her."

"A *little*? What does *ramshackling* mean?"

"You know." Teever looked away. "Cracked up, slappin' her around."

"Jesus." Mary Byrd could not picture either of those kids in such a life. "How badly did he beat her?"

"Well, never put her in the hospital, I guess."

"God, Teever. Like that's *not so bad,* or something?"

"Didn't say that, Mudbird," he said. "You want me to tell you what I heard, or not?"

"But I mean what—how did she kill him? I don't even know that."

"Shot him in the gut."

"Where would Angie get a gun?" She knew it was a dumb question. This was America.

"You kiddin'? I'm the only guy I know who *don't* have one, and I did, 'til I pawned it, back at Christmas, buy some Christmas presents."

"Damn," sighed Mary Byrd. She had rolled her cocktail napkin into a ball and she tossed it into the trash can behind the bar. Christmas presents, my ass, she thought.

"She shoots, she scores," said Chip. He reached up and

changed the channel to the evening news, which was all about the approaching storm front.

She swallowed a gulp of wine and put down a twenty, then added a five.

"Okay, I've got to get home to my tribe." Pointing a finger at Teever, she said, "You behave and take care of yourself. Are you going to be all right in this weather?" She had no idea where he was staying but didn't want to embarrass him by asking.

"I'm always all right, Mudbird. Hey, can I have them smokes?" Teever asked, pulling Mary Byrd's unfinished wine in front of him. "You just a bar puffer anyways."

Mary Byrd tossed the pack to him and clattered quickly down the stairs. She wondered what it would take for her to be mad enough at Charles to shoot him.

Seven

I T HAD BEEN surprisingly easy for Mary Byrd to arrange the improbable trip with Foote Slay, one of the truckers for Valentine Chickens. It was easier than booking a flight, and possibly less risky than a long-distance drive by herself or with Teever. Mann set it up, saying, "You'll have a good time. He'll seem completely insane, but he's a pussycat, I promise. Just don't bring up politics."

Mary Byrd knew a little about Foote from Mann; they'd stopped by his lovely, decrepit family home once to drop off some papers. Mann was intrigued by him because he was that complicated Mississippi hybrid of redneck and blue blood—as blue as blood got in Mississippi. Mann said Foote might use the n-word, but more as a challenge than a slur: he *dared* you to call him any more of a racist than you were, you white liberal poser, deep in your most secret, elitist hearts of hearts. Firmly rooted, or rooting, in the nineteenth century, Foote believed in white supremacy, the right to bear arms, and the sexual superiority of black women, but Mann swore that he could be a gentleman, and was shy and sweet and honorable in his own dishonorable way. Kind of a Rhett Butler in an XXXL Lions of Tsavo T-shirt. He lived alone with a big black cat named Mr. T, a creepy pit bull–bassett hound mix named Frank Booth, and a parrot named Virgil Caine, who, if Foote said to him, "Virge, what were all the people singing?" would answer, "*Naaaa, na-na-na-na-na-na-na, na-na na-na, na-na-na-na-naaa.*" The inside of Foote's house, Mary Byrd had noticed, had been unchanged since who knew when. Heat seemed to be gas space heaters; creaky, spider-webbed ceiling fans the AC. Foote existed there in comfortable, regal squalor—king of his own castle. Empty Ben and Jerry's tubs (their ice cream was the only thing Yankees had ever gotten right, according to Foote) and beer cans crowded his living room, peacefully coexisting with a computer, stacks of history books, and his .44 Magnum he called "the Tabletopper" that was always at the ready in case any of *them* came around unbidden.

Of course Mary Byrd was drawn to it—its wantonness and neglect and one-time glory. She'd perversely had the urge to clean his house and fix it up and get his teeth fixed and cook healthy meals for him and do his laundry. He was handsome in spite of some pudge and poundage, smart, and way funny. His thing was to defy you to like him, Mann said, and Foote saw no reason to lie about anything; he was what he was and you could take it or leave it. But could she actually drive a thousand, maybe two thousand miles in a truck with him? Better that than a trip on Flaming Cartwheel Airlines. Charles wasn't happy about it, but tough for him, and Mann interceded for her. Foote could barrel up there in no time, and weather would not deter a Peterbilt. She could sleep or read. This trip didn't have to be totally a drag. It could be an adventure and a distraction from what awaited her at the end of the line.

Sometimes the most off-the-wall plans were the ones that actually ended up working best, or working at all. Mary Byrd felt all right about it: had she planned to go any other way there would have been a snag for sure. She left at the crack, in the dark, before the children got up, without telling them her mode of transportation. What a chickenshit. Eliza would be appalled; William *might* think it was cool because it was a truck. She'd give them all that: the three of them could have a big laugh and a little contempt-fest at her expense. Fine with her. She didn't have to worry about anyone else knowing about the trip because Charles and the children would be too embarrassed to mention it to anyone.

So, here she was in the gloomy dawn, eight feet above the road barreling along at eighty miles per hour, eastbound on I-40, enjoying the company of Crofoote Slay VI. It felt a little ridiculous; was she too old to be doing this? During the night, a cold rain had begun falling, but they'd beaten the brutal, frigid front that was expected by taking the northern route; the worst of the storm would be south of them. Foote, so far, was companionable and entertaining. He had been shy at first, but his morning pills—he kept a line of Black Beauties stuck on a piece of two-sided tape along the dashboard, or the control panel or whatever it was—made him an authoritative and talkative captain of his ship. The cab was cozy, if smoky, and curious. She felt like she was in a nuclear sub or at NASA Mission Control, there were so many gauges and knobs and cord things hanging around. Behind the seats was the cool little cabin, with a neatly made up bed, pillows, curtains, and a TV. Some photos were tacked on the wall.

"Do they even still make these?" asked Mary Byrd, reverently touching the Beauties on the dash.

"Have you ever heard of Mexico?" he cracked, and then, with not much encouragement from Mary Byrd, launched into his family's history. "My *hay-ruh-tay-uhdge*," he laughed.

The Slay family was from up in Spanish Trap, where they had had cotton holdings—land purchased from departing Choctaws for a few gold coins and easily accessible to the Mississippi River. They had gradually squandered their money on various postbellum enterprises, most notably a riverboat brothel, saloon, and gambling emporium that, because it was on the water, was exempt from all laws but God's, or the devil's. The entire crew, maquerelle, and most of the prostitutes who worked the boat and the riverside brothels had been wiped out in one summer by the great 1878 yellow fever epidemic, but not before spreading their pestilence up and down the river from St. Genevieve to Natchez. From that point on, the Slays had lived from decade to decade, selling off wedges and slices of their valuable land like hoop cheese to get by. On the last parcel was Foote's house, the family seat, a glorified double dogtrot with modest square columns and a broad front porch—the classic, graceful house type that was a hallmark of Mississippi hill country. Which, Foote added, had been mostly frontier when the house had been built. Mary Byrd recalled that the night she and Mann had visited, the cotton fields came almost up to the walls of the house. Woods and underbrush had barely obscured a Texaco Tiger Mart next door, and the county road ran less than fifty feet from the front door. They could just make out the casinos off in Tunica, a glittering mirage in the soybean and cotton desert.

Foote went on. Jerry Lee Lewis, the Killer, lived not far away and had tried to buy the Slay house but Foote wouldn't sell for any price, not this final little scrap of his family's past. He'd gone to some parties at Lewis's place. Once, on an epic binge, Foote said he'd tried to tell Jerry Lee that he knew the rocker was Hernando de Soto reincarnated because he'd been born in Ferriday, Louisiana, and that's also where the infamously cruel cocksucker conquistador had died and supposedly been chunked in the river. Foote thought it was more than coincidence that the Killer had settled near Spanish Trap—Foote suspected that he'd come back for his buried gold. Foote looked over at Mary Byrd, eyes bugged out, and laughed, saying, "And then I told him, 'Your wife got hold of your gold, and that's why you offed her,' and I got the heave-ho, which it took three of his goons to do." Wow, thought Mary Byrd. This will be quite a ride.

Foote talked for about two hundred miles nonstop. He talked about some things Mary Byrd liked hearing about, like the old plantings around his house that he kept going—ancient roses, boxwood, and Cape jasmine—and about the cross-country car race he had won once back in the seventies by driving a van that he'd converted, making the whole interior a giant gas tank so that he never had to stop. He also told her things that fascinated but horrified her, like the dogfights he frequented, which took place in an abandoned academy. Foote had once taken Frank Booth down there to fight, but his bassetness had done him in; he was vicious, but he was too long and low to be quick and a nasty-ass bulldog had torn part of his long left ear off. He'd seen a bobcat and a Plott hound fight there once, and the bobcat, even though chained, had easily won because the deeply gut-bit Plott had kept tripping over its own intestines until it finally gave out. He told Mary Byrd that he suspected that the Chinese, or whatever the fuck they were, who owned the Ha Ha Fresh Café in Tunica, bought and served dog obtained from the dogfights in some of their weird-ass dishes. But was fresh, stir-fried dog meat any worse than ground pig sphincters shipped six weeks earlier as sausage from Iowa, Foote wanted to know. He described his dream of signing up for a refrigerator truck haul up to northern Canada where he'd pick up a polar bear, bring it back to fight at the academy, and make a shit-ton of money. And, he went on, speaking of animal abuse, it seemed like every time he watched any porn lately it involved animals, and it made him ill that dogs and horses were getting more than he was. Mary Byrd couldn't help but laugh at most of it, hoping none of it was true and it was all to pass the time. God— dogfights. How awful. But how different was that, actually, from treeing a coon, or spotlighting or running deer to ground? Or baiting the poor bears that had existed over in the Delta in the old days?

"Feel this," he said at one point, reaching over and grabbing Mary Byrd's hand, scaring her to death. But she let him, with the tiniest twinge of interest, she had to admit, place her hand on his stomach, where she felt a hard, knotty protrusion.

"Hernia," he laughed.

"Gross," said Mary Byrd. "But thanks for sharing."

"Why, you're welcome. Just tell me when I've gone too far." He smiled half-sheepishly.

"I don't think I'll try to tell you *anything*, Cap'n Slay. I'd probably end up back there with the chicken parts."

"But enough about me. How about some music? You wanna tune into that idiot preacher show, 'Healing the Wheeling,' on American Family Radio, or do you want a tape?" He suddenly straightened in his seat, ran a bandana over his face and hair, and composed his features—which had been pinched and twitchy—into a mask of serenity and normalcy. Mary Byrd sensed with relief that maybe his upper rush was over.

"A tape would be good," she said.

Foote had great rig-rock: a mix tape he'd made of dozens of car and road songs, everything from the obvious stuff like "Bobby McGee" and "Deadman's Curve" and "Leader of the Pack" to "Dynaflow Blues," "East Bound and Down," "Lost Highway," and Jimmy Liggins's "Cadillac Boogie," the song, Foote maintained, Ike Turner had ripped off for "Rocket 88," which was on the tape two times. And "Ramblin' Man." Was there anything better for driving and cheering you up than Dickey Betts? One of Mary Byrd's local favorites was on there, too: the old blues singer Fairlane Ford's "Cement Mixer Blues":

> *I want to be a cement mixer, honey,*
> *churnin' it while we drive.*
> *And if you don't mix it with me, baby,*
> *you won't be goin' home alive . . .*

They listened, Foote and Mary Byrd, without saying a word for a long time.

The Beatles singing "Drive My Car" came on, giving Mary Byrd a little jolt; it had been Stevie's favorite song on her *Rubber Soul* album that a boyfriend across the street had brought her back from England.

"Oh!" she said. "This song!" Foote ignored her.

Stevie must have been seven or eight and Mary Byrd had hauled out their mammoth Norelco tape recorder one day. She had wanted to record Stevie singing the song; she'd been babysitting him and trying to entertain them both, and she'd known her mom and Pop and Nick would be amused. They'd all listened to the tape so many times; it always cracked Nick and Stevie up. She still remembered every word of the tape. The two of them had been sitting on the floor in her room, and Stevie had only wanted to mess with the dials and the rotating tapes. She'd interviewed him first, to warm him up.

"Here we are talking to the famous rock 'n' roll star Stevie Rhinehart. How are you, Stevie?" she'd asked.

"Can these wheels go faster, so we'll sound like the Chipmunks?"

"Pay attention! You're supposed to be one of the Beatles, dopey. If you do this, I'll take you to Doc's later for a cherry Coke and a candy bar."

"O-*kay*, Mubba," he'd said, grudgingly.

"And don't call me that," Mary Byrd had said. When he'd first come into the family, Mubba had been the best he could do for her name, and he still liked to use it because it annoyed her and got her attention, although he didn't really get why. To her it sounded too much like "muvva."

She had tried again. "Mr. Stevie, since you're a rock 'n' roll star, lots of girls want to know if you have a girlfriend. Can you tell us who she might be?"

"No-o-o-o," he'd answered slyly. "But it's not Sherrie," he'd said, singsong, naming a girl in his class at school who Mary Byrd had known he had a crush on.

"It's not Sherrie Finkelstein? Are you *sure?*"

"It's . . . *you*," he'd laughed.

Mary Byrd had broken character and laughed, too. "You know your sister can't be your girlfriend, dummy."

"Then it's Mom," he had said.

"And Mom can't be your girlfriend either!" He had been sucking up, but it had made her happy that he liked his step-mother enough to even say that.

Switching back into interview mode, she had asked, "Well, Mr. Stevie, how about singing your favorite song, 'Drive My Car,' for all your fans?"

"Do I have to?" he'd said.

On the tape you could barely hear Mary Byrd whisper, "*Yes. If you want to go to Doc's. Stand up and do it!*" She remembered how great it was to watch him pretending to play the guitar, doing an outstanding imitation of John Lennon's plié playing style. Baby James could do it, too.

Stevie had begun singing in a desultory, gruff voice: "Baby, you can drive my truck. Yes, I'm going to be a duck."

"Stevie, STOP!" she had shouted. "Why are you singing the wrong words?"

"Nick sings it that way!" he had said. "And there are some bad words, but if I sing them you'll tell Mom or Pop."

Mary Byrd had yelled, "Oh, *brother!* You're both *hopeless.*" The tape ended there with Stevie chuckling goofily. She'd listened to it once after Stevie died, then thrown the old recorder and tape out. *Oh, brother.*

Foote watched his gauges and the slick road and the traffic and the signs, and Mary Byrd watched the windshield wipers and the low sky and the landscape and thought about Monday. She'd soon be in an office in downtown Richmond with some deadly serious strangers talking about deadly serious things. She guessed that Foote knew from Mann that she had something bad awaiting her, and that he was trying his rough best to distract and entertain her. Which was nice, even if it *was* dogfights and pig sphincters and hernias; it was still distraction and entertainment.

They stopped to eat at a truck stop. Foote had wanted to stop at a Cracker Barrel because he'd heard they didn't hire queers. "You don't need to tell Mann I said that," he said.

"Gah. That's a pretty . . . *wrong* thing to say." She was pissed, given that Foote worked for Mann. "And Cracker Barrel learned their lesson. Why don't you?"

"It's nothing against them; I'd just as soon they didn't handle my food. I would think you'd feel the same."

Taken aback, Mary Byrd asked, "What do you mean?"

"Never mind."

Jeez. The truck stop café where they finally ended up was good, though. It had a wholesome meat-and-three menu, and she could see that there would be some fruitful trash-shopping in the gift shop. Many of the best presents she ever gave people came out of truck stops and roadside crap-o-toriums. And in the lot next door there was a fireworks store. They went ahead and ordered; Mary Byrd wanted a salad with chicken strips and Foote asked

for the country-fried steak and vegetable plate. When the waitress asked him which vegetables he'd like from the list on the
menu, he said, "Mac and cheese, grits, and bacon."

"Bacon," said the waitress, a pretty girl with too much
makeup.

"Pork is a crop, isn't it?" he asked Mary Byrd.

The waitress went away and Mary Byrd went to the gift area.
There was a profusion of junk of all kinds: the usual stuff like
Confederate license plates and incense and dream catchers and
throat cutters or fish gutters—it was hard to tell what those
things were for—and wooden hillbilly joke items, but there
were a few finds. In with the wolf T-shirts and Tennessee shot
glasses, Mary Byrd found perhaps the sickest thing ever: a shirt
emblazoned with 50,000 BATTERED WOMEN IN AMERICA, AND
I'VE BEEN EATING MINE PLAIN. Oddly, there was only one, and
it had a worn look to it but it didn't smell. She bought it so no
one else could, and because it was so unbelievable. She also
bought a pen in the shape of a finger that farted when you
pulled it and a tiny Chihuahua that lifted its hind leg. Did the
Chinese study us and watch our TV programs and make this
stuff up, or did wacky Americans dream it up and go over there
and have it made? Mary Byrd was ashamed to be buying the
shirt and folded it so the middle-aged lady cashier could only
see the price, not the slogan. While she waited in line, she looked
over the disgusting generic candy selection: long, ropey jelly
snakes, cotton candy in plastic tubs, Nik-L-Nips that looked
left over from the fifties, candy barf and snot. Whatever had
happened to Bonomo Turkish Taffy, Sky Bars, and BB Bats?

The cashier accepted her items, saying, "Isn't that the funni-
est shirt?"

"Unbelievable," said Mary Byrd.

They ate in silence, except for Mary Byrd trying to get Foote
to eat some of her salad, and returned to the truck. Mary Byrd

begged Foote to let her just run into the fireworks store and he said okay, but he didn't turn off the roaring engine. Mary Byrd moved quickly around the fireworks display table and picked up some small ones, a Dragon Fart and a Monkey Drive. She loved the exotic, colorful graphics of the wrappers and boxes. They were gorgeous. William liked fart stuff –who didn't—and monkeys, and he'd be happy to have a little stash; you couldn't buy fireworks in the progressive state of Mississippi except around New Year's and the Fourth of July. Probably she was a bad mother for giving her child fireworks. Big William often said he'd had to fix too many fingers and eyeballs because of them. Little boys adored explosives, though. William and his friends were crazy for them. Nick and Stevie had been, too. Big boys loved them as well, she thought, and that's why we have war.

Back on the road again, headed across Tennessee toward the mountains, Foote and Mary Byrd rode quietly, a little bored and disappointed with each other and amusing themselves by reading off the weird roadside messages and bumper stickers they saw. It had started raining again, and the clouds were dark behind them. The backs of other trucks seemed to have become the new venue for religion and patriotism: 100% AMERICAN and ON DUTY FOR AMERICA and JESUS: LEGAL IN ALL 50 STATES. What did that even *mean*? Foote might be a far-to-the-right kind of guy, but he wasn't a big fan of Jesus. "Jesus," he told her, "was just a big ole Socialist."

CROSSING INTO VIRGINIA they began to see old churches and houses that still dotted the hills, charming as calendar photos, but more common were huge steel structures like airplane hangars or skating rinks. One near Wytheville looked like a flimsy, art deco twelve-plex theater with an electric billboard out front declaring that it was THE CHURCH IN THE NOW. Whatever that meant. As if anything in southwestern Virginia could even remotely be *in the now*, thought Mary Byrd. More like *in the then*. There had been so many more old, abandoned farmhouses along this stretch in the old days. She remembered being sad, twenty years earlier, when they had begun to be replaced by new trailers. Now some of the trailers were abandoned and new ranch-style houses stood by them. She guessed that this meant prosperity and better lives for those families, but still. There had to be so many things left behind in the old places; not TVs or recliners or carpeting, but fireplaces and hearths and caned rockers and hooked rugs, and the ways of making them. And not just tangible stuff, but stories and songs. Food. Blah blah. She stopped herself in mid-romantic-hillbilly reverie. She wondered what Foote thought, although she could guess.

"It makes me sad to see these old houses falling down, and all these people living in these crappy prefab things," she said.

"*Sad?*" Foote said. "You think *they're* sad to have places that are clean and don't stink of all their ancestors' fatback grease? You think they're *sad* to be free of being cold and breaking their backs chopping wood and hauling water and being isolated and shit?" He turned to her and blew smoke out of a contemptuous smirk. "*That's* some folk-ass, Yankee bullshit, right there. Don't be one of those quaint-hounds, girl."

Uh oh. Just as she thought. "Hey!" she said, "I'm not a Yankee! I'm from Virginia!"

"Puh," Foote huffed. "Virginia is for lovers. And Yankees."

"I call bullshit on *that*." She wondered how many soldiers— husbands, sons, brothers, *boys*—had died in Virginia over the centuries. Foote would know, but she wasn't asking. "And you live in *your* ancestors' house."

"Virginia is what Yankees think of now when they think of the South," Foote said. "They don't know the real deal. All that genteel old Virginia colonial horsey shit, and they think they've got so much more history than Mississippi. And my house is no farmhouse, thank you very much."

"I didn't mean that. But Virginia's twice-soaked land, isn't it? It is way older," Mary Byrd said.

"Twice-soaked? What's that mean?"

"You know—the Revolution and the Civil War were both fought and ended in Virginia. And Jamestown—"

"Jamestown? That place was sorry as shit. And hell, De Soto was in Mississippi at least fifty years before, in what? Fifteen forty-one."

"Okay, well, lots of Mississippians are Virginians who went west to settle," she said.

"Exactly." Foote lit another smoke, sucked in, and exhaled. "Exactly. They came out to Mississippi to get away from the federal government, which was too close, so they could do what they fucking wanted. My mother's great-great-grandfather came out of Kentucky—a sorry state that never could decide, by the way—and went to Virginia, where he grew and shipped tobacco on the Richmond and Danville Railroad, and then in the *War of Northern Aggression,*" here Foote enunciated pointedly, "he shipped guns for the Confederacy. The Yankees tore up the tracks, and then *somebody* blew up the arsenal. It blew for six days. He lost fucking everything. They came to Mississippi to start over. They made it the hard way. Mississippians are the survivors. Carpetbaggers poured into Virginia. J. P. Morgan bought the railroad."

"I'm tempted to mention Natchez, if we're talking carpetbaggers," Mary Byrd said. "But I won't. Let's talk about something else."

But Foote went on. "And then, Mississippi was forgotten about. The only time the federal government ever paid attention to us was when they decided we were doing something wrong." Sleety rain was coming down hard now, and Foote bumped the giant wipers up to a faster tempo. Mary Byrd was so glad she was not driving.

"One fifth of the Mississippi state budget after the war had to pay for prosthetic arms and legs for Confederate veterans."

"But come on, Foote. What about all the New Deal—"

"Shit! Roosevelt just wanted to give it all to hillbillies, and," he paused, "*African-Americans*," he added sarcastically.

"Okay! Uncle!" cried Mary Byrd. "All hail Mississippi—the only authentic southern state! I'm a lover not a fighter!" Mann had warned her. "Do you want me to get out here?"

"Maybe. Admit you're guilty."

"Guilty of what?" she asked.

He laughed. "Failure to have been born in the great state of Mississippi, and of being a liberal."

"Fine." she said.

"And here's your sentence," he said, poking the tape deck buttons. "You have to listen to this."

Mary Byrd waited until the tape stopped whirring and began to play "Dixie." She might have known. They both laughed and listened to Black Oak Arkansas's version of the song, the mournful, crudely harmonious opening vocals giving way to metal chaos. She could picture the half-naked band whipping their hair and whaling at their guitars. What an incredible song "Dixie" was, Mary Byrd thought but didn't say for fear of cranking Foote up again. She definitely wasn't going to point out that it had been written by a Yankee and maybe even a black guy. It was still one of the most poignant and stirring songs ever, even sung by Black Oak Arkansas, with the ability to raise the hair on her forearms, to her embarrassment. It was too bad that it had been claimed by a lot of rednecks as a football fight song and that it was now banned. She couldn't help it. "It is an amazing song," Mary Byrd said, with cheesy feeling.

"Yep," said Foote. "The greatest." He knocked the wipers back to a slower pace. As the song came to a close, Mary Byrd said, "What's next? The Elvis 'American Trilogy'?"

Foote laughed. "As a matter of fact, that's on here somewhere. But I need to listen to my CB." He punched off the tape. "So you keep it down, okay?"

Lunch and beer and the hypnotic effect of the wipers made her sleepy. It seemed like a lovely idea to crawl into the bunk and conk out, but it also seemed rude. But she was tired of hearing Foote talk his crazy trash and tired of sparring with him. She was tired of hearing everything she had to say, too; she'd said everything she'd ever known over and over again a million billion times. In a few hours she should be in Richmond. Who was this detective, she wondered. He wasn't one of the original guys; they had to be retired, or dead. She hoped he wouldn't show them anything horrifying, including her diary. She hoped not to cry. She would try not to bow up with attitude. Putting her head down on the crumpled jacket between her and Foote, she hoped Foote wouldn't put a hand on her hair, or on her upturned shoulder. There might be something in the surprise of it. Was this the way people who committed sex crimes felt? Always having inappropriate, wrong thoughts? She willed this one away and thought instead about staying at her mother's house, full of crazy cats, the hard guest mattress, the familiar sniping she and Nick and her mother would do, and the silly comfort she felt there anyway, and she fell asleep.

MARY BYRD SLEPT long and heavily, and when she woke it was nearly dark and the truck was rolling along fast—too fast—approaching Richmond. She had drooled not only on her jacket but had made a sticky spot on some of Foote's papers—a clipboard with receipts and forms.

"Oh, man," she said. "I kind of drooled a little bit on your stuff." She tried to clear the slobber off the papers with her hand and wiped it on her jeans.

"A little bodily fluid never hurt anything, far as I know."

Mary Byrd fluffed her fluffy hair a little and rubbed the crusty corners of her mouth with her fingers. She should put on some lipstick and blusher, which would please her mother. "Wonder what the weather's doing at home?"

"Sounds bad from what I heard on the CB while you were asleep. A lot of ice, roads closed. You never would even have gotten to Mempho, let alone taken off." She wondered how Charles and the children were getting along. William and Eliza were probably having a blast and Charles was probably pissed.

"Wow," she said, seeing a sign for Caledonia. "We're almost there, aren't we?" The dread resurfaced in her groggy consciousness.

"Yep. Where exactly am I taking you?" Foote asked.

"Anywhere in the West End is okay. My mom or one of my brothers can come get me."

"I'll take you wherever, but it's hard for me to get this thing into and out of residential areas."

"There's a little shopping center at Libbie and Patterson. Just take the Patterson exit. I'll show you.

She had suddenly taken it in her mind to go back to their old neighborhood—to Cherry Glen Lane, the house where they had all lived when Stevie died. She wasn't sure why she wanted to do it; maybe to refresh her memory for Monday? She realized that all along she had planned this, and that she wanted to be alone and not with her mother and brothers. The two neighborhoods—Tuckahoe where her mother now lived and Cherry Glen Lane—were a couple miles apart. She'd call a cab from Doc's Drugstore, if it was still there, to take her to her mother's when she finished seeing whatever it was she expected to see, or feeling whatever it was she expected to feel.

"So you've got some unfinished business to tend to up here," Foote said.

"Some . . . unpleasant stuff that happened a long time ago in my family. I'm not looking forward to it."

"Mann told me a little."

"It's no big secret or anything. Just something it's not fun to talk about, and nobody wants to hear about." Mary Byrd shrugged.

"Creeps like that should be fried." Foote shook his head. "I hope they've got the guy. They should let me and Frank Booth interrogate him."

Mary Byrd laughed a little. "You and Frank Booth could get a false confession out of anyone. I'd say *I* did it to keep y'all away from me."

"Fuckin' A," Foote said grimly. "You know that scene in *Reservoir Dogs*? Your guy would *definitely* be stuck in the middle with me and Frank Booth."

Foote was just a little too serious, but she laughed. "I think the case is sort of past all that now," she said. "I don't know a hell of a lot about what's going on. They've reopened it, and I think they might have finally decided they've even *got* a case, and they're trying to move fast and seal the deal before some reporter scoops them."

"The big pedophile barbeque," Foote said. "Save me the heart."

"Good lord, Foote." Mary Byrd rubbed her eyes. She noticed a couple more Beauties were gone from the dash.

"Don't you and your family want to see him sizzle?"

"God, I don't know. No! Back then, maybe I—we—did; I'm not sure. We were all so shell-shocked it was kind of all we could do to just get dressed in the morning. My stepfather was pretty badass; if he'd been himself, and they'd been sure of who did it, he would have torn the guy to pieces and anyone who tried to stop him. But he was so destroyed and drugged-up. He was just *gone*." Mary Byrd drew her feet up under her, hugging her knees, thinking of how hard it must have been for Pop with Tuttle just down the street. "It really did kill him, and he was hard to kill. He survived the Battle of Hürtgen Forest! My mom was still picking shrapnel chunks out of his hip. But losing his kid that way is what did him in."

"And you don't think this fucking freak needs to die?" Foote said.

"I . . . that's just too dark-ages or something. I mean, probably, the guy was totally fucked up by something that had happened in *his* life, right?"

"And he had no choice but to go out and fuck up some other people? Shit, M'Byrd, your bleeding heart is messing up my upholstery worse than your drool."

"I just have to imagine what's it's like to be the parent of a person who . . . does that stuff, and have them get the death penalty. Maybe there should be some mercy in it somewhere," she said, thinking about Evagreen and Angie.

"Mercy's overrated."

"What if he's been doing something good all this time, like in the Peace Corp?"

"Or like a priest or a Boy Scout leader?" Foote said, viciously sarcastic. "Girl, trust me: those fuckers don't change. They *can't*. Don't even *think* that 'but he's a human being too' bull-shit." That thing that happened in West Memphis a few years back? Those three little dudes?"

"Don't remind me of that." The boys had been killed in early May, like Stevie, and the murder had made her jumpy, hovering over William.

"Those punks didn't do it; they're just some loser Death Metal kids. Anybody with half a brain could figure that out. I go in and out of that truck stop over there all the time—the biggest freak crossroads you've ever seen. Somebody really sick and pissed off did that shit, and you think he deserves to live?"

"God, I don't know," she said miserably. "How does *more* killing fix anything? But let's not talk about it anymore. It's too scary for me."

"Okay, but if you ever want me to take your guy out, just let me know," Foote said. "Whoever—*whatever*—he is."

"Okay, Foote," she said, rolling her eyes. "Don't call him *my* guy."

"I'm *serious*," he said. "I have my ways. Don't think I can't hide a processed piece of pedophile in one of the Valentine freezer trucks." Foote laughed. "Sell it to KFC."

She laughed weakly. "O-tay," she said. "O-*tay*." Foote might really be insane. There was silence until Mary Byrd said, "Next exit."

He began down-shifting, making the exit onto the wide street and pulling the behemoth truck over to the curb.

"End of the line, baby."

"Okay, right here is good," she said, glad to be getting out. She needed a little walk.

She zipped her leather jacket and gathered her duffel from behind the seat. "Thanks, Foote. You got my mom's number; call me when you head back. If I don't go back with you, I'll see you around town. Be careful."

"*You* be careful. *Mercy* is an anagram of *cryme*, ya know." Foote smiled. "Never mind. Get outta my reefer, Miss Liberal Lily-liver."

It must have been an odd sight to a passerby; a middle-aged woman climbing down out of a semi on a suburban Richmond street. Or maybe not; it was hard to know what seemed weird to people anymore. But here she was, getting out of Foote's rig at the old bus stop, her red duffel bag over her shoulder, on her uncertain little mission.

Down the road where the woods had been was a tract of townhouses, as they called them up here. She crossed the intersection and turned the corner onto Cherry Glen. In spite of the nagging dread, Mary Byrd felt a little excitement. The cherry trees lining the street had grown enormous. Their branches, even without leaves, formed a thick canopy over the street, which was lit like a tunnel by the streetlights. The thick trunks were taut and shiny with growth and rain and reflected light. A couple of the old houses were gone, and stupid-looking, vaguely "French" McMansions were squeezed onto the small lots, their three stories towering over their neighbors—like Fisher-Price castles or something. But there was the Furmans' house, and the Coles', and the Greenawalts', and Mr. Nance's aka Big Nana's, all looking smaller but spiffier than she remembered. More landscaping, more decorative gewgaws, lots of lighting fixtures illuminating trees, walks, and driveways. Decks were visible in backyards. And there was the Tuttles', which hadn't changed much at all; it was still shabby and mildewed and run-down looking. In all the windows, shades or curtains were drawn. Mary Byrd felt cold, like she had descended into a dark creek bed on a warm day. Was Ned in there? Did Mr. Tuttle still live here? Or Neil, the creepy older brother? Maybe they were all in there together, watching sports, or old Saturday evening monster movies, aging bachelors, eating Healthy Choice dinners on TV trays. Or maybe Ned had been here alone all these years. She hoped he was in custody. Shivering, she walked on.

She stopped when she reached 5117, her own house. It seemed so tiny, as miniature as Eliza's dollhouse. How had they all fit in? The white painted bricks she remembered had been blasted back to bare, and maybe the roof had had green shingles instead of black? A spindly, leafless sapling stood on the hill outside the living room window in front of her mother's slow-growing boxwoods, which were a lot larger. It was amazing that the boxwoods had lived at all after all the Pushy-in-the-Bushy and Sardines games they'd played. There was her bedroom window, where'd she climb out, late on hot nights— only her parents' room had had an air conditioner—and sit on the roof, her hair in rollers, in her mom's black hand-me-down baby doll pajamas, whispering to John Nicholson down below and listening to his older brother practice Kingston Trio songs on his guitar. The wonderfully tragic songs; "Tom Dooley" and "Where Have All the Flowers Gone" drifting across the street from an open window, making them feel like they had a clue about love, then wacky "Coplas" making them laugh. *Lay lay lay umm ole lay* . . . Had that been leading John on, too? But she had actually had a crush on John, and he on her. She wondered what was in her diary about him. Ned Tuttle had seen her one night, sitting on the roof talking to John. At least she thought she remembered that, or had she dreamed it, or made it up? Surely she'd written about it in her diary?

Their front yard hill seemed smaller, too. It had seemed so steep when they sledded on it, and her mother had had to descend the walkway steps so carefully when she was pregnant, which she'd always seemed to be. Mary Byrd remembered how gingerly, as if in slow motion, the ambulance guys had carried Pop down the steps after his first heart attack that summer. And somewhere, maybe in her old scrapbook, there was a Polaroid, spotty and faded, of Mary Byrd holding on to the lamp pole with one hand, leaning away Twiggy-style, the other hand on her hip and her ankles crossed in a pose that she must have seen in *Seventeen* or *Tiger Beat*. The dress had been her favorite: a mod, navy blue voile shift with a round collar and flared cuffs trimmed in cream tatting. Under that dress there would have been a slip—your mother would never let you out of the house without one then, and you wouldn't have considered wearing see-through—and a stupid damn garter belt holding up her pale patterned stockings. In the background, unbeknownst to her, Stevie and Nick had leapt into the photo, looking like the dirty, shirtless, knuckleheaded brats they were, ruining her glamour shot. She had been so pissed. Her mother must have taken the picture. It might be the last photo they had of Stevie.

There had been some happiness in this house worth remembering, she realized, in spite of Pop's drinking and how problematic all their relationships were, and how shockingly their life in this house had ended. Pop had tried with her, before Stevie died, bringing home "Ferry Cross the Mersey," for no particular reason. Mary Byrd felt an unexpected rush of nostalgia for those few years, the last of childhood. She thought of the summer afternoons she'd spent in the backyard, lying on the chaise longue, roasting, basted with baby oil and iodine, trying to pick up Barry Richards on WUST out of Washington on her transistor, reading the Jalna books or watching the babies and Stevie play in the sandbox and wading pool, the divine scent of her mother's Crimson Glory roses mixing with "Unchained Melody" or "Tracks of My Tears" in the steamy summer air. Here's where her first boyfriends had started coming around. Where they'd all watched the Beatles on Ed Sullivan ("a bunch of nellies," Pop had called them), and the shooting of Lee Harvey Oswald right before their eyes, in their own living room—where they'd all had Christmas and Thanksgiving and the babies' first birthdays. Where she'd lain in her bed wondering why losing one's virginity seemed like such a big deal before and such a letdown after. It had been in this house, after all, that she and Nick and Stevie had been part of a real family. A sort of slapped-together family, yes, but still, for Mary Byrd and Nick, their mother and real father having divorced when they were so young, for a while they'd had the traditional deal: a mother and a father and a bunch of kids all under the same roof. With a shitload of dysfunction, but still. A lot of it had felt good. Secure. Normal. It only lasted, what? Five years. And then, overnight, *literally overnight,* it had turned into a haunted house, scarier to them than the smelly Laff-in-the-Dark ride at the amusement park. Nick and the babies huddled in one bedroom, Stevie's room emptied, the door closed for good. Even little James and Baby Pete wouldn't go near it. That whole summer before they moved, Pop had never again gone upstairs, claiming that climbing the stairs was "too hard on his heart." Mary Byrd's own heart clenched at these memories. It was a wonder that they all hadn't had heart attacks that summer.

A man came and stood in the living room window and looked out at her standing down on the street. She wondered what the people living in the house were like. Could be anybody now: a gay couple, a single father with kids, a group of graduate students, an unmarried lawyer couple. Thirty years earlier, with the exception of Mr. Tuttle and Big Nana next door who were widowers, Cherry Glen Lane had been a street of traditional families, most with children. Her mother had heard that after Stevie was killed and the murderer was never caught and signs pointed to Ned Tuttle living right on their street, other families had moved away, too. The man in the window continued to stare at her and she realized that she probably looked suspicious carrying luggage and staring back. Maybe the fear still lingered in the neighborhood? Probably Stevie's death had become folklore: a lurid cautionary tale that still kept families with kids from buying homes in the neighborhood, and those that did always a little on-guard. If there were any kids around, they talked about a little boy's ghost, or maybe dared each other to run up and ring the Tuttles' doorbell, like Jem in *To Kill a Mockingbird.* That's what she and Nick and Stevie would have done, like they used to do to Big Nana. Big Nana surely died years ago. Or had he? He'd seemed old then but was probably in his fifties. They must have made his life miserable.

Mary Byrd moved off toward the shopping center and Doc's, where she could call a cab. The guy in the window had lightish, crew-cut hair. Like Stevie's. Stevie, had he lived, would be about that guy's age, forty or fifty. Or about Pop's age when he'd died. Weird. Life was just fucking weird.

She moved on, circling back to Patterson and continuing past the Horseshoe Apartments, where the scary poor people lived. Big, reeking garbage bins had stood in the parking lot in front of, not behind, the apartments, with broken glass strewn across the pavement. The few residents who took the *Times-Dispatch* in those days often wouldn't—or couldn't—pay Nick when he tried to collect on his paper route, and sometimes they yelled, so their mom had gone with him when he did his collecting. Police cars were often breaking up fights and parties. Kids didn't need to be told to stay away from the Horseshoe and loved to imagine the things that went on there. When Stevie died, that was one of the first rumors, of course: someone in the Horseshoe did it, although they were no doubt as terrified as anybody about the murder. In reality, the 'Shoe was just an enclave of poor young whites, many of them transient construction workers in from West Virginia and little Virginia hill and piedmont and tidewater towns, always working on their cars, raising hell on payday, and trying to get by. As far as Mary Byrd could see, not much had changed in the 'Shoe except the garbage bins were gone, replaced by Dumpsters; some trees had been planted; and some of the people she saw in the darkening winter light looked Hispanic.

At the Libbie Shopping Center, Doc's was Doc's no longer, but a chain store, and the fountain with its cool granite counter was gone, she was sad but not surprised to see. So was the comic book rack; and the magazine rack, which before had held only the *Times-Dispatch* and a few things like *Life, True Confessions,* and *Mad,* now was a brilliant grandstand of slick publications. For ten cents—the price of a Baby Ruth and a cherry Coke in a paper cone, kids had been able to waste an entire afternoon reading comics, depending on who was working the counter. Sal would let you read the comics without buying them, but Estelle and Lloyd wouldn't. She loved *Archie* and *Betty and Veronica* because they were about teenagers and love and had fashion pages, although the clothes were tacky. She preferred girly reality to the Justice League comics that Nick loved. Stevie loved them, too, but he wasn't allowed to cross the big streets to Doc's. Sometimes she looked at *Soldier of Fortune,* poring over stories about torture in World War Two prison camps. The Japs had put a glass tube in a guy's penis and smashed it. Another had a story with "real" photographs of Fidel Castro zipping up after raping somebody. She hadn't been sure what constituted rape, but she'd had bad dreams about it after. For the amount of change she was now having to put in the pay phone she could have had a week's worth of comic books, Cokes, and candy bars. She tried calling Charles first to tell him she'd made it, but there was no answer.

Leaning against the pharmacy's front door, Mary Byrd waited for a cab and tried to pinpoint what she was feeling, as she might examine her arms and legs for cuts and bruises after a fall. She didn't know what she'd expected to feel. Probably exactly what she *was* feeling: a dull, sweet sorrow, and a sharp desire to hit rewind and stave off what had happened. She wouldn't have gone parking with her boyfriend. She would have gotten Nick and Stevie to help her make a Mother's Day cake so that Stevie wouldn't have wandered off. He loved projects, and cake. She could have taken him and Nick to the old Westhampton Theater to see the Sunday matinee of *The*

Sound of Music. The boys hadn't been allowed to go alone and they'd been dying to see it again because the evil Nazis looked like tools. But what had happened had happened. Randomness seemed to be the only order to the universe. If they'd made a cake they might have blown up the kitchen, or they might have gotten run over going to the movie. The only thing to be done now was to offer her two cents in the hope that it might keep what had happened to her family from happening to someone else's. And it *had* happened to her entire family. Each one of them had been molested and some part of them killed off, or maimed for life. If it hadn't happened, they'd all be different people. She heaved a big sigh, startling a woman leaving the pharmacy. "Sorry. Excuse me," Mary Byrd said. The woman didn't speak. Okay. She was through. She'd had her little scab-picking tour and she would now face everybody's most real reality: *mom.*

Eight

CHARLES RUMMAGED IN the refrigerator, which was dead from the storm, looking for something to feed the children, disregarding the Tupperware tub of chili marked EAT ME. It was probably something old. Hadn't they had chili a week ago? There were hot dogs, but he only saw hamburger buns. He knew Mary Byrd had told him what to have, but he'd forgotten. Oh well. He could put perishable stuff in a cooler outside. There were seven boxes of macaroni and cheese on the pantry shelf, so he knew they wouldn't starve. Plenty of OJ and milk and cereal, plenty of cat food and dog food, of course. She'd never let the *animals* go without. Luckily there were some jugs of water; the water and toilets had quit just after the electricity. The phone had been last to go. At least they had the gas. It would be a boring Saturday night with no TV, no ESPN.

He wondered how Mary Byrd was doing. Riding in Mann's semi seemed so batty, but it was true that she wouldn't have gotten out of the Memphis airport if she'd tried to fly; every-thing was shut down. Worrying about her was pointless; she was going to do what she needed to do. This mess with her family was so awful, he felt a little bad that she was having to do it by herself. But even if he could have taken her, his being around her mother and brothers would only have made things weirder. There might be fighting, and yelling, and if he tried to intervene, somehow he'd get blamed for intervening. Mary Byrd could take care of herself, though, and she was tough, something he credited himself with helping her be.

He'd learned that if he let her lean on him in situations about which he could do nothing, she'd lean too much and not figure out how to deal with things herself. But he knew that she knew he was going to be there, no matter what craziness came down the road. He didn't want to be her damned father, though.

Hearing activity in the kitchen, the cats came around and rubbed against his legs. Irene said, "Ow?"

"Oh yeah, *now* you guys love me, right?" The cats paid little attention to him unless Mary Byrd was gone. As he was trying to put some cat kibble into their bowls, Iggy bumped his big fat head against Charles's hand, scattering kibble across the floor. "Iggy, you big dumbass," he said. He didn't pick the stuff up; whatever the cats didn't eat the dogs would take care of.

The dogs. How could they be walked with all the ice and deadly branches crashing down? He saw William's neon green Ninja Turtle bike helmet hanging on a peg by the kitchen door. He put on his overcoat and the helmet, took down the leashes, and whistled loudly. The Pounder and Puppy Sal trotted in hopefully, looking sideways at the munching cats and spilled kibble.

To the dogs he said, "Forget about it, you two. Y'all can clean up when we get back. I just fed you an hour ago, remember?"

Charles hooked them to their leashes and the three of them went out the door, stopping to take in the icy scene, their breaths three white clouds in the dark cold. It was part winter wonderland, part tornado aftermath, and the man and dogs, recognizing an unusual adventure, went forth in wary excitement.

"Okay, dudes, let's have some fun!" Charles hoped that he wouldn't slip and bust his ass. He wished William and Eliza were with him, it was all so amazing, but taking them out in the storm would probably be *reckless endangerment* or something. Mary Byrd would think so. He had a shitload of work to do, but the light table wouldn't be working to view Wiggs' photos, and anyway, he wanted to spend some time with the children. He wished he hadn't let William sleep over with Other William; they'd better be playing board games like they said, and not be out in this shit. When he got back from walking the dogs, *if* he got back and wasn't clobbered by a falling limb, he'd get Eliza to play some Scrabble if she was still awake. They hadn't played in a long time, since the time Eliza had spelled "yoni" and he'd challenged her, only to be horrified when he looked up the word and saw the definition. That was the problem with kids today; they knew too much. Where, oh where, was the goddamn innocence anymore?

ERNEST FELT PUMPED up by yesterday's call from Mary Byrd and the last of Pothus's bottle of Maker's, which the ladies thought they'd hidden. It was getting chillier and the day was turning bitter and threatening, even a little icy shit coming down How bad could it get? He'd seen unbelievable snow in the Dinara Planina south of Sarajevo—snow that fell in clumps for days, covering tanks, cows, houses. Snow in Mississippi was puny and accidental and didn't last. Things never got covered over; you could always still see the ugly kudzu tangles underneath, like piles of chicken bones. But now the early night sky had turned that ominous steely gray he remembered in Bosnia—low and solid and not looking like there was going to be any breaking up to it.

A little weather sure as hell wouldn't have bothered Kalashnikov, who'd lived in Siberia and then worked in some wasteland at the munitions plant, not giving a fuck about the cold and lack of attractive gash as long as he could jink with his guns. Ernest pictured him in his tiny, immaculate dacha, cheesecloth spread out on a table where dozens of oily steel pieces lay scattered like watch parts, or jewelry. Kalashnikov would work at the guns into the night with the wind and the wolves trying to out-howl each other outside his door in the vast taiga, or the steppes, or whatever. In the morning he would gather up a few parts, tying them up in an old babushka, and take them to the factory, where he'd fool with them some more. He would mess with them until he got it right, honing and tooling until the gun became a perfect little piece of clockwork, an artifact of impeccable craftsmanship and satisfying—thrilling—to hold and behold. This was just the way Ernest intended to write his novel, refining each little detail until the whole worked flawlessly. It would be the AK-47 of novels. He would get to work on it seriously again after the weekend. Anyway he'd better get his ass on the road.

Ernest gathered up the things he would need for the night. It was a birthday party at Janky Jill's, black tie, but would they be lame enough to cancel it for a little weather? Surely not. The Lords of Chevron were lined up, and even though all they did was R&B and rockabilly covers, they must have cost somebody some money. It had to be happening. He was out of here. He had had no fun, *zero*, in weeks, unless you counted the night at the boats in Greenville, where he'd lost a wad and glimpsed his father.

Maybe Mary Byrd had already left for Virginia, and he wondered how. The Teever idea was just nuts. He was encouraged by her call; she wouldn't have made it if she weren't still interested, right? She could put that shit in Virginia off for a day or two. Crime always waited.

Ernest threw his tux and batwing of Tanqueray into his MG and stowed his overcoat, hunting boots, and gun in the trunk. He carefully tucked a folded-up Dixie Crystal sugar packet in the glove box. A little toot for the ride back. Backing down the long, rutted dirt drive he stopped to throw back a little white pill. "Godshpeed," he said, chewing. He was off.

The roads were fine and there was no precipitation until he hit Highway 7. Ernest could feel but not see that there was a little ice. The MG was so low to the ground that he could sense the road slipping away beneath him, tire treads unengaged. At one point he fishtailed, sending him into a cheek-stinging adrenaline rush and a lower gear. The little car righted itself and Ernest patted the dashboard. "Good girl," he said, and plugged in a Stones tape. The Stones; you could always count on them to supply intestinal fortitude and a surge of confidence. God bless Mick and Keith, although sometimes Ernest had a nagging fear that they had gone soft on him. He didn't mind all the models—that was good—but all those kids, the health food and tennis and tans, the repaired teeth; what was going on with those guys? Ernest had missed out on the early days; Brian Jones, the incredible drugs and parties; he was just about being born when Marianne Faithfull had done the candy bar thing. He had read about it. Now *that* would have been a party.

The light, Ernest noticed, had gotten really strange, like tornado weather, but that was a good month off. The clouds in the lights of the highway seemed so low, like they were barely clearing the trees. Sleet was coming down in hard little lines, and few cars were on the road, almost none from the opposite direction. Here and there a car had run off into a ditch, or had pulled over. Still, it was just a little glaze—nothing so unusual. Southerners just did not know how to drive on ice. They would try to brake, and they would turn against a skid. Sorry bastards. He was glad his country-boy driving skills were so superior. He took another pull of Tanqueray.

By the time he reached Coffeeville, the dex had kicked in good, which made it hard to deal with the fact that he was creeping along, doing maybe forty, forty-five. What *was* this shit? The trees sparkled even in the low light, their branches drooping. The surface of the road had a high and alarming sheen to it now, as if it were coated with Vaseline. Ernest lit a cigarette and fast-forwarded to "Memo from Turner."

Didn't I see you down in San Antone on a hot and dusty
   night?
You were eatin' eggs in Sammy's when the black man
   there drew his knife

Inspired by Ry Cooder's thrilling slide and Mick's lip-curling snarl, he sucked on the Tanqueray again. Mother's milk. He would probably arrive in time to shoot a few at Purvis's Tables with his bud, Boudleaux. Maybe.

Ernest took the exit at a crawl. For the last half hour he hadn't seen a soul on the road. The freezing rain was falling thickly and noisily now, and trees were burdened with ice, branches bending to the ground. Wires sagged. *What the fuck?*

He decided that first he would go to Boudleaux's where he could change and leave the MG. Boudleaux would know whether or not the party was still on. From there he could walk to Jill's. Clearly there would be no driving anywhere tonight. He could crash with Boudleaux in the unlikely event that he did not get lucky. Or he could get a room at the Ole South Motel, where all the doors had hearts painted on them, and room 14 had the Black Romeo circular bed with lights and mirrors. But that was a waste of cash if he didn't score.

Upstairs, in Boudleaux's little apartment overlooking the town square, Ernest hung the tux on a door and flopped down on a crusty plaid sofa. He brushed away some Sonic foot-long wrappers and a puckered nub of hot dog bounced out and rolled along the floor. He pulled on his gin.

His friend Bryant Boudleaux was a faux Cajun. While still in his tender adolescence he had left his unbearably white middle-class Rochester home to work on the rigs off the Louisiana Coast. Taking advantage of his Frenchy last name, he had managed to pass as a local and to pick up some useful skills. A great singer, he had learned to play a wicked squeeze box from some criminal and learned to cook from a three-hundred-pound woman who he only occasionally had to service in exchange for meat and groceries. She had been a wonder with seafood, from catching it to having her way with it in the kitchen. Boudleaux had felt like just another crustacean in her hands, soft and peeled and defenseless, waiting to be plunged alive into a boiling pot of pungent Zatarain's.

The Tanqueray was about a third gone and, wanting to conserve his gin, he switched to the beer in the fridge. "Ah, PBR," he said, gulping. "Piss, But Refreshing." He shook his head.

Boudleaux came in with a sack. "Hey, man," he said. "Why don't you have a beer?" He began unloading batteries, candles, and more beer.

"All they had at Family Dollar were these red Liberace candles." He carried two beers to the window and opened it. On the outside ledge was a narrow painter's trough for spinning beers. A beer could be spun to icy perfection in ninety-six seconds.

"What in the fuck is happening out there?" Ernest asked. "What's going on?"

"I don't *know*, man." Boudleaux. said. "It's the *weirdest*. I walked back through the cemetery and some kids were in there sledding, and all of a sudden, the trees were, like, *exploding*. The kids were freaked—they were screaming."

There was a huge crash. Ernest jumped up to look out the window where Boudleaux was spinning. "Jesus God!" Boudleaux shouted. An enormous oak had split in half. In the streetlight, they saw a confused raccoon pop out of the tree trunk and scrabble away. All around them was the din of branches and trees shattering and crashing under the weight of the ice. The sound was like gunfire, shots amplified by the lowering sky.

"The power's bound to go," said Boudleaux. "I'd better cook."

"I guess this means the bars will be closed," Ernest said glumly.

"It don't seem unreasonable that the bars might close for the end of the world," said Boudleaux. He was busy taking paper packages from the freezer.

"It's supposed to end in fire and brimstone, not in ice," said Ernest, popping a new beer. "Ignorant heathen. You know— the two hundred thousand horsemen: "And thus I saw the horses in the vision, and them that sat on them, having breastplates of fire, and of jacinth, and brimstone."

"Apocalypse is apocalypse is apocalypse," said Boudleaux, busily starting a roux. "You get that from *Star Wars*?"

At that moment the lights went off and the old Frigidaire quit its friendly hum. Ernest and Boudleaux looked at each other in the gloom.

"I wonder how long this will last," said Boudleaux. "If it's doing this all over town, trees and shit falling on lines, then it's not going to be coming on anytime soon."

There was clumping on the stairs and in came Stovall Bott with more beer. Ernest was glad to see it was an upgrade, but not a big one: good old skunky Rolling Rock. They lit all the candles.

"Where'd you get these pussy-ass candles?" said Sto. "Reminds me of my sister back in high school, smoking dope in her room listening to the Carpenters."

"Valentine's Day," said Boudleaux, stirring. "I hope we don't have to fire up the tar baby." The tar baby was a large brown voodoo candle in the shape of a man. You could light him upright from the wick on top of his head or lay him down and light his dick. Next to his Hohner Corona II, the tar baby was Boudleaux's favorite thing.

"Sto, do you think this party will still be on?" said Ernest.

"Definitely, man. It will definitely be a party," said Sto. "It may not be the *same* party, but it will be one. Who needs electricity?"

"We got to plug into something to be able to play, dumbass." said Boudleaux. "Think about it: the Lords of Chevron unplugged? Acoustic 'Higher and Higher'? Mr. Excitement would die all over again"

"Gentlemen," said Ernest. "This plugging-in thing concerns me. Are there any women in town?"

"Who knows?" said Sto. "Let's get the news and see where this situation is going."

They tried to pick up the local stations on the jam box but there was nothing but static. Finally, they homed in on WLVS from Tupelo. "All the way over to the river—they're having a major *thing*, a major ice storm," said the deejay. "We've been told that the power is out over there and trees are falling on power lines—it's an emergency situation. Folks over there, don't go out of your houses unless absolutely necessary. We'll be giving you more information on that ice storm as soon as we get it."

"Cool," said Stovall.

"Damn," said Ernest. Byrd would be less likely to show with the power out. She better not be on her way to Virginia. If she went with Teever, he'd probably never see her again. Crazy bitch.

"I'm just gonna cook up all this shit," said Boudleaux, bending over to light a smoke on the gas eye. "Or this freezer will get funky. We need gumbo to keep up our strength."

"Put me some oysters in there," said Ernest.

Boudleaux threw everything in the pot with the half-made roux. They sat down and began a game of bourré. For every pat hand, knock, and bourré in the game there was a line from *Deliverance*:

"Now let's you jes drop'em pants."

"You don't know nuthin'."

"Aintry? This river don't go to Aintry."

"Give the boy a dollar, Drew."

"Get on back up thar in them woods."

"Don't say anythang—just do it."

"L-l-l-louder."

"Don't you boys try nothin' like that again."

"I could play with that guy all day."

"This corn's special."

"Panties, too."

The men did Jäger shots in NASCAR jelly glasses. The cheap candles formed bloody puddles and the gumbo simmered forgotten on the stove, a stinking sludge. Boudleaux passed around some ludes, saying, "Lagniappe, boys!" Ernest grew bored with the card game even though he'd been winning. When Sto accused him of cheating Ernest said, "Fuck y'all, bastards. This game sucks anyway with three people," and got up to dress for the party and refresh himself. The smell of the gumbo was unsettling. He was curious about outside, and restless, and wanted to find Byrd. Also he needed more smokes.

When he emerged in his tux, Sto said, "Nice monkey suit, dude. You gone need more than that tonight. Carhartt, Day-Glo vest, boots." He lurched toward the bathroom.

"Clothes make the man," Ernest said, scooping up his winnings. "If anyone comes looking for me, I'll be at the par-tay."

Boudleaux said, "Right behind you."

"Hey!" Sto's muffled voice came from the john. "Who did this in the tub?"

Down on the sidewalk the ice was treacherous. Ernest wasn't sure he could negotiate it, but if he could get to his car he could get his boots on. He grabbed a branch, which helped steady him, but it was slow going. When he reached the MG, he opened the trunk and exchanged his Cole Haan loafers for the hunting boots, which smelled vaguely of dog effluvia. The AK lay there. He might need it. One never knew. What if those frat bastards picked a fight again? He needed to be warm, but he felt that the heavy Danish officer's coat detracted from the formal appearance he wished to present. It had an important feature. Inside was sewn a sturdy holster large enough to accommodate the AK, thanks to its ingenious folding feature designed by Peggy at Peggy's Sew Nice Alterations. Peggy, happy to have something to do other than reconstruct prom and beauty review dresses for Hatchatalla Academy girls with disproportionate boob jobs, had installed the holster in exchange for a deer tenderloin from deep in Antenna's carport freezer. He slipped the pet weapon inside the coat and slowly shuffled on to the JFC.

There was light on at the JFC; they must have gotten a generator. People scurried in and out, some forgetting to slow down when they hit the ice, busting their butts. A group stood talking excitedly in front of the sign painted on the building that said DO NOT STAND HERE AT ANY TIME FOR ANY REASON. Maybe Teever was around, and had something interesting going on.

There was a major buzz in the air; Ernest could hear bits of conversation: "Water's off, too." "Sap was up already from that warm spell at Christmas; they were top-heavy." Inside was like a used car lot, or the fun house at the Mississippi-Alabama State Fair. A few orange bulbs were strung around, not quite lighting the place. Back in the dark aisles people skulked with flashlights. A face would loom out of the dimness, smiling crookedly with panic and excitement, causing him to wonder if he'd done any mind stuff. At the checkout, he saw that they'd been foraging for things that normal people needed in an emergency: batteries, charcoal, matches, diapers, paper plates and cups, coolers. Kids were carrying suitcases of beer. A big damn picnic.

Outside again, he realized that even with his boots on he didn't have enough traction. By the JFC Dumpster lay some pieces of chicken wire. He mashed a piece around each foot and stomped around. It was good. He needed to be *getting* some ass tonight, not busting it.

It was seriously cold. *It's so cold, there ain't six inches of peter on Main Street,* as Pothus always said. But he was comfortable. The Jägermeister antifreeze effect. The glaze of ice on everything was like the ice palace scene in Antenna's favorite old movie, *Dr. Zhivago.* Against that romantic image or any others, Ernest swallowed another dexie. Ludes were nice but his was in the tub, and they had a way of taking the edge off. He liked an edge. He patted his left pocket for the Tanqueray, finishing it off and dropping the bottle. He would have to start over.

Plodding on, Ernest climbed over a few busted trees and dodged a falling limb, which came down slowly and surreally and shattered like glass. The broken trees were silhouetted, their fractured stumps raw and jagged against the icy glitter and the strange sky. It reminded Ernest of those peopleless German landscapes he had seen in the museum in Prague. "This is what the war will look like," his refugee Croatian girlfriend had whispered. "Except that there will be people scurrying like rats, and the bodies of children." He got a rush at the memory— his lovely woman with her pale, celadon skin. When she stood in front of the old brass lamp in his shabby room he could see through her amazing breasts.

He might be able to get Byrd to at least slip out for a cocktail, but how could he get in touch with her? Women were out there: frightened, cold, in a tizzy about the storm and needing the special kind of rescue that only Ernest could offer. It had been, what? Since New Year's eve. *Last year*! Totally unacceptable. If he couldn't find Byrd, he had half a mind to go up to Virginia and take care of that shit for her.

He decided to check out Dead Jerry's and refuel. Normally, Dead Jerry's was noisy with college kids shouting at each other above their loud retread music. The bar had actually hosted some epic live performances—Mose Allison, Junior Brown, David Lindley—but the frat boys just forked over the stiff covers to spin their lips the whole show complaining about the bands that *just did not know how to jam, man*. Ernest peered through the window. The AK banged against the glass. A candle glowed at a table far back in the cavelike room and he could make out the bartenders playing cards. They looked like the seven dwarfs: long hair, beards, toboggans. No sign of any patrons, let alone Mary Byrd or Teever. He went in anyway.

"This is quite the Disney moment," he said. "Where's Snow White?"

The bartenders turned, their glazed eyes half-concealed by drooping lids. "Hey now," said one. "Oh, wow. A giant penguin," said another. "What's with your fucking *feet*, man?"

"It's the latest," said Ernest. "Y'all might think of getting some. Chicken wire goes pretty well with hippie couture. So can I get a drink or what?"

A dwarf whose red lips, moustache, and sparse soul patch made his face look like ladies' private parts said, "Help yourself. Here's the flashlight. We'll take those bitchin' tails in exchange for what you drink." It was well known that when Ernest returned from Bosnia he'd gone on a bender and to pay his immense bar tab, he'd auctioned his costly Harris Tweed jacket. Some dick had bought it for forty dollars then traded it to Teever. "It don't matter, bastards," he'd said. "War is hell on a blazer."

Ernest scanned the rows of bottles looking for the Kahlúa and vodka. A few White Russians were the way to go. Some nourishment, and the syrupy liquor would give him a little sugar buzz. Good: milk in the cooler with a yellow wedge of hoop cheese and a bowl of peeled eggs. He popped one of the eggs into his mouth and, not seeing a knife, bit off a few hits of cheese. Something else floating in the ice water caught his eye: a Baggie. Hoping for contraband he pulled it up and held it to the flashlight. A snout, claws, and dull little eyes looked back at him.

"Goddamn, y'all. What is *this* shit?" Ernest said.

"It bit Randy this morning," said a dwarf. "On his thigh— very close to his stuff. We need to take it to the health department to see if it has rabies."

"Jesus." Ernest spat out the cheese and threw the Baggie back. To sterilize his mouth, he quickly slugged back some vodka, gargling far back in his throat. He built his White Russian and played with the flashlight. On the wall was the usual college bar décor—a Porky Pig cookie jar Ernest knew to be full of multicolored condoms, football gewgaws, cute happies the sorority girls had given the bartenders, a Shriner's hat. What the fuck was Al Chymia? In Bosnia the bars were austere and strictly business. In a real bar nothing should distract you from your drink or your thoughts. Unless it was a woman. At a musty bar in Bratislava there had been an incredible medieval barmaid. For an extra five bucks she would lift one long breast from her dress and, giving a tug not unlike the pumping action on a gun, aim a thin stream of bluish milk into your slivovice, turning it a cloudy lavender. Plums and cream. For another five bucks she'd dip the breast in the drink and allow you to suck it off.

Ernest smoked a couple and polished off another drink. Awash in the milky sweetness of memory and White Russians, he grabbed a napkin and a pen off the bar and jotted down a quick Byronic ode, *Ode on a Gone Byrd*. He'd put it in the literary magazine. He loved Byron; a husband in the background never worried *him*, not even when the husband was his brother-in-law.

He felt fortified, but instead of the sugar rush he'd expected, he felt a sinking spell coming on. Rummaging around in his breast pocket, he found some blue pills. He couldn't remember what they were, but it didn't matter; they would alter the mood one way or another. Ernest shook them in his hand like dice, popping them in his mouth. He chewed them—time suddenly seemed of the essence—and washed them down with a swig of vodka. Deftly swiping the Kahlúa bottle, he tucked it into his cummerbund, hoping he wouldn't fall and disembowel himself, or worse. He moved to the door. Party time. Backing out, Ernest drew the AK from his coat, snapping it in line. He fired at the Shriner's hat and hustled quickly into the dark. The dwarfs screamed like girls.

Back on the dark street he worried that the bartenders might flag down some popo, but Hap West ought to have his hands full tonight with better things to do than harass decent partygoers who, after all, had the right to bear arms, especially on an unpredictable night like this. At the very least they'd confiscate the AK. At the worst—Christ, a night in the county jail. With no electricity. He needed to stay off the streets—but how? If anyone saw him creeping through a yard they'd think he was a burglar. A *looter*. He'd just have to keep low, stay on the trail, but not in the middle, off to the side, dodging into the brush at the approach of enemy vehicles. Okay. It could be done. He'd done it before.

The sky was weirder still—that bizarre orangeish glow from an unknown source. Transformers were blowing close by and in the distance and exploding like rockets. The fall of branches had slowed so that the crashes were more separate and distinct and more nerve-wracking. Even more like a war zone. Kalesija.

Ernest slunk along, tensely cradling his gun and thinking about Bosnia. He remembered a night like this. He had been trying to reach his room after drinking with Danish soldiers in the village café. Fighting had been going on intermittently all day a few streets away, near the river. But suddenly, it was in his street, all around him, and the few people who were out ran for cover. He had continued on stealthily through the village, ducking into doorways at every burst of gunfire. A young Serb with a shaved head, wearing only a sweatshirt, had toppled out of a darkened stoop, slumping to the street. Looking in the direction the shots had come from, Ernest had recognized one of the soldiers from the café, who'd been covering his ass. The soldier had looked Ernest in the eye but had given no sign of recognition and had moved off into the night. Ernest had crossed the street to the wounded man. A crummy knockoff Kalashnikov lay next to him. His stomach gaped through the shirt below Willy DeVille's face and the guy's heart pumped out his life across the icy, glittering cobbles.

Ernest shook off the gruesome memory. Just ahead were the silhouettes of several people standing around, looking like a group of meerkats. Damn. Too many sizes and shapes for it to be the police; a family? Each held something: Guns? Baseball bats? They turned to him, shining clublike flashlights. They moved up and with relief he recognized a familiar group of retarded guys from the local halfway house. What were they doing loose on a night like this? He recognized most of them, each of whom had a distinct public persona. There was a municipal worker guy, a suburban leisure guy in a powder-blue jumpsuit, a large set of cowboy twins, and a small, pin-headed black guy. Two more men he didn't know; they had no act and might have been caretakers; sometimes it was hard to tell. Encountered individually the men were meek and amusing, but in a pack like this? Less like meerkats than surly bears startled out of hibernation by the storm. He readied his hand on the right places of the AK, but tried to hide it behind him. "Evening, gentlemen," he said pleasantly. They moved in closer—too close. One said, working his hands, "Theter gun?" He had to move or shoot. He turned on the ice, heading back to another street. They let him go, calling out, "I like to have that suit!" and "Don't go, mister! We fixin' to make us a ice fort!"

He needed to get to that party. South Eleventh Street was iced but smooth—the city must have cleared it—and he pried the chicken wire from his feet. Without the booties but with the energy of the mystery pills and the grace of the White Russians, he found he was able to glide down the street. Only a few branches were in his way, and Ernest elegantly leapt over them. He gathered speed and confidence, an Olympic distance skater with the AK held behind his bent back, his right arm swinging in time to his strong, measured glides. He relaxed and held the gun before him and across his ribs, like a fur muff. The wooden stock of the AK was oddly warm in his hands and icy air and adrenaline burned his cheeks. The sky had finally cleared and stars twinkled gorgeously against it. Byrd, where the hell you at, girl? He didn't want to rescue someone else. If he couldn't find her tonight, if she'd gone up north, he was hatching another plan. She needed his help.

"It's darker than Egypt," he said to himself. All the broken pine and cedar made the air smell like Christmas. Lovely! He sailed down the long street. Hans Brinker on the canal, on his way to put a finger in, well, he hoped not a dyke.

He turned a corner onto the side street where the party was supposed to be. He saw the party house, softly lit, the last bungalow on a dead end. It looked like home, and he couldn't wait to get out of the cold and confrontation. He could see a few people outside but they looked very small. Damn, he thought, this had better not be a platoon of mini-tards or something. It was three kids—little dudes frozen in place, arms held out stiffly from their sides by overbundling. They stared at the gun. Happy that he wasn't going to be fucked with, he said, "What are you kids doing out here?" Maybe they were actually frozen. "I'm a nice guy. I'm not going to mess with you." Ernest opened his long overcoat and stashed the gun in its droopy holster. He pulled out the Kahlúa, guzzled the last of it, and threw the bottle in the bushes where it shattered glassily.

"What's the matter? Tongues all froze up?" He grinned, a substance-driven rictus of teeth and gum, and wagged his own tongue to amuse them.

Their eyes widened, and one little boy spoke up. "We . . . we're going home. We were just looking for good places to sled tomorrow. There's a good hill behind that house." The boy gestured with one inflated Michelin Man arm at the party house.

"Huh," Ernest said. "Well, maybe you guys want to come inside and get warm? There's a party in there. There's beer." He laughed, a high-lonesome sort of whinny.

"Um," the boy said. "We've got to go home now."

"Well, okay then. If you're sure."

"Okay," said the little boy. He swatted one of the other boys, and they began back-stepping off the sidewalk, into the brush, turning and breaking into a run, scrabbling through branches and tinkling ice.

Ernest tried to think of a cool sendoff that the boys would appreciate, coming up with "My dear penguins, we stand on a great threshold! It's okay to be scared, many of you won't be coming back. Thanks to Batman, the time has come to punish all God's children!"

The boys were quickly out of sight, although he heard one screech, "Williams, wait up! Don't ditch me!"

He didn't really get kids. They always seemed so unsociable.

Nine

ALL THE LIGHTS were on at her mother's; the sunroom shone blue from the eternally-on TV. Mary Byrd's mother's neighborhood was exclusive but not really ritzy, but the country club and the Presbyterian church were not far, and this set the tone for the subdivision. Her mom didn't care about all the WASPy and clubby crap, she just wanted security, a nice yard to root around in, and to be close to Nick and James. She didn't really know her neighbors. The homely colonial-ish house had been chosen because it had a small, manageable backyard for her birding and gardening, and its rooms were small, uncomplicated boxes.

Marisa D'Abruzzi Rhinehart opened the door to her daughter with a hug and a kiss. Mary Byrd was anxious to get the inevitable beat-down over with as quickly as possible and pulled back a little. It was also a little awkward to hug her mom because she was so tiny, just under five feet and shrinking, and

Mary Byrd, feeling enormous, had to bend over for the hug, sticking her butt out.

"*Eeew*," her mother said. "You smell like cigarettes."

"I know," Mary Byrd said. "I'm sorry."

Her mother still looked beautiful, even though she insisted on so much tanning that her naturally burnished olive skin had become opaque. But her silver hair, loosely gathered into a bun, set off her pale green eyes, astonishing in such a dark face. She was wearing silky green pajamas.

The familiar scent of cat box and tuna was just discernible under the stronger aroma of garlic and olive oil. Eliza and William referred to their grandmother's basement, where the cat box was, as "Teetee World." Her mother's cats weren't allowed to go outside because "too many bad things could happen," and they'd eat her birds. Mary Byrd set down her duffel, removed a personal-size bottle of Sutter Home cab— not the martini she craved, but thank god she had it—and went straight to the refrigerator, the age-old homecoming ritual of all children, no matter what age. Her mother followed. Mary Byrd was more desperate for a drink than for food. She looked around in the fridge, taking out a jar of pepperoncini and fishing one out with her finger.

"Did you really ride up here with a *trucker*?" her mom asked, the same contemptuous smirk on her face that she'd had the last time they had seen each other and she had plucked at Mary Byrd's ratty Levi's jacket, a favorite that had been Charles's in junior high, and said, "Are you still wearing this? You might think that this jacket is cool, but it's not."

"*Yes*, Mama. He's a guy we know who works for Valentine Chickens, Mann's company. It was fine. It was actually kind of interesting."

"I just think it's *very weird* that you did it."

"Ma, it's *good* to do weird things sometimes. Besides, it didn't cost anything, and because of the weather I never would have gotten out of Memphis if I'd tried to fly, which you know I hate anyway. And you do weird stuff all the time." Mary Byrd was suddenly really tired.

"Not that weird. And Charles wasn't happy about it either. I made that hummus just for you."

"Yum. Thanks. Charles is never happy about stuff I do. How do you know? Did you talk to him?" She sank down at the table and poured the cheap red wine into a glass, restraining herself from taking a giant gulp. Her mother was a teetotaler.

"I called this morning to see when you were coming, since you hadn't called me. You'd left *practically in the middle of the night*, Charles said." Her mother paused for emphasis. "Here's some wonderful olive bread. Put the hummus on that. And I made podotoli soup. Your favorite."

"I tried to call Charles but it just rings and rings," Mary Byrd said around a mouthful of bread and smushed chickpeas. "You know they're having a huge ice storm down there. The phone lines are probably down." She was glad to have the conversation change course. What she really wanted was to drink and go to sleep.

As her mother went to the stove Mary Byrd noticed that she limped a little. "What's wrong with your leg, Ma?"

"Oh," her mother laughed. "I have *gouty tophus* on my toe. It sounds like something out of Dickens, doesn't it?"

Or out of William Byrd's diary. "Does it hurt?"

"Not much; it's just ugly," her mother said happily, showing her the big knob. She loved medical crap.

"Yuck, Mom!"

Her mother dished up some soup and set it, a spoon, and a napkin in front of her daughter. "Here's the grated cheese. It's delicious."

Meatball soup wasn't her favorite, it was Nick's, but she dutifully spooned up the meatballs, carrots, celery, and maca-roni. It *was* super-delicious and Mary Byrd said so. Her mother was the greatest cook. "Thanks. I'm eating this and then I'm going to bed. I'm exhausted."

"Nick and James will be over tomorrow afternoon. They didn't know if they'd get to see much of you." She sighed. "I wish Pete were here." There was never any question of Pete coming. He'd been a baby, and though what had happened had clouded his life in many ways, he didn't even remember Pop. He wanted it all behind him, and had moved far away, to Portland, as soon as he could. That Pete was probably gay—they knew so little about his life—could only have deepened his estrangement and unease within the family.

"If you'd get over that flying hang-up," her mother went on, "you and the children could come up more often. We're never together anymore."

"I know, Mom," said Mary Byrd. "I'm sorry. But I've got to go right back. Eliza's in a play. She'd be really upset if I missed it. And we've got to do something to help Evagreen. I guess Charles told you about that."

"Yes, it's just terrible. I wouldn't have thought Evagreen and her family were . . . *those types,*" her mother said. "You're not going back in that truck, I hope."

"*Mom,*" she warned. "I'm not sure what I'm going to do. Maybe I *will* fly if the Memphis airport is open." Annoyance added a little defiance to her voice. "So how will this meeting work on Monday?"

"Who knows?" her mother said, shaking her head as she cleared up dishes. "Who knows. That's such a shame about Evagreen. Charles said he's going to try to find a good lawyer for her daughter. *I* told him what they need is that Johnnie Cochran guy who got that big . . . *jerk* off the hook."

"Well, that won't be happening unless Evagreen wins the lottery. But what about us? What about this meeting? Is this going to be over now, do you think?"

"I don't know. They certainly seem in a hurry all of a sudden. I don't know if it's because of this reporter who wants to write a book about the case, or because they've figured out how to finally charge Ned Tuttle."

An enormous Maine Coon cat, wide as a hassock, waddled into the room and bunted the backs of her mother's green pjs, leaving a visible swipe of fur. "Oh, Mrs. B! There you are! Mary Byrd is here to see you!" she said in the high, enthusiastic voice she used for cat-talking. She picked up the always-open can of human-grade tuna in the sink and put some in the kitty dish.

Mary Byrd's face flushed at the mention of Tuttle. She didn't even know for sure if her mother had ever known what the police had suggested about her cock-teasing Tuttle. She didn't know if her mother had seen her diaries, either. If she weren't such a pussy, she'd ask. She got up to pet Mrs. B, who gave her an accusing look and lumbered off, probably to hide in the basement wall where she spent most of her time. "Isn't there some sort of statute of limitations on this kind of stuff?" she asked.

"It doesn't really matter, if what they're worried about is this reporter scooping the story and solving it herself, which would make them look terrible. James says there's not a statute of limitations on murder." Her mother scraped more tuna into the cat's dish. "I guess she was expecting ham," she said sadly.

"They already look pretty terrible," Mary Byrd said, stretching out her legs. "If all this time they've thought it was Tuttle and haven't been able to charge him before now." She added, "That kitty does *not* need more food, Ma."

"But maybe that's what's going to happen. Maybe they can do the DNA thing or something. I hope that doesn't mean . . . exhumation, though. And that kitty is still just a kitten. She's growing." Her mother huffed indignantly.

"*Jeez*, Mama, surely not!" she said. "Do we even know who Linda Fyce is? Is she from Richmond? Do we really have to talk to *her* again, too?"

"Oh, you'd remember some of her articles—I've sent a few clippings to you. She wrote for the *Times-Dispatch*, then for the *New York Times*. Local color stories about, oh, you know, 'Southern things.'"

Mary Byrd said, "Oh, I know who you mean. She's a . . . quaint-hound—does stories on barbecue and inbreds who drive Trans Ams and handle snakes." She pulled impatiently at her boot laces. "Stuff that people in New York and California get all excited about so they can have things to talk about at dinner parties. What Meemaw and Peepaw and them down there are up to now. That sucks."

Her mother said, "Do you need to say that?"

"Yes, I do," Mary Byrd said. "*Someone* needs to."

"Well, anyway, she's one of those Fyces from over in Fewtheyville, the ones who have that big mobile home dealership out on the highway, I think. I talked to her a little bit, although Detective Stith asked that we not talk to anybody until we'd talked to them—him—first." Her mother thought of herself as a respecter of titles and authority as long as those people agreed with her.

Stith. So *that* was the guy's name. Mary Byrd started peeling off her boots and socks. "That's what he said to me, too, so *I* didn't talk to her. So why did *you*, Mom? Do we really want this to be a book, or on TV or something?"

"Well, she called me first. And as far as I'm concerned, I don't really care who finally figures it out and gets whoever convicted, just so someone does." Her mother began deconstructing her hair for the night. "I think it would make an interesting book or something. She told me she's working on that show, *Medical Detectives,* about solving crimes. I love that show. They're filming an episode right now on the Southside Strangler. They *finally* executed that man, you know." She put the tuna can in the trash. "But I didn't talk to her very much."

"But, Ma, it will *never* go away then. If it's on TV, or whatever, it will be right in our faces all the time. We will have to be *that poor family* again. What do we have to gain by that?"

"Oh, I think the truth is always important to tell. And from my point of view, the story has an interesting psychological angle," she said, pausing provocatively, her head down while she fiddled with her bun. A pile of hairpins had accumulated on the table.

"What do you mean?" Mary Byrd asked cautiously. A throw coated in cat fur was draped on the chair next to her and she pulled it over her. The sneezing would begin any minute. She was only allergic to her mother's cats.

"I was . . . relieved," her mother said, slightly rueful, but also slightly triumphant.

"What are you saying?" Mary Byrd asked. She felt the hair on the back of her neck—her hackles—rising.

"I was relieved that he was gone." Her mother raised her head to look directly at Mary Byrd.

"Mom, *Mom*, why would you *say* that?" Mary Byrd wailed, covering her eyes with her hands.

"Because it's true."

"Even if it's true, why would you *say* it?"

"Because I need to be honest with myself."

"Okay, that's *yourself*," Mary Byrd cried. "You don't have to *tell* every true thing that you feel, do you?" She thought she knew where this was coming from. If her mother thought that her higher power meant for her to take twelve steps into a vat of boiling monkey vomit, she'd do it. She wondered if her mom went to some church-basement meeting, everybody proudly confessing their worst shit to each other, the air thick with affirmation and cigarette smoke. "Don't you think there are just some things that are better left unsaid?"

"Stevie created so many problems with Pop," her mother went on. "I resented the fact that Pop favored him over you and Nick. And over *me*."

"Mom, Pop was a widower with a three-year-old," Mary Byrd protested. "Of *course* he favored Stevie over me and Nick. Even back then, we got that."

"Well, maybe it's just this mean streak that my sisters and I all have." She shrugged, pulling at her bun.

Maybe what her mother wanted was the melodrama, or to be upbraided for having *low self-esteem*, or some other pop psych garbage. Mary Byrd wasn't taking the bait. Her mother's self-esteem was fine.

"Maybe Pop was just trying to protect Stevie from us. Nick and I tortured him so much." Had they? Maybe they'd teased him a little too relentlessly, but it had seemed like normal sibling abuse at the time. She and Nick had done far more sadistic things to each other than the teasing they had subjected Stevie to.

"Oh, Pop knew how I felt," her mother said. "Those terrible rages when he was drunk."

"Well, I never saw it from you. I mean, that Pop favored Stevie and resented us, I saw. But I never saw any mean stuff from you."

"I was good at hiding things," she said. "Like my drinking. Anyway, that's how I felt. It was very hard for me having Stevie in the family. I did try. I went to a therapist for a long time."

"*Uhhh*," Mary Byrd moaned. "God, Mama. I hope you didn't say anything like that to that woman."

She looked Mary Byrd in the eye. "I only said that we each had our own issues to deal with about what happened." She tossed the hairpiece on the table, where it lay like an arctic gerbil.

Mary Byrd scrubbed at her eyes with her fingers, dislodging a contact. "Well, will you please not bring this up with the detective? It has nothing to do with the case." She popped out the other contact, absently wiping them both into her napkin. "It can't help anything."

"Okay," her mother said, shrugging. "I just thought you should know."

Her mother's revelation made the squirrel executions seem charming and warm-hearted. Mary Byrd couldn't hear anymore. "Okay. I've got to go to sleep. See you in the morning." Mary Byrd gathered her socks and boots and duffel, heading for the guest room. At the kitchen door, she turned abruptly, went to her mother, and kissed the brown cheek that was offered. There was nothing else to say, and nothing to be done until Monday.

"'Night, darling. I'm glad you're here. I love you," her mother said pleasantly, as if they'd just been sitting around watching *Seinfeld* or the Animal Channel.

"'Night, Ma. Luvyatoo," she said, but thought, 'Night, you scary mother.

IN THE GUEST room, Mary Byrd popped half a Xanax, even though being at her mother's usually made her sleepy and she always slept well, even on the thin, shifty mattress and even when there was disturbing stuff in the air, like tonight. She wasn't sure why she slept so well here; at home it was lightly and fitfully. Maybe the relief from responsibility: this was her mother's domain and all problems here were hers to deal with. Or maybe it was the lack of annoying disturbances like a husband, children, and pets. Her mom had the cats, but they had "emotional problems" and hid out when anyone was around, so they wouldn't be scrabbling at her door or patting her face in the morning like Iggy and Irene did. Maybe it was just because here she was always a child, and always would be, even if she was doddering around at seventy-five and her mother a ninety-three-year-old crone in a wheelchair. Better to be on the safe side with the seepy-seep pill than to toss and turn all night, worrying. Or dreaming, god forbid. She suddenly sneezed three times.

The guest bed looked prissy and crisp and so inviting. She started to undress, but she caught the smell of cigarette smoke, exhaust, greasy food, dirty hair, and sharp, anxiety sweat coming off her and realized she'd have to take a shower. She could never sleep when she smelled bad or felt gross, even with a pill.

After scalding herself, washing her hair, and breathing deep breaths of clean, steamy air, she felt somewhat better. How had women ever endured life without hot running water? Imagine the chronic funk. She knew the pill would kick in any minute and neutralize the adrenaline her mother had stirred up, so she allowed herself to think about her. Had she made her disturbing confession to her brothers as well? She doubted it. Those special hollow-tipped bullets were saved for Mary Byrd alone, and her mother liked to fire them when Mary Byrd was least expecting them, or least needed to hear them. Was it possible her mom was nuts, and maybe had hardening of the arteries or something? No, it couldn't be that—she was whip-smart in all kinds of ways—it must just be that she was old enough that some of the filters had rusted or loosened, or fallen away. Old people flaunting their vast superior life experience and not giving a shit about saying or doing whatever; they'd be dead soon and they'd earned the right to terrorize, and to exercise their last chances to set the world straight.

There was a list Mary Byrd had kept over the years, for fun, really; she'd intended to show it to her brothers someday and they'd all have a good laugh. It was a list of all the stuff her mother had said, mostly while visiting Mary Byrd and Charles and the children. As Eliza once had complained, "Nana walks around the house and tries to control stuff." And Mary Byrd had seen her mom and Evagreen conferring disdainfully about laundry, shower curtains, cat and dog hair, et cetera, et cetera. There was no choice but to laugh about it.

If you don't get that ivy off that dogwood it'll die.
It smells too much like feet in here.
If you don't hurry up the ice cream will be all melted.
Why do you let them do that?
You have to prepare the soil.
It doesn't look like you had many daffodils this year.
I think that happened to me, too, when I was taking
     Lipitor.
The grits are a little bland.
If you get tan enough those age spots won't show.
You get that from me.
You get that from your father.
Are the shrimp and grits spicy? I don't like spicy things.
I've got a stiff neck, too.
Why do you let him do that?
You'd better get that ivy off the house.
This pillow has slobber stains. Guests don't like that.
Go to the bathroom before we drive home.
You should clean off your grocery cart with the wipey
     things.
This is not fresh.
You boiled the eggs too long; they're gray.
That *stove.*
Don't eat regular mayo, eat fat-free.
Was he drunk?
Don't use whole wheat bread crumbs in the stuffing; it
     gives it an ugly taste.

You need to mulch.
She must have been drunk.
These need water.
You're turning her into a princess.
You probably pruned too late.
It's freezing, can you turn down the AC?
We need some air back here!
I can see your butt in that skirt.
He's gay, isn't he?
Wow. At home these are only five dollars.
That *shower.*
They must be gay.
This pillow smells like men's heads.
Why do you let them just run off like that?
This thing is so rusty it can't be operated properly.
Your skirt is hanging down too low.
That's because you won't take calcium.
That's because you don't know anything about investing.
You've parked way out in the street.
That light is *yellow*, not green.
You *love* animal prints.
Water this. It's going to die.
You're not supposed to put olive oil in the pasta water,
    you know.

Her mother terrified her sometimes—the power she wielded over them all. Her potent ability to wound or frustrate. But her mother was a good person. Mary Byrd loved her and knew that so much of who or what she herself was—good and bad—she'd taken from her mom. Meanness? Jeez. She hoped not. Mary Byrd could be plenty mean, but with small, furry animals or helpless stepchildren? Was Eliza going to inherit that? From her mother she'd also learned tons of stuff about plants and flowers and cooking and fossils; a love for cats and antiques and reading; her sense of humor; and, in spite of her mother's occasional politically incorrect remarks, the importance of rooting for the underdog. Unless the underdog was a squirrel.

She guessed everybody pretty much felt this confusion about their mothers, more or less. But why *was* the relationship women had with their mothers so often the most complicated relationship they ever had? With your mother and your mother only, you shared the strongest, simplest, and most intimate bonds that two human beings can share. You've shared blood, you've shared flesh, you've been as much a part of your mother's body as her liver or her heart. You've shared the awful abattoir scenario of birth, and after that her fluids sustain you. But with a girl and her mother, the tension and competitiveness. Of course she knew that that was exactly why it was so complicated: it was a lifelong struggle for both of you to separate and become two distinct women, and to gain male attention in the family. Duh, duh, duh. She could see it with Eliza already: Eliza desperately needed her mother but often wished her dead, Mary Byrd knew, and she remembered having the same feeling. With Charles, Eliza was relaxed and happy, even a little flirtatious. Charles could do no wrong in Eliza's eyes. Well, almost, she thought, thinking of the Mann-kiss joke. And if he did do something wrong, it was going to be Mary Byrd's fault. Why are so many little cruelties built into us?

Mary Byrd wanted to believe that her mother hadn't really been glad that Stevie had died. Surely she had just felt more intensely what Mary Byrd and Nick also had felt: a certain relief that the friction and fights between their mother and stepfather had stopped. They'd stopped all right. But there was no possible way that any of them could have been relieved about *why* they'd stopped.

She sneezed again. She wished she were back at home, at the birthday party. The loud drone of Foote's truck was still in her head and she tuned to that frequency and fell asleep quickly and slept, as they say, the sleep of the dead.

ELIOT NELSON HAD brought Mary Byrd home in a rain shower that was brief but came down heavily; the bottom seemed to have fallen out of the night sky. She felt a twinge of melancholy as she often did on Sunday evenings. Undone homework. School in the morning, and for four more mornings. And Sunday was tense; a family day. But it would only be another month before school was out for the summer and she'd be free from the stupid junior high, and algebra, forever. There would be end-of-the-year dances and parties. She and Eliot would have more nights like this one and they would have them all summer long. She hoped.

They cruised slowly in the convertible through the cherry tree–lined neighborhood. The blossoms lay thick on Cherry Glen Lane, like snow. It seemed a shame to be driving over them, crushing them into a gray mess.

Mary Byrd could see a lot of cars parked in the middle of the block in front of her family's white brick house. The Nicholsons, the big family that lived across the street, must be having a Mother's Day party, she thought before realizing that the cars were Richmond police cars, and her grandparents' pale pink Cadillac, and her aunt and uncle's woody station wagon. A large rescue truck, what her cousins Kath and Susan called a "glamour truck" because of all the lights and loudspeakers and crap they had on them, was parked farther down the street, and now she heard loud static and walkie-talkie conversations. A few neighbors stood around in their yards and a policeman was talking to Big Nana, the scary next-door neighbor. Mary Byrd looked at her boyfriend, who looked horrified. She wanted to say "Go!" and keep driving and driving and pretend she hadn't seen anything, but instead, without a word, she jumped out of the car and ran up the driveway, running a hand down her dress to be sure all her buttons were done, and into the open front door. The small living room was full of standing men. Her mother sat on the sofa between her own sister and mother. Had she been crying? Mary Byrd couldn't tell; the only time she'd seen her mother cry was when Kennedy died. Her mother wore the dumb turquoise housedress that she'd gotten when she married Pop. Her housewife costume.

"Stevie's gone," her mother said. "We can't find him." She turned to her sister, Marie, who wrapped her arms around Marisa and looked up at Mary Byrd with wide, blank eyes.

"Where are the babies?" asked Mary Byrd, looking around the room. "Is Kath here?" She desperately wanted her to be. She was glad she didn't have any sisters; her cousin was her closest friend.

"The babies are asleep," said her aunt. "The girls didn't come."

Nonna, Mary Byrd's grandmother, solemnly smoked a Viceroy with the usual long, drooping ash. If only it were one of those afternoons when her mother and aunt and grandmother sat at the kitchen table, smoking, sipping Cutty, and laughing at the new Frederick's catalog. "Daddy Sam and Angelo and the big boys and Nicky are out looking," she said.

The warm evening and the making out had made Mary Byrd hot and sweaty but now she shook.

"I'm going, too," she said, but before she could move, a man stepped in front of her. He introduced himself as detective somebody, Richmond police, and in a low, quiet voice said that he needed to ask her some questions. He wanted to know if there were secret hideouts or forts or gathering places in the neighborhood where kids liked to go. Had Stevie mentioned any plans he had that day? When had Mary Byrd last seen him?

Where had she been since dinner? What was the boyfriend's name? Where was the boyfriend now? Mary Byrd blushed. She wasn't telling this guy she'd been parking, not in front of her family. She just said, "Riding around. He dropped me off and went home." She said his name. The detective took notes and, without raising his head, looked her up and down. She shivered again, the wet spot in her underwear cold as ice.

"On Mother's Day?" he asked.

She ran down the street toward the woods and the creek, calling Stevie's name, which seemed so dumb. He had to be somewhere. He *was* somewhere, but where? Accidentally locked in a shed or a basement. Dopey kid. Rode his bicycle too far away and was lost. At the worst, maybe was hurt, had been knocked out and couldn't yell back. A logical dumb-kid explanation for which he would get his butt beaten by Pop when they found him.

When she got to the end of the road and crossed to the woods, she was stunned to see, in the streetlight, her grandfather's small, shadowed figure dragging the deep part of the creek with a rake—the rake he used when he came to get their leaves up in the fall. He painted all his tool handles acid green, and the rake seemed to glow. They looked at each other but said nothing. Her grandfather's pants were rolled up and he wore his goofy summer straw hat to keep the rain off. He looked like he looked when they went crabbing at the bay every summer. Mary Byrd stifled an abrupt urge to laugh and the laugh stuck in her throat and burned. She watched her grandfather, wondering why the sight seemed dreamlike but familiar—not the crabbing, but something else—and she remembered a painting they'd talked about at school. Charon, rowing his boat across the River Styx into the unknown dark. How could she possibly be watching her grandfather dragging the creek, looking for her brother's body?

Daddy Sam said to her, "Go look in the creek on the other side of Willow Lawn."

"But he's not allowed to cross Willow Lawn," Mary Byrd replied stupidly.

Daddy Sam looked at her like she was an idiot and said, "Go look. Look every single place you can think of, or that *he* might think of, even if he wasn't allowed, chooch." He wouldn't be calling her a dumbass if he was really worried, would he? She was heartened that her grandfather would say something so ordinary, one of his Sicilian epithets, as if she'd left a door open or water running.

She crossed Willow Lawn to their school bus stop on the bridge and looked down into the black water. The creek was rocky and shallow. Someone lying there would be easy to see. Stevie wouldn't have gone any farther up the creek because he was afraid of the dark culvert. They had always told him that a thing like the Loch Ness monster from the *World Beyond* had been sighted there. She wasn't going in that slimy thing by herself, either. She was wearing her new Villager dress with pink and green flowers. But it wasn't that; she was afraid of the culvert, too. The red-headed twin hoods from the Horseshoe Apartments had covered the culvert walls with alarming sex graffiti and drawings. She took a deep breath and smelled the rain and the light sewage funk of the creek, and she smelled the boyfriend's dried saliva around her mouth. In the morning she would be standing in this same spot, waiting for the school bus, talking excitedly with the other kids about what had happened the night before, how Stevie had gotten lost but had been found safe and sound, dumb kid, man, was he in trouble, my stepfather almost killed him! It would be that way. It had to be. For now, all she could do was keep looking and calling, like it was just one of the games they all played on summer nights, Sardines or Pushy-in-the-Bushy, or Freeze Tag.

She turned from the creek and looked around the big, wide intersection. Deserted late on a rainy Sunday night, the usually busy streets seemed sinister and forbidding. When they were younger, it had been a fun spot on the predawn mornings she had helped Nick do his paper route. A bunch of them would get up in the dark and meet here where the paper bundles of the Sunday *Times-Dispatch* were dropped. It had been exciting; they were being allowed out in the dark—practically the middle of the night. They'd serve the papers but they'd also make the traffic lights—they seemed like party lights—change by jumping on the sensor plates. They'd lie in the road, they'd yell cuss words, they'd moon each other. Now the lights were warnings, like something to do with the emergency, signaling on and off, on and off, and reflecting their colors in an eerie way on the wet, empty street, revealing nothing.

She found Nick, who was searching with their older cousins. They went around the elementary school, and behind the Horseshoe. They searched King Stalks, the big bamboo forest that stretched from the Nicholsons' backyard to the Fleshmans'. They spread out, calling and walking, and then they'd go somewhere else. Off and on it rained and they were soaked and cold. They'd straggle back to the house, sure they would be greeted by happy shouting and police cars driving off. Then, stunned more deeply that nothing had changed, they'd go back out into the night.

Mary Byrd did not see her mother or her stepfather. She didn't want to. She didn't want to know what they were doing, either. Finally, one of the detectives said that everyone should stop for now and start looking again at first light, which was only a few hours off. Then, he said, they'd have to notify the media and widen the search. Everyone would need some rest.

Mary Byrd knew she'd need to help with the babies, who'd be getting up before long, so she went to her room and lay on her bed. Never had she wanted anything more in her life than to wake up to a Monday morning as usual, babies crying, chaos in the bathroom and the kitchen, she and Nick and Stevie bumbling and flailing around, rushing to make their buses and avoid their mother's wrath if they missed them. She'd go to school and have a good excuse for not having her homework, and then the boyfriend would pick her up after school and put the top down and maybe they'd go out to Kentdale Road or even farther, and just drive and drive and drive and drive. Mary Byrd opened her eyes suddenly and from the slow movements and murmuring downstairs she knew they were all still in the nightmare. Something inside her, her heart or her stomach, seized up, her mouth watered, and she thought she was going to throw up.

At her window she saw that two TV trucks blocked the driveway. What little light there was outside was gray with fog. The rain had stopped, though. She supposed that was good, but she wasn't sure what anything meant anymore. The ordinary touchstones of daily life seemed to mean nothing. Yesterday's pair of spotted underwear was balled up in an old potato chip bag at the bottom of her trashcan. She pulled on clean cutoffs and a sweatshirt and went downstairs, realizing she'd again forgotten her glasses when she saw all the people who'd assembled in the living room. Relatives, some police and other official people, she guessed. She was glad she couldn't really make them all out, she was so blind.

Her mother seemed almost normal and was in the kitchen feeding the babies. Nick had gone back out with Pop and the searchers and Mary Byrd was relieved not to see him. There wasn't anything to say. She stood watching the babies and eating a Pop Tart while her mother did the dishes. Only she and Stevie liked Pop Tarts. There were two in the box and she left one.

James, who wasn't really a baby anymore, struggled off his chair at the table and took his juice beebah to the bedroom to watch cartoons. He was old enough to be ashamed to have a bottle and would hide it if someone came into the room. The real baby, Pete, banged loudly on his high chair to alert everyone that he was finished pincering up his Cheerios one by one. Mary Byrd freed him from the high chair and set him down. He had recently started walking and wore blue corduroy overalls that were almost white from many washings and handing-downs. They hadn't been snapped up the legs, so it looked as if he were wearing a tiny evening gown. He staggered around like Frankenstein, going to the drawer where he had his own set of miniature pots and pans to play with. Mary Byrd took a deep breath with the rush of love she felt for him, and also envy. For him nothing had changed. The world was still a good place.

While she and her mother cleaned up after the babies and dealt with all the doughnuts and coffee and cigarette butts in the kitchen, Mary Byrd heard her stepfather's familiar, heavy tread, a sound she never liked hearing, in the hall. She and her mother turned and there he was, his bulky body filling the doorway. He stood there with his head to one side, hands hanging down, smiling a big smile, she thought—she still wasn't wearing her glasses—the identical pose he'd strike when he came home from work and spied the babies eating dinner and he'd laugh and say, "I see monkeys!," making them squeal and chuckle. She held her breath, but he didn't do that, and instead he brayed loudly, "He's dead." Her mother leapt to him and they sobbed, and Mary Byrd scooped up Pete and ran out of the kitchen—where was James?—and flew up the stairs, taking them by twos even with the big, fat baby in her arms.

Ten

IT SEEMED TO Teever that he'd been leaning in front of the
JFC for an hour with the weather and his foot getting worse
by the minute. Some city trucks passed, Solid Waste guys throwing out sand; nobody was going out now unless they had to. He
knew them, but they just lifted a finger off the wheel and went
on by. If he couldn't catch a ride soon, he decided, he was going
to fall down and just lay there, he was feeling so poorly. Mr.
Johnny might come out and pick him up, but where would Mr.
Johnny carry him? All the phones were out, he couldn't call
Mudbird or Charles, couldn't reveal his hooch in the graveyard,
couldn't even get back to the graveyard with this foot. He'd
made just enough cash working for Mr. Johnny to get some
food and beer. The night before, a little loaded, he'd jumped
down from the loft in the graveyard shed in his sock feet and
had landed on an adze, tearing his foot wide open. He'd packed
it with clay the way his grand had done with cuts—but he didn't

have her special clay—and now it was bad. He needed to get it seen about.

As Teever was thinking about what it was going to be like lying there in the muddy ice with tobacco cuds and cigarette butts, a gold Dodge pickup came slowly down Lamar and pulled over to where he had propped himself. The window slid down, the ice on it cracking off and falling to the street, revealing a wizened red face with a cigarette hanging from it. Loud music blasted from the dashboard. It was L. B., a local fireman.

"Man, Teever, you look terrible. You all right, bro?"

"Ayyy, L. B.," Teever said weakly. "Not too good, not too good. Can you carry me out to the Mexicans?"

L. B. looked disapproving. "Why the hell you need to go out there?"

"My foot gone bad, man. They can take care of it, fix themselves all the time. I seen it," Teever said. "Can't call nobody anyway, phones all be out." As if he had somebody to call.

"Why don't I just take you by the hospital? Don't that make more sense?" L. B. said. "What about the V.A. hospital?"

"Hospital—that just axing for trouble. Lost my V.A. card last time I was down to Parchman, got to go to Tupelo or Memphis or somewhere to get a new one. Come on, man. This thing *killing* my ass."

L. B. tossed his butt aside as he got out of the truck. "Okay, dude. Get your sorry self in the truck." He helped Teever off the wall and to the passenger side and half-lifted him in. L. B. was an ex-Marine, and like a lot of jarheads Teever had known, he was a little scrawny guy, but strong as an ox. His mama and Teever's sister had worked the C-shift together out to the Retard, as the state home was uncharitably known. Inside the cab it was wonderfully warm and smelled of scuppernong jelly, or toilet cake.

Driving slowly down the slippery street, L. B. looked Teever over and asked, "What did you do to that foot?"

"Stepped on a adze, working," he said.

"Yeah?" L. B. said. "An *adze*? What the hell you doin' with an old-school thing like that?"

"Just bustin' some shit up," Teever lied. To change the subject he said, "What *you* doin' out in all this mess?"

"Just low-ridin', checking things out. I got to go in to work in about an hour. There gonna be plenty of fires to put out tonight."

The terrible white-boy music throbbed in Teever's leg and skull. "What the fuck we listening to?" he asked. He put his hands up to the heat vents to warm them and felt the music in his fingers.

L. B. chuckled. "Slobberbone. They played at Jerry's the other night and gave me one of their tapes. You don't like it?"

"More like *Clobber*bone, to me. Shit's hurtin' my head *and* my foot," Teever said.

L. B. laughed again and turned the tape off. The big hospital building rose before them, every window a coldly glowing, fluorescent square. "*That's* where you need to be, bro. The ER. Their electricity don't never go out." He pulled up at the D & L Package Store across from the hospital.

"No way." Teever shook his head. In the ER he'd have to wait for hours, and there were always too many cops around. "No way," he said again. Now that the music had stopped, he hated to get out of the cab and its smoky, grapey coziness. Drops of sweat crept from his temples, but he was stone cold.

"You really think these Mexicans gonna fix you up?" L. B. asked. He got out again to help Teever climb down. "At least that sleet shit has quit."

"I'm good," Teever said. "I'm like a worm in hot ashes; I got to keep movin'. Thanks for the ride, bro. I appreciate it. Look out for those fires, now."

"Man, you sure you're not gonna end up in a enchilada?" L. B. grinned.

"I'll be okay." He tried to smile back at L. B. To himself he added, sure do hope so.

L. B. cranked up his Slobberbone and drove off into the night. Teever dragged the foot across the parking lot. The package store was open, of course, and lit with dinky, colored Christmas lights. Dog and Lena must have a little generator, he thought; maybe he'd borrow it for the hooch after the storm. He felt seriously in need of a drink. Dog and Lena were smart; put a liquor store across from the doctors. Doctors had to have their toddies, buy shit by the case, in and out of there twenty-four/twenty-four in their green doctor pajamas. One time he had even seen a patient coming out of the store, a brown bag and a smoke in one hand and using the other hand to hold together one of those butt-crack hospital shirts. He hoped the Mexicans at least would have enough liquor or beer to knock him out. He felt like his heart was beating in his toes.

Teever limped around the big ice bin to the side of D & L. The front trailers were set like a wagon train circled up in a cowboy show. More trailers were rowed up in the woods beyond, and a path that wasn't really anything but an old pig trail led to them. Somebody had paved the path with flattened Bud Light cans set in the mud in a kind of pattern, with some of the cans flattened length-wise and others stomped into disks. They picked up whatever light was around—not much—and shone blue and silver in the night. Two hooptie vans sat off to the side and some old bikes covered in ice leaned against a tree. Rising up from the circled trailers was the Mexicans' sad *Zorro* music, smoke, and sprays of golden sparks. They'd already built a kind of teepee bonfire to burn off all the skinny pines and junk that had fallen in the storm. The warm, orange glow of the flames lit up the scrubby blackjack and bare sweet gums that were still standing around the outside of the camp.

The trailers looked horrible because they were owned by Booger Britches. They were the most pitiful, raggedy-ass ones in town. Broken windows were patched with cardboard, mangled blinds hung in many. A few had sagging window units that probably didn't work, and some had no steps, just cinderblocks stacked to the doors. The trailers sat, rusted and peeling, back in the brush on the dirt lot, which in summer was a baking dust bowl and in winter a muddy bog. Black folks wouldn't live in a Booger Britches property; only these guys or students who'd use them for parties or fuck huts. But Mexicans had a lot of shit figured out. Had the front trailers set up for different things, separate from the ones back where they really stayed. There was a store trailer where they could rent leaf blowers or weed eaters to make extra cash on weekends, and they could buy beer or bread or Cokes or candy, whatever. They could live off the land, too, selling squirrel and birds and deer parts out of a freezer chest in the store trailer. Teever knew that for a while they had had a deal with some rednecks who were spotlighting deer and selling them to the Mexicans, who processed them and sold them again to each other. Another trailer might be a party trailer where they played their music and watched TV; and another, Teever was pretty sure, was a church because the blue and white spray-paint sign that said IGLESIA DE DIOS PENTE-COSTES MONTE DE LOS OLIVOS had some crosses on it. In a few months, some new Mexicans would come and these old boys would move on to better trailers, or wad up together in a pitiful house. Edna Hill, his brother's mean-ass ex, owned a lot of them out on Old 7. She was like a black Booger Britches.

Teever limped on into the circle where a handful of men sat on milk crates and lawn chairs around the fire. Meat sizzled on a jinky grill. The pieces were long and bony, some kind of nub or claw on one end. Not like anything regular folks ate. Their food always smelled delicious, but Teever knew better than to try it unless he could see that it was an animal he knew. He wasn't sure if Mexicans ate dog like the gooks did or not. Anyway he was not hungry and the idea of strange meat brought on a powerful quease. He began to salivate in a bad way and had started to shiver and wanted to be closer to the fire. Moving in, he swallowed and said punily, "Aayyy amigos. Que pasa? This storm somethin' enough, ain't it?" to the men, who looked at him blearily. He always liked the way they had different outfits: some of the young ones dressed like gangsters or students. A couple older dudes sported straw cowboy hats. One pointed to Teever's foot and rattled off some Spanish, another reached back behind him and with one hand retrieved a milk crate and tossed it to, or at, Teever without even looking at him. Teever decided to interpret this as a welcome though he wasn't sure.

"Thanks, amigo, but I'm gone to have to stand or lay," he said, not sure that the pain in the foot would allow him to lower himself to milk-crate level. The men looked away. They all had Bud Lights and were studying the bonfire. Two liquor boxes of empties sat next to the grill, and pop-tops were scattered thickly in the mud like coins at the bottom of a fountain.

"Y'all got a extra beer?" he asked. What he really hoped for was some of that homemade shine he knew they had for special occasions. *That* shit was *stout*. He really needed to take the edge off, bad. His whole damn leg was hurting. Someone passed him a beer, which he popped and chugged gratefully. Pointing at his gimped leg with its sorry, raggedy bandage, he said, "Me footo choppo." Pantomiming a big machete slicing his foot, he added, "Son of a bitch *killing* my ass." He grimaced and grabbed his leg to make the point. "El medicine-o?" he queried, tipping an air shot to his lips. A couple of the men looked at him and looked back at the fire, ignoring him.

The two youngest-looking guys, just kids, spoke to each other, and one got to his feet and started toward a trailer that a tree must have fallen on. Blue plastic was spread across the crushed part of the roof. The kid called out "Antonio!" as he went inside. Teever sucked down some more beer. The *Zorro* music played on—guys singing with old-school acoustic guitars. Everyone seemed glum. Teever could see it wasn't going to be party night at the trailer-ios.

A new Mexican emerged from the smushed trailer with the young dude behind him carrying a jar of clear liquid. He held the door with his elbow for a rooster the size of a turkey vulture who hopped down and began pecking in the frozen mud. The new guy was heftier and older, a little sinister, with a massive head and an unhappy face on the front of it. He approached Teever, holding up a plastic Walmart bag. Teever was surprised to see the guy had a silver grille. "No fucking *way*!" He laughed a little and shook his head. He hoped that jar was filled with shine. The guy pointed at Teever's trashed foot and said some Spanish—*Pinche chupacabras cayó en una trampa*—that made all the Mexicans laugh. "Y'all laugh all you want, amigos," he said to the headman. "Just please, please, *please* help me out, bros." The headman came closer, pulling a big Coke bottle from the inside pocket of his beat-up hunting jacket. The liquid inside looked like Gatorade, greenish but thick. The rooster followed, and stood beside the man. Both regarded Teever carefully. Rummaging in his bag, the Mexican brought out two dried yellow flowers and a small dinged-up metal bowl. After crumbling the flowers into the bowl, he poured a finger of the pale greenish liquid from the Cock bottle over the buds. Using his big fingertips like a pestle, he emulsified the mixture and then bent down to nestle the bowl in the glowing coals.

The headman gestured to the rooster and said, "Es Muhammad Ali," and handed the Coke bottle to Teever, miming for him to drink. "He ees thee greatess." On cue, the rooster crowed.

"I can see he a badass," Teever said. This shit did not taste like the other shit he'd had with Mexicans before, which tasted like the cough syrup Mudbird gave him, but he figured it was best to do whatever dude said. With the bottle still upturned, he cut his eyes over at the headman before swallowing to be sure he was doing right. The guy waved his hand and nodded, wanting Teever to hit it again. After four or five pulls, the headman reached for the Coke bottle and capped it. He ordered one of the men off a chaise and gestured for Teever to sit down. Most of the nylon webbing was busted out, but he slung his ass into it—the pain was excruciating—and tried to situate the throbbing leg and watermelon foot. It had become so swollen and hurt so much it was taking on a life of its own—a separate, faceless, limbless, and cruel being. Someone threw a Stuckey's Indian blanket on him.

As the headman began unwrapping the sodden bandage, the kid lit a cigarette and handed it to Teever. Teever gave him a bright, grateful smile that he hoped signaled international goodwill. He said, "We are the world, dudes. Fuckin-ay."

Out of another deep pocket, the head guy pulled a biggish knife with a broad, shiny blade. On each side was a cutting edge and it was pointed, like a leaf, broad in the middle. More like a spear. The handle was darkly stained and crudely carved with a figure on all fours. It looked familiar to Teever but he couldn't think why. With his wide, brown fingers the Mexican began slicing through the twine and dirty T-shirts to get at the wound, the whole time talking and laughing with the other men around the fire.

Teever was sorry to see the T-shirts get cut; the outermost one was his favorite. Even though it said KKG-SAE SWAP 1993 PIMPS AND HOS, there was a picture of Shaft and Foxy Brown. But he was pretty relaxed and feeling better now, so whatever. That shit is *goood*, whatever the fuck it is, he moaned to himself.

Now Teever could see that the guy did not have a grille but that each of his upper teeth was actually silver. The yellow and red flames reflected off the silvery choppers and inside the dude's mouth his red and blue tongue was globular and fleshy. Like that flying, flaming heart thing they prayed to, Teever thought. Could this dude be some kind of preacher?

"Hey!" he said woozily to the headman. "What's your name, amigo?" Teever pointed at himself. "Teever." Then he pointed at the guy and raised his eyebrows. The Mexican laughed, showing his mouthful of silver and juicy heart again, and said something Teever couldn't begin to pronounce. It sounded like "queer and arrow."

"Naw man," he said, shaking his half-fro. "Far as I'm concern, you Dr. Bernardo." Teever called most Mexicans "Bernardo" after the best character on *Zorro*, the weird little bald dude in the bullfighter suit who couldn't talk but knew everything that was going on. He liked him because Bernardo was always saving Zorro's gay ass and fucking with that fat fuck, Sergeant Garcia.

"Sí," Dr. Bernardo laughed. "Sí. Bernardo." He pointed to Teever and said, "Mayate loco," cracking the other men up.

Teever grinned. "Y'all can speak all the spickish trash at me y'all want to long as you keep passing that bottle."

The mummified foot was now unwrapped and the disgusting, clay-caked wound was revealed, causing all the men to make sick faces and shake their heads. One muttered darkly, "Ayy, asqueroso." It smelled some, but not too bad. Roadkill, or the nasty water in the zinnia jar when his grandma had thrown dead flowers out. Everyone was looking at the foot. It was porno. The toes were swollen to bursting like purple grapes, and the angry slash ran from the ball of Teever's toes to his heel, red and gaping and oozing. A guy on the far side of the fire pointed at the foot and said something and the others chuckled but didn't look too happy. "Yeah, I know,' said Teever, "look more like bad leftover pussy than foot." Maybe Mexicans had never seen black folks' feet, how different they were, black on top and baby-ass pink on the bottom, nor somebody with such funky toenails. Ever since Nam his toenails had looked like Fritos, thick, yellow, and opaque, the nails on each toe the size of a nickel. Couldn't blame them for looking ill. He looked around at the Mexicans' hands, stubby and tan all over. Funny how that was. Black folks' hands and feet told the whole story of black and white, how they had both in them, and these guys had nothing but pure, one-hundred-percent brown Mexican.

An ambulance wailed and Teever was glad not to be in the emergency room, even if he didn't know what these guys were fixing to do. The kid set down the jar of clear stuff.

"What's that shit?" he asked. The liquid looked oily.

"Awah." Dr. Bernardo shrugged.

What the fuck was *awah*, Teever dimly wondered. Dr. Bernardo grasped Teever's leg just above the ankle with his left hand, while the right hand brandished the knife. He said, "Hiss no good," and shook his head. Teever was now alarmed. Did "awah" mean "amputate" or "chop" in Mexican talk? He suddenly remembered where he'd seen a knife like that. Didn't have a fancy handle, but it had had that weird-ass spear-shaped blade. A guy in Nam had gotten it from his daddy, who'd gotten it in World War Two. The dude had called the knife "Mr. Smatchett," like it was a person, and had talked about all the atrocities Mr. Smatchett was capable of inflicting on Germans and Cong. It could cut like a motherfucker, for sure, both sides.

"Goddamn, Bernardo, don't cut the foot, now, bro," he said. "I will be *too* sorry without no foot." He'd made it through the jungle and land mines and all kind of gook traps and snaky-ass swamps and now he was fixing to lose a foot in his own American-ass hometown?

Dr. Bernardo looked squinch-eyed at Teever and solemnly said, "Tecpatl." Then he spoke to the two kids, who stepped up with mean smiles. One got behind him, resting his hands on Teever's shoulders. The other squatted down and gripped the bad leg at the shin with both hands. He winked evilly at Teever.

"Oh, man, no way, no way, no way, no way," Teever protested, wagging his head from side to side. He crossed his arms over his chest and knew he couldn't rise up from the chaise even if they hadn't had a grip on him. These wetback fools gone take my foot and I'll be bleeding to death, he thought. Shoulda listened to L. B. Overcome with disappointment more than fear—that this was how it was all going to go down, the pitiful end he was going to come to—he continued to chant, "No way, no way, no—"

"Hiss okay," Dr. Bernardo said, cutting him off in a soothing whisper. "Hiss hoka-y-y." A helpless silver simper lit up the headman's big brown face. "Hiss no good," he said, shrugging and pointing to the awful foot. "No good. Cállate ahorita. No hagas más ruido."

The Mexican slowly raised the knife to his face, where Teever saw that on one side a sideways smiley-face was drawn. What the fuck. His own incredulous face was reflected in the wide blade, too; and behind it, the huge gripped fist, and the flames. A tiny portrait of himself facing the devil in hell. Teever didn't think he believed in the devil or any of that shit, but he had not expected the devil to be Mexican or any other kind of colored person. Maybe this wasn't even *about* the foot; maybe they were just fixing to stob him for the hell of it.

"Man, I know that foot is gone bad but please don't shank me, bro," he pleaded. He looked around the fire at the other men, hoping for support. The men sat languidly, watching the scene and smiling. Dr. Bernardo swung a thick leg over the chaise and now straddled Teever. He slowly brought the knife to Teever's neck.

Prepared for the worst, Teever closed his eyes. It couldn't hurt much worse than jumping on the adze. He remembered that at least he was fucked up and maybe wouldn't feel much. Why these guys had to fuck with such a good buzz was a goddamned shame, he told himself. Teever felt the cold insistence of the blade against his gullet. *Oh Lord. Sarah. Grand.* The rooster crowed again, three times, as the pressure of the blade slowly increased.

All of a sudden, the kids tightened their grips, and the headman shouted with Halloween-monster glee, thrusting both arms up into the air, waving the satanic, smiley-face knife. Teever hollered with shock and anticipated pain, expecting to see a gusher of his own blood before him. The men howled and hooted, slapping their legs and holding their sides. The kids backed off, laughing. Teever grabbed his throat, hoping not to feel anything warm and wet. He looked at his hands. Nothing. Dr. Bernardo babbled happily, reaching forward to give Teever's shoulder a friendly shove. Dismounting, he moved to the end of the chaise and squatted. With the knife he began gently scraping the clay, pus, and blood from the swollen foot, sprinkling it with the awah from the jar. Teever, so happy to find his throat unslit, began laughing along with the guys around the fire who were reenacting the joke and cracking each other up. The pain in the foot began to subside.

"Hi-fucking-larious, motherfuckers," Teever said, wiping his sweaty forehead with a sleeve. "Y'all belong on Leatherman or somebody. Stupid Mexican Tricks." He was pissed but he couldn't *stay* pissed, it had cheered the Mexicans up so much, and he himself was so lightheaded and giddy with relief. He was sheepish that he'd fallen for it. Mashed the fool button *good*, he thought.

"Crazy cocksuckers," he said.

When the wound was clean, the headman produced the drinking bottle again, offering it to Teever, who swallowed mucho more. He gave it up and felt complete trust in the Mexicans. They'd had their fun. He wanted more of the shit in the bottle—it was *too* good—but it was making its way around the fire. Joints were being passed. The mood was cheery, almost festive. Somebody changed the music to the kind Teever liked, noisy and happy and horny. He thought the evening had become special for the men, too.

The guy who'd changed the music jerked his chin at Teever and pointed to the jam box. "Banda," he said, giving a thumbs up.

Teever said, "Yeah, man, it's a good banda all right."

"Descansa un poco, compadre, hasta que esta porquería este lista," said Dr. Bernardo. "Vuelvo en un momento." He rose and went back into his trailer. Muhammad Ali flapped over and the door opened, taking him in.

Teever settled back in the chaise, hoping that the doctoring was over. He felt great. In fact, he felt *wonderful*. Beyond buzzed. He hoped he could cop at least one more swig of the pop-skull shine. Taco backwash wasn't even going to bother him. One of the guys cut an audible fart. Or was it the fire crackling? Teever laughed, "Dude, you puckerin' string got too much slack in it."

Some time, minutes or hours, passed. Somebody changed the music again. For a while a man sang beautifully from the jam box. One of the men said to Teever, "Julio Elias. 'La Voz de Dios.'"

Teever nodded solemnly. His head felt heavy, in slow motion. Did he smell gasoline? Had someone stoked the fire? The singing stopped and the sad music began again. The men sat, pretty quiet now, like they were watching TV instead of fire. Teever could see why. The flames were incredibly beautiful, like something alive, and danced to the mournful thrum of the hollow guitars. Teever had never seen a desert, but he knew this was desert music. He felt no pain now; he could feel nothing physical at all. He felt so good, he allowed himself a thought he tried not to have. Sitting around a fire like this, a bunch of dudes drinking, smoking weed, horsing around, made him think of Nam. At least the good part of it: the buddies, the feeling of belonging to something unknowable to anyone but the dudes *right there* with you *right then*. The trust. He had that feeling. He was sure that what had happened so long ago—that mess at Hill 937—had to happen, but he wasn't sure why. Why that candy-ass white kid, just off his mama's titty, from somewhere up north would be officer over a bunch of badass poor black and white guys from Mississippi, he didn't know. Send 'em out to be bush bunnies. Some of those guys had had less to go home to than he did. *Nothing* to lose. Nothing waiting for them but crack and gangs, just like Nam. None of them cared about much besides not wanting to be shot down like doves in a cornfield because some West Point kid didn't know shit from Shinola, wanted them to take some worthless hill, Charlie all up in it, waiting. It was a fucking shame. A fucking shame.

Teever stared down into the coals. He could see past the yellow flames and blue wisps through every glowing piece of wood. They seemed like fiery, orange cubes of ice or Jell-O, and he saw through them all the way into the heart of the fire where it was bloody red. No use thinking about that old shit now, Teever thought. At times like this, he wasn't even sure that night had even happened, or that it had happened the way people said. He didn't remember much. They all had been so fucked up, every night and day, and the fighting had been so crazy. They'd *talked* about doing it, no doubt, but exactly who'd done it, what had taken place, nobody really knew. Since he'd been back the story had become a part of who people thought he was, how people, even his family, explained him away; and he'd just given it up. Easier for everybody. He was proud that he felt good enough right now to think about bad things and feel sorry about them.

The fire popped loudly and a glittering fountain of sparks went up like a Roman candle. Instead of burning out or floating off into the trees, the golden sparks swirled together, a little golden tornado over the flames. The goldness of the sparks was unbelievable. They were a gold that mesmerized Teever, a color that was more a feeling than a color, never before seen, but also familiar. Was gold even a color? The sparks swirled together and became a mass, but not a mass. He thought of the soft, battered gold of Grand's old ear hoops—they had teeth marks where all her babies, black and white, had chomped on them— and of the cheap, promising dazzle of Sarah's fake fingernails and the shiny spinning rims on Fairlane's car. He thought of the dark, bronzy gold of the coppernose and chinquapin he and Grand had caught in the old days at the dam, scooping them up with ice chests in the spillway when it was opened, and of the evening sun going down on the water and lighting up the tree-tops as they sat together other days and fished from their special clay bank. He thought of the golden cat-eye flecks at the back of Sarah's green eyes when he had kissed her, way back in the day before he gave up on kissing. He thought of the sexy, money color of the gold watch as it had slipped off the lieutenant-boy's wrist, and he thought of the gold teeth of the beaver hound kill-dog at Parchman, of which he'd been so afraid. Longing and lust and remorse seized him for a second, but without any real sadness or nature to it; just the strong feeling that the past is dead, bad and good, no going back.

The mouth of the whirlwind dropped into the fire and flames were sucked up into it. Bigger sparks flew out, flickering on and off. Lightning bugs, Teever thought, until they bloomed into brilliant orange wings veined with black, opening and closing. Fucking butterflies! Old Mudbird would love to see this! They flitted around the glittering vortex. The thing now seemed to be stretching out, forming a tall, pulsing shape, drawing out all the colors of the fire; the goldness was shot through with reds and blues and even green—the unlikely green of that split-second flash at sunset when the sun dips below the horizon on Sardis Lake. Teever could see through the twister to a vast, barren landscape of rosy rock. Was this what guys back from Desert Storm talked about? How did they call it—a mirage? Coiling in upon itself, the spindling whorl took more shape, and the colors began to come together to define smaller shapes that began to define details: eyes, a face, a whole head appeared at one end. If my body can't feel nothin', why my eyes seeing and my brain workin'? Teever thought to himself. Then Teever stopped thinking at all. There was no fear or even wondering, only watching now. It was alive, a being that contorted its powerful body into massive 3-D curves and then pulled them straight, slithering in midair. Teever could see the beast from all sides, and through it, but knew for sure that it was real, as real as anything he knew. He felt himself as his baby self, smooth fat padding his limbs, the big soft spot on his head pulsing, his eyes huge with amazement. A pattern began to show on the long, tapering body. Scales? No! *Feathers!* Elegant, gorgeous, strong feathers, each one alive and moving on its own like fingers, but also rippling sensually together with the body's coiling and uncoiling. The unearthly green feathers came together into shapes—wings!—while the face grew large and blood-red. The thing dipped its head into the fire and torqued around to face Teever, foreshortened so that it appeared to be only a giant mask before him. He understood that there was something for him and he was not afraid. The fiery, beaklike jaws opened and a blue forked tongue lashed out. With a sound like fifty slot machines disgorging their jackpots, out spewed a torrent of greenish-gold coins. The noise they made and their dull, lichen-colored patina made Teever feel their heaviness, and that they were very, very old. Solid. On each coin was a splash of darkest red; he *felt* that it was blood. The jaws closed and opened again and out came the ribbon of tongue wrapped around a new gold thing, a cylinder. Unfurling itself, the blue tongue revealed the object, whose gold was not brilliant or metallic or smooth or shiny, but bumpy and deeply, richly yellow. Fleshy. Succulent. Earthy. *Corn!* An ear of corn with fat, bursting kernels in rows like gold teeth. Teever reached toward it but as he did, the tongue and cob snapped back. Once more the beak opened and in a split second the tongue unscrolled again and flickered, blue and wetly glistening, lapping at Teever's poor foot. The mask stared at him as if waiting for something. Teever could see its iridescent gator tail lashing behind it. He was overcome by an urge to speak, to communicate with the thing in some way, but he could not think of a single word. Opening his mouth, Teever felt sound— an old, familiar tune coming up from deep in his gut and exploding in a loud, *Exorcist* yawp:

Estaba perdido, pero ahora me he encontrado
Estaba ciego, pero ahora ya veo.

There was another loud bang from the fire and an explosion of sparks, and the thing was gone, taking its fantastic orange retinue of butterflies with it.

Stunned, Teever looked around the fire, but he knew that the corn and coins were nowhere, and that nobody else had seen what he had. There was no rosy desert, just the cold and mud of a deep, icy Mississippi winter night. The storm had cleared and the moon was out now, a minstrel grin in the blackface sky.

His throat throbbed from his ecstatic song. The men sat slumped and passive, more committed to their torpor. How much time had gone by? He couldn't tell if there were more beer cans on the ground, or if the fire was any smaller. The one thing that he was sure of was that he'd had a message or an omen—something. *But what the fuck?* he thought. *What the fuck?*

The flower concoction bubbled in the coals. It smelled like ass. Or maybe it was the baking, sour foot. Dr. Bernardo was back outside, his sidekick strutting and pecking behind him. He picked up the steaming bowl with his bare hands and dumped the contents on the foot, patting the poultice into the gash. Teever flinched, expecting pain, but then blissfully remembered he could no longer feel either of his feet at all. Or his hands or face, for that matter.

"Don't smirch the pants, bro," he said very slowly. The men mumbled but were over it now, smashed and settled. Reaching into the Walmart bag again, Dr. Bernardo brought out a Light Days maxi pad. On his arm, like a giant bracelet, he wore a wheel of duct tape, and he yanked out a long piece, biting it off with the silver choppers. He held the two sides of the nasty wound together and taped the maxi pad tightly over it. A kid came over and tugged a big, floppy tube sock on over the whole thing. The empty Walmart bag went on with more tape for waterproofing, and a flat flap of old tire made a sole. Stepping back, the two Mexicans grinned at Teever, who wanted to look thankful but wasn't sure his face knew how. He put a hand up for high fives but only slapped air.

"Otra véz mañana, hokay?" Dr. Bernardo said, pointing at the foot and making a circular motion with his index finger. From the army Teever knew *mañana*, so he assumed that it was okay to spend the night. The gangster dude came over with a plate of meat and a new beer. He might could eat a little now, if he didn't really think about it.

"Okay then," he said. "Yum yum eatem up." He thought he was smiling his most friendly, appreciative smile, but he couldn't be sure. Looking around the fire at his new brown friends, the new niggers of this world, he thought that this might be as good as it gets. The graveyard hooch was okay, but he was glad not to have to stay there on this crazy night. He was happy his foot no longer hurt and that his fever had broken and that he was wasted and keeping some pretty good company.

"Okay then, all y'all kimosabes," he said, "Muchas gracias. Muchas *muchas* gracias."

THE PARTY SEEMED to have been going for some time, or it was way later than Ernest thought. Janky Jill's living room was illuminated by a few stubs of candle. The air was sooty and smelled of pot, bourbon, burnt sugar, burnt hair, and gas space heater. A wood fire was petering out. From the ceiling hung an oil lamp that swayed and smoked like the censers in Sarajevo's cathedral. Bessie Smith moaned from an old jam box, complaining about men. The song dragged a little as if both Bessie and the jam box batteries lacked the will to go on.

Catching a glimpse of himself in a mirror over the mantel, Ernest noticed that his mousse-stiffened golden coif glowed regally in the candlelight. He imagined himself, for a second, as the Emperor Jones. Or Kurtz. A few people were dancing, wrapped together tightly. Others had tumped over like the trees outside and lay on the floor. A man stumbled past him, going out the door—a music guy, a sort of backcountry Phil Spector who despised him. Good; no problem there. Everyone wore coats and boots. Ernest scanned the room looking for friends and opportunity. He was disappointed—sorely—not to see Byrd but he was in dreadful need of a woman. Sto was hitting on a French graduate student who reclined on some pillows in a corner. He remembered a night with her last summer. She was good-natured and easy, too easy for him. She'd let him wear her yellow panties as an ascot afterward, but she had bored him to death with her graduate student babble about Derrida, deconstruction, postmodernism, all that shit. What the fuck was postmodernism anyway? Besides, he said to himself, the French? Losers. Fuck 'em.

Maybe Byrd was in the kitchen. He made his way to the back of the house where he recognized more late-night people: the vicious dude in the wheelchair who also hated him—how could he be out in the storm?—a line chef from the Bear dancing sensuously with a waitress from Ajax; a young doctor; a shaggy, smelly blues enthusiast; the girl and the two guys who played in Blue Mountain; a handful of pale, scrawny boys in dresses. Ernest thought them not to be gay, or even sexual at all, but he shied away from them anyway. Sorry bastards. Damn. No Mary Byrd. Someone had lit a small fire in the sink, and the two groupies for the Lords of Chevron, Holly Springs girls known as Hump and Pump, were toasting tiny marshmallows with roach clips. Ernest admired their skanky pulchritude. Healthy, pretty girls, they worked hard at maintaining their sickly, fluorescent pallor. Their hair was mayonnaise-colored; one was buzzed soldier-short, and the other's hair hung lankly on one side as if it had been pressed, the other side short and oddly frizzled. Grayish straps always hung out of the few clothes they wore although tonight they were wearing what appeared to be dog-fur coats.

"Ernest!" the frizzled one said in a cheerful voice. "Want some marshmallows? We're on a bourbon and marshmallow diet." Her eyes glittered with reflected candlelight and god only knew what else. "That's all we've eaten for two days. Unless you count the X."

"Girls, I'll just skip the sweets if you don't mind," he said, reaching behind them for a jug of black Jack. "I'm on kind of a liquid regime, myself. Anyone seen Teever?"

"It's not, you know, totally unlike, you know, a mint julep," the other girl said, raising a glass in which some blackened marshmallows floated. "But without the mint. Maybe we could throw in an Altoid."

"I haven't seen Teever in forever," said the buzz-head. "Maybe he's back in the pokey."

Ernest poured a big plastic cup half-full of sour mash. "What the hell happened to your hair?" he asked Hump. Or Pump.

"Caught fire in a marshmallow-related incident," the girl said. They laughed.

"Scorch becomes you," said Ernest. "Na zdorovye."

Jill was in the pantry with Boudleaux and one of the dress boys, a waiter with a shaved head named Porter. They were smoking a number and offered it to Ernest, who declined. "I've got some X, if you'd rather," said Jill. "Or a Dilaudid? Or one of these?" She pointed to a few flat little packets about the size of a half stick of Juicy Fruit. Each was stamped WHITE BRONCO.

"I don't shoot, but I think I'm in some pain," Ernest said, chewing a proffered pill.

Porter, who had what looked to be either a busted lip or a small disease, was leaning slightly on Boudleaux.

"Are y'all ever gonna play?" Ernest asked him, trying to focus his eyes on Jill.

"Man, we just played for an hour!" Boudleaux said. "Where you been?"

"Jill," said Ernest. "You look lovely this evening." He took in Jill's long, skinny form and scant but downy, freckled cleavage. A hot glow came over him and he sprang an equine tuffy. "Happy birthday, darlin'." He tried to thump himself down but it wouldn't go.

"Some thing, this ice storm, eh?" said Jill, smiling at him, checking him over. "You clean up pretty good, too, Ernest. Want to see something cool?"

"Uh, sure," said Ernest, thickly. He was suddenly finding it difficult to speak.

"Watch." Jill stood a flashlight on end and held her fingers close over the lens. Each long, witchy fingernail was punched through with a tiny star. Shining through the stars, the flashlight beam projected a little Fourth of July galaxy across the ceiling. Ernest was transfixed. Jill moved her fingers as if casting a spell. The stars danced sensuously. Ernest thought he'd never seen anything so wonderful. Fuck Byrd.

"Porter and I were just saying, in an emergency like this, nothing is true, everything is permitted," said Jill. "None of the rules apply." She smiled; not young, but beautiful.

"Ernest don't go by rules anyway," said Boudleaux. "*Pimp* law, maybe."

Ernest tried to say, "Son, I take exception to that," but his jaws had gone numb. He could only manage to mumble between teeth that were beginning to clench.

Porter said, "Ernest, you okay? You want to go lie down?"

"Prayer," he muttered as his legs gave out and he sank to his knees in front of Jill. He buried his face in her long coat. "Lil prayer." The AK clanked heavily against the floor.

WHEN ERNEST CAME to, he was on a bed with Jill and Porter, sandwiched between them. His shirt was open and his pants were undone. Good god. He was freezing. He vaulted sideways over Jill's comatose form, pulling his clothes together. His coat lay on the floor and miraculously still had the gun swaddled inside. Jill and Porter were wearing their coats but both of their dresses had hiked up. No underwear. He sniffed the air for clues and tried to focus on his various orifices to see if anything seemed amiss. Everything seemed to hurt, but nothing hurt inordinately, except his head. Maybe his pride. Ernest left the house in a hurry, hoping nobody had seen the threesome on the bed. He'd never live that down.

Once he was on I-55, heading back to Wallett, he relaxed a little. The interstate was a longer haul but he'd stupidly tried the back roads and they were a mess and he'd had to turn around. On I-55 the pines had been bowed to the ground and had been chainsawed back to the shoulder of the road, their pale cut ends turned to the traffic like hundreds of clock faces. Beyond them, scattered around the edges of the cotton and bean fields, the hardwoods stood, stripped and raggedy. By Dundee things were considerably improved: the trees, all but the tall, skinny loblollies, looked okay. The landscape was frosty, but not crystalline like last night. By Coffeeville, it was completely clear. He stopped at the Stuckey's in Vaiden for beer, smokes, and some BC powder, and he mentioned the ice storm to the woman taking his money.

"What ice storm?" she said.

The beer and BC eased his headache a little; his head felt cleaved. Taking the Dixie Crystals sugar packet out of the glove box, Ernest unfolded it, tapped the contents onto his fist, and held it up to each nostril. He chewed the packet and swallowed it. Feeling around to see if he might have sustained any wounds, he located nothing other than a small, scabby knot on his head. It would take a little extra mousse to make his hair lay back and cover it, was all.

By the time he crossed the Hatchatalla County line, it wasn't even cold. The sun shone warmly and there was no ice on the ponds. It was a drag not to have hooked up with Mary Byrd; it would have been a totally different night if he had. She must have gone ahead up north, goddamn it. He wondered how that shit up there was going for her. That sicko was going to beat the rap even if they caught him. He really ought to go up there and see what's up; he could find the sick fuck and turn him in, and the bounty would be Mary Byrd, in gratitude. And it would be good to lay low for awhile after last night.

No use thinking too much about whatever had happened. What happened in the storm stays in the storm, he decided. It was really a gorgeous day. The red MG buzzed along on the wide, dry road, perfectly ten miles over the speed limit. The sky was blue. He could go home, sleep some, get fresh clothes, and drive to Virginia in the morning.

Ernest reached to put in a tape. He wanted to hear "Tangled Up in Blue" and think about his bounty-hunter trip. He couldn't seem to punch the track up. As he turned off onto the long, ascending exit for Wallett, he was fiddle-fucking with the buttons, finally finding the song. *I helped her out of a jam I guess . . .* He bent his head to light a cigarette and looked up to see a beat-up pickup truck coming at him. Maybe it wasn't moving at all. The cigarette fell to his lap. He had time to yell, "Wrong way, bastard!" and then Jack Ernest was sailing again, remembering last night's magical skate down the icy street, the sparkling winter wonderland of frozen trees and the stars in the deep, infinite night sky, twinkling and winking at him like so many beautiful, beckoning women.

"EVERYBODY LOOKING FOR something in this world," Teever said to himself out loud. He knew he'd have to find a way to be useful to the Mexicans, make a place for himself, if he was going to hang with them. He had keys to shit, knew things, jungle-war things that could come in handy, but these dudes probably knew that kind of stuff—desert *and* mountain shit. It was all basically about the same thing: fucking people up before they fucked *you* up, finding and taking what you needed to survive. There was nothing he could offer them: substances, maybe, but with no money and if he couldn't find Ernest, he had no game. Teever's heart clamped into a tight fist of regret. He knew better than to think he was anything but a loser.

His thoughts turned back to the glorious, coiling monster thing that had risen out of the fire. Suddenly he understood what it had wanted him to know. Like he'd put a key in the ignition, his heart loosened and gave a violent chug. *A garden!* He'd make these dudes a big-ass fucking garden just the way he'd helped his Grand make hers. It was time—nearly past time—to set out collards, onions, sweet potatoes, peas. Peppers and tomatoes first weekend after Easter. These dudes would be jonesing for peppers, no doubt, and he could find out what those beans were that they liked, plant some of those. And *corn!* Big, juicy sweet corn! Tools from his hooch, manure from Big Lars and Yimmy, who he'd borrow—have to muzzle that biting-ass muvva Lars—to turn up some rows by the trailers. While all these guys were out working on condos, laying bricks, making other people's gardens, he'd make theirs. He thought about it, ideas popping in his head like firecrackers. When they returned from work in the evening they could all shuck corn and drink beer and shell peas—beans or whatever—and shoot the shit. Some of them would cook. He could cook! He cooked in the army for a lot more guys than this! Then they'd all eat around the fire and chunk in bones and cobs and drink more beer and piss in the fire and listen to their music—the happy kind—with all the brass and shit. Go to sleep in the back in their trailers; he'd even be happy to sleep in the one with Muhammad Ali. He knew about chickens, too. He'd get some of those chicks off Cong, he thought. They could have eggs. Boil eggs, devil eggs, fry eggs, poach eggs, scramble eggs, egg and olive sandwiches, egg McMexicans with that saucy shit and melted rat cheese on them. Hatch some and have more chickens. Fatten 'em up with the corn! For a second he thought about raising some to fight—hook 'em up with that Ali—but that wasn't really his way. He didn't like to see anything get hurt, or die. Unless, of course, it deserved it.

Teever closed his eyes to get the visuals and drew the Stuckey's blanket up to his neck. It would be so badass, his Mexican trailer garden. Plenty to eat, some to sell. *Maybe* even put a little chronic between the corn rows. Maybe Ernest would help him move some of that. They'd all get healthy and happy as heifers in deep hay. Maybe Dog and Lena would let him put a little stand out in front of the liquor store, catch some of that doctor action, and Mudbird might get some ladies to buy his vegetables. O-fucking-kay, then. But *now* I see! He heaved a big, raggedy sigh that started him coughing and he kecked a big wad into the fire. The loogie, dark and big as an oyster, sizzled for a second. In spite of his excitement, he realized he was tired. No one had said anything for a long time. The music had stopped. Keeping his eyes shut, Teever hoped for sleep, even though he knew that in an hour or two that damn trailer rooster would be crowing for real, and he'd wake up at the crack by a heap of cinders, lying in his chaise longue alone, all the other chairs and crates empty, frosty weeds between the trailers all glittery in the sun's first rays of the new day. He didn't care. He did not *care*. That was *mañana*. He'd worry about *mañana* mañana. Fuckin' ay. Right now he was home, because home was where they might fuck with you but for some reason they'd let you stay. Okay then, he sighed to himself. O-fucking-kay, then.

Eleven

WHEN MARY BYRD woke on Monday morning she had to think to remember where she was. Her mother's rose-colored, frilly guest room. Recalling that, and what her mother had told her Saturday night, and what the day had in store for her, she closed her eyes and drew herself up into a ball. Her heart pounded and goosed up her pulse so that she knew she wouldn't be going back to sleep, which was all in this world she wanted. From the wicker nightstand she reached over and pinched up the Xanax half she'd left there the night before and swallowed it with a swig of water. Later, she promised herself, she'd take another. When she got back home she'd ask Ernest for some more.

Outside the guest room came the sounds of her mother bustling around, talking to the cats over Howard Stern's annoying yammer. Her mother and James loved Howard Stern, but whenever she listened to him it was always about big tits or his small dick. Now she heard the back door and heavy footsteps in the kitchen. Mary Byrd rolled over and looked around the room. Her mom had good taste but it had started getting Target-ish. Maybe when you got old you just lost the will to be original and went instead for easy and inexpensive. Your *things* just became a pain in the ass. She was already feeling it sometimes with her own stuff, which was about to bury her. Her grandmother went around labeling things with masking tape so the family knew who got what, but if she could make you take it *now*, she would. "My life is over, my children are gone," she'd say. "I can't take it with me. No ice buckets in heaven. Maybe you can use it." To which Mary Byrd's uncle would tease, "Jesus, Mama. What makes you so sure you're going to heaven, anyway?" and Nonna would pretend to be hurt.

Sunday with her family had passed peacefully. They had been sad, and tense, but glad enough to have some time together. The ordeal before them hadn't been brought up, and they had treated each other politely, if not tenderly. Mary Byrd and Nick had been careful to avoid politics or current events. They had reminisced, telling the same old funny family stories, and Stevie and Pop had come up in some of them, but it was as if they were like Pete: alive and well, just off someplace else, just not with them at the moment.

In the afternoon while the boys watched sports, Mary Byrd had walked around the yard and had listened to her mother talk about her plants and her birds, and then in the kitchen they'd cooked and talked recipes. They ate the delicious but random dishes their mother had made—no main dish, but a little of this, a little of that—something to please each of them. They had talked about their children and what they were up to, and watched tapes of their favorite old *Twilight Zone* and *Little Rascals* episodes on the new VCR they'd given their mother for

Christmas, laughing as if they hadn't seen them dozens of times before. They'd teased their mother and mocked her admonishments, given out as if they were still children: "*Handwashing is very important.*"

As Mary Byrd had lain in bed afterward, she'd thought about how they had so little in common with one another, family anecdotes, mom-mocking, and TV shows aside. They didn't see each other often, and her brothers weren't married, although Nick had been, briefly, and had only one child—a great kid in spite of being smothered and overprotected. There was no tribe of cousins like she and her brothers had grown up with. She'd wondered how different things would be if they'd grown up more normally. Or more happily. But there were no *normal* families, were there. Why hadn't Stevie's death brought them closer together? She thought that it must be true that happy families are all alike. If a family didn't have a dead child, why *wouldn't* it be happy?

Monday, Monday. Mary Byrd's mother rapped on the door and Mary Byrd cringed. "I'm up!" she called. One of the demented cats was yowling somewhere down the hall. On Cherry Glen Lane in the mornings, her mother had awakened Mary Byrd to get a head start in the bathroom before the boys by banging the broom handle on the kitchen ceiling, which had been right under Mary Byrd's bed. The sound she hated most in the world, that broomstick reveille, and now she meanly used it on William and Eliza.

"The boys are here," her mother called. "It's seven thirty. We need to leave the house in an hour."

"Okay, I'm coming. I hope there's coffee," she yelled back. Somehow she was the only person in the family who drank it. She wished she could say, "If there's not coffee, I'm not going" or "I can only go if there's an original Chanel suit, navy blue bouclé shot through with white, size two, hanging in the closet for me," but she shuffled out barefoot, her black curls all wacky, wearing the old flannel nightgown she kept at her mom's, to greet her brothers, drink coffee, and sit with them silently for a few minutes until it was time to dress and go downtown and talk to some strangers about the murder of their brother and stepson.

THE FOUR OF them sat in a dingy police waiting room. A little dulled out from the pill, Mary Byrd wished for more coffee to face whatever this meeting was going to be. While they waited, the boys looked at leftover *Times-Dispatch*es and a smattering of testosterone publications. *Varmint Masters*. *Guns and Ammo*. "Couldn't they at least have some fishing magazines?" Nick said.

"Not enough blood," said James.

Their mother silently crocheted a granny square. She'd made dozens of afghans—they each had several—and they were the only pretty ones Mary Byrd had ever seen. The yarn was getting fuzz on her mom's navy blue Chanel suit, size zero, and Mary Byrd picked it off. She smoothed her own suit—her black Banana Republic she wore to funerals and meetings.

A police lady came in. "Y'all can just go on in and take a seat. Detective Stith will be right with you."

Detective Stith wasn't in his office when they sat down. Mary Byrd looked around for some clues about the guy. Other than a big piñata—a Halloween spider that hung in the window—there wasn't much: a stack of *Sports Illustrated* and another of *Vanity Fair*. *Vanity Fair*? she wondered. Must be because they had all those great murder investigations and muckraking articles cleverly stashed in between the reeky perfume and celebrity gossip. Or maybe Stith was into perfume, fashion, and celebrity gossip. Her head started to hurt. On the wall behind the desk hung some certificates and diplomas, and she rose and leaned forward to make them out. UVA BA, UVA Law, Virginia Institute for Criminal Justice, John Jay College of Criminal Justice Crime Scene Academy, something from Penn, something from the FBI, blah blah.

All were awarded to Sooraji Mehta Stith. An Indian guy? But if he was a Stith, there ought to be an ancient FFV connection. William Byrd had had a friend named Stith back in the day. A small, framed piece of needlepoint was propped on the console behind him. It read: A STITH IN TIME SAVES NINE. A funny guy, too. He'd better get his smart, funny ass in here.

The door opened and in walked a handsome black guy with a bright, bruisey complexion. His lips were purple and his ears stuck out boyishly, framed by hair clipped so close it made his head appear to be flocked. Mary Byrd was intrigued by the mix of people he seemed to be.

"Hi," he said, tossing a pack of Marlboro Lights on the desk. "Sorry to keep you waiting. Got that Marlboro monkey on my back." Good old Philip Morris. Keeping Richmond, doctors, and hospitals everywhere afloat and population numbers down.

He loped easily to the window where a coffee pot sat on a mini-fridge. "Coffee? Or a Coke?" He popped open a can of Diet Dr. Pepper, taking a sip and raising it to them.

"Nothing, thanks," her mother said. Mary Byrd resisted her own desire for coffee. She'd only have to go to the bathroom.

James said, "We're good."

Stith was a skinny guy, or *poor as a snake,* as Teever might say. A dark red sweater, navy corduroy jacket, and khakis gave him a little gravitas, but he still looked way too cool and way too young to be a detective who had a clue about anything. She didn't know what she'd expected—someone off the TV, past his prime, seedy, cockeyed, gimpy or bald. A gut, crappy clothes. She thought of the detective who'd questioned her the day Stevie died. Had he been the one who'd suggested the connection between her and Ned Tuttle, and asked for her diary? She couldn't remember. They'd all seemed creepy.

"*Diet* Dr. Pepper?" she asked him, wrinkling her nose.

"Diabetic." He smiled. "Dr. Pepper is like me: '*so misunderstood.*' A cold-case guy isn't the most popular guy on the force." Quickly, all business again, he said, "I want you to be comfortable with this. I won't keep you long, and I don't want this to be too much of an unpleasant experience."

She felt a smirk twitching at the corners of her mouth. "Is there the possibility that this could be pleasant?"

"It can be really *un*pleasant, stressful, and pointless, or it can be not too bad, and useful." He sat back in his chair and looked at her—what? Reprovingly? "Your call."

"Let's do this," said James. "We're ready."

"I could have explained a lot of this when I called each of you last week," Stith said, "but the department is trying to keep these cards close to our chest. For this to have the best . . . the most productive outcome, I figured that to have you all here at once would be the way to go. I hope you agree."

Mary Byrd spoke up again. "But isn't this mostly so y'all don't get scooped by that reporter and look lame and inept? You must know about her, right?" She knew she was being a jerk and needed to stop. Let Nick be the asshole.

Somewhere outside the door, men laughed and walkie-talkies crackled. "This is not exactly going to be a great chapter in the history of our police department. Maybe in the Annals of Great RPD Bungles of the Twentieth Century. But we need to be the ones to solve it, make it public, and get it right. Then she—or anyone—can do what they want with the story. Reporters are not the law, and can't bring this case to a resolution. We can, though, and I think we will."

A policeman in uniform opened the door and said, "Hey Sunshine—oops! Sorry, Raji. Want anything from the Sonic?"

"I'm good, thanks," Stith said. The cop left.

"Sunshine?" asked Nick.

"Yeah," he smiled. "My motto around here is 'sunlight is the best disinfectant.' It beats being called 'Mud' I guess."

They didn't smile. They were focused on the word *bungles*. James shifted uncomfortably on his small chair and said, "I have to admit that I feel a huge amount of anger at you guys— not you, but all these people who were involved then, and never figured this out, and here we are again. Or at least, here are most of us." He gestured at Mary Byrd, Nick, and their mother. "I was only three, and our brother Pete was just a baby."

"I was in diapers myself when this happened," Stith said. "But I sure heard about it all my childhood. My mother never let me or my brother out of her sight. The boogeyman was still out there. That has something to do with why I'm personally so interested in this case." He paused. "I certainly understand how you feel. You're entitled to that," he went on. "We—"

"Really? You think you really do understand?" Nick said. His eyes narrowed and his jaw worked.

"Look. Balls were dropped, and a lot was overlooked, for sure. I can't explain exactly how or why. Not everything, anyway. The guys who were working on this case then are dead or retired, or clueless; their memories can't be trusted. But that's my job now— to clean up some old messes. I was brought back down here from New York, where I worked on the Etan Patz case, and I worked the Southside Strangler case, if you remember that. We finally got that . . . taken care of. That dude is *gone*."

"They did a great job on Etan Patz," Mary Byrd sniped. "When was that? The seventies? and this is nineteen-ninety-six." She had avoided knowing much about the case, but she remembered that the little New York boy had never been found.

"That case is still open, it's true, and the investigation is ongoing." Stith lifted his chin slightly, looking pissed. "But we've got DNA now, and all kinds of forensic technology and labs and computers, even here in Richmond. We can do a lot now that we couldn't do then. In Steve's case, most of what was needed was all right here, in these files. In *most* cold cases, that's true; you just have to start over and review everything. Somehow, through negligence or stupidity or oversight, or, I'm sorry to say, deliberate obstruction—and I think it was all those things—nothing happened. Until now." Stith picked up a pencil and drummed impatiently on the pile of old, discolored folders in front of him. "So bear with me, okay? That's why you're here, so let's just get to it."

"Obstruction?" James asked.

Ignoring James, Stith went on. "There are some pro forma things that we need to take care of first before I can discuss any new information. I want to be absolutely sure everything is done by the book this time—no fumbles or mistakes that can prevent prosecution and conviction to the fullest extent of the law. Which is why I don't want this going public just yet. I'll ask questions; just tell me what you remember."

He opened a binder from the pile in front of him and placed his right hand on a tape recorder. "I'll be taping our conversation. Mainly because my handwriting's too sloppy and my typing's too slow." He grinned, a challenging display of teeth. "That okay with everybody?"

Nobody said anything.

"Okay then," Stith said. "Rolling."

Stith spoke for a few minutes, recounting the day of the murder, finding the body the following day, questioning the neighbors, and, Mary Byrd was shocked to hear, Eliot Nelson. *Finding the body.* Dear god, don't let him bring out any pictures of that little body, Mary Byrd prayed. Did any of them have any information they hadn't revealed at the time? They all shook their heads, and he carefully looked at each of them.

Stith seemed deliberately casual, almost uninterested, like a doctor asking about your bowels or libido, but was he looking more pointedly at her? Was it about her diary, and Tuttle? Remembering standing in the Cherry Glen Lane living room, answering that smarmy detective's questions, she felt her face go hot. Blushing wasn't something she did often.

Stith picked up a folder. "Photos. Let's review some of the things I believe you looked at in 1966. You don't need to look at anything graphic. Unless you want to."

"No!" said Mary Byrd, looking over at the others, hoping they'd say the same.

James hunched his shoulders and said, "I don't think we need any of that."

Stith held up a photograph of a dirty, striped beach towel. "Is—was—this towel familiar to you?"

Nick spoke up. "It's familiar only because they showed it to me and Mary Byrd then. They said it had blood and semen on it. It didn't belong to us. I think someone in the neighborhood said they thought they'd seen it hanging on the Tuttles' clothes-line. I'm not sure."

"I guess I remember that," Mary Byrd said miserably.

"I never saw *anything*," their mother said. "They hardly talked to me at all."

"What about this footprint?" Stith held up a photo of a mold of an unclear footprint with treads that looked like they'd been made by a tennis shoe.

Nick looked at Mary Byrd. "No," he said. "I don't think I saw that. But what would we recognize? It's not like sneakers now— they were all alike back then."

Mary Byrd shook her head.

Stith flipped open a notebook of five mug shots, men in their thirties or forties. "Do you remember looking at these before?"

"Yes," she and Nick said at the same time. They remembered all too well.

Nick said, "These were the known sex offenders in Richmond then, right? Potential suspects?"

"Right," Stith said. "You should see how many there are now—two whole binders, at least, and more in our new computer files."

"But isn't that because you lump twenty-two-year-old guys who've been seduced by seventeen-year-old girls in there, too? Those guys are *not* pedophiles and they're *not* dangerous." Nick's voice was thick with disgust.

"We're not here to open up *that* can of worms right now," Stith said dismissively. "But were these five mug shots shown to you then?"

"I remember that Nick and I were freaked out because the guy in the bottom left corner was Mr. Canter, who was a married guy in the neighborhood with kids," Mary Byrd said. "But these guys were eliminated because they'd figured out, I think, by the footprints that the . . . the murderer was a younger guy wearing smaller tennis shoes?" She was getting slightly queasy. Maybe she should have eaten a bagel. No crying, no throwing up.

The detective held up another photo. "From the old filing system, F-B-six-seven-A," he said to the recorder. "What about this one? Were you ever shown this?"

Before them was a photo of an older teenager, ordinary looking except for a vicious case of acne, the kind people didn't get anymore. What kids used to call a pizza face.

They all looked, and shook their heads. "No. Don't know him," said Nick. He passed the photo back.

Stith coughed and shuffled through the folder, drawing out a small photo. He said very clearly, "S-R-six-six-B," and came around his desk, stopping in front of Mary Byrd. "This one?" he said to her.

Her face burned. They all turned to look at her. "That . . . that was my boyfriend," she said. "Eliot."

"You gotta be kidding," Nick said angrily. "Where the hell is a mug shot of Tuttle?"

Stith asked, "So you weren't told anything about Eliot being a suspect?"

"Why are we talking about these guys?" James spoke up. "Can we cut to the chase?"

"I'm getting there," Stith said. "Eliot Nelson—"

"Eliot Nelson?" their mother said vaguely. "He seemed like . . . a lovely kid." She looked at Mary Byrd, who crumpled into herself, horrified.

"Eliot and the other guy I showed you were suspects along with Tuttle. I'm not sure why you weren't informed of that. Eliot wasn't a sex offender, but the lead detective had determined that he was homosexual, and he had an . . . incident in his history." Stith leaned over his desk, retrieving another photo. He held it up. Tuttle. The sad, moon face stared dully out at them. "S-R-six-six-A," he said.

"*Finally*," said Nick.

"Yes, finally, Ned Tuttle." Stith took a deep breath and continued. "His tennis shoes match the footprints, the stained towel was thought to be from his family, and, although he passed a lie detector test, his father had dosed him with Valium when he took it. I'm guessing you weren't told that?"

They shook their heads. Nick, pissed off, said "No. We weren't." Mary Byrd's heart beat crazily. She was confused— what was he saying? Eliot? Tuttle? Either way, she was afraid awfulness was about to crash down on her.

"And of course, there's the odd letter he sent Mrs. Thornton after Steve was killed," Stith said. "Which Tuttle dated so it would appear that he was away at school and couldn't have been involved."

Mary Byrd tried to control the shaking that seized her. James's knee was bouncing up and down. He said, "So. Game over? The rest of the physical evidence seals the deal on Tuttle, right?"

"There's a couple more things I need to show you." Stith leaned back to grab his Dr. Pepper. He took a long drink. Putting the Tuttle photo down, he picked up a page with a transparent plastic covering, saying, "S-R-six-six-C-O-M-P. Is this familiar?"

It was an amateurish composite sketch in pencil. Nick rubbed his face with his hands and said, "I don't remember it, but it doesn't look much like Tuttle."

Stith moved closer. He had the composite and another sheet in his hands. Not saying anything, he held them up side by side. Then he said quietly, "That's because it isn't. This is the guy. *This* is Steve's killer."

They were stunned and speechless. To the recorder Stith said, "We're looking again at F-B-six-seven-A, with the composite." It was the unnamed suspect that Stith had shown them before Eliot. In the inept composite, the size and shape of the head, and the eyes, nose, and mouth, looked similar to the photograph, but could be anyone. But the violent acne in the photo and the drawing were unmistakably alike. Mary Byrd looked more closely. The expression on the face in the photograph was blank, but as she focused on his eyes, she thought she could see that they were not quite empty. There was a pinprick of something there, something she couldn't interpret or give a name to, maybe because she'd never seen it before. The silence was long as they all leaned forward, staring.

Nick was the first to speak. "How? How is *he* the guy?"

Mary Byrd couldn't take her eyes off the simple, plain face in the photo, with its terrible, baroque eruptions. "How is it not Ned Tuttle?"

"It was *never* really Ned Tuttle. But I want to—"

"Is *acne* supposed to be some kind of proof?" James interrupted. "Why didn't you just show us this guy from the first?"

Nick said loudly, "What do you *mean*? Tuttle . . . he's the only person the cops ever told us about."

Stith went back around his desk and put the composite back in the folder, leaving the photo on the desk in front of them. "I realize that now. I didn't really get that until I started going through files and I found . . . things that were actually from other cases, both before and after Steve was killed." He took a deep breath. "I needed to show you the other photos to determine what you hadn't been told. This will be clearer to you in a minute, I hope, as I explain."

They waited for Stith to go on. Their mother whispered, "Dear God in Heaven."

"Ned Tuttle was almost immediately discounted as a prime suspect even though some things pointed to him. The police were aware of this other guy, and all suspicion became focused on him, but they didn't know who he was. I can't explain why your family wasn't told about this, or why the papers never picked up on it. I do have some ideas, which—"

"*Ideas?*" said Nick, his voice rising. "Are we still going to be talking about *ideas*?"

Stith rubbed his skinny neck, like he had a crick. "Look," he said, "I know this is shocking. But I'm laying it all out, if you'll let me. And I'm going to tell you right now, it's gonna get worse. But let's try to get through it. I'll try to answer any questions you might have. If I can. But there are things I don't have any answers for; at least not yet. Can I go on?" He looked at them flatly. "Please."

Nick sat back, arms folded. James's leg began jiggling again. Mary Byrd wished desperately that she was anywhere but trapped in the dreadful room.

Stith said. "Here are the facts."

They sat, tense but quiet, while Stith began to unscroll for them the truth—finally, the truth—of how Stevie had been molested and murdered; the technical details of exactly how the delicate little machine that was Stevie had been stopped: stabbed in the neck with a four-inch knife blade more than twenty times, he had choked on his own blood. His shorts—Mary Byrd remembered the kind he wore; baggy brown or navy blue ones with elastic waists, saggy because of all the junk he kept in his pockets—and his underwear had been pulled down around his ankles. Although the coroner hadn't been able to find evidence of penetration, dark head and pubic hairs had been found on the beach towel, stained with blood and semen, on which Steve had lain. Scrapings from under Steve's fingernails had been taken.

"Here," Stith said, "is where Steve's story ends. Until now. The known pedophiles were discounted and Tuttle was dropped as a suspect, which you were never told: the physical evidence didn't match up. He never really was the prime suspect. But this man, Jeffrey Zepf, was. Is."

Stith continued. "They hadn't been able to catch Zepf—they knew he was out there, but they didn't have a name for the face at this point—but they pretty quickly figured out that Steve's killer was the same person who'd molested a series of boys over the previous year, right up to a few weeks before Steve's murder. The composite was made then, before Steve. All the attacks were in woody areas within a mile of Cherry Glen Lane, and those victims—at least the little boys who dared to come forward—all reported that in spite of knowing better, they'd gone with Zepf, who had said he was looking for his lost bike. He'd offered them a reward. Once he got the boys to a secluded spot, they would be molested at knifepoint. Although none of those boys had been hurt—"

James interrupted, saying sarcastically, "You mean by *hurt* that none of them was slashed or stabbed?"

The detective said evenly, "Yes. Of course that's what I mean."

Mary Byrd could see that James, easily angered but who'd learned better than his brother or sister how to rein it in, was bowing up. Poor James. He'd just been the clueless old baby at the time, but Stevie's death had haunted him like it had haunted the rest of them. She put her hand gently on his thigh to stop his jitters.

"All the boys reported that the guy had a bad complexion," Stith said.

Her mother spoke up. "If all this had happened—if this Zepf person was loose in our neighborhood—why wasn't there some kind of alert? I can't get over this. We never heard a *thing* about this going on. Were the schools told? There was an elementary school and a public playground nearby. We never heard *anything*. All we knew about was Ned." She began sniffling and rooted in her bag for a Kleenex. "Ned. Poor child."

Stith looked tired. "I'm guessing that the families of the boys who'd been molested didn't want anything made public, to protect the boys. A couple parents didn't come forward until after Steve's murder. There were almost certainly other boys who never told anyone at all. These incidents are so traumatic for families. Maybe if more parents and more boys had spoken up, maybe if the department had insisted, as it should have, that every attack be made public, things might have been different. Everybody wants to talk about getting mugged, or their home being robbed, but nobody wants to talk about a sex crime. Victims and families just want to forget about it and go on with their lives, as you know too well."

Mary Byrd felt shame at how she had balked about coming to Richmond to deal with this. *Pale at no crime.*

"In fact, one victim—he was thirteen at the time but looked younger—could never get over what had been done to him, and later killed himself," Stith said.

"But Stevie was the only boy this guy killed?" Nick asked.

"Up to that point. Steve—Stevie, if I may—apparently resisted Zepf and struggled, or angered or threatened him in some way." It was weird to hear Stith say *Stevie*, like he'd known him.

"But if it wasn't Ned Tuttle, what about the N on Stevie's shoulder?" blurted Mary Byrd.

"It wasn't an N," Stith said. "It was a Z. I don't quite know how the guys on the case fumbled that. Stevie and Zepf lay on their sides, Zepf behind Stevie, his left arm under Stevie to hold him, and with his right hand, he clumsily slashed the Z. If Stevie had been upright or flat on his stomach during an autopsy, the slashes would have appeared to make an N, unless you considered the position they'd been in. The coroner blew that. And other stuff."

Mary Byrd shuddered; so that had been done when Stevie was still alive. How could they even be *just talking* about it.

"Jesus Christ," said Nick. "Who was the coroner? Helen Keller?"

"If you want names, that's your prerogative," Stith went on. "Like I've said, most of the department guys who worked this case are gone, or clueless. So let's just—"

Nick interrupted again. "They were *clueless*, all right. Is this asshole still out there?"

Stith looked down. "Please. I'm going to give it all to you." Mary Byrd could see that he was struggling to be patient. This must really suck for him, too. What a fucked-up job: digging up old dirt and bones and awful tragedies and department mistakes.

They sat stonily—even Nick seemed deflated—and listened to Stith tell them more about Jeffrey Zepf.

"Even though they knew this guy was out there, and they had a pretty good description of what he looked like from victims, and all the attacks were in the same area, he still wasn't caught. Since there was no publicity about any of the attacks before

Stevie, there wasn't much to go on. Even the FBI had gotten involved—because they investigate all kidnappings—but nobody could ID him. At that point."

"We had to move," her mother said quietly. "I—we were all terrified of Ned. Some of the neighbors moved, too."

Mary Byrd remembered that James, a solemn little guy, had become silent and angry. Her mother and Pop had never let the boys out of the house alone that summer, before they were able to move, and had monitored them every minute. They had been afraid of Tuttle, and they'd been just as afraid of the closed door of Stevie's room. Only Pete the baby had seemed okay.

Stith gave them a breather, drinking from his Dr. Pepper. He walked from his desk to the window, touching things. Mary Byrd knew he wanted a smoke. She did, too.

He resumed. "About a year to the day of Stevie's murder, there was a break in the case," he said. He puffed out his cheeks in frustration and exhaled. "Look, I'm just going to read all this to you, as I've written it up and summarized for your family. You'll each get a copy. Nobody here except the chief has seen this. Let's be careful; I can't emphasize how important it is that we not let this get out just yet. There are sensitive legal issues involved here, and what we don't need is reporters and public- ity complicating things, or scaring off the people we need to interview before we can get to them."

Mary Byrd was sure Stith was only thinking about his depart- ment saving face. He picked up a blue folder and said, "Okay. Here's the rest." He began reading, his voice businesslike and clipped.

Sometime in May 1967, eighteen-year-old Jeffery Zepf
first noticed fourteen-year-old Freddy Brickle, a boy who
appeared to be two or three years younger than his actual
age. Over the next several weeks, Zepf began following

Freddy home from school and hiding beneath an open kitchen window at the Brickle house. By eavesdropping, Zepf learned all about the comings and goings of the Brickle family, and especially about Freddy—his schedule, interests, and when he would be alone in the house. On the evening of June 12, knowing Freddy's parents were going out and leaving him to babysit his younger sister, Zepf phoned Freddy. Knowing Freddy's hobby was building and flying radio-control model airplanes, Zepf pretended to be a member of a radio-control airplane club and convinced Freddy to meet him in an empty lot several houses away to look at some planes and discuss Freddy's possible membership in "the club." Excited, Freddy left his house at dark, about 8 P.M. Arriving at the empty lot, he found nobody there. Turning to leave, he suddenly felt something painfully sharp poked into his back. Zepf told him to keep quiet and still or he'd be killed. Zepf then blindfolded Freddy with a bandana and dragged him into the shrubbery, and lay him on top of a sleeping bag. Freddy's pants were taken down and Zepf lay down behind him and began fondling him.

Stith paused. He looked them over quickly. Nick's jaw was working again and James cracked his knuckles, but they sat quietly listening.

Zepf told Freddy that he'd been stalking him and said he couldn't help himself because he was attracted to blond, blue-eyed young boys. Freddy, thinking quickly, told Zepf that he had VD, something he had recently learned about in health class. Zepf went no further than fondling, but kept Freddy for approximately an hour. Still blindfolded, Freddy could not see Zepf, lying behind him, but he reported that he could feel Zepf's rough acne as Zepf rubbed his cheek against his.

Mary Byrd shivered, feeling the flesh of her arms tightening into goose bumps.

Zepf proceeded to tell Freddy that he had no friends his age, he was the "black sheep" in his family because they knew about his homosexuality and that his only friend was an older man named Chuck Richards, an attorney. Zepf told Freddy he would release him, but said, "I've killed before and I'll kill you if I find out you told anybody." Zepf then commanded Freddy to count to 1,000 before removing the blindfold, and he fled the scene.

The detective stopped again, and Nick burst out, "And why do we have to hear details about other disgusting things this son of a bitch did?"

"*Nick*," their mother said.

Stith raised a palm—*just hold on a minute*—and continued.

Freddy Brickle's parents called the police. Lacking a good physical description, except for a report of acne, detectives told the Brickles that if Zepf should again contact Freddy, Freddy should arrange another meeting whereby police could immediately apprehend Zepf. Zepf did phone Freddy again later that summer, telling him, "I feel bad about what happened and want to make it up to you. You like firecrackers, right? I've got some really cool ones for you." Police were notified, a sting was set up, and Zepf was arrested at the scene on August 3, 1967. He was carrying a four-inch knife and in his car police found rope, a sleeping bag, and a toy truck. He was found to be wearing size eight tennis shoes, the size of the footprint found at the scene of the attack on Steve Rhinehart.

Jeffrey Zepf was charged with the sexual assault and the attempted murder of Freddy Brickle. One of the arresting officers punched Zepf and Zepf used a bandana to stop the bleeding from his nose. During initial questioning at the station that night, Zepf admitted to stalking Freddy. Detective Fahey, now deceased, told one of the officers to discard the bloody bandana. When it was suggested by other officers that immediate comparisons should be made between dark brown hairs found at the scene of both Steve's and Freddy's assaults, and between Steve's fingernail scrapings and the blood on Zepf's bandana, Detective Fahey disallowed this, puzzling the arresting officers. The officers declined to challenge a superior, assuming there was a legal explanation for Fahey's decision. Jeffrey Zepf went to trial for the sexual assault and attempted murder of a minor, Freddy Brickle, on April 2, 1968. His attorney was Zepf's aforementioned "only friend," Chuck Richards, soon to become a U.S. District Court judge.

Despite the strong case presented by prosecutor Bill Cates, Judge Thomas Fairborn sentenced Zepf to a two-year suspended sentence and two years' probation. Freddy Brickle's parents were so shocked by the lenient verdict that they told their son that Zepf would be "imprisoned for many years" and would not be a threat to him any longer. Inexplicably, the arrest and trial of Zepf were not reported in the *Times-Dispatch*, allowing Freddy to believe this.

"Jesus," James said. "*We* weren't told about Brickle? It wasn't in the papers? Zepf gets a slap on the wrist for attempted murder of a child? How can this *be*? Why wasn't *somebody* raising hell? *Inexplicably*?"

Nick said, "That's what Linda Fyce plans to do. It will sure be in the papers now."

Stith said evenly, "I'm sorry. Let me go on." He glanced at his watch. Poor guy, thought Mary Byrd. He should get one of those new nicotine patches. She had begun to feel sorry for him—for the ugliness of what he was having to do. Stith—the whole RPD—would become another circle of victims in the whole tragedy. Crime upon crime, infecting more and more lives, on and on. The ruining that keeps on ruining. Detective Fahey—that name suddenly was familiar to Mary Byrd. She was sure he was the one who'd questioned her that day. She was glad to hear he was dead; she hoped he'd died from quartan fever or the bloody flux. And the Brickles—god. Would her mother and Pop have been able to come forward like that, if Stevie had only been molested? Pop was from an old-school Irish family in a hard-scrabble steel- and mine-worker neighborhood in Pittsburgh. If Stevie had been Freddy, could Pop have let what happened be public, or offered him up for a sting? A more chilling thought came to her: what would she and Charles have done if it had been William? She wiped her clammy hands on the coat in her lap, catching a whiff of sweat from her sweater. Stith picked back up with his report.

For as yet undetermined reasons, Zepf spent only three nights in jail for the attack on Brickle. Later in 1968, Zepf moved to Bloomington, Illinois, supposedly to attend college there. In 1977, Bloomington police were looking for the murderer of a young boy whose sexually molested body had been found in a cave near railroad tracks. The details of the crime were very similar to those of the two assaults in Richmond. Bloomington police were unaware of Zepf and the fact that he lived six blocks from the child's house and one mile from the murder scene. There were no leads in that crime until June 1986, when Zepf was arrested and charged with molesting a young boy he was babysitting. At the same time, an RPD detective began reopening and reviewing all cases, including Steve's, around Richmond involving unsolved sex crimes against children and repeat sex offenders.

Stith looked up to say, "That detective, by the way, was my predecessor and is deceased."

Learning that Zepf had relocated to Bloomington, the detective called police there to inquire about any crimes involving young boys. It was only then that Zepf was connected to the 1977 murder there. The RPD detective flew to Illinois to interrogate Zepf regarding Steve's case. Zepf denied involvement in Steve's case, and passed a polygraph test, although the polygraph technician determined that Zepf had been coached on manipulating results by altering his breathing patterns. There were no arrests in the Bloomington murder or in Steve's. On November 8, 1986, Zepf received twelve months' probation and paid a $375 fine for molesting the child he had babysat in Bloomington. For reasons unknown, none of these facts was made public by the Bloomington police, or again in Richmond.

Around this time, Zepf moved to the San Francisco area where he sold drums and gave music lessons to young boys. There he was a suspect in numerous other sex crime investigations, none resulting in convictions. Zepf returned to Virginia and began using Compuserve to seek out and arrange meetings with underage boys. According to a 1987 chat log between Zepf and a sixteen-year-old boy, Zepf wrote, "I hope you don't tell anyone I've sent you these pictures. I don't ever want to go to jail and be Bubba's love slave."' In July 1987, Zepf initiated contact with an FBI agent posing online as a fourteen-year-old boy. Zepf was arrested in December 1987 and charged with crossing state lines to engage in sex with a minor. Zepf pleaded guilty in U.S. District Court and was sentenced to eighteen months in jail. FBI agents searched his home and found more than six thousand porno-graphic images, many involving boys, enabling the FBI to build a second case against Zepf, who admitted to having sex with a thirteen-year-old boy, photographing him, and sending the photos from his computer. For this second charge, Zepf was sentenced to nine years in the federal penitentiary at Butner, North Carolina, where he is today. These two cases mark the first and only time Zepf was actually incarcerated for his many actions as a child molester and suspected murderer.

In my investigation, I've determined that Jeffrey Zepf has been the primary suspect in 125 cases of the sexual molestation of children in several states, of the murder of Steven Rhinehart in 1966, and convicted of the attempted murder of Frederick Brickle in 1967, for which he was incarcerated for only three days.

His lips pressed together grimly, Stith closed the report folder and added, "And of course we will probably never know how many other victims there were, most of whom would not have been attacked if Zepf had been caught and convicted of killing Stevie, or if he'd been appropriately sentenced for his attempt to kill Freddy Brickle."

"*Suspect*? *Suspect*? Are you fucking kidding me?" Nick was going Sicilian and practically shouting.

"When did *loud* ever help anything," Mary Byrd said, channeling Charles. But she also wanted to shout something; she couldn't think what. She looked over at her mother, whose tanned face was pale.

"It's a good thing Pop died," their mother said. "If he'd known this creature was out there, and all these . . . *mistakes* had been made, there's no telling . . ." she trailed off, shaking her head. "Poor Pop." She began crying.

"Ma," said Mary Byrd, putting her arm around her mother's shoulders. But it was true. Pop would have wanted William's flame thrower, too. And he would have used it on Zepf *and* the police. But not on her—she was free of that now, at least, it suddenly occurred to her.

James rose and walked stiffly to the window, his broad swimmer's shoulders and back ropey with muscle and tension. "So, *now* game over?" he said quietly. "He's already in jail."

"Yes, he's in jail now," Stith said. "But that nine-year sentence is nearly over."

James turned to face him. "What do you mean?"

"I mean: Jeffrey Zepf is eligible for parole." Stith knocked a fist on his desk. "In April. Two months from now."

Nick threw his hands in the air. "And you people know all this about him, and someone's going to *let him out*?"

"It's hard to believe, but those two Internet convictions are all we've got. That's all that's ever stuck to him. But *this* is why we're doing this. *This* is why I've been in such a hurry. We have to go forward with this information and try to get a conviction in Stevie's case. If we do, he will never be released. It may be hard without the physical evidence, which would contain the DNA to make an unquestionable ID on Zepf, but I'm committed, and absolutely determined, to keep this guy locked up. At the very least. And to give y'all some closure."

"What do you mean, 'without the physical evidence'?" James said. "What about the towel and the . . . other stuff?"

Stith's face sagged, and he shook his head. "The physical evidence—the towel, Stevie's clothes and fingernail scrapings, the knife from the Brickle arrest, Zepf's polygraph results—it's all missing."

"How could that happen? How could that happen?" Nick said, dazed.

"No wonder," Mary Byrd's mother said. "We . . . I should have paid more attention. I should have been asking more questions. I was just . . . I don't know." She dropped her head and cried again.

Oh my *god*, can this get worse? Mary Byrd reached for her mother's hand. "Mom, don't." She selfishly wanted to know if the diary was gone, too. *It's not about me.*

"You mean the evidence and the polygraph results were lost, or they were 'disappeared'?" asked James.

"At this point, I don't know. That part of it will be an ongoing investigation, and is one reason I needed to know what, exactly, you all were shown, or told, in nineteen sixty-six. If the evidence was tampered with, or if the judge was influenced in some way in the Brickle case, or if any department guys or Chuck Richards were involved in a cover-up of the lost evidence, I'm going to get to the bottom of it." Stith stepped back from his desk and opened the middle drawer. "But we do have this." He took out a Baggie with a small object and held it out in his long, pale palm. A small green and yellow metal dump truck worn to the metal. "Do you recognize it?"

Mary Byrd closed her eyes, feeling tears. "That . . . that was Stevie's Tonka truck. Or he had one like that. Same colors, and beaten up like that."

"Definitely," Nick said. "'Pickin' up dirt . . . Brrrrooom . . . dump truck.' That's what he'd say. He played with that thing all the time."

Their mother said, "Yes. That's his truck. I don't know how many times I had to take it out of his pants pocket when I did his laundry."

"Even I remember that truck," James said, surprised. "Sometimes he let me play with it." He smiled a sad little smile.

"So you feel sure it was his?"

Mary Byrd reached for it and he allowed her to take it. "Please don't take it out of the bag."

She thought of William, who always seemed to have a few of his tiny war machines in his backpack, or parked neatly in front of his plate at meal times. "Yeah," she said softly. "It was like a good luck charm. He loved to load it up and make it dump stuff." Like English peas he didn't want to eat—William had tricks for that, too—or roly-polies, or Japanese beetles her mother paid him a penny apiece to pick off her roses. Pumpkin seeds. Her eyes and nose watered and she sniffed hard.

"It was evidence from Freddy Brickle's case," Stith said. "Those clowns hadn't even inventoried it or cross-indexed it with Stevie's file. It wasn't Freddy's, so I had a hunch that it must have been Stevie's. Zepf kept it as . . . a kind of trophy, I guess. But if you're sure it was Stevie's it's going to be a very important piece of evidence."

She squeezed the little truck in the bag with her sweaty palm and moved its tiny dumper thing.

"I . . . I actually have a picture of him with it. And some of his other trucks," she said. "I was looking at it the other day."

Stith's eyebrows rose. "I really need to have that photo, if you'll send it as soon as you can."

"Okay." Mary Byrd handed back the bag. She wondered if they'd ever see it again, or if they wanted to.

James, at the window with his back turned, gave the hanging spider a push. "What is it that you think might have happened to the other stuff?"

"There are a number of possibilities. One is that the evidence was lost innocently enough, however ineptly, by Detective Danvers, who transferred it from the RPD to the FBI, which at that time made its labs and forensic experts available to small police departments. You know—left in a box in someone's trunk, or in a locker and accidentally thrown away. The records here show the evidence being signed out and signed back in to the department, but they might have been altered. Fahey, the lead detective, knew the evidence for Stevie's case was lost—or was 'disappeared,' as you say—but wanted to cover up that fact, therefore disallowing comparisons between Stevie's finger-nails and Zepf's hair and blood when he assaulted Brickle. That's why Fahey had the bandana discarded. And there's the possibility that there was something even more . . . criminal going on."

James gave the spider a harder push—a punch. Stith looked over but went on.

"Possibly one or more of the detectives involved were . . . *encouraged* in some way to lose the evidence, although we have no proof to that effect. Zepf's father was a wealthy developer and his uncle was a county executive. Both were large contribu-tors to the local Republican Party. Judge Fairborn was appointed by Nixon. Chuck Richards, Zepf's 'best friend,' who was Zepf's defense attorney in the Brickle trial, later received an appoint-ment as a U.S. District Court judge, also from the Nixon admin-istration. It's also possible that Richards and Zepf had a sexual relationship, which of course Richards, who was married with a family, would have made every effort to conceal. Some or all of these things could account for what did, or did not, happen, including why no one in the Zepf family was ever questioned in either of the two boys' cases, and why your family and the public were never made aware of Zepf. Why, when Stevie's case was reopened when Zepf was a suspect in Illinois, these . . . injustices weren't discovered, and why no reporters were made aware of these events, particularly Zepf's trial for the attempted murder of Freddy, and why the prosecutor put up with being prohibited from connecting Freddy's case to Stevie's. It's also true, but no excuse, that by 1987, everyone around here was . . . preoccupied with the Southside Strangler. There's some stuff we'll probably never be able to know. I, speaking personally and as a member of the department, could not be sorrier. I hope that eventually an official apology will be made to all of you, and to the public, for what's been a tragic failure to protect this community, and other communities, from crimes like this, for what that's worth. Although those other communities—in California and Illinois— need to face up to their own failures as well."

"Eventually?" Nick said. "There'll be an apology in another thirty years maybe?"

"We need a conviction first, right now," Stith said. "And look, in no way do I want to be defending the officers involved, but I've got to say that at the time, in 1966, the RPD was a podunk operation. These guys didn't have adequate training in homicides and forensic science. Most small police departments still don't have access to proper training and facilities. This is a personal soapbox of mine. We've come a long way. Now there's the Virginia Institute of Forensic Science and John Jay College's Crime Scene Academy."

James interrupted, "And that helps us how?"

Stith was unflustered. "Unfortunately, these crimes will not stop happening, but the more we know, the more we can prevent them."

"Maybe even in this century," Nick said. He cleared his throat, and Mary Byrd hoped he wouldn't spit.

Their mother picked up her crochet bag and started fiddling in her purse for her keys. She was done. They all were.

Stith wasn't, and preached on. "Things move too slowly because the legal system is overwhelmed. There's a big difference between a child taken by a parent and one snatched by a predator, and there's a difference between real predators and a nineteen-year-old kid who has sex with a sixteen-year-old girl, as Mr. D'Abruzzi pointed out, and the law needs to catch up. I say this somewhat lamely because I know that nothing can bring Stevie back. I am so, so sorry for what you've been through. I have children. If we can keep Zepf behind bars, and I think we can, maybe that will be some comfort to you." Stith looked exhausted and genuinely sad.

Except for their mother rattling her keys, they sat limply while Stith briefly laid out the plan to retry Zepf. He asked them to be patient and wait a little longer, saying again that he hoped they would resist talking about it. They had his promise that he was doing everything he could to stop Zepf's release, but if he failed, they could—should—go public with their story in any way they wished. It was their story, after all.

"One more question," Nick said, standing to go. "Can this guy still get the death penalty?"

"It's not likely," Stith said. "But it's a possibility you might want to think about." He reached over and snapped off the recorder.

They left the room wasted and sad, their tough mother forging ahead, Stith following them. Like a beaten dog, thought Mary Byrd. He rushed ahead of her to speak to her brothers and mother. She lagged behind, struggling with her coat.

Stith waited for her to catch up. "Can I talk to you a sec?"

"Okay," she said doubtfully. What fresh hell?

He smiled gratefully and held the door open. "I could use a smoke."

Outside he said, "Wow! Pure, frigid oxygen!"

"Let's ruin it. What I *really* need is a drink," Mary Byrd said, taking the Marlboro and the light he offered. She sucked in the soothing smoke. "Have y'all ever thought of putting in a bar? It might help with confessions. Let a detective pose as the bartender."

Stith looked surprised. "I'd expect you to be a little more . . . circumspect, at the moment."

"What should we be doing? Ululating? Tearing out our hair and beating our breasts?"

"I'm sorry you had to come so far to do this, but your mother insisted you'd want to."

"My mom is great at deciding how I feel," Mary Byrd said.

Stith smiled, but said apologetically, "This had to be . . . grim."

"It couldn't have been very fun for you, either. And I'm guessing it's going to get worse when everything is out there."

"It's what I was hired to do." Stith shrugged. "There's some satisfaction in it."

"How do you *do* this stuff, day in and day out?"

"Somebody has to," he shrugged again. "Maybe it makes me a better person, if that makes sense. Like, if you can understand— or I guess *confront* is a better word—the worst in people, you're better able to appreciate the best? I admit there's a rush when you solve a case. I'm no superhero, but I'd *like* to be one." He grinned. His teeth looked perfect and white; weird for a smoker.

"I sometimes think about how . . . lucky we are, because at least Stevie was found the next day. I can't imagine how the families whose children are never found get through life."

"They hope," he said. "Even when they know, they hope."

"What about Tuttle? He's been blamed all these years."

Stith nodded. "I'm going to try to locate him and set that straight."

No telling how Tuttle's life had been fucked up. Mary Byrd shook her head, stepping on her cigarette butt, then picked it up and put it in her pocket. "Well, we all thank you very much, even if we seemed to be hating your guts."

Stith smiled. "When we no longer need the little truck, would you like to have it?

"Oh. Yes, sure." She wasn't at all sure.

"I just offered to send it to your mom or brothers, but they didn't want it; they said you might because you have a little boy. And your mother said, 'Yes, she'll want it. She's a *terrible hoarder.*'"

"Guilty," Mary Byrd said. "I like little things." She felt tears. "My son might like it, but he's more into tanks and planes. But thanks. I would really like to have it. And I'll send you that photograph of it as soon as I get home."

"There's something else." Stith drew something from his pocket. "They're yours."

He handed her a small green book with gold edges, and an envelope.

"Oh, jeez," she said, recognizing her ancient, pitiful diary. Embarrassed, she could only think to say, "Thank you."

"I don't know why they were never returned," Stith said. "Or why they were asked for. They were never needed."

Seeing the old envelope addressed to her in Tuttle's boyish scrawl, she said, "I don't think I want this."

"It's yours to destroy."

"They told me . . . Did they ever even really think that Ned Tuttle had killed Stevie to get back at me?"

Stith looked puzzled. "I don't know what you mean."

"That's what a detective told me. That's why they took the diary." She wondered if Stith had read it.

"Are you sure you're remembering that right?" Stith asked. "Sometimes, when people are so traumatized . . ."

"I've been remembering it correctly for thirty years. It's not something a girl would forget." Eliza would kill anyone who looked at her diary.

Stith put his hands in his pockets and looked down. "I would let that go. I'm just glad you have your things back."

He raised his head and looked her in the eye, honest and stern, like a dad. Or a shrink.

Mary Byrd made up her mind to do what he said. It was time.

They shook hands. She noticed his nice wrists. What was wrong with her? Stith said he would stay in touch until it was over. Mary Byrd ran to catch up with her family, who she knew would be fuming in the car, pissed off at her for keeping them waiting, her big, middle-age brothers crammed and doubled up in the backseat, her pipsqueak mom at the wheel, insisting on driving in spite of the gouty tophus, taking the lives she'd given them back in her bony little hands.

Twelve

EVAGREEN SAT ON her porch in the weak winter sun, smoking a Salem. They were burying Rod; she hadn't gone. She couldn't, although L. Q. and Ken had. She'd used the excuse that somebody had to stay back with Desia. Desia, Angie's girl, sat on a blanket on the walk playing, having given up trying to ride the plastic Big Wheel Ken had brought her. L. Q. and Ken had cleared most of the fallen branches, but the trees dripped a little from melting ice.

Evagreen had plaited Desia's soft hair with pink beads and a few yellow jessamine blossoms that, being so close to the house, had survived the storm. The tiny girl looked so much like her father, something that Evagreen knew would haunt them all forever. Girls look like they daddies, she'd heard somewhere, so their daddies don't turn on them. Eliza Thornton look just like her daddy, too, thought Evagreen, so maybe that true. Maybe so.

Desia was trying to arrange some sticks, oak leaves, and an empty Salem pack to make a little house, managing a sort of hut. From a pile of old chinaberries that had blown down during the storm, she took three. "This the mama and the daddy," she said. "My mama and daddy gone love to see this, Granmama." She looked up at Evagreen and grinned.

Evagreen smiled back. They hadn't told Desia yet. What you gone tell a four-year-old? she'd said to L. Q. and Ken. She just like me. All she want in this life is a nice home, a family that act right, be good to one another. They had let it drop for the time being. Evagreen hoped Desia hadn't seen much of the ugliness between her parents. Whatever happened with Angie, she and L. Q. and Rod's folks were going to make a happy home for Desia right here.

Ken and L. Q. had taken Evagreen to see Angie in Memphis. All Angie could do was cry, cry, cry. Evagreen hadn't even been able to hold her; had to stay across the table in the visiting room. And she'd had to be strong; she'd told herself; wouldn't help nobody, all of us be crying. L. Q. had prayed, and Ken had promised he would work things out the best he could. They could count on that, he'd said. The guards had led Angie away, and all she had been able to say was, "I'm sorry, Mama." That moment, taking her good baby girl away, had hurt Evagreen more than anything. She thought it might have hurt less if Angie had died. "Hope and strength what I'm lookin' for," she said out loud. "That, and some a that mercy they always be talking 'bout."

Desia looked up at her solemnly, and with a big breath, like she was blowing out candles on a birthday cake, blew at her stick-and-leaf house. "I huffed and I puffed and I blowed our house down!" she said. The sticks fell apart and the three chinaberries rolled away in different directions.

Thirteen

THEY WERE A little late to Ernest's church, although the service hadn't started and the musical warm-up was going on. Teever's giant old Bruzzi Boots made a lot of noise as he clumped along, so they slipped quickly into the very back pew, which is where they wanted to be anyway: easy in, easy out. They were both a little uncomfortable being in church, but the simple space, just a cube of whitewashed beaded board ceiling and walls and a rough plank floor, was so plain and informal that they relaxed a little. A young girl dressed in a long granny gown stepped up with her little violin to play an almost-perfect "Ashokan Farewell"—an off-key note and her wide blue eyes enhancing the sweet PBS poignancy of the tune. Then an old man played a buzzy keyboard and a big lady in a blue-bird-colored robe rose from the side of the altar, swaying and singing in a strong, even jazzy, voice about mercy, salvation, God's love, and life everlasting. It was rousing and lovely, even if the lady looked more like Mary Byrd's old Carolina-blue VW Beetle than an angel, and even if the message was the spiritual version of Corelle.

Mary Byrd was surprised to hear Teever's gravelly voice join in softly when the whole congregation began to sing. He leaned over to say proudly, "I remember some o' them old songs, Mudbird." She realized that at some point long ago, Teever must have had something that resembled a normal family and home life—church, regular meals and baths, and work, and maybe even school—although he never talked about it. Not to her anyway. She wondered at what point things had gone off-road for him. He hadn't just stepped out of a cotton field. Vietnam? Or maybe before that—the Meredith crisis? Either one was enough to make a kid go wrong. Maybe she'd ask him some stuff on the way back.

It was amazing how little the country church resembled the cold and scary Catholic church of her childhood—about as much as a square dance resembled a ballet. It wasn't even like the Episcopalian and Presbyterian churches Charles's family attended, either. There wasn't a lot of mumbo-jumbo, or bowing and scraping, or fancy trappings and incense. Presbyterians were pretty plain. But they were still pretty stiff. And when did they start doing communion, for god's sake? Here—did this little church even have a name?—the *otherness* felt similar to Mary Byrd; the feeling of *them* and *me*. They knew the drills and she didn't, not unlike the Latin masses of her childhood. But in this old rickety place, where they seemed to value light and air, and even on this dreary wintry day, it wasn't forbidding and gloomy inside. It reminded her of Evagreen's church. She supposed that not having a lot of dark wood beams and chiseled stone and drapey crap made the difference. The stained-glass windows weren't advertisements for wealthy church families, but each pane was simply glazed in

rectangles of blue, red, or yellow. Did people need all the trappings to feel more serious about their religion? The opposite
ought to be true. No distractions. She didn't care about any of
it, but the plainness of this space seemed so much more—*something*. Holier, or homier. A holy kind of home, maybe.

The only decoration in the place, other than winter greenery—magnolia leaves and cherry laurel—was some kind of icon
on the wall above the altar. She could barely make it out from
so far back. The flat, expressionless face, its features crudely
painted on, looked just like the Jesus face she'd seen in the spec-
tacular cathedral at Kizhi, built all of wood without a single
nail. This Jesus looked like a big rag doll that had been loin-
clothed and arranged in the crucified position, although the
arms of the thing were a little too straight-up—more Superman
than Jesus. Or maybe the arms were supposed to be raised up
to the dingy cotton-ball clouds across the top. What looked like
actual bird wings stuck out from behind each shoulder, and a
broken piece of chain, ends dangling, hung around its middle.
Plastic greenery arched around the sides of it, and in the two
bottom corners, printed large, were the Greek letters A and Ω.
The background was either old sprigged blue fabric or patterned
wallpaper bordered with large, faded gold something—rick-
rack?—the whole thing framed in pine with stars, or darker
wooden crosses at the corners. Block-lettered on the wall
beneath it were the words AND GOD SO LOVED THE WORLD.
Really? Mary Byrd thought. What father would ever have sacrificed his child? But it was a very amazing piece, and it was sort
of more amazing that some folk art picker asshole hadn't come
around and bought it or stolen it and sold it in Atlanta or New
York for a zillion dollars. She pictured it in her living room or
kitchen, looking wrong but very cool.

It dawned on Mary Byrd that even though the ankles of the
icon were crossed, and it looked like there were spots where the

stigmata ought to have been, it was not a crucifixion, but an ascension. She thought of the famous ones she'd seen at the Uffizi; one by Mantegna, maybe? It was a triptych, and one of the panels showed Jesus standing on a solid cloud as if he were on a cherry picker, his robes perfectly shaped and intact. He was holding a flag and surrounded by putti, and with his right hand he made the gesture he always made, a sort of gentle, instructional, palm-out-and-up gesture: "Hark, listen up, everybody." In those old paintings, Jesus was natural and life-like and the scenes often so graphic that you totally got it about Jesus's humanity and suffering. In the odd little puppety thing here, Mary Byrd was struck by how the figure sort of clobbered you in the same way, somehow transcending its toyness and commanding attention to the earthly lessons of Jesus's life, and to the mystical and supernatural properties of Christianity itself, blah blah. Well, she thought, it was just a rag doll, scraps, and a Walmart glue gun, and she was just flashing on her William and Mary Renaissance Art lectures. Sometimes a weird rag-doll Jesus was just a weird rag-doll Jesus. But it did have a kind of sacred, mummy-in-the-mvsevm thing about it, some powerful voodoo appeal. Some redneck Giotto knew what he—or she—was doing.

Mary Byrd noticed that Teever was staring at it, too. She wondered if he could read the sign. Curious, she whispered to him, "Wonder what that's about, up there."

Without looking away from the thing he said, too loudly, "Easter." A couple of church members turned to look back at them.

After a moment, Teever whispered more. "Mean, Jesus dead, going to heaven to be with his daddy, where people like Ernest and you an' me *not* goin'." Surprisingly, his voice was a tinge rueful. He cut his eyes over at her and gave her a meaningful look. Mary Byrd still couldn't tell if he could read the message on the wall or not, but she guessed he didn't need to. She wondered what Teever's idea of hell might be. Parchman? She'd always joked that hell for her would be having to spend eternity tailgating in the Grove on a game day. Ha. There was probably way worse waiting for her.

She wasn't sure why she'd decided to come to Ernest's funeral; it wasn't a great idea, since she'd already been gone from home for days. And then, it felt disloyal, of course. Even though it would just be an afternoon, getting away again had been a pain in the ass: arranging for picking up the children, having Charles on alert while they were home alone, feeding and walking the dogs, food, homework, same old. But partly, she truly felt the need to *mourn*. She was curious about Wallett, Ernest's little town, and his family. And Teever had wanted badly to go, and there was no one else to take him. But she hated funerals and she hated church and there had just been so much death and awfulness going on. Had Evagreen and L. Q. gone to Roderick's funeral? she wondered. Could Christians be true Christians and forgive a child's murderer? Jeez. Teever hadn't gone to Rod's funeral; he'd been dealing with his hurt foot or something, and he wouldn't have been welcome, probably. She hadn't even seen Charles since she'd gotten back from Richmond; she'd come in the previous night, and he had let her sleep in and had gotten the children off and gone to work. So she'd just gone ahead and come to Wallett.

Mary Byrd and Teever had ridden down the interstate toward Wallett mostly in silence. It was alarming to see all the damage the ice storm had done to the landscape close to town. Trees down on houses and cars, more cars abandoned on the road, hedges and decorative shrubs broken up, people out with chain saws trying to push all the dead trees into bonfires. Coming back from the airport the night before, Mary Byrd hadn't been able to see the craziness of the damage in the dark. She'd commented to Teever that it looked like a war zone, and he'd snapped, "Un-uh, no way. How you know what a war zone look like? Those people look dead to you? War zone, ain't *nuthin'* alive. This here just a bad storm, just branches be piled up, not people. It ain't *nuthin'* like a war zone."

But fifteen, thirty minutes away everything had looked pretty normal. It was so odd to Mary Byrd that she'd missed the apocalyptic storm that people would be talking about for years. Lots of people, she'd heard, still didn't have electricity. The damage seemed so weirdly biblical, as if some vengeance were being wreaked in a narrow swath west to the river. On whom and for what? Or maybe it was just a reminder that there was always a monkey wrench that could be thrown into the existence that everyone pathetically believed they had some control over. A cosmic smack-down, known to many as *an act of God*.

When they'd gotten close to Wallett, they'd seen that a roadside memorial had already been put up at the exit where Ernest had died. A white cross, a plastic wreath, some antlers. A little cedar had been planted where the storm debris had been cleared. Mary Byrd had glanced over at Teever, wondering what he was thinking. It was tempting to think that he wasn't thinking at all, which was what most people who knew Teever probably thought, but she knew better. The inside of that head was wired and streamlined for sizing things up quickly, manipulating, and surviving. He didn't waste a lot of time or brain cells worrying about things he couldn't do much about, or cluttering his thoughts with nonessentials like art, love, responsibility, or hog futures—crap that caused people misery, ulcers, and heart attacks. But what did she know? There was a little flotsam in Teever's hair, Mary Byrd had seen; god knows where he'd spent the night. Or any night. Otherwise, he looked presentable. She was surprised to notice how gray he was getting; he was too old to be doing yard work. Mary Byrd had tried to avoid breathing in the air close around Teever in the warm car, but she was pleasantly surprised that he smelled of wood smoke and, faintly, gasoline. Maybe a little beer. He had on some wrinkly but fairly clean khakis, a wrinkly but fairly clean blue button-down shirt, an expensive-looking tweed jacket that he said he'd "traded-up" for with a dude who'd gotten it off Ernest, which he wanted to wear for the sentiment of it, and a nice tie of Charles's. He'd asked to borrow one that she'd gotten for Charles at Barneys years before; it was deep blue, with tiny, barely discernible black skulls all over it. Mary Byrd had suggested that it might not be great for a funeral, but Teever had said *he* thought it was just right.

Breaking the silence in the car, Mary Byrd had said, "Okay, so tell me again exactly how you hurt your foot the other night?" She expected a variation on what he'd already told her.

"I tole you: tryin' to help Mr. Johnny break up some ground for a lady's garden," he'd lied. "Stepped on a tool blade."

"And it cut you that badly?" she had asked suspiciously. "Through your shoe?"

"You seen them shoes, Mudbird," he'd said. "They was rotten." Teever had groaned and shifted on the seat. "Man, this thing still *hurtin'*, too."

"God, I'm sure it does," Mary Byrd had said almost sympathetically, knowing what was coming.

"Don't you have somethin'?" he'd asked. "*Anything?*"

"Damn it, Teever," she'd protested. "I think I have a Xanax. A Xanax. With her right hand she'd rummaged in her bag for a Tylenol tube. She didn't want him handling all her pills but she couldn't drive and open the tube. "Here," she'd said grudgingly, handing it to him.

Teever had shaken out the assortment into his palm and had flipped through them with his index finger: Tylenols, a pink

Benadryl, two Ritalins, a green capsule, a blue Xanax, and some white and yellow pieces.

"Take *one*," she'd said.

He'd put all the pieces quickly in his mouth, letting the Xanax drop to his lap. "Okay, but I see all these halfs in here," he'd said, chewing. "You ain't foolin' nobody." He'd shuddered. "*Oowee*. Bitter."

"Well, thank god they're bitter, and expensive, or we'd all be dead," Mary Byrd said. A huge truck had passed them on the right, doing about ninety, just inches from Teever.

"Shit!" she'd shouted. "Did that seem really, really close?"

"Um-hmm," he'd answered, unconcerned. He'd been fiddling with the pills, pretending to be trying to get them back in the tube and stashing the Xanax. "Seem a shame. Ernest still around, we'd have *plenty*. No tellin' what he leff behine."

Mary Byrd had been occupied with trying to drop back behind another insane truck. "What is the *matter* with truck drivers?" she'd said, thinking of Foote, hauling major ass around the country, never hitting anything, stately in his expert careenage.

Teever had replaced the tube in her bag and settled back. "They jus' like everybody else. Trying to get where they goin' fast as they can." He sighed. "Man, I feel better already."

Teever's foot had been scary when she saw it this morning. It didn't look infected and he felt fine, but he needed stitches and antibiotics. Mary Byrd decided she would make him see a doctor the next day. He'd said it had been much worse but he'd gone to the Mexicans and one of them had doctored on it and it was going to be fine. That could be the truth, or not. They'd been in such a rush to get off to Wallett, and she hadn't wanted to get too close a look, but she'd made him come in the kitchen and take off the nasty bandage and poured peroxide over it, even though Big William had scorned peroxide ("It's just water with bubbles," he'd said).Then she'd made him squeeze in half a tube of Neosporin and she'd given him a fresh Light Days maxi pad and adhesive tape and made him tape it on whether he liked it or not. She'd retrieved Charles's old pair of Bruzzi Boots; Mary Byrd's father sent everyone a new pair every few years. The size twelves could accommodate Teever's short, flat feet even with the bandage. It would be fine for the funeral; in messy winter weather country guys always wore boots, even with tuxes. Teever had been happy about the boots and looked the part of the Delta planter. Meanwhile the Quarter Pounder had stolen the disgusting alleged Mexican bandage and had been gnawing on it in the dining room. What was the matter with *dogs*, she'd thought, changing lanes again to avoid a large, blackened roadkill loaf.

A FEW PEOPLE, even later than Teever and Mary Byrd, had continued to file into the church. The choir lady had stopped singing, but the keyboardist played on. Let's get this show on the road, Mary Byrd said to herself with a sigh. She was exhausted from the Richmond trip and knew she had no business coming to Wallett. But she also felt strangely energized and buoyant in a way that was so unfamiliar. To have gone to Richmond, done what she'd done, and heard what she'd heard was such a relief. She felt a mix of feelings: liberated, but a tiny part of her was sad to have to let go of the comfortable guilt that was so much a part of her and such a convenient excuse for so many things. And in a lesser way, the news of Ernest's sad death was the reverse: her heart had broken a little and she knew she'd miss him, and maybe awfully. Their silly, unsettling attraction for each other was erased. There had been no crimes, not really, and now no footprints remained on the slippery slope she'd walked. Mary Byrd realized that into the ground

with Ernest she could dump a whole lot of the shit that had
been weighing her down. She knew Ernest would be happy to
take it all with him, even the stuff that had nothing to do with
him, like her guilt about Stevie. She could hear Ernest saying,
"Baby, just put it all on me. I can handle it. Where *I'm* going, I
can just chunk it all on the bonfire."

There would be more Richmond crap to deal with; Mary
Byrd knew that. Linda Fyce had her beady eyes on the prize.
She'd put something out there. More people might bother
them or want to talk to them. But they didn't *have* to talk to
anybody anymore. Zepf, the murdering, child-molesting
asshole, was safely behind bars, and it was clear that Stith was
going to try to keep him there. Ned Tuttle wasn't guilty after
all, and he wasn't coming after anybody. How different would
life be if the murder had been solved in 1966? Maybe Pop
wouldn't have frozen her out. Maybe he wouldn't have had a
heart attack and James and Pete would have had a father.
Maybe she wouldn't have had nightmares all these years. She
wouldn't have felt like a complicitous, white-trash slut. She
imagined Eliza in her place; she'd sheltered Eliza and Will in
ridiculous ways. Their lives were so stable and innocent. There
was still what had happened and her heart hurt so much for
Stevie, and for all the other boys and their families. And for
Tuttle—pitiful, dorky thing—and his family. Mary Byrd
understood how even Zepf himself was a victim; no doubt
some sort of unlucky and terrible circumstances had occurred
in his life to cause him to become a victim of his own monstrous
and uncontrollable urges. She felt her eyes sting with stupid
tears and she had to cough back what she thought might be
some gross noise rising in her throat. Teever looked over at
her and awkwardly pawed her shoulder. He would be thinking she was choking up over Ernest, which was fine; but there
was really no point in crying over Ernest, who'd courted

disaster as if it were one of his women, and had clowned around with death every day of his crazy life.

Teever tried some Richard Pryor—"Eulogy"—to comfort her, leaning over and whispering, "And it seems that death was quite a surprise to his ass," but she didn't get it. One thing Mary Byrd was grateful for: she'd learned early that this is the way the world works, randomly and chaotically, with billions and trillions of stories overlapping and colliding and entangling so that one could never feel that one's own story was one's own. Everything that happened was like a stone thrown in a pond, rippling out, or an earthquake causing distant tsunamis. There was no black and white, yours and mine, almost no good or bad. But who threw the stones and heaved up the earth? Pssh, she'd exhaled, dismissing the lame, Zennish drift of her thoughts. Was she having an acid flashback or something? If there *was* a god, he was a player and a cruel asshole. A real trickster dickhead. Someone who, if he'd been in your fraternity, you'd have hated. God may work in mysterious ways, she reflected, but a lot of those ways suck.

As if in punishment for this thought, there was a loud, feedback buzz from the keyboard at the front of the church. Mary Byrd jumped, and Teever looked at her and laughed silently, his tweedy shoulders heaving. The service got under way at last, although the little church was only about a third full. There were lots of empty rows between the congregation and the back-row rat pack who were Ernest's buddies. That included Teever and Mary Byrd, she supposed, although they sat on the other side of the aisle from the posse. As the keyboard guy played a hymn (Mary Byrd knew she wouldn't know most of the Protestant songs), Ernest's family straggled in to take their seats in the front pews. There were Ernest's two aunts, or grandmothers or whoever they were. A tall, skinny one who looked nervous, and like she might be smelling something bad, and a short, plump one who looked placid and composed, but sad. Uncle Pothus came last, an old colonely-looking guy in a suit with a bow tie, a neat white beard, and longish white hair. He looked somewhat out of place in this crowd, like Ernest would have. Or did: Mary Byrd could see that in the coffin he was similarly decked out. The uncle limped a little—she remembered that Ernest said he had the jake leg—and was visibly, but not, thank you Jesus, audibly, weeping.

Mary Byrd knew Ernest didn't have a mother and did have a father, but who knew where he was. Ernest had never met him but knew his face from pictures. He'd seen him at the casinos a couple of times over the years. His father didn't know him, but Ernest told Mary Byrd he didn't care. Could any man not care about having a father? That was it for family, except for the aunts and uncle. How weird it must have been to have grown up around nobody but adults. No wonder Ernest did whatever he pleased and expected to get what he wanted. Spoiled, orphaned only child. That's probably where he'd gotten spending money, too, from the relatives. He always had plenty, but to Mary Byrd's knowledge he'd never worked. He'd always said he had "oil rights" from some family property in south Mississippi, Lux or Sumrall or somewhere.

The funeral proceeded slowly. There was more hymn-singing and scratchy tapes of certain of Ernest's favorite songs—"To Live Is to Fly," "No Expectations," "Tom Ames' Prayer," the Neckbones' "Cardiac Suture," "Free Again," and "Lawyers, Guns and Money"—which caused Mary Byrd and Teever to nudge each other, amazed that the old ladies had been okay with having that stuff played. Surely they wouldn't play "Jack on Fire," Ernest's anthem, which had some really bad lines. Then, a raw, lovely song by somebody, or some group—she couldn't remember the name but it had "nails" in it—a song that Mary

Byrd recognized because she'd heard it coming from Eliza's room, and it had been so haunting—*my empire of dirt*—that she'd stopped in her tracks outside Eliza's door to listen to it. She'd had to take the tape away from Eliza because the next song had been about somebody's big gun or big dick rubbing on someone's face. Then the jam box played Jim Mize's crusty love song "Drunk Moon Falling" and "Simple Man," which Mary Byrd was surprised about because Ernest had thought Skynyrd was *déclassé*, and Green Day's "When I Come Around," which probably meant he'd recently been messing with some coed, but she didn't see any likely suspects in the small crowd. An annoyed, weary-looking preacher had given a sermon, claiming that they'd all come to "celebrate the life of John Pothus Ernest," but his message had been a sad spiel of resignation about the fact that even if you'd started life as a good boy, a great baseball player and turkey hunter, and a good student, as Jacky-boy Ernest had once been, if you *strayed from the flock,* you were bound to come to an end like his, because of *God's plan.* Hardly a celebration. Ernest's life *was* the celebration! And as if they *all* weren't ending up in a box or an urn no matter how much drinking they did or didn't do, how many other people's spouses they fucked, or Sundays they didn't show up in church. It seemed ... un-Christian to Mary Byrd, and unfair because Ernest wasn't there to defend himself, and if *she'd* been Ernest's kin, she would have prayed for a bloody flux to be visited upon the preacher. No one in the church seemed to mind, though, so maybe they all agreed.

She glanced across at the rat pack pew but none of them seemed perturbed, either. They were either dozing, drunk, or daydreaming about their next drink. She recognized some of these guys from around town. They'd told Teever and Mary Byrd they were having a huge wake for Ernest that night back in town, where "a virgin will be sacrificed, except that we can't find one."

The jam box played Handel's "Sarabande," which Mary Byrd knew Ernest had thought to be the most beautiful song in the whole world ever since he'd heard the Chieftains' version in one of his top five movies, *Barry Lyndon*. Who'd put together this mix tape? she wondered. Probably Ernest himself, before he'd gone off to Bosnia, half-hoping to be blown to smithereens and martyrized forever. She'd started on her own funeral playlist on the plane, with her will. We're all so stuck on ourselves.

The flight back from Richmond, once she'd made up her mind to do it, had gone well. True, she'd had a Bloody Mary and a yellow crumb of Valium, but still. Waiting to board the plane, she saw something you often saw on flights to or from Memphis; a little kid, one with a bald blue head sitting on his or her mother's sweat-suited lap. A soccer-mom pietà, no doubt on their way to one of the children's hospitals. What right did Mary Byrd have to be fearful about her own selfish self taking a simple plane ride? She resolved to get a grip. Mann had called her at her mother's with the bad news about Ernest, so death was even more on her mind, if that was possible. As the plane had climbed on takeoff over the city, she thought she could make out Monument Row— Jeb, Jeff, Stonewall, Bobby Lee—and the construction site where the new Arthur Ashe statue would soon stand facing his stadium. Look away, poor Arthur: you showed us, didn't you? And somewhere below—they passed over Appomattox, the last dead boys, and the justly inevitable surrender, where, she recalled, Grant had sadly regretted his grungy uniform facing the impeccable and impassive Lee. It wouldn't have surprised Mary Byrd if the plane had crashed, but at least she hadn't felt absolutely positive that it would. Instead of putting herself in a coma as she usually would have, she'd stayed awake and used her captivity in the hurtling Delta tin can constructively. On her barf bag she'd jotted down a short will, which gave her a sense of control although of course if she went down, the will would go with her. But if she had to be thinking so much about death, she might as well put the preoccupation to work.

FINAL INSTRUCTIONS FOR ME

1. Bury or cremate—whatever's cheapest. Make absolutely sure I'm really dead before you do anything. If you bury me (don't send me to Richmond) pls get Don D to build me a plain pine box, or bury me in the trunk Liddie gave us that we use for the coffee table, unless someone wants it. (Coffintable! Hahaha.) If no room in your family plot, put me in the black section on the hill where the old cedars are. If that's OK with them. If cremated, throw ashes into my zinnia bed or get one of my bros to dump some in the Ches. Bay where we used to go, or Mann could scatter a pinch in the KGB Bar in NY. Pablo could make a ceramic headstone. A little music would be good—maybe Lucy would play a little. If you or the children want a poem or something, fine. No speakers!

2. No visitation, church, or preacher. Graveside only. Must have a bouncer with a list—no assholes dancing on my grave. You and Mann and Lucy know who I mean.

3. Wish people wouldn't send flowers unless from their yards, better to donate to Humane Soc, St. Jude or Cntr for Missing & Exploited Children. If winter some cedar with blue berries and magnolia leaves is fine. Pls plant me a little cedar or a dogwood—the old ones in cem. probably clobbered in storm.

4. Give something from my jewelry to cousins Kathy and Susan, Lucy, and Mann and whatever my bros want—I don't know what. Eliza can help.

5. If there's a wake at the Bear, play all my favorites! (As much Everly and Neville Bros. as you can stand.)
6. Don't dance on my grave, either, Chaz! If I die doing something stupid or bad, try to forgive me, and don't let E &W hate me. Luvyabye! Mary Byrd D'Abruzzi Thornton, from somewhere in the sky with barf bags.

Mary Byrd slipped a hand in her purse to feel the folded bag still tucked there as Ernest's sad little family trio and cousins trudged up to the coffin to touch him a last time. Pothus worked something into Ernest's jacket pocket, and spoke out in a quavery voice, "We had us some fine times, didn't we Jacky-boy? I'm going to be missing you like front teeth, yes sir, I will." He cried softly and the aunt ladies tended him. Others began filing by the coffin. He was loved. It was nice to know that.

Mary Byrd whispered to Teever, "What do you think his uncle gave him?"

Teever whispered back, rubbing his thumb and fingertips together, "Foldin' money. Wish I had somethin' to put in there, too. Crown, Marlboro, *somethin'*."

Mary Byrd kept quiet but thought to herself that what she'd have put in, knowing the one thing that Ernest would want from her, would be her underwear. Preferably worn.

Teever rose suddenly from the pew and limped up the aisle to the casket. He brought something out of his pocket and put it in the coffin. When he returned, Mary Byrd cocked her head and widened her eyes.

"You don't got to know everything, Mudbird," he said. "He was some dude, whatever he was. I'm not gone see nobody like that again."

She would miss Ernest. The world wasn't a better place because of him, but it sure had been more interesting. I should have slept with him, she thought. Who would have been hurt? Where did scruples get you? He was the fuck not taken.

Mary Byrd and Teever sat a little longer, listening to Al Green sing "Amazing Grace" and watching people cluster up around Ernest's kin. That would be the right thing to do, to go up there and speak to the family, but she wasn't going to. She wasn't going to get that close to the body, and she just wasn't going to anyway, for a million reasons.

There was no point in trying not to think of Stevie's funeral—his tragic little self was so much on her mind—so Mary Byrd let herself go there. She didn't think she'd ever, over all these years, tried to remember it, and she didn't remember much.

It had been a lovely May day. The sun had been shining warmly but she had shivered, and had drawn a deep breath to will her teeth to stop chattering. She had been sick with the fear that it would be raining and they'd have to bury Stevie in the mud and that would make everyone even madder with grief. How did they get to the funeral home? What did she wear? She had no idea, although she thought it would have been important to her at the time. Or maybe not. The babies hadn't gone, but she wished they had because they'd have given her something real to focus on.

Across the parking lot of the funeral home they'd seen the trucks from the local TV stations. The cameramen had kept a respectful distance but Pop hadn't cared anyway; he had looked as if he'd never care about anything again. He was taking tons of sedatives and Angelo and her mother had walked with him. Of the service, all she could remember was that the sight of the small white coffin had made her want to cry, but she wouldn't. She'd shrunk away from her family on the pew. Her mother had cleaved to her stepfather, and Nick had sat fidgeting and craning his neck around, trying to make eye contact with their cousins. At the grave, Mary Byrd had taken off her glasses so that, sitting behind her parents, she wouldn't see the hopeless, gaping finality of the half-size hole so clearly, or Pop's face, or the faces of her friends and teachers, and Stevie's classmates and teachers from Longwood Elementary and so many others spread way up behind them on the hill. Was the boyfriend there? She hadn't cared.

The boy cousins had been horsing around inappropriately, so they'd been dismissed by the adults. They all had walked to Doc's for cherry Cokes and candy bars. Neither children nor boys, Mary Byrd and her cousin Kathy had drifted along with the rest of the pack, Kath holding her hand and watching her anxiously. She wasn't going to cry and she didn't want to talk, she just wanted to be somewhere, anywhere, else. At Doc's, the boys had broken down in a hysterical, choking giggle fit over nothing, or the usual joking about the Kotex and douche bags in the "ladies' products" aisle, drawing shocked stares from adults in the store who all knew who they were. Mary Byrd had frozen at one point, thinking she saw Tuttle watching them, peering through the soaps and shampoos in another aisle, but the round moon face had instantly disappeared. How could he be walking around freely, she'd wondered, eating Mars Bars and reading comic books and hanging around as if nothing had happened? Was it even him? Nothing was real anymore. She'd been scared and had hurried back home.

After Stevie's funeral, their house had been horridly empty, and she and her mother had watched the evening news. There they were on TV. She had been shocked, she recalled, at how unrecognizable and diminished her family had looked without the three littlest boys. Small, hunched, and only the four of them. Her overweight stepfather had seemed to have lost a hundred pounds in the few days since Stevie had died. The notion that she was never really going to have a warm and safe place in the family, or even in the world, had come over Mary Byrd like ice settling into her stomach and chest and bones.

THE JAM BOX stopped and Ernest's family and the church people began moving out to the cold hole where he'd be buried in the deep, red clay. In her head Mary Byrd took the memory of Stevie's funeral as if it were a bad page of writing off a yellow legal pad, wadded it up, and lobbed it at Ernest's coffin. The throw was high, but Ernest reached up from the casket and snagged it with one hand, the hand with the diamond signet ring he was so proud of. He winked at her with his right eye, and she blew him a very small kiss with her middle finger. Pallbearers rose, closing and then lifting Ernest's coffin, and shambled slowly out the door.

The fat lady began singing,

> What have I to dread, what have I to fear,
> Leaning on the everlasting arms?
> I have blessed peace with my Lord so near
> Leaning, leaning, safe and secure from all alarms
> Leaning, leaning, leaning on the everlasting arms

Mary Byrd's heart began thudding and her breathing quickened and she turned to Teever, clutching his arm. "Teever! I'm so, so sad!" she said desperately.

Startled, Teever looked hard into her distraught face for a moment before saying, "It gone be okay, Mudbird. He in a better place now. Like that lady jus' sung: he got blessed peace and he safe and secure. Don't somebody in the Bible say, 'Weep not?'" Teever stood. "I'm gone get a smoke off them guys. It gone be okay, you hear? This life ain't nothin' but a bale of tears." He lurched across the aisle to the posse. "Wassup, spleen? Got a smoke?" she heard him rasp to one of the guys as they slouched out.

One of the goofballs sighed, "Zed's dead, baby. Zed's dead."

Still breathing hard, Mary Byrd watched the men troop

outside. The church was empty. She felt powerless to move. She was overcome by a frightful, suffocating urge like a ferocious sneeze or a terrible cough that could not be suppressed and she began weeping big heaving sobs and gushing tears. Head in her lap, she wept and wept, a bale of tears, full-on blubbering like there was no tomorrow. Or like there was.

THE DRIVE BACK from Wallett on I-55 was way too long and more boring than the ride down, when for the first half hour or so they had had all the storm damage to see.

Going back, the day had cleared, the clouds opening up to reveal one of those glorious Mississippi winter sunsets, which seemed an appropriate ending to the day and to Jack Ernest's time on the planet. It would be hard, Mary Byrd and Teever both knew, to not be expecting to see Ernest up at the Bear, or at the late-nights, or skulking around on the periphery of some literary event. Even if you didn't see Ernest that often, it was comforting, somehow, to know he was out there, the antidote to too much wholesomeness and small-town charm and polite society. Their dark sides were important and Ernest had nourished that.

Mary Byrd found herself in a strange place. Now the world seemed lighter—still fragile and land-mined with the unexpected, but there seemed now to be more space, more navigable paths to choose, and more fortitude for any obstacles or skirmishes or forays ahead. But she newly grieved, or re-grieved, for her lost stepbrother—her *brother*—and for what he'd endured, small and alone, terrified, in pain and drowning in his own blood. That would always be with her, with all of them, and she knew it would continue in their lives in ways they couldn't yet imagine. It was like the jagged little bit of grit that got into an oyster and no matter how much the nacre of time smoothed it over, it was still going to be there—a pearl of pain. Now what had happened at last had a definite face and name, and it had nothing to do with her.

It dawned on her that if her mother had ever known about the nonsense about her leading poor Tuttle on, she would certainly have said so, her mom being her mom. Why hadn't this ever occurred to her before? Why had she clung to that guilt?

If Stith was to be believed, her family was going to have a chance to strike back. But Mary Byrd found it hard to accept that she also grieved for Zepf, another ruined life, and for everybody, for the whole world, which was a place where people did unspeakable things to each other, for reasons that must be a part of whatever it is that makes humans human, but not necessarily humane. Was the real difference between humans and other animals that humans gassed each other and butchered each other or forced sex on each other for reasons other than survival? What a world, what a world.

"*Wooo*," she twitched her shoulders. *Basta*. Time to lighten up. She exhaled loudly. "I'm glad that's . . . behind us."

"Me too," Teever said. "What we gone do now, Mudbird?" She knew he meant without Ernest.

"Man, I don't know," she said. "But I can tell you a lot of things we're *not* going to be doing now," she said wryly. "Did you score any smokes from those guys?"

"Jus' that one. Sorry," Teever shook his head. "I *had* a carton last night," he lied. "Mexicans cleaned me out. Need to quit, anyway. Clean up my act."

"Are you serious, Teever?" She thought he wasn't, but he did have that cough, and maybe even he was worried about it. She hoped it wasn't contagious. TB cooties would be pinballing around in the car right now. "You're going to quit smoking and drinking and stuff?"

"Aw, hell no, Mudbird. Jus' kiddin'. I'm gone always be a kind of a wretch," he said. He should have kept his mouth shut. If he said he wasn't going to straighten up, they'd all be amazed when he *did*. No point in jumping the gun. He wanted to feel the rush of resolve he'd had that night around the bonfire, but daylight always had a way of sapping things, stealing your nature, like you were a vampire. "I might *never* get found," he said to Mary Byrd, wondering if he could get the good feeling back.

The light was nearly gone. Teever squinted, focusing his eyes on the horizon beyond a vast soybean field.

"Hola!" he suddenly yelled, thinking he saw that unearthly green flash as the fiery disk of sun disappeared. "Thought I saw somethin'. N'mind." But the flash, or flashback, gave him a surge of confidence and well-being. "I do got options."

Ignoring what seemed just another Teever non sequitur, Mary Byrd asked him, "Where do you think Ernest is?"

"He somewhere," Teever said.

"Yeah, but like *where?*"

"Don't know." He thought a second. "But I do know that there's things folks aren't spozed to know 'til they *need* to know 'em."

"You think?"

"I *know*. We all knew how things gone turn out, where we gone end up, wouldn't be nothin' to keep people from acting the fool twenty-four twenty-four."

Mary Byrd laughed. "Isn't that what we do anyway?"

"It would be way, way more worser," he said. "Trust me."

"For some stupid reason," she said. "I pretty much do."

They drove on in the interstate gloam, not talking, finally exiting onto the last annoying stretch of two-lane between Batesville and their town, where new faux chateaux vied for highway frontage with double-wides, Tool Central, Toyota, the Eureka True

Vine Church, and 1950s pretend Taras that made the 1980s pretend Taras almost look good in comparison. Once this had all been the beautiful old Riverdale Cattle Ranch, where velvety Limousin cows had stood posing in the emerald fields as if it were Barbizon and they were waiting for Millet to paint them.

Mary Byrd wanted to take advantage of Teever's thoughtful, sober mood. It almost never happened. She wanted him to talk seriously about himself, but something told her that his private life was maybe one of those things that he thought "folks aren't spozed to know."

Instead she asked, "Well, what about Rod's funeral? Did his family have trouble getting down here because of the storm?"

"What you *think*, Mudbird?" Teever said. "You dumber'n a box a mud. Course they had trouble—folks got to drive from way up north. You think everybody got the money to fly around like you and Charles? "

"Take it easy," said Mary Byrd. "I didn't mean it like that." She felt dumb and white. "But what about Angie? What's going to happen with her, do you think?"

"Hard to say. Hard to say. She do *not* need to be in no jail in Memphis, I know that."

"Yeah, I know. I hope Evagreen and L. Q. are okay. And Rod's parents. Jesus."

"Not *ever* gone be okay for them," Teever said. "No way." He coughed wetly into his tweed sleeve. "But I got a feeling *something* gone happen with Angie."

"What do you mean by *something*? Something good or bad?"

"Don't know, Mudbird. *Something*. Like I say, there's shit we ain't spozed to know. Sometimes, hard to tell when a thing be good and when it be bad." He shrugged.

"Ha," she said sarcastically. "Where's all this coming from? You channeling the Dalai Lama or something?"

"Who she? I'll channel her anytime," Teever said, allowing Mary Byrd a second to look over at him to see if he was serious. She couldn't tell. "No way—I'm channeling the *Tolliver* Lama, Mudbird."

"Sounds to me like you're channeling Amos, or Andy." So much for serious.

He shrugged again. "Shit happens. Maybe up to us to make it turn out one way or the other."

"I don't see how any of Angie's mess could turn out good for anybody. It's so awful. Think about Desia, her little girl."

"Maybe so," he said, heaving a sigh that rattled his throat but didn't catch. "Why you asking all these questions, anyhow? Can't we just drive in peace?"

"Okay then," she mocked him. It made no sense at all, she thought. Someone like Zepf, who'd killed and molested at least one innocent child, might be released from prison, and somebody like Angie, who'd been pushed over some dreadful edge and killed her husband in self-defense, would remain in prison for who knew how long. Was it possible that Angie could get the death sentence? Mary Byrd's shoulders hunched in disgust. She reached for the radio buttons. "It's time for NPR. Let's just listen to that."

"Not them people with them crazy names—Carl Kasell, Korva Coleman, Calvin Cockamamie."

"I love NPR."

"Zo listen to that stuff all day down to the Iko Theater. Them two dudes talk about cars—white folks' nice cars, like yours. Puh. Don't know shit. Need to put some black guys, some Mexicans, on that show, talk about some *real* cars and car problems."

"Well, I'm sure as hell not having *that* kind of conversation now. Why are you being so cranky?" Mary Byrd poked the buttons until she found WEVL out of Memphis, which they could just barely tune in. This was as crazy as driving with Foote.

The deejay's voice shouted from the dashboard, "Okay, people, some funky stuff comin' at you, take us back to nineteen fifty-seven. Don't be afraid, don't be afraid, but if you don't like the racy stuff, now is the time to *spin your dial*. Here's Andre Williams doin' his signature song, 'Jail Bait.'"

"Okay, here's my attempt at racial reconciliation," Mary Byrd laughed.

Teever perked up. "Oowee, I have not heard this song in *too* long. And this not his best song. There's one that's *too* nasty; everbody knows it. Cain't even say it front of a lady. You a lady, Mudbird?" He laughed.

"Shut up, Teever," she said. "Okay, we'll listen to this so we can have racial harmony in this car. Where's *your* attempt to reconcile?"

"Mudbird, I would only be *too* happy to let you get to know the pleasure of a black man's company, you know, *personally*," he said, grinning. "*Too* happy. There my attempt to reconciliate."

Mary Byrd laughed. "That's *another* conversation we're not having. You never give up, do you?"

"No ma'am, I never do," he said. "Not Teever. No way."

At least he never played the race card like some of those guys did out at Junior's juke joint—trying to guilt-trip the little white coeds, who were so pleased with themselves for being adventurous enough to be in a black club, into dancing with them: "Oh, you jus' don't wanna dance with a *black man*."

"I don't give up on *nuthin'*," he said, "no way, no way, no way."

Fourteen

THEIR RAMSHACKLE—THAT WORD was never going to be the same for Mary Byrd—old house was inviting and a comfort to return to after Ernest's funeral. Warm, relaxed, full of people and dogs and cats and lower forms of life scuttling through the big rooms, requiring Homer, the vigilant Orkin man, to visit every other month. The ice storm had knocked the power, plumbing, and phone out for a few days, and Eliza and William had hauled ice to melt to flush the toilets and had enjoyed themselves until they began jonesing for TV. Their old gas Chambers stove had become a sort of communal hearth for the mostly electric neighborhood and people had come in and out to make coffee or heat their suppers. Now things had gotten more or less back to normal, except for mud and the thick spatters of wax on the rugs.

When she'd gotten home from Richmond the night before in her stale suit, she'd peeled it off and gone straight to bed. In the morning she'd only had time to doctor on Teever's foot, empty the fridge and freezer of ruined, smelly food, and zip herself into a short but demure tweed skirt before taking off again with Teever for Ernest's funeral. There would have to be a big cleanup day tomorrow, a Thursday without poor Evagreen. She needed to remember to get Evagreen's checks to her as long as she needed to be gone. Was it time for Evagreen to retire?

She and Charles had not really had a chance to talk at all about the events of the past few days. Although Mary Byrd knew they could easily never get around to discussing any of it and could just pick up where they had left off, as if nothing unusual had been going on. That would be absolutely okay with Charles, and very near okay with her. She was talked out.

Charles for some reason had ignored her chili but had kept some stuff cold outside so it was still good, she hoped. Now he had a garlic omelet ready for her, which was one of the four things he cooked really well, the others involving flames, sizzling skillets, or a powerful blender. He liked his omelets runny inside, though, and Mary Byrd didn't, so she did what she always did: scraped out the runny stuff into a pool on the side of her plate and ate the rest. When Charles wasn't looking, she'd let the puppies lick her plate. Charles could not bear for the animals, especially the cats, to use people dishes but would occasionally give the Pounder or Puppy Sal a bite of steak or offer them a nub of fat right off his own fork. It was something about the cat's *fur licking* that especially disturbed him.

Mary Byrd looked down at the floor, where Iggy the fat little cow milled around, hoping for treats. He sniffed at her shoes— her favorite Charles Jourdan pumps with the Pilgrim buckles that were now ruined, crusted with thick red Mississippi clay from standing at Ernest's graveside, sniffling and drying her eyes with one of Liddie's old lace hankies, firmly stuck to the earth.

"Well, Iggy, these have about had it, don't you think?" She kicked them off, a few small clods falling away, which Iggy investigated as well.

"Wow, I'm so exhausted. Aren't you?"

Charles poured her a little more wine. "Nah. It was actually kind of fun. Life on the frontier. Reading by candlelight. No TV. Melting ice to flush the commodes. I think the boys might have sneaked out one night, according to the Dukes, but I didn't say anything to William—how could they resist?"

She was too tired to register alarm or be pissed. "I guess that's why there's wet spots, mud, and wax everywhere."

"Yeah, Eliza and William were flailing candles around before I put some in the bathrooms for them," he said. "There's probably some pee on the floor, too. William can't aim in the dark."

"William can't aim, period," she said. "Gee, I'm really sorry I missed all the fun," she said, rolling her eyes. "*Not*."

Charles wore his old Washington and Lee sweatshirt and pajama bottoms, which was something of a departure. Normally he stayed in his street clothes until he went to bed. He seemed relaxed and happy, she was surprised to notice, having expected him to be annoyed with her because he'd had to deal with things while she was gone, and because she'd gone to the funeral. Usually, Charles was never around when stuff went wrong. The storm had been good for him, although she felt slightly slighted whenever the three of them were able to get along fine without her. It was funny that Charles seemed to do well in her absence, when the opposite felt true for her. But in the long run, she told herself, things would go down fast without her. Dogs' and cats' accidents would go undetected and would accumulate, tape and scissors and tools and kitchen things would become misplaced or lost, dark and white laundry would be mixed together and the whites would become dingy or pink and the darks would have bleached spots. No, if she died, or she was gone, Evagreen would take over and the house would be more efficient and organized and cleaner than ever. They'd all be better off, probably, except the animals, which Evagreen would dispatch immediately. They'd even eat better—all Evagreen's fried chicken and catfish and *real* mac and cheese and chess pies and meatloaf that they loved, on the rare occasions when Evagreen cooked for them. It bothered her a little to realize that she couldn't do without Eliza and William, and probably Charles, even if they could do without her.

Charles poured himself a little more Maker's. "What's wrong? I mean, besides the obvious. You look miserable," he asked.

"Oh, I'm not," she said, straightening up and smiling. "Just so tired. The funeral was nice, actually, super country, with great music. And things went all right in Richmond. There was a little weirdness with Mama. Of course. I'm too wasted to go through all the details tonight. They've found the right guy, a totally different guy, and they just have to prove it somehow, which won't be easy since they—get this—*lost the evidence*, and they've got to bring him to trial or at least keep him in jail by civil commitment, whatever that is, or he could be free again this summer. That's why they're in such a hurry."

"Jesus! I don't get that—how could they *lose* the evidence?"

"Oh, it's *way* worse than that," she said. "I'll show you this detective's report tomorrow. It's so fucked up, you couldn't even make it up. But it's going to be . . . over. We *think*."

"God, I hope so. What a mess. Do you want a nightcap? Maker's?"

"Okay," she said. "What about Wiggs? How did that end up going?"

"He was fine," Charles said. "After he got back to Memphis and settled down a little, and figured out that his nose wasn't broken. I'm going up to pull the prints, and we'll probably do the show in May." He poured a finger of whiskey into her wine glass and raised his.

"Chaz! That's great!" She leaned up and clanked glasses with him. Whew, she thought. At least she hadn't screwed that up.

They sat silently for a minute. Mary Byrd heard water rushing in the pipes upstairs. One of the children flushing. She wanted badly to see them. They didn't know she was back, or they would have come downstairs, or maybe they didn't want to hear whatever she had to tell them about her trip. Or maybe they were miffed that she'd gone off to Wallett.

She finished off the last of her omelet. She could have eaten another one, she'd been so hungry. "Did you go to Rod's funeral?" she asked.

"Of course I did. They somehow got all their people down here from Gary and Chicago by Monday, in spite of the storm, and they went on and buried him."

"Was it okay? Did Evagreen and L. Q. go?"

"L. Q. and Ken were there, kind of in the back, but not Evagreen. I guess it was as okay as it could be, under the circumstances. But I did get to speak to Ken, and he's got someone great to represent Angie."

"Who?" she asked. "The Mongoose?" The Mongoose was a scary and highly successful criminal lawyer in town.

"Nope," Charles laughed. "Ruby Wharton."

"Who's that?"

"She's an African-American lawyer in Memphis, married to AC Wharton, the hotshot attorney up there. They're both famous for civil rights cases, and Ruby has done some women's stuff, like she wrote one of the first laws about domestic abuse. It's kind of a brilliant move on Ken's part."

"How will they do it?" Mary Byrd asked. "Self-defense?"

"I guess." said Charles. "But I don't know."

"Wow! That's great. What about Evagreen and L. Q? They must feel so much better about it. What about Desia?"

"How *good* can they feel about it, really? I think Desia is coming to live with the Kimbros and Evagreen and L. Q., 'til it all gets figured out. Call Evagreen tomorrow." Charles extended his hands on the table before him, slapping both palms down, a signal that it was time for the conversation to be over. He took his plate to the sink.

"I told Ken a little about why you had to go to Richmond, in case they were wondering why you hadn't been by with food or something." He yawned and stretched. "I'm going to bed."

"Tell Eliza and William I'll be up in a minute," she called to his retreating back, already in the next room. He didn't answer. In the morning she would make some bread and pimiento cheese for each family. Pimiento cheese sandwiches could sustain people in a crisis. Under stress, when you weren't able to eat rich, gloppy pies and cakes and casseroles or big, heavy slabs of ham, you could always eat a nice, neat, square pimiento cheese sandwich on homemade yeast bread. Of course, Liddie had taught her this. And she'd take something for poor little Desia—a toy or some books or something.

Charles reappeared in the door. "This was in the mail slot this afternoon." He handed her a plain white envelope with MS. MARY BYRD printed on the front in Evagreen's old-school handwriting. The envelope was lumpy with more than just paper. What on earth, she wondered. "Here's the rest of the mail, and a phone message Eliza took today." He tossed a stack on the table.

Charles retreated. Mary Byrd put her plate on the floor and watched Iggy pad over. The dogs followed the cat hesitantly and Mary Byrd said sharply, "No, Iggy. Go on." Iggy reluctantly backed off and the dogs moved in, clearing the eggy plate in seconds.

She looked at the note from Eliza, written in sorority-girl handwriting: Is dotted with circles, each letter cheerfully bulbous.

MOM, A KIND OF ANNOYING LADY IN RICHMOND WANTS YOU TO CALL HER ASAP.

The number, of course, was Linda Fyce's. Mary Byrd snapped her wrist, index finger pointing at the message, and said, "Bitch, I will call you *if* and *when* I feel like it." She carefully slipped the note in the silverware drawer, hoping she'd remember where she put it. She might have some things to say.

Flipping through the few pieces of mail that had accumulated while she was gone—a surprising amount, given the storm—Mary Byrd pulled out a stout manila envelope postmarked Clarksdale.

Inside was a photograph that she recognized as Evagreen and L .Q.'s house, and a note written in an almost illegible, fountain-pen scrawl:

My dear Mary Byrd,
    Please accept this gift as an apology for my, shall we say, unfortunate behavior on a recent evening. Like M. Popeye, "I yam what I yam," don't you know. Looking forward to seeing you and Charles again soon, and to the show in early summer.
    Grazie mille,
    Edward Freeman Wiggsby

AMAZING. THE PHOTO was, of course, stunning. The Bons' small house glowed softly in a violet night sky. The porch light illuminated the huge tangle of early-blooming Carolina jessamine climbing up and over the little portico, the vines a dazzlement of canary-yellow blossoms. How had she not noticed them that unhappy night? She couldn't wait to show it to

Charles. And Eliza, who *might* be impressed enough to cut Wiggs a little slack. She'd give the photo to Evagreen and L. Q., or maybe to Ken, to remind him of home. Or to Angie, if she wasn't going to be coming back. Ugh. She didn't want to think of it. Maybe the photo wouldn't make any of them too sad. And what was this envelope from Evagreen?

She opened the envelope carefully and removed some folded tissue paper. Wrapped inside was a handful of little tan globes. Unfolding the enclosed note, she read:

I am praying for you and your family. These from our chinaberry tree. You plant them in your yard NOW, where they will get Sun, to honor your Little Brother. Who is now an angel in Heaven. Ms. Evagreen Bon.

She piled the chinaberries on the windowsill with the other tiny things. Picking up a pad of stick-it notes, she wrote PARK- ING RESERVED FOR STEVIE'S DUMP TRUCK and stuck the note beneath them, wondering how long it would be before Stith sent the truck.

Mary Byrd wanted her bed. As tired as she was, she thought she'd better check in with Mann first; he'd be worried. And curious, but that could wait. It was late, past his usual early bedtime, but she went to the phone. E-A-T C-H-I-X. It rang a couple of times and Mann picked up, saying groggily, "Hey, it's really late."

"I know. I'm sorry," she said. "But I know you were worried sick about me."

"Uh-huh," he said. She heard the inhale of a big yawn. "You okay? How was it?"

"Creepy, but fine. I'll tell you tomorrow. I'm just checking in."

"How's your family?" Mann said.

"Everyone's pretty okay. At least for now. And Ernest's funeral was . . . weird. Did the storm mess up your house at all?"

"Just a tree on the deck. No big deal. I had some hot chicken stuck in Texas, though."

"Did Foote get back okay?"

"Yeah, he's back. Oh—he said to tell you that he and Frank Booth are 'at your service.' What's that about?" Another yawn.

"Oh, god! Mann, he is so crazy! I mean, the trip was fine, but he says some insane stuff. He's kind of a homophobe, among other things."

"Yeah?" Mann said. "So who isn't? A lot of the junk he says, he's just showing out."

"Maybe. It doesn't bother you?"

"He's a good driver. He's a nice guy around me. Nicer than Wiggs, your well-educated, sophisticated friend. Anyway, I doubt Foote really cares about gays much one way or the other, but he does care about his paycheck."

"I'm exhausted. Go back to bed. Call me tomorrow."

"Sweet dreams," Mann said.

"Yeah. I hope. Luvyabye."

Heading upstairs to her children, as she passed the bookshelf where they kept assorted reference books—the French diction-ary, *The Readers' Encyclopedia,* the pill identification book. She pulled out *Mississippi Trees.* Evagreen's gesture touched her deeply, and she loved the old-fashioned dooryard trees. Chinaberry flowers smelled like her mother's favorite perfume, Fracas—rich and wonderful, but almost overpowering. People didn't seem to grow chinaberries much anymore. She knew she'd better read up on how to plant and grow them properly, or else.

Mary Byrd knocked softly at Eliza's door and opened it. Eliza was already asleep in her poofy cocoon, the mosquito net drawn around the bed, or she was pretending to be asleep, because just a few minutes earlier Mary Byrd had heard her laughing. She had the greatest ha-ha-ha laugh but they didn't hear it often these days; of course she had been on the phone with one of her friends. Mary Byrd decided to leave her daughter be; she didn't have the energy for any skirmishes. They could talk the next day.

Passing the bathroom, she saw Irene lapping at the little puddles left in the tub; probably they'd forgotten to melt some ice for the kitties while she was gone, and Irene and Iggy hated drinking dog water. Who wouldn't. Irene looked so cool and colorful. She loved how calico cats were sort of pieces of different cats patched together—a black-and-white tuxedo cat leg here, a marmalade tabby leg there. She went in to pet Irene and saw that she had what the children called "rainforest butt": leaves and twigs were tangled in the long fur around her fluffy ass. Mary Byrd tried to pull the junk off, but Irene was having none of it and jumped out of the tub and ran off. "Suit yourself, skanky-butt," she sighed.

The toilet seat was down, but there were no dribbles on it, so the flush she had heard from downstairs had most likely been Eliza. They really had to talk; she knew Eliza wanted to know, and should know, really, what had happened in Richmond, but couldn't bring herself to act interested enough to ask, and would just pump William for information in the morning. William, his father's son, would reduce all the details Mary Byrd gave him to not much more than "yes" or "no" or "I don't remember; ask Mom," which would make Eliza crazy. Maybe there'd be some one-on-one time after drama, while her daughter was captive in the car and before she picked up William from soccer. She knew Eliza would also want to know why she'd gone to "that guy's" funeral. It was a good question that Mary Byrd would give half an answer to, if she could think of something.

William's door was wide open and he was looking at a book by the beam of his bedside light, an old railroad engineer's lamp that Mary Byrd had found rummaging around in a junk shop.

"Hey!" She walked over and sat on the bed and kissed him.

"Hey."

"How is everything?" she asked. "How was the ice storm? I bet you guys did some great sledding."

He kept looking at his book. "It was pretty cool. At first we could sled, but then all the trees and branches fell down and it was scary. Mom," he added, "you don't smell that great."

"Oh, I'm sorry. Dad just made me a garlic omelet. I'll try not to breathe." She pulled the sheet over her mouth. "Dad said y'all were like pioneers, with all the electricity and water off."

"Yeah. But then it got boring with no TV and only peanut butter and soup and hot dogs. We had to eat the hot dogs on hamburger buns. And then Dad made us help pile up all the branches." Taking notice of *Mississippi Trees* in her hand, he asked, "What's that book?"

"It's that book about trees; you know, the one we used for your leaf identification project last fall," she said. "Evagreen gave me some seeds and I was going to read about how to plant them."

"I hate that book. It's boring," he said.

"Okay, Contrary. You don't have to *hate* something just because it doesn't interest you."

"What's 'contrary' mean?" he asked.

"You know, like Eliza acts: cranky. Or like how Evagreen sometimes acts. It's not exactly that they're *mean*, they're just *against* a lot of things. Like Evagreen likes things to be her way. She thinks she knows the best way to do things, and she's *contrary* if you don't agree."

William said, "You mean like Nana?"

"Exactly. It doesn't mean they don't care about you, or they're mad at you, they just like to control things and want things their way. Kind of strict, or bossy; they like to disagree with stuff."

"One time I saw Evagreen playing with my airport and my planes," William said. "I was contrary about that."

"Really? Huh." Mary Byrd thought about that for a second. "She was probably just dusting them. Or maybe she's interested in planes, too."

"She was talking to them."

"Well, remember Ken, her son? He's in the Air Force and used to fly planes. Maybe she was thinking about Ken," she said. "Why don't you ask her, maybe? When she comes back." Mary Byrd fervently and selfishly hoped that she would come back.

"She'll probably just say, 'Mind your own beeswax, Little Mister Man,' like she always does," William said. "Did Ken really fly planes? In a war?"

"Hmm, I'm not sure. I think so, for a little while, in Desert Storm."

"Did he bomb people? Or was he a spy?"

"I don't know." Jeez, William. "Ken's a really good guy, but in the military you've got to do whatever they tell you. But let's not ask Evagreen about *that*. She's got enough . . . sad stuff to think about right now."

"Spies aren't sad," he said. "And you always tell us, 'Don't be afraid to ask questions.'"

"Well, just don't, okay? Sometimes there are things that grown-ups don't like to talk about," Mary Byrd said. "There's a difference between school questions and personal ones. You could ask Daddy about Ken. He probably knows." Pass that hot potato. Why did so many things she told her children come around to bite her in the ass?

"So, what are *you* reading, Will?"

"I'm not really reading." He scrubbed his pajama sleeve across his face. "It's a book about Greek myths. We're doing them at school. It's got some cool pictures."

"Like what?" she asked, covering her mouth with her hand. "Which gods and goddesses do you like?"

"Well, *no* goddesses." He turned back a few pages. "This guy is cool."

Mary Byrd took the book and turned it around to see the picture. "Oh, Mercury. Yeah, he does look cool. What do you like about him?"

"Look," he said pointing to Mercury's feet, which had wings attached to his sandals.

"Oh, yeah, now I get it." She smiled at him behind the sheet and tried to turn the book back around, but he closed it and set it aside.

"I wish I had those. You could go anywhere, and if I didn't like something, or something bad happened, I would just fly away." William smiled a little sheepishly, knowing he might be too old to think something so fairy-taleish and impossible. "Would you like it, Mom?"

"Are you kidding? I'd *love* it," she laughed. "What kind of shoes would you have?"

He thought a second. "Remember my glow-in-the-dark, cheetah Converse high-tops that I had when I was little? Those."

Mary Byrd felt a pang. Little—he'd only outgrown those shoes a year or two earlier. "Those would be perfect." She wondered what had ever happened to Stevie's little blue PF Flyers, always untied.

"What would you have?"

"Hmm," she said, striking a thinking pose, chin on fist. "I think I'd have red Prada lizard high heels."

"What's a Prada? Is it a kind of lizard? Like a Komodo dragon?" he asked hopefully.

Laughing from behind the sheet, she said, "No! It's the name of an Italian fashion designer who makes fabulous shoes."

His little face took on a scornful look. "High heels would be dumb," he said. "You couldn't do anything fun or even *walk*."

"Hey, if I had red lizard Pradas with wings, I would *not* be walking!"

William reached over to his bedside table and picked up one of his special little planes—the Russian Seagull—parked there and began examining it carefully, as if he didn't already have every micro-millimeter of the thing memorized. Maybe, Mary Byrd thought, he didn't like the idea of his mother ever wanting to fly away, or of her having any reason to want to. Or maybe he was just waiting for her to talk about Richmond. Or maybe he was just a little eight-year-old guy, sitting in his bed with a toy, waiting for his mom to go away so he could play with it.

"Well, on second thought, I probably don't need those shoes," she said. "I'd love for *you* to be able to fly, but I think I'm just fine right here with my family in our cozy house on this dumb old earth." She brushed his stiff, tousley hair, so like Charles's, and not, she could smell, washed, back from his squinched-up forehead.

"Dumb?" he said.

"Oh, you know, dumb; like lots of times things in life are crazy, or don't make any sense." She gave him an opening. *He should bring Stevie up, not her. Was that right?*

"Are things always spozed to make sense?"

"Hmm." She thought. Which way to go now, Dr. Spock? "No, I don't think so. People *want* everything to make sense, and that's what people try to do—figure stuff out. Why things happen, what the reasons are, and how things can be fixed. We want life to be nice and neat and sometimes it's not. Sometimes it's dumb. And messy. And sad." Mary Byrd picked up one of his hands. "God, these fingernails! They are so gross. What have you been doing, William, working on an oil rig?" She pulled open the little drawer in the bedside table and rummaged around for clippers. "What's under your nails could be your next science unfair project. Hey, I hope you guys got your proposals in?"

"Yeah. I'm going to do a new kind of Humvee with more stuff to keep guys from getting blown up."

"Very cool," she said, still looking for clippers.

"Yeah. Eliza said I could use her glue gun."

"Oh, great! What's her project?"

"Something dumb about germs and lip gloss, I think."

"Huh," said Mary Byrd, finally finding what she thought were the clippers. "What is this blue gunk all over these nail clippers? Yuck."

William rose up to look. "Oh, that's the shark I made with Play-Doh. See? The clipper part is the jaws. That red stuff inside is part of a person he ate."

"Jeez, William." She picked the Play-Doh off the thing and began clipping.

William watched her. "You mean the world is messy like my fingernails?" he asked. "Like they get dirty, and we cut them, and they just get dirty and long again anyway?"

His mother laughed. "Hmm, maybe a little like that. But really I mean more like complicated-and-unhappy-messy. Like what happened with Angie."

"But that's grown-ups, right? Things for kids aren't unhappy, right? Unless you're a kid in a Nazi concentration camp."

"Well, that's the way things are *supposed* to be. That's the way grown-ups *want* things to be," she said.

William looked at her solemnly but slyly. "Not *all* grown-ups."

Okay, here it was. He was thinking about what had happened to Stevie at the hands of a grown-up. He knew nothing specific, of course, but all kids knew about sexual abuse now. Had knowing about Stevie hurt William in any way? Maybe the children should never have been told until they were older.

She sighed. "No, you're right. But *most* grown-ups want kids to be safe and happy. But that's what I mean about messy. There are always going to be people who are crazy, and they make things happen that are bad and hard to understand. Like Hitler, right? Sometimes there aren't any answers about why bad things happen." She was practically quoting Teever.

Now his eyes looked directly into hers. "What if something bad happens to me?"

Her heart thumped hard inside her chest. It was awful for a child his age to have this fear. "Oh, darling, it won't." She put her arms around him. "If you're thinking about Stevie or something you saw on TV, those things almost never happen." She'd give anything to say, "*never, ever.*" She thought of Freddy Brickle's parents lying to him about Zepf's ridiculous sentence. "There's a bigger chance of you being run over by a school bus driven by chimps than of those things happening to you." Probably not true, but they laughed. It's a hard line to walk with a child, she thought, that line between truth and comfort. They so easily saw through the comfort. "And Stevie made a mistake. He talked to a stranger, and you know better than to do that, right?" The nail clipping resumed matter-of-factly. "You should be more worried about getting the Ebola virus from what's under your nails."

"That would be cool because then my eyes would bleed."

"Yeah, very cool. Ha."

"So if Mrs. Barnes comes in our classroom and asks me a multiplication and I can't think of the answer, can I say, 'stuff in life doesn't always have answers'?" He grinned. Braces were in his future, she noticed for the first time. She'd let him keep his passy too long.

"Uh-huh. Go ahead—try it." Children called Mrs. Barnes a math terrorist because as principal, she cruised the classrooms and the cafeteria, randomly demanding answers to multiplication tables. If you didn't know, you got After-School. Somehow she was related to Evagreen, but Mary Byrd wasn't sure how. "But you get what I was trying to say, don't you, Will?"

"Yeah." Raising the plane into the air, he buzzed her face a little too close, maybe not accidentally.

"Hey!" she protested. "Do you want a one-eyed mother?"

"Cyclops," he said. "Are you sad about Stevie?"

"Of course. But not like I was. You sort of . . ." she paused. ". . . get used to the sadness. That was a really long time ago."

He was zooming the plane around, avoiding looking interested. "What was he like?"

What *had* he really been like? she wondered. What kid stops to think about what his or her brothers or sisters are *like*? "Oh, he was regular. A pain in the booty for his sister, but sweet," she told her son. "He came to live with us when he was practically still a baby, and he was cute, with blond hair and blue eyes and freckles, and Uncle Nick and I were really excited about having a new brother. When he got older, he was really funny. He loved goofy jokes. He liked sports. And he was crazy about trucks the way you're crazy about planes and tanks." It occurred to her she might not want William to have Stevie's little dump truck, or that *he* might not want it.

"Did y'all torture each other, like Eliza and I do?"

She had to laugh and say honestly, "Of course. I was really too old to be doing it, but Nick and I loved to scare him." A slight breeze of regret chilled her for a second. "You know—we did Halloween kind of stuff, like putting scary masks in his closet, or sneaking up behind him when he was watching *The*

"Hmph." He landed the little plane and picked up his book again.

Mary Byrd leaned over and kissed him. "Three more pages and lights out." She walked to the door and said, "Love you, Air Force Captain William Thornton," keeping it breezy.

"Okay," he said, covering his face with his book. "Love you, too, Cyclops Mother." She left his door open a cat's width, the way he liked it.

As Mary Byrd headed to the stairs, she felt, for a minute, a little of the old, pointless sadness that seemed to be part of her, like her bones or blood. The world was not a great or easy place and it was stupid and pathetic to think that it was. But she also felt oddly high, as if she'd had a Xanax; had she? No, she remembered that the last Xanax had gone with Ernest. Teever hadn't fooled her. She was thinking that what goodness and happiness and rightness there was could be claimed, but you had to work hard at finding it and hanging onto it. She wanted her children to know reality, up to a point, but she didn't want them living darkly or fearfully. For too long she'd let her own self get distracted by guilt and fear. Some measure of that seemed lifted from her. Oh, there would always be plenty of crap to feel guilty about. Making good sport, speaking lewdly, committing uncleanness. Drinking, smoking, pills. Leaving dishes in the sink for Evagreen. Lies. And plenty to be scared about: second-story fires. The New Madrid fault. Hurricanes and tornadoes. Mini-strokes and colon cancer. Cooties of all kinds. Her mother. But fuck all that. The old dumb earth could tilt and spin all around her but she was really going to try not to fly off her own personal axis. She just plain felt better, in spite of everything. She hoped it would continue.

On the landing she stopped to look outside at the night. The windows were smeary; for some reason William had to put his cruddy hands on any window he looked out of, as if he had eyes on his palms. She'd call the Window King tomorrow about doing all the windows; spring needed to be seen. Where was the screen? She hoped William hadn't been on the roof again; maybe Eliza had been laying out on warm days already, soaking up ultraviolet rays that would activate Uncle Junior's melanoma that lurked in her DNA. Mary Byrd cranked open the big casement window to get a fix of night air and see the moon more clearly. It was a silver crescent against a deep blue, nearly black, sky. It looked like one of William's nail clippings that had fallen on his navy flannel comforter. William's Braves jacket hung on the newel post and Mary Byrd put it on, wanting to step out onto the roof.

The night air was colder than she'd thought, or she'd gotten too warm in William's stuffy little lair. She was glad for the jacket; it smelled of William, and, oddly, of her lavender. Charles had gotten it big for him to grow into. Shoving her hands into the pockets, she felt a familiar shape she couldn't for a split second identify. Goddamn it—a lighter. That little asshole, she thought. But maybe it was Evagreen's. She might be the one smoking on the roof. Or Eliza? Either smoking, or trying to frame William for fooling around with a lighter. Oh, whatever. Some things will never be known, all right. She let the aggravation fall away. *Playing with fire* seemed such an innocent transgression now, an old-school crime from her own childhood, although a dangerous one right up there with *crossing without looking both ways*. She couldn't even remember saying those things to Eliza and William, who hardly walked anywhere and were way more interested in Game Boys than fires, but surely she had. She wondered what had happened to poor Eliot Nelson, just another boy, really. She could have asked Stith, but he wouldn't have been right to tell her; it wasn't her business.

A huge limb lay on the roof. Charles could deal with it whenever. Teever couldn't because of his foot. She wondered where he was spending the night. He wouldn't stay with them and had wanted her to drop him near the cemetery, for some reason. She had refused and had taken him to the JFC, where he could get a ride somewhere. He was going straight to the doctor in the morning, if she could find him. She sat down on the old tin with her legs up against her chest, not caring if she got roof crud on her tweed skirt. Off in the woods beyond their yard an owl hooted—*hoohoo hoo hoo hoo*—and she was glad to hear it. Teever said the owls and foxes were all gone because of the new condos. She hoped she might hear a mourning dove, her favorite bird call, or actually the only one other than owls she recognized. In Richmond, their sad song was a summer sound, but they didn't all migrate in Mississippi and sometimes she did hear one on a winter evening, like a lonely Indian flute off low in the trees. It was too early for the night birds—what were they? Whippoorwills? Her mom would know; she'd call her in the morning. They were so weird, singing in the dead of night. It was nice to hear them if you were up late, nursing a baby or something, but if you were having trouble sleeping you wanted to kill them.

A foot or two away lay the screen, and in the old, rusted gutter were some butts—Salems, and a couple Camel Lights. One of the Salems was only partly smoked, so she picked it up and lit it, surprised that the damp nub lit. She'd actually always like menthols. It tasted great. Gazing down at the backyard, Mary Byrd realized Charles must have hauled most of the big downed limbs out to the street; the yard looked pretty okay from what she could see. They'd lost a cedar; its torn flesh showed *edible pink* in the porch light. There'd probably been ten million chain saws going all over town since the storm. Her perennial bed, a mess of dead stalks she should have cleaned out forever ago, lay almost directly below her and was palely illuminated, brown from the hard freeze. Mr. Yeti, the wild boy, was waiting in the bed, hoping someone would appear at the back door with one last late-night snack before he retreated to the woods. Or wherever he spent his nights. Around the raggedy yellow cat, in front of the dead leaves and stalks, Mary Byrd could just make out the strappy narcissus and the blue-green tips of the daffodils barely emerging. Cold and bleak as it was now, spring was only a few weeks off. It could be a hard season for her; its memories had always made her blue and anxious.

The big quince bushes at the back of the yard would soon be an almost imagined mist of palest salmon. Every year after she cleared away all the Christmas crap, she'd cut quince branches and bring them inside to force. The bright little flowers seemed to buck everyone up as a reminder that the gaudy excesses of December were past, and the dreariness of January and February would soon be, too. She used to force paperwhites, but Eliza, who had inherited a hot bird-dog nose like her mother's and grandmother's, complained that they smelled like cat shit. She was right, Mary Byrd had to admit.

Then before much longer she could have cut flowers in the house again, and the bittersweet, fragrant spring would unfold. She loved the way certain flowers bloomed in tandem. Mann said it was as if God were an old queen, the pairings all spring were so perfectly matched: the Scrambled Egg daffodils and spunky spiderwort, the leggy spirea and forsythia that looked so good in Evelyn's old bronze urn, then iris and azalea. She loved the old flags—Lucy had given her some rhizomes from her grandmother's Louisiana garden—and the George Taber azaleas with their sweet fragrance like cotton candy. Then came the assault of the spicy chinaberry—now she'd have her own—and cummy privet, their killer, sexy perfumes making up for their pale, uninteresting blossoms. The best duo of all, the one that for Mary Byrd signaled the best of spring and summer, was the gold-and-cream honeysuckle and the flat, deep pink Choctaw roses. If she could beat the damn deer to them, she'd cut armloads of roses and honeysuckle for the house, and the scent of the honeysuckle was sometimes so strong in the night that it would wake her up and fill her with a confusion of happiness, sadness, and longing. Who knew for what. The rest of the summer would be too hot for anything but zinnias, and even those had to be tended to make it. After August, she could always count on periwinkle ageratum and watermelon-colored spider lilies, a sassy antidote to the dry Septembers.

Stubbing out the butt, Mary Byrd opened *Mississippi Trees*. There was enough light from the landing for her to read. She looked up "Chinaberry, *Melia azedarach L.*" Under "Habitat," she read that the trees came originally from the Himalayas. That was cool. As for "Timber Value," the wood had been used for auto bodies, musical instruments, matches, tool handles, and cabinetry, and the seeds had been used for rosaries. Rosaries? She remembered the little seed-pearl rosary that Nonna had given her when she was a little girl; she wished she still had it. Chinaberry extract had been used long ago to cure roundworms and had anti-viral and anticancer properties. She was sure that William Byrd hadn't mentioned chinaberries in his diaries, but maybe they hadn't yet been brought to the colonies in the early eighteenth century. Wondering if Evagreen knew all these things about her little gift, Mary Byrd read on to "Propagation." Chinaberries could be grown by seed or cuttings, were tolerant of drought but not shade, and grew rapidly. Perfect. Mary Byrd read down to where in bold-faced red letters it said:

WARNING: Classified by the Exotic Pest Plant Council as a Category 1 species that invades and disrupts natural plant communities in all states. Considered as an invasive pest.

All parts of the Chinaberry are poisonous. Eating as few
as 6 berries can result in death. Songbirds that eat too
many seeds have been known to become paralyzed.

She stared at the warning for a minute, thinking. Then, she
said out loud, " Evagreen! *Really?*" Mary Byrd grinned like the
Cheshire Cat in the cold, clear night. She'd give the Chinaberry
prime real estate, and would plant them where the cedar had
stood.

She sat a few minutes more, looking out over the town and
toward the university on its hill. Closer, she could see the rude,
overkill light of the Chevron and the colored neons of the Sonic.
All the electricity seemed to be back on again, but many of the
silhouetted trees looked ragged and torn, with large limbs
dangling like badly broken arms. It was late, and a Wednesday,
so there weren't a lot of headlights, or houses lit up. Students
and working people had gone to bed, resting up for the morning's eight-o'clock classes and bank openings and sidewalk
sweepings and all the regular weekday business of the little—
not so little anymore—town. Mary Byrd liked to think about
everyone sleeping, stacked up in beds in every house on every
street, in every town in Mississippi, in every state across the
country. Everyone checking out horizontally for a few hours'
respite from the exhausting, battering, busy business of living.

Something small but desperate suddenly screamed and
abruptly went silent. Goddamn it—probably the owl, or Irene
or Iggy with a rabbit. Old Mr. Yeti looked toward the sound
but was unmoved; he'd given up the hunting life for his regularly delivered meals at the back door. The darling homeboy
kitties killed for sport, the Tonton Macoutes of the backyard.

Out there, she knew, at this moment, maybe even in this
town, things were happening to children; they were crying,
alone, scared, in pain or enduring silently, rendered

not-children by one thing or another. She knew that a husband was probably beating a wife, or a wife was thinking of killing a husband, and if it didn't happen tonight, it would some other night. Everyone had reasons, secret or unconscious, or plotted and deliberate. The world *was* a crazy, round place. There weren't any neat, even lines to make things clear, or corners to hide in. It was precious and horrible, swollen and wobbly with craziness, whirling along in spite of death, and everybody just had to hang on *for dear life*, hoping the ride wouldn't be too centrifugal, or too bumpy, or more than one could stand. It was exactly like Mr. Natural used to say in *Zap*: "The whole universe is insane." It had been a week of dreadful revelation, as if she had been *in* Revelation. Mary Byrd was tired and wanted to check out horizontally herself. Stepping back through the window, she hung the Braves jacket back on the post, but did not replace the lighter.

Downstairs, she put back the tree book and made her rounds, putting dishes in the dishwasher, turning off the five hundred lights that had been left on, herding Puppy Sal and the Pounder into the kitchen for the night. She passed William Byrd's portrait and the little hieroglyphic diary page on the wall, and stopped before it.

Was life better then or is it better now? she wondered. So much had been simpler then, at least for white people, but they had worked their asses off, even if they did have slaves, their terrible non-secret. All the sickness, too. Byrd's baby son Parke had died of something as simple as a fever when he was only ten months old. *My wife had several fits of tears for our son but kept within the bounds of submission.* Jesus. But life had to go on. Byrd, so much like Charles: straightforward, a control freak in a mostly good way, taking care of bidnes. She thought to honor Byrd, there in the darkened hall. She danced, doing a couple jiggy steps and a pirouette that she thought might resemble an eighteenth-century minuet or a contra dance. She curtsied to him. Then, to honor Stevie, she went all interpretive, bending and contorting, throwing her chin to the ceiling, and drawing her fists to her heart in anguish, and then she Monster Mashed and Monkeyed. For herself and her youth on Cherry Glen Lane, she Swam and Ponied, and for her children she did a little Cabbage Patch and a Bus Driver that would have horrified them. All solo, partnerless dances, she realized. Charles was a good dancer, but he preferred to dance solo, sixties style, too. Did they even remember how to dance with a partner? Did they even want to?

She climbed the stairs once again, so tired, to their bedroom. There was Charles's long sleeping form, snoring softly. After undressing and slipping on her nightgown, which smelled soothingly of herself, Mary Byrd eased into bed so as not to wake Charles, who probably had a zillion things to do the next day and needed his sleep. She didn't; just the usual. She closed her eyes, resolving to have good health, good thoughts, and good humor, thanks be to God Almighty. Before falling quickly to sleep she thought, Ha.

Acknowledgments

THE THING ABOUT teaching old dogs is true. This book was written in longhand on yellow legal pads, and only with the technical assistance of Katie Morrison, Megan Prescott, Elizabeth Dollarhide, my son, Beckett Howorth IV, Lee Durkee, Bernard Kuria at Safari Wine and Spirits/Copytime, and, especially, my daughter Claire Howorth has this book been made presentable to the twenty-first-century world. I thank them for their expertise and extreme patience.

For answering questions, I thank Les Standiford, Detective Joe Matthews, Ollie Carrothers, Andy Howorth, Padgett Powell, Dent May, Tim Junkin, Tucker Carrington, Dolph Overton, Ken Coghlan, Tom Rosser, Dr. T. Starkey, Doug Roberts, Davis Kilman and the Richmond Public Library, and WFS. A heartfelt apology goes out to FB.

I thank Laurie Stirratt, Diana and Gary Fisketjon, Joey Lauren Adams, Anne Rapp, Jim Dees, Claiborne Barksdale,

Mike Nizza, Inge Feltrinelli, Janie Wells, Karl Ackerman, and Katie Blount for reading, listening, and laughs, and for keeping my spirits up. I'm grateful for the regular ass-kickings I received from Nicky Dawidoff, Kristina and Richard Ford, Doug Stumpf, and my mom, Claire Del Vecchio Johnston. Sarah Crichton and Alex Glass gave me invaluable attention. I thank Jon Massey and Jeff Dennis for their care and 'vigilance. My husband, Richard, and my daughter Bébé helped me and put up with negligence and smoke. Thanks to the Virginia Historical Society for permission to quote from and take liberties with *The Secret Diary of William Byrd*, and to the Mississippi Forestry Commission for *Mississippi Trees*. I hope the late Townes Van Zandt would have been okay with me swiping the title from a great song, and thanks to his son J. T. Van Zandt for his blessing.

I was given wonderful places to write by Darrell Crawford and David McConnell, Thomas Verich, and Debra Winger and Arliss Howard. The MacDowell Colony gave me not only time and space but the confidence to go forward with my writing.

During the writing of this book, we lost some important Mississippi writers who have inspired me in many ways: Larry Brown, Barry Hannah, Willie Morris, Lewis Nordan, and Josephine Haxton (Ellen Douglas). I miss them and am so grateful to have had their friendship. The late Dean Faulkner Wells, who published her fine memoir just before she died at seventy, showed me that it was never too late.

Thanks, of course, to everyone at Bloomsbury USA and UK, especially my editor, Nancy Miller, who kept the faith, and George Gibson, Lea Beresford, Laura Keefe, Nate Knaebel, Patti Ratchford, and Summer Smith; and all at ICM, particularly Dan Kirschen and my badass agent, Lisa Bankoff.

I thank my family—Johnstons, Neumanns, Valenzas, Del Vecchios, Woods, and Howorths—for their love and support.

My late sister-in-law, Susan Barksdale Howorth, gave me an iPod (loaded by my nephew Stewart, who won't let me live down the fact that I excitedly first put the iPod to my ear) for easy access to the music I needed. Special thanks goes to one of my bros in particular, Sam Johnston, without whose pursuit of the facts concerning the still unsolved murder of our brother, Steven Francis Johnston, I could not have written this book.

I hope I haven't left anyone out. If I have, blame my sketchy memory and not my lack of gratitude. For you all, or at least most of you, my love's bigger than a Cadillac.

—L.N.H.

A Note on the Author

Lisa Howorth was born in Washington, D.C.,
where her family has lived for four generations. In
Oxford, Mississippi, she and her husband opened
Square Books (*Publishers Weekly*'s 2013
Bookstore of the Year) in 1979 and raised their
three children. She received the Mississippi
Governor's Award for Excellence in the Arts in
1996 and a MacDowell Colony Fellowship in
2007. Her writing has appeared in *Garden & Gun*
and the *Oxford American*. This is her first novel.